SET THE NIGHT ON FIRE

Moving toward the door, Joe braced himself for what he knew might be the last few moments of his life. Yodmani followed with the RPG, his shirt still open, burns and bruises seemingly anesthetized by violence.

Sheng's rifle squad was nearly in position when Joe cleared the doorway, creeping nearer in an effort to surprise their enemies and save the arsenal. Their leader tried to get a shot off at the moving targets, but he never had a chance . . . Joseph set the night on fire.

He swung the nozzle of the flamethrower to the right and cut a fiery swath in front of him, igniting canvas, plywood, human flesh.

Yodmani ran ahead of him, already firing with his M-16 at shadow men along the wire. Lee torched a line of tents and caught a pair of sentries in the open as he followed. He felt the searing heat reflected on his hands and face, but he gave no thought of easing off the throttle. . . .

Bantam Books by Michael Newton
Ask your bookseller for the books you have missed

CHILD OF BLOOD
KOREA KILL

CHINA WHITE

BY
MICHAEL NEWTON

BANTAM BOOKS
NEW YORK • TORONTO • LONDON • SYDNEY • AUCKLAND

CHINA WHITE

A Bantam Falcon Book / August 1991

FALCON and the portrayal of a boxed "f" are trademarks of Bantam Books, a division of Bantam Doubleday Dell Publishing Group, Inc.

ISBN 0-553-29173-4

Published simultaneously in the United States and Canada

Bantam Books are published by Bantam Books, a division of Bantam Doubleday Dell Publishing Group, Inc. Its trademark, consisting of the words "Bantam Books" and the portrayal of a rooster, is Registered in U.S. Patent and Trademark Office and in other countries. Marca Registrada. Bantam Books, 666 Fifth Avenue, New York, New York 10103

PRINTED IN THE UNITED STATES OF AMERICA

RAD 0 9 8 7 6 5 4 3 2 1

1

San Francisco, August 1995

The night he almost bought it, Joey Lee was sitting in the fog waiting for a dealer known as One-nut Ma to take delivery on a load of China white.

The dealer's parents didn't name him One-nut. They had called him Thomas, and they died together in a freeway accident when he was nine years old, before they ever saw the kind of sleazy shit their only son turned out to be. An uncle on his mother's side adopted Tommy Ma and did his best to raise the boy with a respect for family, but there was nothing he could do about the wild streak that produced erratic and rebellious conduct, first at school and later on the streets.

The "One-nut" tag resulted from a bungled teenage B-and-E in North Beach. Tommy Ma was crawling out a window with his bag of goodies when a uniformed patrolman took him by surprise. The kid was packing heat, but he was nervous, and his shot went wild. The officer took time to aim—for Tommy's leg, he later testified, but he would only grin if anybody asked which one—and the physician at emergency receiving said he couldn't have performed a cleaner nip-and-tuck himself. The court suspended Tommy's sentence in consideration of his loss, and One-nut started working overtime to cultivate a reputation as a cocksman, but the nickname was too colorful to die.

One thing he learned along the way, aside from how to cross his legs and keep from pulling sutures, was the mortal risk involved in burglary. It could have been some trigger-happy bastard with a twelve-gauge, just as easy, and he wouldn't have had to think about nicknames. Headless bodies don't need them.

It was about that time, three years ago, that Tommy One-nut went for a career change and began to deal in pharmaceuticals. Less risk involved, if you observed the rules, and there was money out the ass.

"You think he called it off?"

Lee's partner, Eddie Hovis, was behind the wheel, an open package of Doritos and a thermos full of lukewarm coffee between them on the seat.

"He'll be here."

Eddie checked his watch, a bargain digital. "It's getting late. Somebody shoulda made a pass by now."

"Relax. No reason to believe we made their action, they don't need to make a pass. It's cool."

"You hope."

Their undercover rent-a-wreck was parked on Mission, facing the Embarcadero and a giant smudge that should have been the World Trade Center. Everything beyond the looming hulk was *terra incognita,* lost in fog. Lee figured that it had to be a righteous deal for One-nut Ma to venture out of Chinatown on a night like this.

"It's gonna be a fucking miracle if we can even *see* his ass."

"We'll see him fine."

"I need a smoke," said Hovis, but he made no move to light the cigarette that would have given them away.

"You smoke too much."

"It's something oral." Eddie grinned, another handful of Doritos going down. "Like I was telling Meg this afternoon—"

"He's here."

They scrunched down in their seats, on instinct, even knowing Tommy One-nut couldn't see them in the dark and fog. Lee recognized the dealer by his walk—a cocky swagger—and the wide-brimmed hat he always wore. He was carrying a gym bag, and it seemed to weigh him down. Two hundred thousand dollars, give or take. He checked the street and ducked into the shadowed doorway of a shop a half-block down.

They weren't concerned with busting Tommy Ma tonight. In fact, they could have hauled him in a dozen times within the past three months, but all their work so far was leading up to this. Ideally, they would watch and wait, identify the dealer's contact, trail him home. Another link toward the completion of a chain.

"They think we're jerking off, downtown."

Lee pinned his partner with a glare. "Somebody tell you that?"

"Nobody had to tell me. You can see the way they look, you mention Bobby Chan."

"We make him, I don't give a shit how anybody looks. He'll still be ours."

"What's this?"

A dark sedan was turning left, off Steuart, southbound onto Mission, headlights blinding in the fog before the driver cut them off and pulled in to the curb across from Tommy Ma, his parking lights like yellow eyes.

"It's showtime."

Tommy One-nut swaggered into view and checked the street each way before he crossed, just like they taught the kids in school. He made it to the center stripe, halfway, before the muzzle flash of semiautomatic fire erupted from the driver's side of the sedan, like strobe lights in the fog. From where they sat, the narcs could see him jerking, spinning like a poor man's Michael Jackson to the music of the guns.

And they were stunned, both groping for their weapons in the darkness, Eddie with his left hand on the latch and spitting out Doritos as he muttered, "Holy shit." They never saw the second car approaching from behind them, running dark, until it pulled abreast.

By that time, Eddie had his door wide open, nothing in the way to save him when the gunners opened fire. Two submachine guns, they decided later. Maybe Uzis, maybe not. They raked the car in tandem, punching abstract patterns in one side and out the other, Eddie taking most of it and screaming in a voice that didn't sound like his at all.

Lee's holster must have worked around behind him somehow, but he had the automatic now, and he was thumbing off the safety when a bullet drilled his shoulder with the impact of a hammer stroke. It drove him backward, and he lost the pistol, his good hand clawing at the inside handle. Anything to get away from there, as someone kicked him in the ribs, and once more at the hip.

Some kind of moisture on his face—had it been raining?—and he registered that some of it was Eddie, some of it his own, before he found the latch and threw his weight against the door.

Deadweight.

Another solid blow, beneath one arm, but there was still no pain. Incredible. He should have been on fire.

The door gave way and spilled him out, a flaccid, dying thing.

He seemed to fall forever, into darkness streaked by blood-red shooting stars.

2

The pain came later.

First, he was aware of drifting in a state of semiconsciousness, his body weightless, blessedly anesthetized. Around him there was mist, but it was not the gray, polluted fog of Mission Street. He would have said it was a *friendly* mist, if that were possible. It had a fragrance he could not identify, a sweet relief from car exhaust and cordite. The uncompromising, gritty pavement was replaced by something soft but firm, supporting him without abrading skin or bruising muscle.

There were disembodied voices in the mist, a few of them familiar, but he couldn't concentrate enough to pick out Eddie's as the babble faded in and out. He tried to listen with an ear for Mandarin or English, but the words were gibberish, a language he had never taken time to learn.

From time to time the mist retreated and his body felt like molten lead. The pain intruded then, but it was never bad enough to make him scream. Not yet. He recognized the bed, with metal railings on the sides and stiff white sheets drawn up around his chest. An IV rig above him, the transparent hose attached to something in his arm.

There always seemed to be a face above him when the mist pulled back. He understood that some of them were people he should know, but names eluded him. They spoke to him and smiled, but there was cotton in his ears, a side effect of the sedation. Others came to study him and ask him questions he could not interpret, much less answer. He ignored them.

Drifting.
In and out of mist that smelled like flowers.
In and out of pain.

The first two he could clearly focus on were strangers dressed in white. The woman—nurse—was pretty, fair complexion with the barest hint of freckles, sandy curls beneath a starched white cap, her smile encouraging. The nameplate on her breast was black and read "L. Reilly."

The man was tall and thin, his long face thickened by a beard that came in white around his chin. It made a striking contrast to the darker foliage on his cheeks, and neither matched the chestnut hair above, meticulously styled. His wire-rimmed spectacles reflected the fluorescent ceiling lights. A stethoscope, protruding from his pocket, was the only badge of office he required.

"Good morning, Mr. Lee. I'm Dr. Beck." Still fuzzy, but at least the words made sense. A radio announcer's voice. Lee wondered if he practiced with a mirror. "We've been hoping you might join us."

"Long."

His throat was parched, and it felt bruised inside. The question came out sounding like a feeble belch.

"How long?" Beck seemed to give the weighty matter deep consideration. "This is Sunday morning; you arrived on Wednesday night. Let's say three days."

He tried to swallow, lubricating rusty vocal cords, before he asked, "Where am I?"

"San Francisco General. It's a private room. We moved you out of ICU last night."

Lee knew the question he should ask, but could not bring himself to face it, so he compromised. "How bad?"

A signal passed unseen between doctor and nurse. She flashed Joe Lee another smile and left the room. Beck waited for the door to close.

"You were in critical condition on arrival, but we've scaled that back to serious and stable. Major blood loss was a problem, but we've got no shortage on Type O. You want the gory details?"

"Please."

"Okay. In essence, you were shot four times, producing seven wounds. One bullet entered on the left side of the thorax, just below the armpit, broke two ribs, and left an exit wound beneath the nipple. You could say the fractures saved you. Give or take a centimeter, and it would have passed between your ribs. All kinds of nasty things in there."

Lee cataloged the dull, insistent ache beneath his arm, the wad of bandage like a sagging breast.

"Another bullet struck you in the left side of the upper back. It chipped the scapula—no problem there—and pierced your lung. We had to reinflate, but you've been breathing on your own since Friday noon. You should expect discomfort for a while, but it'll pass."

His groggy brain identified the pad of gauze and tape below his shoulder blade. More pain, though still remote. A stuffy pins-and-needles feeling on the left side of his chest when he inhaled.

"Okay." His voice was stronger now. He almost sounded like himself.

"The other wounds are more complex. You took a bullet in your shoulder." Beck's finger tapped his lab coat on the left. "The movies tell you shoulder wounds are no big deal. Clint Eastwood stops a bullet, and it barely slows him down. The truth is something else. Shoulders are among the human skeleton's most delicate and complex moving parts. You've got the clavicle and scapula to deal with, plus the joint itself, the deltoid muscle and trapezius. Cut the subclavian artery, and you're talking lethal hemorrhage in four, five minutes, tops."

Lee got the picture. "What's the verdict?"

"Bottom line, we had some luck. The wound was through and through. It missed the bones—don't ask me how—but there was major damage to the muscle tissue. Once the sutures are removed, you'll have to work on learning how to use that arm again."

"That still leaves one."

"Left hip," Beck said, an index finger demonstrating on himself. "This bullet struck the ilium—your hipbone

—and disintegrated. Part of it came out in back, above the buttock, and a smaller fragment pierced the bowel. We cleaned that up, and you're receiving antibiotics as a hedge against peritonitis. It shouldn't be a problem."

"But?"

"Exactly. The projectile split three ways on impact, and the biggest piece—we estimated forty grains—was driven downward, into contact with the joint itself. Are you familiar with anatomy?"

"I took biology in college."

"Fair enough. The hip joint is a ball-and-socket type." Beck demonstrated with a fist and the opposing palm. "It rotates, so. Intrusion of a foreign object limits that mobility, of course, and violent impact is potentially destructive to the mechanism."

"Can you spell it out?" The left side of his body still felt numb between the waist and knee.

Beck frowned, considering his words. "The femur's head was shattered, with corresponding secondary damage to the innominate bone—that is, the socket. In the circumstances, there was no alternative to total hip replacement."

"Jesus."

"On the up side, with some healing time and therapy, a bit of coaching, you should be as good as new. In fact, considering the quality of our materials, you may be better."

"Stainless steel?"

"A brand-new polymer. Less weight and nearly zero friction. Any difficulties you encounter will be caused by muscle damage to the gluteus."

"How long until I'm mobile?"

"We should have you on your feet in three, four days. Then, therapy. The pace depends entirely on your stamina and personal determination. Right?"

"I hear you."

"Excellent. I'll check on you again tomorrow. In the meantime—"

"One more thing."

He caught Beck turning toward the door. The doctor hesitated.

"Yes?"

"My partner."

It took everything Lee had to speak the words, and he could see the answer written on Beck's face.

"I'm sorry, Mr. Lee, there wasn't anything—"

"Okay."

"I know how difficult this is, but you should really try—"

"The funeral?"

Beck drew a blank. "I'll check that, if you like."

"Yes, please."

"The best thing you can do right now is rest."

His chest and shoulder had begun to throb, three wounds in close proximity. Lee thought his hip was waking up, on top of everything, but he determined not to let it show while Dr. Beck was in the room. Alone, he simply didn't care enough.

It should have hurt more, lying there, instead of feeling faraway and dulled by the residual effect of local anesthetics. If it hurt more, enough to make him cry, then maybe he could shake the guilt that came with survival. Eddie Hovis cooling in a drawer somewhere, and he was lying there with tidy bandages, an IV tube, and a plastic hip.

Alive.

It was the relief, immediate and undeniable, that made him doubt his own humanity. Instead of being racked by grief at Eddie's loss, he felt like cheering for himself. And might have, if his wounds had not prevented it.

"Goddammit."

"Sorry?"

He had missed the door, Nurse Reilly coming back with something in her hand. A plastic throwaway syringe.

"I don't need that."

"A sedative," she told him. "Right now, sleep's exactly what you *do* need."

Searching for a vein and giving him the mickey with an

angel's touch. He hardly felt the needle, alcohol before and after, cool against his skin.

"I ask you something?"

The mist was coming back, but he could see her face and hear her say, "Sure."

"You ever feel like cheering, when you know you should have died?"

He floated through an endless fever dream, where time and space were stripped of any concrete meaning. Still in bed, he saw himself at twelve years old, the summer that he broke his leg. His mother brought him tea and egg-drop soup with oyster crackers. All the television news breaks, in between the innings of the Dodgers game, were Nixon politics and Vietnam. They seemed impossibly remote to Joey Lee.

Like death.

His mother came again, to fetch the dishes, and she brought a visitor. He welcomed Eddie Hovis with the logic of a dreamer, not at all surprised to see a dead man more than twenty years his senior in the room.

"You look like shit," his partner said. "What happened?"

Joey had to blush as he explained about his bicycle, the pothole that had jogged him out in front of traffic.

"Barely clipped me. I'm going back to school on Monday."

"Never mind all that. I got a lead on Bobby Chan."

Lee's stomach tightened with excitement. "Really?"

"It's the big one, man. You'll have to skip that test in algebra." Wolfing down a handful of the oyster crackers. "Have you got your piece?"

"It's in the bathroom."

Crawling out of bed, he gimped across the carpet in his walker cast, a five-foot Frankenstein. His mother would have worried if he left the pistol lying out, so Joey kept it in a plastic bag inside the toilet tank.

Before he crossed the threshold, he could hear the shower running. Steam inside the bathroom, warmer than the mist that formed the borders of his dream. A pale, familiar shape behind the plastic shower curtain.

"Nancy?"

"Joe, I couldn't wait." She drew the curtain halfway back to let him in, and he could see the water glisten on her shoulders, on her breasts. One perfect drop suspended from her nipple, like a jewel. "Do you forgive me?"

Glancing down his naked body, toward the swelling he could not disguise.

"I take that as a yes."

He pulled the curtain shut behind him, stepping into Nancy's arms. The steam enveloped them, her body molded tight against him, muscles rippling beneath his hands. She tasted good enough to eat.

"I felt that."

Reaching down between their bodies, Nancy found him, stroking. Joey wasn't sure if he could take it, but she knew just when to stop. A squeeze to break the rhythm, and she slipped one arm around his neck, her body weighing next to nothing as she locked her thighs around his hips and guided him inside.

Warm velvet.

Pressing Nancy back against the tile, he gave himself to the sensation, rutting desperately. He found it hard to breathe, with all the steam, but Joey didn't care. It didn't matter if he suffocated there and fell down dead, as long as he could finish first.

"You ready yet?"

The voice behind him, Eddie Hovis standing in the shower with his clothes on, dripping. Rusty swirls of blood around the drain. He had a pistol in his hand, extending it to Joey Lee.

"Let's go."

"Hold on a second."

Turning back to Nancy, and she wasn't there.

"C'mon, we're late."

Lee recognized the street as part of Chinatown, bright neon signs imparting colors to the fog. It must be eight or nine o'clock, with all the people on the street, and none of them the least bit interested in the gun he carried or the fact that he was naked. Eddie steered him toward an alley where the streetlights did not penetrate, rough gravel underneath his feet.

"We're almost there."

Above them, searchlights blazed and swept the alley with their blinding beams. One of them overshot the mark and came right back, the others burning down on Joe and Eddie like a multitude of suns. Hot needles in his eyes, but he could still see well enough to note the blood that soaked through Eddie's shirt and jeans. His partner turning with a shuffling zombie walk to shout, "Surprise!"

His eyes snapped open in the darkness, spilling tears across his cheeks. The pain was coming back, but he refused to buzz the nurse. He lay there staring at the ceiling, still awake when day's first light came slanting through the blinds.

That morning, Leland Kephart paid a token visit, stopping in before his driver took him to the Federal Building. He wore gray for the occasion, custom-tailored wool, with a Masonic pin in his lapel. His tie was silk, wine-colored, with a perfect Windsor knot. Dark, wavy hair combed back without a part. Lee could not see his shoes, but knew they would be polished to a mirror shine.

"How are you, Joseph?"

"Better, sir." What could he say?

"You had them worried for a while."

Not "us." The Northern California regional director of the DEA did not allow himself to worry over trivia like dead and wounded men.

"I must've missed it, sir."

"Good man." The politician's smile clicked on and off. "I wanted you to know we're working overtime to clear this up. It's top priority. No stone unturned, you have my word."

"Yes, sir."

Kephart already moving toward the door, his duty done.

"If you need anything at all . . ."

"I'll let you know."

"You do that, Joseph. Take your time and follow doctor's orders, now. We've got your caseload covered."

Thanking empty air as Kephart disappeared. Ten or fifteen seconds for the air-conditioning to deal with his cologne, and there would be no proof he was ever there.

•

Ray Christy wandered in about an hour later, while the nurse was checking out Lee's vital signs. She didn't seem tremendously impressed with his credentials, and she let him know that it would be ten minutes, max, before he got the boot. A little smile for Lee before she left the two of them alone.

"Not bad." Ray cocked a thumb in the direction of the door.

"I guess."

At forty-five, Ray Christy could have passed for ten years older, maybe fifteen in a pinch. His craggy face was topped by salt-and-pepper hair run wild around the ears and collar, looking vaguely scruffy even on the rare occasions when he had it trimmed. The half-moon scar beneath one eye stood out in pale relief against a tan that came from working on the streets whenever possible. He wore an old, familiar houndstooth jacket with a tie that clashed.

"The man came by?"

"I caught a glimpse."

"That guy, I tell you." But instead, he asked, "How are you, Joe?"

"Fucked up, I guess."

"I came to see you two, three times before, but you were always out on something."

"Lots of dope around this place. You want to raid it?"

Christy smiled. "The doctor wouldn't tell me much of anything, you know their bullshit, but he said you ought to get around okay, you do some work and all."

"That's what I hear."

"At least you've got insurance, huh? No raise this year, but anyway, you're covered if the fuckers blow you up."

"It could be worse."

That brought them back to Eddie, Ray about to light a cigarette before he flashed on where he was and put the pack away. "The funeral was Saturday," he said.

Two days ago, while Lee was drifting in the fog.

"You talk to Chan?"

"I called his mouthpiece for an interview, he tells me when I get a warrant we can ask him anything we want."

"So, get one."

"Based on what?"

"The bastard set us up."

"*You* say. The judge, he's not so sure."

"And what do you think, Ray?"

"I think you're right, but what the hell do I know? Take a hunch to federal court, they have themselves a laugh and point you toward the street."

"So that's it?"

"Not quite. We found the shooters' car—one of them—in McLaren Park. Reported stolen when the owner got off work that afternoon. No prints or pieces, but they left all kinds of brass inside. Nine-millimeter. We can match the firing pins and the ejectors through ballistics, if we ever find the guns."

"Don't hold your breath."

"Guess not. The way it looks, somebody made you working Tommy Ma and set you up. Decided what the hell, let's waste him too, in case he's playing footsie with the narcs."

"A leak?"

Ray frowned. "I hate to think so."

"Still . . ."

"Time's up." Nurse Reilly in the doorway, giving Ray the evil eye.

"Okay. Stay frosty, kid." He cut a glance at Reilly, winked back at Joe. "Not bad at all."

It was amazing how a simple conversation could sap a grown man's strength. Before he drifted off again, Lee thought about the setup that had taken Eddie's life. His partner, three months' work, and One-nut Ma, all shot to hell in ten or fifteen seconds.

Christy didn't want to think about an inside leak, okay. That didn't mean there wasn't one.

It was an angle, anyway, and something for his mind to work on when he finished counting holes in the acoustic ceiling tiles. It pissed him off, and that was fine. The anger gave him focus, and he nursed it, like a precious candle in the dark.

Right now, he needed light to find his way.

3

Lee gave the nurse a closer look that afternoon. Christy had a point: she wasn't bad. Lee recognized her perfume as the fragrance of his early dreams, before he found out where he was and knew that he was still alive. A meager scrap of knowledge, but it helped, somehow.

She checked him every hour or so, and brought his medication in a Dixie cup, with juice to wash the capsules down. Lee was not cleared to solo on the toilet yet, and so Nurse Reilly also helped him with the bedpan, wincing like she meant it when his wounded hip produced reluctant sounds of pain.

Lee figured bedpans had to be the worst. No dignity for anyone, where bedpans were concerned, but Reilly kept it casual. No big deal, like she had seen a thousand men in backless gowns who couldn't take a leak or wipe themselves without a helping hand.

Which, Lee supposed, was probably an underestimate.

Reilly worked the day shift. She was on the floor when Lee woke up, and left about the time they brought his dinner on a plastic tray, with lids on everything to make it seem like he was dining in a fancy restaurant instead of sitting up in bed and scarfing down the blue-plate special. Sometimes she looked in to say good-bye before she left.

Sitting up was an improvement, anyway. Nurse Reilly checked him out on the controls before she let him operate the superbed alone. No trick at all, unless you jacked it up too high in back and put unnecessary pressure on the hip. That woke up the gremlins and got them busy with their implements of torture, spreading to his bandaged shoulder if they had the time before his medication came.

Lee did it all one-handed—eating, coping with the bed and the remote-control TV, making small adjustments to the bedpan—while his left arm alternately throbbed or lay there playing dead. His fingers followed orders to a point, when he commanded them to curl or straighten, but the shoulder gave him hell if he tried to lift his arm.

"You'll get it back," Nurse Reilly told him when she caught him at it Tuesday afternoon. "It won't be painless, but you'll get there."

"That a promise?"

"Absolutely."

Glancing at her nameplate casually enough that Reilly wouldn't think he was measuring her bra size.

"What's the L for?"

"Guess."

"It wouldn't be Loretta."

"No."

"You don't look like a Lois."

"Thanks, I think."

"Lorraine?"

"Strike three."

"I'm working with a handicap."

"That's no excuse. You need the bedpan?"

"No. Lucinda?"

"I'll be back in half an hour with your medication."

"Chances are, I'll be here."

Reilly hesitated in the doorway, turning back.

"It's Lisa."

"Hey, all right."

On Wednesday morning, after breakfast and the bedpan, Lisa brought a wheelchair to his room.

"You're missing someone."

"Nope, all yours. We're going for a ride."

"Says who?"

"You're getting pale in here. A few more days, you'll look like an albino."

Lowering the right-hand rail and skinning back the

sheets, she helped him out of bed. It wasn't half as bad as he expected, with his good hip taking all the weight and Lisa helping to support his legs. She didn't bat an eye when Joey's floppy gown rode up around his hips and flashed her.

No big thing, he was about to say, and then she had him on his feet beside the bed, a double jolt of pain exploding from his hip and shoulder with the change in altitude.

"Okay?"

"The votes aren't in."

"Don't try to walk. Just stand there for a second. Hold the rail, that's right."

She got the chair around behind him, set the brake, and caught him underneath the arms to help him sit. The strength she had, for such a slender woman, Lee imagined she could stand him on his head and shake him till he rattled, if she wanted to.

"How's that?" she asked when she had his feet in slippers, resting on the foot plates, with a blanket on his lap.

"Not bad."

"One dose of sunshine, coming up."

It was the first time Lee had seen the corridor outside his room, pastels, yellow over orange, a stainless handrail running horizontally between the two. She wheeled him past the nurses' station to the elevator, and her touch lit up an arrow pointed toward the ceiling. When the spacious car arrived, they had it to themselves.

He was expecting competition on the roof, but they were all alone, the sky a washed-out blue with scattered clouds like wisps of shredded cotton trailing in a wind Lee couldn't feel. The sun was warm against his face, its sudden brightness forcing him to squint.

She wheeled him over green-painted concrete to reach the parapet, complete with metal railing that would never have discouraged a determined jumper. Distant freeway sounds told Lee that he was facing east, before he ever caught a glimpse of morning traffic bustling over Highway 101.

"Okay?"

"It's fine," he told her, studying the layout of Potrero

Hill and straining for a glimpse of San Francisco Bay beyond. He expected to be left alone, but Lisa showed no signs of going anywhere.

"You like your job?" he asked, for something to say.

"Most times. When I can make a difference, it's terrific. Florence Nightingale, you know?"

Her small, self-deprecating smile minimized her commitment, just in case a stranger caught her caring and decided she was weak instead of kind.

"It must be nice," he said. "To make a difference."

Lisa turned to face him with her back against the rail, arms crossed beneath her breasts. A transient breeze slipped underneath her pristine skirt and offered him a glimpse of knee, with supple thigh above.

"Police work must be similar," she said. "I mean, you're out there helping people every day."

"I used to think so."

"Has the shooting changed your mind?"

Lee met her eyes and had a feeling she could look inside him, sorting truth from lies. Somehow, the feeling did not put him on his guard.

"I grew up in Los Angeles," he told her, working toward an answer in his own good time. "Fourth generation, but my parents spoke Chinese around the house, like they were two days off the boat."

"You speak Chinese?"

"What else? I tried some Spanish when I got to high school, but it wouldn't take."

"What made you choose police work?"

"It was there." He thought about it, didn't know what else to say. "I finished college with a lame B.A. in history and had a choice of teaching school or doing something else. A month of student teaching settled that. LAPD was signing on minorities like we were going out of style, and that was it."

"No secret fantasies about fighting crime?"

"You don't give that a lot of thought in the academy," he said. "Police work in a city like L.A. is mostly traffic, crowd control, and settling domestic beefs. I saw my share of bodies, but we always left them for the suits to handle."

"Suits?"

"Detectives. LAPD's motto is 'Protect and Serve.' That means you mostly stand and wait."

"It doesn't sound much like TV."

"Five years, I had one high-speed chase, one shooting, seven days apart in 1985." He saw the skinny black kid aiming with a piece that didn't look like plastic in the dark. "The rest of it was pretty much routine."

She didn't ask about the shooting, whether anyone had died. Instead: "What made you switch?"

"The DEA was hiring, and I knew some people in the L.A. office. Asian syndicates were on the rise—still are—and there I was. Between their hiring quota and the second language, I was what the doctor ordered."

"And you saw a chance to do some good?"

Lee shrugged. "It was a change from rousting drunks and tagging speeders. Graduation day, you know? It takes a while to figure out that no one cares."

"Do you believe that?"

"Look around. The best year DEA has ever had, we intercepted maybe ten percent of the narcotics smuggled in from Mexico, Colombia, Iran, and Southeast Asia. Never mind the home-grown weed or any of the crack the bikers cook up in their floating labs. The president goes on TV a couple times a year and talks about the 'war on drugs,' but all I see are dealers making bail, a new crop standing by in case we ever lock one up."

"I'm sorry about your partner."

Hearing Eddie's scream again, he told her, "These things happen."

"Have you been in San Francisco long?" A tactful change of subject, backing off thin ice.

"Six years last April. How about yourself?"

"A native, born and bred. One year of school in Oregon, and back to stay."

"I don't think I've ever met a Frisco native."

"San Franciscan," she corrected him. "First time for everything. And, while we're on the subject . . ."

"Uh-oh."

"Dr. Beck wants you to start your therapy this afternoon."

"You'll be there?"

"Bet your life."

He thought of Eddie jerking to the sound of gunfire. Bobby Chan relaxing by his swimming pool in Daly City, thinking he had it made.

"You're on," he said.

The workout room had everything. A universal gym and heated whirlpool bath. Free weights, a treadmill, stationary bikes. Equipment Joe Lee didn't even recognize.

"Don't worry," Lisa said, "we'll take it slow at first. You need to get some strength back in your arm and leg before we really go to town."

"Truth is, right now I feel like staying home."

"I told you it would hurt. But the worst of it was getting shot. You're over that. So if they couldn't kill you, they're not about to keep you down."

"I like your confidence."

She steered his chair across the room, a thick athletic mat beneath the rubber wheels. Parallel bars in front of him, hopelessly out of reach.

"A little stroll, to get you started."

Lisa set the brakes and knelt to fold the foot plates out of his way. A glimpse of cleavage as she straightened, leaning close to slide her hands beneath his arms. Soft hair against his face.

"You'll have to help. Don't try to use the left side yet."

He struggled to his feet, lopsided, listing to the right. Without support from Lisa, he would certainly have tumbled backward, but she kept him upright, backing in between the wooden bars and forcing him to follow.

"Both hands, now. It doesn't matter if the right one handles all your weight at first. Just concentrate on taking one step at a time."

It hurt like hell, the muscles in his wounded hip emitting jolts of pain each time he moved. Three halting steps, and he could feel the shoulder chiming in, despite the fact that he was barely clinging to the guide rail on his left. Before he got halfway, a sheen of perspiration glistened on his forehead, and his jaw was aching where he clenched his teeth against the larger pain.

"You're doing fine."

"Oh, yeah?"

"A few more steps, you've got it made."

One more, and then another. When he lost it, Lee could feel his bad leg folding under him, but there was no way he could catch himself. Before he knew it, Lisa had a shoulder underneath his arm, supporting him, her round breast soft against his ribs.

"Just catch your breath. It's nothing."

"Feels like something."

"Every step you take, you're getting stronger. Each one hurts a little less."

In fact, every step hurt a damn sight *more*, but Lee was not about to let it show. He made it to the end without another stumble.

Lisa flashed him a killer smile. "Okay, just take a breather now, before you head back."

"Back?"

She pointed over Joseph's shoulder. "Your ride's back there, unless you feel like walking to your room."

So much for Florence Nightingale.

He made the turn without relying on his wounded side, a simple pivot on his strong right leg.

"That's tricky. I can see you're good at thinking on your feet."

"One of them, anyway."

"Let's try them both, then, shall we?"

Back along the narrow runway, dizzy, pain from head to foot.

"Once more."

"Are you for real?"

"Believe it."

Lee was near exhaustion by the time he traveled up and down the bars a second time, almost collapsing in his chair.

"Not bad, for starters." Lisa took a moment to release the brakes and wheeled him toward the universal gym. "Before we quit, let's see what you can show me on the weights."

His gown felt clammy on the ride back to his room, but Lee was thankful for the perspiration drying on his skin. The chill of air-conditioning helped compensate for nagging aches and pains, the flush of physical exertion that had made him feverish in the workout room. He felt like shit, but he could not deny a small sensation of accomplishment.

"Okay, champ, here we go."

It took more help from Lisa this time, but he wallowed into bed and tugged the floppy gown around his knees.

"Don't bother, it's a write-off," Lisa said. "You've got a fresh one coming, and it's bathtime anyway. Right back."

She disappeared, returning moments later with a plastic tub of soapy water and a sponge, a folded gown and several terry towels tucked underneath one arm.

"Now, wait a second—"

"Not to worry, Joe. I've bathed you twice already, and you're still intact."

"So, where was I?"

"Out cold, as I recall."

"You haven't got an orderly around here somewhere? Like, a man, let's say?"

"They're all tied up right now. You're stuck with me."

She raised the bed till he was upright, more or less, the towels and tub of water resting on a tray. Resigned, Joe offered no resistance as she pulled the sweaty robe down to his waist.

"Lean forward, please."

She kept the sponge just damp enough to do its job and followed with a towel, his back and shoulders finished in a dozen firm but gentle strokes.

"Sit back."

She mopped his face and dried it, moving to his chest and down along his belt line, where the gown lay folded. Concentrating on the vacant television screen, he tried to make his mind a blank, ignoring Lisa's touch and memories of the recurring Nancy-dream.

It didn't work.

"Right arm."

He raised it, and she sponged his armpit, down along his rib cage to his flank.

"Now, left."

More difficult, and Lisa had to help him. Pain throbbed from his sutures, and for once he welcomed the discomfort, hoping it would cover his involuntary reaction to the sponge bath.

"Here we go."

She slipped the fresh gown over his arms and tied it off behind his neck, the other whisked away and gone. He lost his focus on the television, searching for a new spot on the ceiling as she let the bed back down.

And lost that, too, when Lisa said, "If you could just turn over, to your right."

He did as he was told, cool air against his buttocks and behind his knees as Lisa bathed him, blotting with the towel.

"Lie back."

Lee closed his eyes, embarrassed as his half-erection pressed against the gown. She didn't seem to notice, telling him, "We're almost finished now," and starting at his ankles, sponging up along his thighs. A draft as Lisa drew the gown above his hips and finished up. New color in his cheeks as she dropped the gown back into place and drew the sheet up to his waist.

"All done."

His eyes came open.

"It's another hour, yet, before your medication. If you need it, I can see about a little something for the pain."

"I'm fine."

"Okay." She hesitated, turning toward the door with the pan, the towels, and the rumpled gown. "You did all right today. Tomorrow we'll try a little harder."

Harder, right.

"I'll do my best," he said.

The door swung shut behind her, and he reached for

the remote control. Soap operas, anything, to take his mind off the conflicting stimuli of pain and sexual frustration. He would have to master both, one inescapable, the other absolutely out of place. And concentration was the key.

Watching a mindless game show, he turned out thoughts of Lisa, Nancy, Eddie Hovis, and concentrated on recovery, the first step past survival, and the next step after that.

The road that led him back to Bobby Chan.

That afternoon, Ray Christy paid another visit. He was carrying a paper bag with grease stains on the sides.

"I snuck a couple burgers in, some fries, in case you wanna try them on."

"They didn't shoot me in the taste buds, Ray."

While he attacked the junk food, Christy briefed him on the progress of his case. Which was to say, no breaks, no leads, no further evidence of any kind.

"The man thinks maybe One-nut made you, tipped off his contacts, and they got overzealous. Dusted Tommy too, for being dumb enough to let you cover him."

"That's bullshit. If he was slick enough to make us, he'd have tried to set us up some other way. He wasn't any rocket scientist, I grant you, but he wasn't suicidal either."

"Well . . ."

"Whoever burned us, they decided Tommy was expendable. They'd rather cut their losses, and they weren't afraid of heat from wasting federal agents."

"Chan, again?"

"Who else?"

"We haven't found a goddamn thing to tie him in."

"He wouldn't leave a trail. By now he's got the shooters tucked away somewhere, or maybe buried."

"Then we're screwed."

"On his end, maybe. I'd still like to know who gave us up. Find that one, squeeze him hard enough, you've got Chan by the short and curlies."

"We're putting all our snitches through the ringer, but I gotta tell you, Joe, we're getting nowhere fast."

"Leave some for me, okay?"

"You've got enough to do, just healing up."

"As good as new, the doctor says. Don't write me off."

"Nobody's writing anybody off. We've got a team, remember? No James Bond, no solos. Take five while you can. The shit's not going anywhere."

"I know," Lee told him. "That's the problem."

4

"Again. Let's do it right, this time."

Lee strained against the leg press, biting off a curse as new pain flared inside his wounded hip. The weights responded sluggishly, but they were getting there. Another inch. One more.

"That's it. Now *ease* them down, don't let them drop."

Worse yet, resisting gravity and all that weight, when he could simply let it go and never mind the ringing crash. The muscles in his hip and thigh were burning. One more second, and he knew his bones would crack beneath the strain.

"Okay, let's take a breather."

Nearly out of breath, he found the strength to say, "I hope I'm not exhausting you."

"A sense of humor. That's encouraging."

She sat beside him on a metal folding chair, legs crossed, the crisp white skirt providing just a glimpse of thigh. She didn't seem to take offense at Joe's grousing; she must have heard it all before.

He let himself relax, surprised to find his hands were cramped from clutching at the rubber grips protruding from his chair on either side. He flexed his fingers, bringing circulation back, relieved to note that he felt nothing in the way of major protest from his wounded shoulder. Not until he tried to raise the arm above his head.

It was another Wednesday, seven days since Lisa had introduced him to the workout room. She had brought him back for longer sessions every day, and this morning he had made the rounds with isotonic exercises on the shoulder press, the thigh and knee machine, the hip flexor, finishing off with the leg press. An hour, overall, and he was reasonably pleased with the results.

On Monday, suddenly aware that she had worked the last nine days without a break, he had asked about her schedule. Lisa told him she had traded weekends with a friend who had some things to do at home, and he accepted it without argument. No reason to believe that she would skip days off to put him through his paces, when she could have had the free time with her boyfriend—lover? husband?—to relax.

No reason in the world.

She didn't wear a wedding or engagement ring, but that proved nothing. Many women viewed rings as symbols of possession and refused to brand themselves, requiring trust instead of ornaments to seal a bargain. On the other hand, no ring *might* mean no man at home.

Lee stopped himself, surprised. Where was he going with that train of thought? A date, perhaps, when he could walk again without a cane? A love affair, inspired by . . . What? His gratitude? Her pity?

Not a chance.

Patient-nurse infatuations might be routine, especially in cases where the duty nurse was also therapist, companion, friend, but he had to keep the whole thing in perspective or he'd wind up looking like a goddamn fool.

The lady was assigned to work with him until she had him on his feet and out of there. She had sponged him down the first few days, as she had done a hundred or a thousand men before, because he could not bathe himself. Last weekend she had worked extra days to help a friend. Case closed.

And yet . . .

He found himself drawing parallels between Lisa and Nancy—who had nothing in common. Nancy had been dark-haired and petite, the classic Oriental bride; Lisa was tall and fair. Nancy's smile was hesitant, reserved; Lisa's came and went at will, a physical expression of her zest for life.

Lee's marriage to Nancy, in the spring of 1982, had seemed a love match at the start, but he had spent the past nine years dissecting it with twenty-twenty hindsight. Now he was inclined to think that he had mistaken lust for love. His friends were married or engaged, some bailing out of college in their haste to tie the knot. His parents had encouraged Joe's decision after hinting broadly that he should have let them choose his bride.

For Nancy the marriage had seemed preordained. The product of a traditional Chinese home, she had been groomed to marry from the time she was old enough to walk. Her parents would have liked to pick her husband, but this was America, so they were grateful that she wasn't smitten with an Anglo boy. Nancy had abandoned junior college on the day she became engaged, returning two years later when her doctor told her there could be no children. It was an escape from sitting around the house alone all day, and sometimes through the night.

Her education—liberation, really—drove a wedge between them, but if Lee had had to cite a single cause for the divorce, he would have blamed his job. Police had always boasted a high divorce rate, a concomitant of the stress, erratic hours, and sporadic violence in their lives.

"I'm not cut out for this," Nancy had told him on the morning after Lee shot the black kid in an alley off Sepulveda. "My fault, okay? It isn't you. I'm sorry, Joe."

They'd parted friends, and Lee still sent her little things at Christmas, but otherwise didn't keep in touch. It was just another fact of his life, like going to the dentist, paying taxes, gunning down a kid and getting himself shot.

"Let's try the bike," Lisa said, cutting through his reverie.

"Feel free." And when she said nothing: "You're killing me, you know that?"

"Joe."

"Okay, I'm going. Can you help me up, at least?"

"You have the cane. Left hand, this time, for practice."

"Thanks."

"I'm right here if you need me," Lisa said. And smiled.

• • •

Lee showered by himself these days, a safety railing close at hand in case the wounded hip betrayed him. It was awkward, but the left arm was coming back and he didn't have to do the job one-handed any more.

His first time in the shower, he had concentrated on his balance, hardly moving as he shuffled in a tiny circle, once to wet himself, again to rinse when he was finished with the soap. The second day, it was a little easier, and yesterday he had let himself relax, enjoying it.

The fantasy came next, a mix-and-match amalgam of the Nancy-dream and Lisa bathing him, his own hand standing in for hers until he caught himself. He had a choice, to finish it or not, and he had savored the decision for a moment, finally opting for an icy spray that set his teeth on edge and left him shivering.

Willpower.

It had carried him this far, with Lisa's help, and it would see him back on partial duty in another week or so, if all went well. From there, continued exercise at home should whip him into fighting trim, but the workouts would not be the same.

He felt a pang of loss, and dismissed it as a patient's natural dependence on a therapist. Lisa had nursed him back from somewhere in the close proximity of death. His was a normal and predictable response. It happened every day.

But not to *him.*

That afternoon, when Lisa brought the wheelchair, his muscles were groaning. "Too much," he told her, making up his mind that nothing she could say would make a difference. "Once a day is all the torture I can stand."

"No exercise," she said. "A little ride. I've got somebody you should talk to."

"Who?"

"The trauma counselor."

"No, thanks."

She frowned. "It's doctor's orders, I'm afraid. And your employer was insistent."

Damn.

A trauma counselor was no more than a shrink renamed, and Lee had no use for doctors of the mind, with all their bullshit dream analysis and building up a simple case of anger into something they could poke and probe for weeks on end. He had been through it all before, about the shooting in L.A.

Catharsis, hell. It was a kind of sterile self-abuse, but he would have to play along with Dr. Beck and his superiors downtown before they cleared him for release and a return to duty. One more exercise, to supplement his workouts in the gym.

"Okay, let's go."

He could have walked, but there were rules involved. Insurance, Lisa said, and he had pushed himself enough for one day, anyhow. She wheeled him to the elevator, down one floor, and back along a corridor to a door marked "PRIVATE." Lisa knocked and waited for a woman in her mid-forties to appear. No lab coat over her tweed and cotton, and gray-streaked hair worn fashionably long. Designer spectacles that magnified lively eyes.

Across the threshold, Lisa left him parked and set the brake. "I'll see you in an hour or so."

"That should be fine," the stranger said, a whiskey voice like something from a Bogart film.

Alone with Lee, she took her seat behind the desk. "I'm Dr. Janeway. You may call me Paula, if you like." A quick perusal of the open folder on her desk. "It's Joseph, isn't it? Or Joe?"

"Whatever."

"Please feel free to walk around the office." The divan, a bucket chair, the window, all included in an airy gesture of her hand. "I know about the rules, but we're adults here, after all."

Lee stood with the assistance of his cane and shifted to the other chair, regretting it at once; the unfamiliar contour shot needles through his hip.

"I understand you're doing very well in therapy."

He echoed Lisa: "I'm getting there."

"Determination is important to the healing process. Too many patients languish or expect the therapist to do it all."

"I'm determined," Joe said. So far, at least, he hadn't been compelled to lie.

"Outstanding. Were you briefed on why you're here? I mean, right now?"

"For trauma counseling."

"Correct. Could you define that for me, Joe?"

He scanned his memory, retrieving the appropriate response. "Cooperation toward adjustment and reintegration after some traumatic episode. To wit, the fact I saw my partner die and nearly got my ass shot off."

The doctor's noncommittal smile remained in place. "You've been around this block before, I see."

"Los Angeles, about ten years ago."

"Would you describe the circumstances for me, Joe?"

His file was lying on her desk, but Lee continued the charade. "I had a shooting, in the line of duty. Fifteen-year-old kid held up a liquor store and met me coming out. His gun was plastic, mine was real. He died."

"And how did that make you feel?"

"Relieved to be alive."

"That's all?"

"The doctor in L.A. kept waiting for a breakdown, like he was hoping I couldn't take it. Guilt reaction, nightmares—anything. I think I disappointed him."

"Because you felt no guilt? Or were you simply able to conceal it?"

"Guilt for what?"

"You killed a man—a boy, in fact. Some people, in your place, might doubt themselves, regardless of the circumstances."

"I was on the job. He had eleven priors at age fifteen."

"So, he deserved to die?"

Lee felt the color rising in his cheeks, determined not to let his anger show.

"I didn't say that. He was stupid. Taking down the liquor store was bad enough, but pulling on a cop? I mean, he *knew* the gun was plastic, didn't he?"

"And now, another shooting. That's uncommon, isn't it?"

"It happens. Anyway, I didn't pull the trigger this time."

"No."

"I mean, it's more like being in an accident, you know? I walked away, if you can call this walking."

"But your partner didn't, Joe. How does that make you feel?"

"I miss him. We were friends."

"Close friends?"

A flash of Eddie, shit-faced, hitting on a barmaid after work and getting nowhere. Both of them together, doubling, with women Lee couldn't remember if his life depended on it.

"Yes."

"It's natural, in such a case, for the survivor of a crisis situation to experience some transitory guilt. You may have asked yourself, 'Why Edward?' "—she had clearly read his file—"or, 'Why not me?' "

"His name was Eddie."

"I apologize."

"For what?"

"My point is, your doubts and questions are completely natural. It's not your fault that Eddie died and you're alive."

"I know whose fault it is."

"Which brings us to the question of response. Assuming that you know the guilty man—or *think* you do—what action should you take?"

He saw the trap and stepped around it.

"I just want to do my job."

"Which is?"

"Arrest narcotics dealers. Put them out of business if I can."

"Of course, but in respect to the specific case at hand?"

"I want to do my job," he said again.

"Aside from misplaced guilt, there is a tendency in such traumatic cases for survivors to experience an impulse toward revenge."

"I see."

"In my experience, I've witnessed victims with desire

for retribution aimed at individuals and corporations, lifeless objects, even God. For tragedy to be endured, it must be logical. Responsibility must be assigned."

"Somebody *is* responsible."

"In your case, yes. But *you* are not responsible for bringing him to justice single-handed."

Letting her believe that he believed it.

"No."

"I hope that's clear?"

"I'm with you, so far."

Dr. Janeway's smile was skeptical. She jotted something in his file.

"Let's talk about your dreams."

The fog was back, with drizzling rain besides, and Lee was tired of waiting in the car for Eddie to return. They should have stayed together, and to hell with any risk of being spotted. If the mark could pick them out in this soup, he deserved to get away.

Lee checked his watch, confirming that the action should have been wrapped up by now. Another miss, and Eddie standing out there in the fog and rain somewhere, content to wait for hours if he thought it would do the job.

He cursed beneath his breath and stepped outside, remembering to close the door behind him quietly. The mist felt warm and clammy, but at least the rain was letting up. He had to get his bearings, take a fix on where his partner was supposed to be, or they might miss each other in the fog. Some stakeout, wandering in circles, up and down the block all night.

He leaned against the car and flinched, cool porcelain against his naked buttocks. Reaching for his gun, he came up empty, somehow understanding that he must have left the shoulder holster with his other clothing when he stripped. He turned to face the bathroom mirror, wiping at the cloudy glass until his face appeared. The funny part, he hardly recognized himself.

"I couldn't wait." A soft voice from the shower, teasing him. "Do you forgive me?"

Lisa Reilly pulling back the plastic curtain, sleek and naked, with an invitation in her smile.

"I take that as a yes."

Inside the shower, stifling heat, but Joseph didn't care. They stood together, fencing with their tongues and eager hands exploring, Lisa twitching when he found a spot she liked. A glimpse of Nancy when they broke the kiss, but Lisa coming back again with soap and sponge in hand.

"We have to get you clean."

She seemed to take forever, concentrating on his genitals, and Joseph thought he would explode before she finished rinsing off the soapsuds.

"You look good enough to eat."

She knelt before him on the tile, considering the task at hand before he ever felt her tongue. Lee closed his eyes, surrendering to the sensation. Soft hands sliding up to cup his buttocks. Lips and teeth and Lisa working, moaning something with her mouth full.

This time, when the curtain parted, it was ripped away with force enough to scatter plastic rings across the bathroom floor. The rod broke free and clattered to the floor at Eddie's feet.

"For Christ's sake, Joe, it's going down! You with me now, or what?"

The bathroom door slammed open, flying off its hinges. Lee saw dark shapes moving in the fog at Eddie's back. He recognized the firing squad, his partner swiveling to face them. There was nowhere he could run and hide. His shoulders pressed against the sweating tile with Lisa still attached to him, a human shield that would not even save the family jewels.

The guns went off, and—

Lee jerked upright in his bed, the sudden movement lighting flares of pain inside his hip and shoulder. Darkness all around him, with the perspiration beading on his face despite the air conditioner. The loose robe plastered to his body.

"Joe?"

The voice familiar. Lisa coming into focus, moving closer to the bed and switching on a lamp.

"Are you all right?"

"A dream," he said. "It's nothing."

"Are you sure?"

"It must be late. You're out of uniform."

The blush was obviously his imagination, eyes adjusting to the light.

"I left some things behind this afternoon and had to pick them up. While I was here, I thought I might as well look in. If you need something for the pain, to help you sleep . . ."

"I'm fine."

"Well, if you're sure . . ."

"A dream can't do me any harm."

She touched his hand, her fingers there and gone almost before the feeling had a chance to register.

"I'll see you in the morning, then."

"More sweat and toil."

"You bet." She killed the light. "Good night, Joe."

" 'Night."

The door hissed shut behind her, cutting off a wedge of faint illumination from the corridor and leaving him alone.

I left some things behind and had to pick them up. Why not? Forgetfulness was part of life. It happened all the time. He had no reason to believe she had come back just to check on him.

But thinking it, believing it, helped Lee back to sleep again and kept the dreams at bay.

5

The next nine days were gone before Lee knew it; tasteless meals and sweaty workouts ran together with the dreams that woke him every night. When Lisa took him to the gym, he made a point of striving for exhaustion, hoping it would let him pass a night without the images of sudden death, but all in vain. Only time would wipe the memories away, and he resigned himself to wait.

He wasn't fooling Dr. Janeway with his cheerful-patient act. Her questions took a different tack each time they met, but in the end she always worked her way around to Eddie and the shooting, Lee's reactions in the days since learning of his partner's death. She doted on his dreams—the censored versions, leaving Nancy out, and Lisa—offering interpretations that were seldom helpful, never news.

His dreams were an expression of survivor guilt, spewed up by his subconscious while he slept. Dream bullets never touched him, never would, because his guilt and sense of loss were intertwined. He came away unscathed each night—or woke before the guns went off—because, subconsciously, he felt he should have died in Eddie's place.

Lee knew the drill. He frowned and nodded like a student putting the important bits together for himself, but Janeway wasn't buying it. Each time they parted, he could see the disappointment in her eyes, a mission unfulfilled.

No matter.

She would sign him out because she knew *he* knew

precisely what was happening between them. Lee was not the first cop who had ever walked away from counseling without a major breakthrough. Cops were tough to crack, and Dr. Janeway had to know the only sure-fire cure for his depression was getting back to work. If he went off the deep end six months down the road, and ate his gun, at least she would have done her best.

It wouldn't happen, though. The last thing on his mind was suicide.

The morning they checked him out, a Saturday, he kept expecting Lisa Reilly to appear and see him off. The weekend nurse—J. Fairchild, early forties, mousy blond—was competent and nice enough, but Lee was hoping for a chance to say good-bye, see Lisa's smile again, and etch it in his memory before he left.

She didn't show, but Dr. Beck came in with breakfast, letting Lee's powdered eggs turn cold while he discussed the need for further exercise at home. Lee shook the doctor's hand and pushed his food around the plate awhile, then dressed himself, with only minor protests from his hip and shoulder, after Fairchild came to fetch his tray.

It didn't matter if he said good-bye, though. Lisa must have a hundred patients on the floor, every one of them a special case. He had been conning himself, imagining a special bond between them. Grasping straws each time she pulled an extra shift or smiled at him while he was sweating out another session in the gym.

It was her *job* to smile, for Christ's sake, comforting the lame and hopeless. What was he expecting from a nurse?

"You decent, Joe?"

Ray Christy in the doorway, shopping bag in one hand and the other jingling keys.

"I like to think so."

"Hey, three weeks and then some. Had enough?"

"I'd say. What's in the bag?"

"Your piece. We couldn't leave it with your clothes and all. I took it home."

"Okay." He looked around the room again, an old man leaning on his cane. "I guess that's everything."

"Not quite. If you'll excuse me . . ."

Fairchild with a wheelchair, nudging Ray aside and waiting. "Mr. Lee?"

"Don't tell me. Regulations."

They were silent in the elevator, Fairchild waiting with them while he signed releases and insurance forms downstairs. Lee caught himself shooting hopeful glances up and down the hallway, seeking Lisa.

Stop it.

Automatic doors hissed open, and he stood without relying on the cane. The nurse's smile clicked on and off; then she was gone.

Outside, the sun was warm against his face, a light breeze ruffling his hair. He smelled the grass, fresh humus in the flowerbeds, warm asphalt. Slipping on a pair of shades, he scanned the parking lot for late arrivals, knowing that he could not pick out Lisa's car.

"You coming, Joe?"

"I'm right behind you."

He lived on Seventh Avenue, two blocks from the Presidio. Five miles in half an hour through the weekend traffic, Christy driving north on Highway 101 to catch Turk Boulevard, then east, the university surrounding them for several blocks until they left it all behind. Across Arguello, Turk became Balboa, picking up an alias. Six blocks, and right on Seventh, past Arguello Park, to reach the small apartment house where Lee had three rooms on the second floor.

His car was parked out front, a '92 Toyota, three weeks out of action. He considered giving it a try, to check the battery, and then decided it could wait.

Ray parked across the street and killed his engine, listening to metal tick beneath the hood. Their conversation in the past half-hour had been desultory, sparse, but he was bound to try again.

"You live upstairs?"

"Those windows on the right."

"If you need some help, I don't mind coming up."

"I've got it covered, thanks."

"You need anything at all—"

"I'm fine."

Another lag before Ray said, "You're coming back on Monday?"

"That's the plan."

"They wouldn't kick, upstairs, you took another week to settle in."

"I've taken all the time I need."

"A thing like this, it hits you when you least expect it."

"Ray, I'm coming back."

"Okay. I won't deny we're short."

"You're always short."

"It hasn't been the same."

"I know."

"We all miss Eddie, Joe."

"I know you do."

"I never told you this, but back in eighty-four, about a year before you transferred north, we worked a bust together on the waterfront. It was a Friday night, Pier Twenty-three—the Foreign Trade Zone—and a couple of Colombians were bringing in some heavy flake. We counted three, four Cubans waiting for the shipment, and we let 'em bring it in."

Ray lit a cigarette and flicked the match out through his open window.

"Anyway, we jumped 'em, and you know the way things go. We had one cuffed behind a warehouse, to a rail or something on the loading dock, and two more out in front. All Cubans. The Colombians, we had to chase 'em for a couple hundred yards on foot, but Eddie caught 'em both. One tried to cut him, stupid fucker. Eddie broke his nose, a couple of his ribs, before I pulled him off."

"He had a temper."

"But the funny part, we ran 'em back downtown and started filling out reports. I'm halfway through, the usual hunt-and-peck, when Eddie says he'll be right back, there's something he forgot to do."

Lee saw it coming, but he didn't interrupt.

"Half-hour later, Eddie's back there in the office with another Cuban." Christy chuckled to himself. "Would you believe it? All the running, kicking ass, and taking names, we went and left that fucker cuffed behind the warehouse. If Eddie hadn't thought of it, he could've sat around till Monday morning. Maybe chewed his arm off like a wolverine and got away."

They laughed together, winding down, before Lee said, "I miss him too."

"There was nothing in the world you could've done to save him, Joe. Shit happens. No one's blaming you for anything."

"I'll see you Monday."

"Right."

Lee took the shopping bag, his pistol with the extra magazines inside, and crossed the street. Felt Christy watching as he reached the outside stairs, and turned to wave again before the federal four-door pulled away.

Lee took the stairs as they had taught him in the hospital, his right leg first, the cane to help him, and his free hand on the rail. It wasn't all that far to climb—he counted eighteen steps—but he was winded by the time he reached the top.

There was an advertising flier anchored to his doorknob with a rubber band, and Lee removed it as he fumbled with his keys to let himself inside. The combination living room and kitchen had a musty smell, and it was dark, the curtains drawn on sliding doors that served the tiny balcony. Lee dropped his weapon on the couch and threw the curtains back for light, the left-hand sliding door for air.

He would have mail downstairs, but it had waited this long, it could wait another hour. He was looking forward to a breather and a beer before he hit the stairs again.

Lee moved around the breakfast counter, barely limping, to examine the refrigerator. Sour milk and mustard on the door, with two eggs he had meant to fry the morning after trailing One-nut Ma. A partial loaf of rye bread, showing spots of mold, beside a package of bologna that had surely turned, by now. Inside the crisper, half a head of lettuce that had taken on a new life of its own.

At least the beer was safe. Lee popped a can and

drained it where he stood, three weeks of abstinence providing the suggestion of a rush. Not bad. He grabbed another, full can in his right hand, empty in his left. If he was breaking training, Lee decided, he should do it right.

For Eddie's sake, if nothing else.

He stooped to throw the empty can away, and met a killer fragrance emanating from the cabinet underneath the sink. The kitchen trashcan, nearly full, had gone untouched while he was in the hospital, its contents ripening in darkness. Joseph held his breath and sealed the liner with a plastic twist-tie, kneeling to inspect the cabinet for any uninvited guests who might have been attracted to the feast. None visible, and he was toasting his good fortune when the doorbell rang.

The landlord, he decided, ready with a spiel about the rent, now three days overdue. Lee set the beer can down, considered hobbling on his cane for sympathy, and thought: To hell with it. Four years in one apartment, and the first time that he ever missed the rent, he had been lying in the hospital with bullet wounds. The old man wants to bitch and moan, tough shit.

He was prepared to let his landlord set the tone and go from there, but nothing had prepared him for the sight of Lisa Reilly standing on his doorstep, both arms wrapped around a jumbo shopping bag.

"Hello, yourself," she said as Joseph stood before her, staring silently. "Can I come in?"

Inside, she said, "Nice place," not sounding like a joke.

Lee closed the door behind her, suddenly aware of dust, the lingering aroma in his kitchen.

"Thanks."

"Before you ask, I tracked you down from your admission forms. It was a toss-up, whether I should see you off or do the shopping, but I thought, three weeks, you might be running low on food."

"You didn't have to do this, Lisa."

She ignored him, moving toward the kitchen with her bag of groceries, and she spied the open beer can on the breakfast bar.

"You're celebrating?"

"More or less."

"Alone?"

"So far."

"I'm sorry, Joe, if you're expecting someone—"

"No."

He watched her blush, enjoying it.

"This really isn't me. I've never done this kind of thing before."

"I'm glad you came."

"I feel like such an idiot."

"What's in the bag?"

"The basics." Lisa started taking inventory. "Eggs. Some Campbell's soup. A loaf of bread—whole wheat, I didn't know what kind you like."

"It's fine."

"Some fruits and vegetables, this and that."

"What's 'this and that'?"

"Fresh shrimp, wild rice. A bottle of Chablis."

"For lunch?"

"Or dinner, as you like."

"I should've paid attention in my cooking class."

"You'll manage."

"I don't know."

"Of course, if you were *really* free this afternoon—"

"I promise."

"—I suppose it wouldn't hurt for me to walk you through the tricky parts."

"That's all I ask."

He watched her putting things away and took the opportunity to stuff his bag of trash inside the pantry, out of sight.

"You spoke with Dr. Beck this morning?"

"Briefly. He was making sure I don't forget my workouts."

"It's important, Joe. You've made tremendous progress, but you can't afford to let it slide."

He said, "You made me what I am today."

"That's silly. You did all the work."

He moved in close enough to smell her perfume, almost touching-close.

"I don't know whether I can pull it off, without my coach."

"As I recall, you've got determination."

"What I need right now is some incentive."

"Oh?"

He hadn't planned to kiss her yet, but breathing in her scent and standing close enough to feel her body heat, Lee couldn't wait. If Lisa was surprised, it didn't show, her lips responding cautiously at first, then parting to admit his tongue. She moved against him, straining, as his hands moved down to cup her buttocks, working at the faded denim of her jeans.

Her face was flushed, eyes shining, when they broke for air.

"I don't see any shortage of incentive here."

"About my therapy . . ."

She slipped a hand between them, trapping him.

"I think I've diagnosed your problem."

"Is it curable?"

"Unfortunately, with our latest methods, I can only offer you a brief reprieve."

"It's a recurring problem, then?"

Her warm hand squeezing, stroking him.

"I wouldn't be surprised."

"And you'd advise that I should keep these treatments up?"

"Indefinitely."

"Ah."

He worked her shirttail free, smooth flesh like velvet to the touch, and Lisa squirmed against him as he sought the closure on her bra.

"In front," she whispered, nipping at his ear while Joseph kissed her neck.

He took his time, excited by the feel of supple flesh encased in silky fabric, Lisa's nipples making exclamation points against the thin material. She trembled as he found the catch and worked it open, nudging lacy cups aside.

"The bedroom?"

"Back there, on the left."

"Why don't you show me?"

Shadows, with the curtains drawn, their only lighting from the open bedroom door. He left it that way, hungry for the sight of her, afraid that he might lose her in the dark. Lee's hands were trembling as he started on the buttons of her shirt.

"Let me."

He couldn't tear his eyes away from Lisa as they stripped, perhaps a yard apart, ignoring twinges from his hip and shoulder in his haste. Another moment, and they stepped together, flesh on flesh, her body fitting his as if she had been tailor-made.

He loved the taste of her, a flavor all her own, the mental images of Nancy banished as he flicked at Lisa's nipples with his tongue, bent lower. Going down on his right knee, first, to ease the pressure on his wounded side.

"Oh, God."

She tangled fingers in his hair and pressed his face against her, thrusting with her hips to meet his tongue. The muscles in her thighs were rippling, and he wrapped both arms around her waist to ease her gently backward, onto the bed.

"Right there. Don't stop!"

His hands moved up to stroke her breasts, and Lisa arched her back, a purring feline.

"Mmmm."

He registered the little sound of disappointment as he switched positions, changing as he eased himself between her open thighs. A slender hand came down to guide him.

"Faster, now."

"Like this?"

"Uh-huh."

She braced her heels against his buttocks, thrusting.

"Harder."

"I don't want to hurt you."

"Hurt. I need. Like that."

"Oh, Jesus."

"Aaaahhhh!"

They lay together, afterward, Lee's index finger tracing lazy patterns in her pubic hair. He said, "You're out of uniform again."

"I noticed."

"Nice."

"You have a certain flare, yourself."

"My coach gets all the credit."

"All?"

"Well, maybe half."

His hand slipped lower.

"Mmm. We shouldn't overtax your strength."

"I have to build up my endurance."

Reaching for him. "Such determination."

"Work hard, play hard."

"So I see."

"I'm out of practice. Maybe we should try again, make sure I've got it right."

"You did just fine."

"I'm shooting for perfection."

"What about a shower?"

"After."

"During?"

"Ah."

She kissed him firmly on the lips, then bolted for the bathroom. "Last one in . . ."

6

The Federal Building, at McAllister and Hyde, stands opposite the San Francisco Public Library. Its underground garage has spaces numbered and assigned, with thirteen slots on Level 2 allotted to the working agents of the DEA. When Lee arrived at half-past eight on Monday morning, there were two spots left.

One of them Eddie's.

He was running late and didn't care. He had been up at six, with Lisa making breakfast after spending Sunday night, but they had been distracted from the eggs and lost an hour, somehow, in between the kitchen and the bedroom. Lisa called it necessary reinforcement for his first day back at work, and he was not inclined to argue with success.

All weekend, he had waited for the nightmares to return, but Lisa had been running interference, holding them at bay. Lee knew it wouldn't last, but he was grateful for the respite, time to lick the wounds that didn't show.

And if it *did* work, having her around—what then?

They seemed compatible in every way, but two days didn't prove a thing. Three weeks, if Joseph counted every day since he woke up in San Francisco General, Lisa standing by his bed with Dr. Beck, but everything before the last two days was business, duty nurse and patient, by the book. Despite their history, it felt like starting out from scratch.

Lee did not have the words that would prepare her for a string of broken dates and nights alone, the gnawing dread that would accompany every stakeout, every raid.

She had already seen him close to death, a situation Nancy never had to face while they were married, and he questioned whether Lisa's clinical detachment could survive another shooting.

Begging trouble.

Next time—if there *was* a next time—Lee intended to be ready. When they wheeled the stretchers out, he would be standing on his own two feet. The one who got away.

And where would Lisa be?

He took the elevator up to number five, ignoring the directory. The corridor was cool, impersonal, familiar. IBM Selectrics clacking at him from the open doors of offices he passed along the way. His destination was the next-to-last door on the right.

The Drug Enforcement Administration is charged with execution of the many federal laws pertaining to importation, manufacture, sale, and possession of "controlled substances"—narcotics and other dangerous drugs. Perpetually understaffed and underfunded, the DEA makes do as best it can, sometimes employing confiscated cash and weapons, vehicles and real estate, to prosecute its war against the syndicates responsible for moving tons of heroin, cocaine, and other drugs throughout America.

Depending on an agent's duty station, he may spend his days pursuing dealers in marijuana, methamphetamines, barbiturates, or LSD. His adversaries are Jamaican, Haitian, Cuban, Puerto Rican, and Vietnamese, along with good ol' home boys who have spied a signpost on the road to instant wealth. Colombians import cocaine from Bogotá and Medellín, while Rastafarians sell weed as part of their religion. Members of the Dixie Mafia have graduated from the moonshine still to high-tech marijuana farms, and chemists hired by outlaw bikers manufacture speed in makeshift labs from coast to coast. An average thirty thousand yearly busts for dealing and possession don't even begin to faze the smugglers, dealers, and their countless customers.

From time to time, a new administration orders studies

of the problem, gathering statistics on arrests and seizures, tabulating federal dollars spent against results obtained. Prognostications on addiction are broken down by age and income groups, geography, religion, sex, and race. Regardless of the party or the president in charge, the bottom line remains predictable: America in crisis, coping with the modern plague. A call to arms.

In Northern California, heroin is still the drug of choice among discriminating junkies, and the purest form is known as "China white." Historically, despite its several points of origin, the potent drug's chief handlers have been—and remain—Chinese. In San Francisco, during the summer of 1995, the traffic was coordinated by a smiling businessman named Robert Chan. No record of arrests, indictments, or convictions.

Yet.

The office was familiar chaos, several agents milling in the bullpen as Lee entered, others typing reports or phoning contacts in the double line of open carrels on his left. The smell of coffee, gun oil, sweat, and cigarettes.

"Hey, Joe!"

Conversation lurched to a halt, all eyes on Lee, his friends and fellow agents looking for a sign that he was still the man they knew from grueling hours on the job and all-night parties afterward. With Eddie dead and buried, each of them required some private affirmation of his own invincibility. Joe Lee was living proof that any one of them could take a hit—hell, four or five hits—and walk away.

Lee was relieved that he had left his cane downstairs in the Toyota.

"Joey, how's it hanging?"

"Welcome back."

"Too bad about the Ed man, Joey."

"Gonna kick some ass, we pin it down."

He shook hands all around, showed nothing when they slapped him on his wounded shoulder. Mouthing the expected macho crap about how being shot and nearly killed was nothing special. Piece of cake. No sweat. They all knew it was a lie even as they ate it up.

"You made it, Joe."

He turned to see Ray Christy emerging from his tiny office at the far end of the room, beyond the carrels.

" 'Morning, Chief."

"A minute of your time?"

Ray closed the door behind him, hooked a chair around, and Lee sat facing him across the cluttered desk.

"How are you, Joe?"

"Fine."

"How are you *really*?"

"Ray, I wouldn't be here if I couldn't do the job."

"Okay, I had to ask." He lit a cigarette and left the lighter on his desk. "The man left word he wants to see you, first thing."

"What's going on?"

Ray shrugged, his eyes evasive. "Standard welcome back, for all I know. Don't keep him waiting, huh?"

"On six?"

"Where else?"

"I want the file on Bobby Chan when I get back."

Rank has its privileges, including segregation of commanders from their troops. In Leland Kephart's case, one floor made all the difference in the world. On six, he could rub shoulders with the FBI and HUD, a better class of suits than he employed to root out dealers on the streets. If all else failed, he could pretend to disengage himself from the routine of buys and busts his people spent their duty hours laying out downstairs.

It was the second time Joe Lee had been required to visit Kephart's private lair. The first occasion, two years earlier, had been a simple one-on-one that followed Kephart's transfer from New Orleans. Kephart had seen them all together in the fifth-floor bullpen, but the private chats were meant to foster the illusion of accessibility. Each visitor, in turn, was reassured that Kephart valued teamwork and expected all his men to run their operations strictly by the book. If they encountered any problems, Kephart was behind them all the way.

In fact, the man remained aloof unless a heavy seizure

brought him out to preen before the media, his secretary posting commendations for the men whose victories were registered in Kephart's name. When there were problems with a warrant, friction with the FBI or local agencies, Ray Christy worked it out. If anybody crossed the line and needed whipping into shape—a reprimand, or worse—the word came down from six and Christy had it covered, leaving Kephart free to meditate on higher things.

Like moving on.

The man had eyes on Washington, and everybody in the building knew it. San Francisco was a stepping stone between New Orleans and the payoff, privately defined by Kephart as promotion to the Seat of Government. Another year or two, a few more decent headlines to complete the portrait of a slick administrator on the rise, and he was gone.

For Joseph and the other grunts on five, it couldn't be too soon.

The outer office looked familiar, beige and brown, with imitation leather furniture. No smoking while you waited for the man. The magazines were new, and Kephart's secretary was a different blond, a later model than the one Lee had met before. She took his name and passed it on, inviting him to have a seat.

Ten minutes, browsing through a *Newsweek* background article on China's year-long border war with India, before the man decided Lee had waited long enough.

"Excuse me? If you'd step this way . . ."

He liked the new blond better, in her thigh-high minidress that could have been mistaken for a second skin. She led the way to Kephart's inner sanctum, introducing Lee as if the two had never met, then disappeared.

"Please, have a seat."

The man made no attempt to rise or offer Lee his hand. Behind him, flags to left and right, wall-mounted photos of the president and the attorney general. His desk was twice the size of Christy's, but it showed no evidence of ever being used for work.

"How are you, Joseph?" Like an echo from the hospital.

"I'm fine, sir."

"Feeling well, I take it?"

"Yes, sir."

"Frankly, we were all a bit surprised to hear that you were coming back so soon."

"I'm tired of sitting on my duff."

"Of course. I had a word with Dr. Janeway Friday afternoon."

Lee waited. There was nothing he could say, no way to second-guess the counselor.

"She tells me that you're fit for duty, Joseph, but we shouldn't overload your circuits for a while. You take my meaning?"

"No, sir."

Kephart frowned. "A shooting is traumatic. All the more so when your partner . . . well, you follow me, I'm sure."

"I think so."

"Dr. Janeway feels—and I concur—that it would be advisable to make your comeback over time—in stages, as it were. Some desk work for a week or two, a bit of light surveillance afterward."

"With all respect, sir . . ."

"Yes?"

"I disagree."

"How so?"

"I'm ten years on the job," Lee said. "Before that, five years on the street, in uniform. I'm not some shrinking violet, fresh from the academy."

"I know your record, Joseph. It's exemplary. That doesn't change the fact that you've been gravely wounded, seen your partner killed. It hasn't been a month since they had you on machines in ICU. Forgive me if I question any man's ability to go all-out, in your condition, on his first day back at work."

"I have a job to do."

"Precisely. And it's my responsibility to guarantee that that job gets done. I can't allow your zeal, commendable as it may be, to jeopardize the other members of our team."

Lee swallowed the impulsive words that came to mind. If logic knuckled under to emotion now, in front of Kephart, he was lost.

"The night that Agent Hovis died, we were approaching the conclusion of a major case."

"With Tommy Ma. I've read the file. Somebody beat you to him, Joseph."

"Ma was only part of it. I'm after his connection."

Kephart shifted in his swivel chair and heaved a weary sigh.

"The tongs, again?"

Lee shook his head. "The tongs are nothing but a cover. Old men playing fan-tan, children putting on parades in Chinatown. We're looking at a Triad operation here. I'm talking Bobby Chan."

"We've had Chan underneath a microscope the past four weeks. I won't pretend he's squeaky clean, but we've got nothing we can use to hang him, either."

"Nothing *yet*."

"He owns a chain of restaurants and laundries in the city, south to San Jose and Santa Cruz. Last year he gave back ten percent of everything he earned to different charities."

"I know that."

"Did you know that Chan had dinner with the mayor two weeks ago? They average eight, ten times a year. Old friends, it seems. His Honor carried Chinatown with sixty-eight percent of the recorded votes, last time around."

"Is that what this is all about? Connections?"

Kephart stiffened in his chair. "Don't be insulting, Lee. Nobody pulls my string at City Hall."

"Okay, no problem."

"Wrong." The regional director's lips had narrowed to a bloodless slash beneath his nose. "The *problem* is, that *I* won't use *my* team to prosecute a personal vendetta.

Nothing we've uncovered in the time since you were shot leads back to Chan or anybody on his payroll. We've been fishing for a month, without a single bite."

"You need new bait."

"Forget it, Lee. Your judgment has been skewed by personal involvement. Understandablc, of course, but there's no way I'd let you run this case, assuming that we *had* one."

"I spent three months working Chan. My partner died because we got too close. You're telling me to write it off?"

"It's not the first time that a lead went sour," Kephart said. "Won't be the last."

Lee shook his head. "Not good enough."

"I beg your pardon?"

"Chan's as dirty as they come. He's Triad, all the way."

"Too bad you couldn't prove it."

"Give me time."

"No way. This pipe dream has already cost me one good man and several thousand hours of investigation, at the taxpayers' expense. The end result is one dead dealer, and the other side bagged *him.* It's finished, Lee."

"I can't accept that."

Knowing he had overstepped his bounds, not caring.

Kephart forced a narrow smile. "The matter is not open to debate."

Lee met the regional director's gaze, unflinching.

"I work Bobby Chan," he said, "or I don't work at all."

"I've never been impressed by threats," Kephart said. "You're about to make a critical mistake, career-wise."

"Chan, or nothing."

"That's your final word?"

Lee nodded.

"Have it your way. You're suspended, as of now, until a formal hearing is convened on insubordination charges. Two, three weeks would be my own best estimate. I'll take your shield and weapon now."

Lee placed the wallet with his badge and I.D. card on Kephart's desk.

"I bought the piece myself. It stays with me."

"Whatever. Bear in mind, you're a civilian now. No carry permit, no authority of any kind. I'd hate to see you make things worse by playing vigilante."

"I'll remember that."

"Please do. My secretary will advise you of the hearing date, by mail."

Dismissed. He closed the heavy door behind him as he left, the blond delivering a smile she offered anyone who came to see the man. The elevator seemed to take forever, and he rode it down to the garage without another stop on five.

I'm unemployed, he thought. Suspended, minus pay, until a board convened to make it permanent. The impact of his stubborn outburst hitting home.

Was it too late to double back and plead insanity, before the paperwork was filed? Ten years, for nothing, and the insubordination charge would blow his partial pension, if it stuck.

Too late.

The moment that the shooting started, Eddie dying on the seat beside him, it had been too late, his options limited to one. The DEA was writing Eddie off, a total loss, but Lee could never let it go at that.

His sights were fixed on Bobby Chan, the men behind him. He would have to do it on his own, and that meant there was no more time to waste.

The telephone was ringing when he entered the apartment, Christy furious and breathless on the other end.

"For Christ's sake, Joe, have you been snorting up the evidence, or what?"

"Don't sweat it, Ray."

"Terrific. Have you thought about this thing you're doing? Did you think it through at all?"

"It's done."

"I talked to Kephart. Joe, he's not unreasonable. Drop your beef with Chan *for now,* and you can start from scratch tomorrow. No suspension, nothing in your file. He's calling it a stress-related lapse in judgment."

"Where'd he go to med school?"

"Jokes, now? Let me guess. You're pissing off ten years —your pension, everything—to be a comedian. Are you fucking crazy?"

"Eddie died to make a case on Chan. I owe him one."

"We'll get the bastard *later.* Guy like that, he always fumbles, somewhere down the line. I guarantee, we'll be there waiting for him. In the meantime—"

"No. I want his ass for killing Eddie."

"How about a citizen's arrest? Just let me know your next of kin before you try it, will you?"

"Ray, I'm busy."

"Dammit, Joe—"

"I'll call you."

Cradling the handset long enough to clear the line, he left it off the hook before he cracked a beer. Let Christy fume in private for a while. His arguments were logical enough, but Lee had moved beyond the point of operating in his own best interest.

He had work to do, but he couldn't proceed without a cover and a plan. It was the kind of problem he might have shared with Eddie Hovis, kicking it around until they solved the puzzle.

Still, every riddle had its own solution, if you thought about it long and hard enough. The key was trying every angle in the book, and some that weren't, until you let the problem solve itself.

Determination.

Concentration.

The answer, when it struck him, was simplicity itself.

7

The offices of Ace Investigations were on Campton, north of Union Square, a neighborhood that still showed traces of the killer quake of '89. A face-lift made the building look brand-new, but Lee could never ride the lift without a thought for joists and trusses, straining to defy the law of gravity. The elevator smelled of mildew, and its layers of whitewash never quite kept pace with rude graffiti.

Charlie Maddox was the "Ace" of Ace Investigations, thirteen years a San Francisco cop before his overzealous questioning of a suspected child molester put him on the street. These days, it was impossible to picture Maddox in a uniform, his squat 350-pound physique encased in suits he custom-ordered from a big-and-tall shop on Columbus. Seldom found without his trademark cheap cigar, a sprinkling of ash across his garish tie, he might have stepped directly off the screen from any one of half a dozen Bogart movies.

"Joey, man, how long's it been?"

"Two years?"

"I don't believe it. Shit, I must be getting old."

Their first encounter had been job-related, Maddox staking out the husband in a high-society divorce while Lee and Eddie Hovis tried to make the guy for dealing in cocaine. They lost out all around when their intended drove his classic Jaguar off the Bayshore Freeway at an estimated speed of ninety-seven miles per hour, but the friendship had endured. Lee had turned to Maddox more than once for information he could not obtain by means of lawful warrants, and they had been known to close the North Beach bars from time to time.

Two years.

Too long.

"I can't believe you pulled the pin," Maddox said after they were seated in his office, a fifth of Seagram's open on the desk. "Fed up with all that bureaucratic bull?"

"I'm on suspension, Charlie."

Maddox cocked a bushy eyebrow, sipping from a coffee mug that had been decorated with a cartoon vulture and a caption reading "FEED THE HOMELESS . . . TO THE BUZZARDS."

"Tell me more," he said.

"I've got an angle on the guy who wasted Eddie, but the brass don't want to hear it."

"I was gonna call you when I heard, but what the hell is there to say?"

"It's done. The thing is, now I'm on my own. No paperwork, in case I need my piece; no cover while I work it out."

"And on the side, you've gotten used to seeing food a couple times a day."

"That too."

"No sweat. You're on the payroll, as of now. My license covers you on the investigative end. The carry permit takes a while, but we can speed it up with reference to your law-enforcement background, if the brass don't raise a stink."

"It could go either way."

"I've got a couple friends downtown. I'll see what I can do."

"I owe you one."

"Forget it. You can do some work around the office here, you get the time, when you're not on this other thing. Which, by the way, I never heard of."

"That's affirmative."

"We're set, then."

Maddox tipped the Seagram's bottle over Joseph's paper cup and raised his own mug in a toast.

"Here's to the assholes at the top," he said. "May they all get hemorrhoids."

"You quit your job?" More curiosity than shock in Lisa's sleepy voice.

"It's no big deal."

They lay in bed together, Lee's place, naked, in the euphoric afterglow of sex.

"You seemed so anxious to get back." Not chiding him. Still curious.

"They wanted me on desk work, filing, anything to keep me sidelined while they run around in circles and pretend to look for Eddie's killer."

"Why 'pretend'?"

"Because the man responsible has money and friends at City Hall and who-knows-where. He's hard to tag, and authorizing tons of overtime without results would make the brass look stupid. Why go after Mr. Big when you can bust a crack house every night and keep your batting average high?"

"You told them that?"

"We talked about it."

"Suspended isn't fired."

"Even if I'm reinstated, it could mean a pay reduction, probably a transfer."

"Oh?" Her voice was smaller, with a hint of worry.

"Either way, I'd still be sitting on my hands. The DEA can't drop a net on Eddie's killer, so it won't hurt for me to take a shot."

"But if you lost your job—"

"I found another."

"That was fast." Suspicious now.

"I called a friend. For all I know, you're looking at the city's first Chinese P.I."

"You're teasing me. Like Magnum, on the late show?"

"I don't wear Hawaiian shirts."

"Oh, God, you're serious."

"Why not?"

"Isn't this a job for the police?"

"If they were on the job, the man I'm after would be

taking all his meals in jail instead of having dinner with the mayor."

"I haven't made a study of it, but there must be laws. I mean, restrictions on civilian interference with police investigations."

"Anybody asks, I'm running down a missing person, maybe working a divorce. Our paths cross here and there, it's just coincidence."

"And they're supposed to swallow that."

"They have to make a case against me. In the meantime—"

"You could easily get hurt again. Or worse."

He pulled her closer, shifting his position so that they were eye-to-eye, his left knee wedged between her own, his free hand resting on her flank.

"Ten years I worked with Eddie. I was only married five before we split. I knew him better than I knew my wife, and now he's dead. The man who killed him walks, unless I make a point of stopping him."

"High Noon? This isn't Tombstone, Joe, and you're not Wyatt Earp. The San Francisco vigilantes gave it up a hundred years ago."

"I'm not the last avenging angel, Lisa. All I'm looking for is evidence that won't fall flat in court."

"And if you find it?"

"I deliver to the prosecution on a silver platter. They don't even have to thank me."

"Dammit, what am I supposed to do with you?"

He smiled and slipped his hand between her legs. "I'll show you."

"You're just trying to distract me."

"Is it working?"

"Mmm. That isn't fair."

"Life's hard."

Warm fingers found him, working. "So are you."

"I feel a little feverish."

"I'd better check your vital signs." Another squeeze. "Your pulse is strong enough."

She rolled him over, mounted with her back to him.

"Blood pressure, satisfactory. Let's see about your temperature."

"You feel a little warm yourself."

"I'm burning up. Must be contagious." Moving slowly, up and down.

"Is this a new technique?"

"Experimental. Trust me."

Shifting underneath her, making Lisa arch her back and close her eyes.

"I love a patient who cooperates."

"I aim to please."

Three months in Chinatown, and he had barely scratched the surface, but he knew his way around. Enough to get him started, anyway. With any luck, enough for him to stay alive and see it through.

The district covered forty-odd square blocks, from Broadway on the north to California on the south, the other boundaries marked by Taylor on the west and Kearny on the east. Inside that magic box was a different world, with ancient rules that bore no correlation to the present time and place. A world where old and new had come together with a clash that echoed on the streets.

In Chinatown, familial piety was still the cornerstone of daily life, but it was showing cracks. Some marriages were still arranged by parents, some careers still chosen for the young by elders of the clan, but increasingly, the youth of Chinatown rebelled against a system that regarded them as carbon copies of their parents, spare replacement cogs for an eternal wheel.

Some made the break through education, finding new directions for themselves and moving on as soon as they were able. Others stayed in Chinatown and registered their individuality by turning renegade, defying cultural tradition and established law. Sometimes they roamed the streets in packs, like feral beasts of prey.

Historically, the Chinese neighborhoods of major Western cities have displayed exemplary respect for law and order, boasting crime rates well below the average. That stoic mask of calm disintegrated in the late 1970's, with youth gangs on the rise and brutal violence flaring up on an unprecedented scale. When Chinese hoodlums robbed the local market or a fan-tan parlor, they displayed a tendency to slaughter all witnesses. Extortion kept the gangs in money, and they spent a hefty portion of their loot on modern arms, the better to defend their turf from rival tribes. Within a few short years, the quiet streets of Chinatown became a free-fire zone.

But through it all, one ancient rule remained inviolate. Mistrust of strangers—and of round-eyes in particular—ensured that secrets stayed secure in the community. A daylight murder on a public street would have no witnesses, because police were aliens, outsiders.

The atmosphere of morbid silence thus created was a fertile breeding ground for crime, and the anarchic youth gangs weren't alone in Chinatown. The Triads—older than the Mafia and founded on the same rough code of clannish loyalty unto death—had reached the New World sometime in the 1850's, dealing opium before it was proscribed by law, establishing casinos and recruiting teenage prostitutes for dead-end lives that smacked of slavery. Masked by their affiliation with the tongs—benevolent societies created to protect Chinese immigrants in urban America—the Triads prospered in the early 1900's, fielding "hatchet men" against their rivals in a bloody chain of conflicts that foreshadowed Prohibition's gangland mayhem. Driven underground by stricter drug laws and protected by the silent walls of Chinatown, the Triads were forgotten as the Mafia and bootleg gangs took center stage.

But they had never gone away.

Maintaining strong familial and commercial contacts in the East, the Triads were prepared when heroin supplanted opium in the United States, creating some two hundred thousand addicts by the end of 1924. The fall of Mother China to a communist regime in 1949 drove Triad leaders from their homes to Burma, Thailand, Singapore, Malaysia, and Taiwan, but the narcotics trade survived and grew. The so-called "Golden Triangle" of Burma, Laos, and Thailand was controlled by warlords of the ousted Kuomintang, supporting their eternal war against the communist regime through sales of opium and heroin abroad. The war in Vietnam secured new trade routes and a vast new market for the potent China white supplied by Eastern Triad brokers through their contacts in Toronto, San Francisco, London, Amsterdam, New York. An estimated half-million American junkies in the late 1980's financed their habits through burglary, mugging, and selling themselves on the street.

Round-eyes sniffing after drugs in Chinatown became as conspicuous—and every bit as welcome—as a black man at a rally of the Ku Klux Klan. Joe Lee, and others like him, were recruited by the DEA in an attempt to break the stalemate, but their progress had been marginal—a contact cultivated here, a meeting infiltrated there, falling short of the desired result.

But it was progress, all the same.

Joe Lee had no authority in Chinatown, since his suspension, but he still had contacts. People he could squeeze, if necessary, to obtain the information he required. If he was cautious, minding every step he took on unfamiliar ground, it just might be enough.

And, then again, it just might get him killed.

The chosen mark was Daniel Ming, a junkie car thief busted half a dozen times for heroin possession by the time he turned eighteen. At twenty, he had mastered the technique of singing for his supper, staying out of jail and detox by providing information to police and sheriff's officers, the DEA, and anybody else he thought could make his life a little easier. A tip from Danny Ming had put Lee on the track of One-nut Ma and led him, ultimately, to a foggy summer night on Market Street.

The follow-up was overdue.

Joe found Ming at the Chinese Playground on Pagoda, watching out for his connection and pacing up and down the way a junkie does before the nerves turn into hunger and begin to gnaw the marrow of his bones. Dark shadows underneath the darting eyes that heightened Ming's resemblance to a walking corpse.

No hurry.

Daniel wasn't going anywhere until he scored, and Lee preferred to catch him holding. It increased his leverage, with a double threat of jail and smack denied, the nightmare of withdrawal in a holding cell.

No rush at all.

The dealer drove a red Suzuki, rolling west on Sacramento with the one-way traffic, cutting off his engine as he made the turn and coasted to a stop against the curb. Before he had a chance to set the kickstand, Ming was in his face, offering a wad of crumpled bills.

The dealer took his time and counted through the money twice, enjoying it, before he palmed a glassine envelope and passed it over in a handshake. He kicked the cycle back to life and made a U-turn in the middle of Pagoda, chrome and leather disappearing with the traffic's flow.

By that time, Ming was pacing east on Sacramento, turning north on Waverly, too wrapped up in his need to notice Lee behind him. Ming was known to guard his address, moving frequently to dodge police and creditors, the countless people he had scammed for cash, but he would not risk fixing in a public place. A block behind his quarry, closing, Lee was certain they were going home.

A cheap hotel on Grant, wedged in between a laundry and a barber shop. Lee didn't want to go inside, risk losing Ming, so he made his move outside. An easy jog to close the last few yards, and Joseph had his arm around the junkie's shoulders, pinning Ming before he had a chance to bolt.

"Long time," he said, all smiles.

"Not long enough."

Ming tested the restraining arm, but Lee held fast, his free hand tucked inside his jacket. Letting Danny feel the gun.

"Be cool."

He steered Ming past the laundry and along a littered alley, stopping halfway down. A Dumpster covered them from anybody passing on the street, as Lee went through the junkie's pockets, lifting out the glassine envelope of heroin.

"You blew it, Danny."

Speaking Mandarin, to drive it home. Ming staring at him, hollow-eyed, a living scarecrow propped against the filthy wall.

"We make a deal?"

"Depends. Last time you put me on a guy, his luck ran out and nearly took me with it. Someone killed my partner, Danny. You have much to answer for."

Ming's lower lip was quivering. "I heard about the shooting, after. There was nothing I could do. You know I didn't set you up."

"Who did?"

Ming tried to shrug, and Joseph slapped him hard across the face, a bleat of pained surprise escaping from the junkie's lips.

"I want a name."

"You think they talk to me? The triggerman for that was *kuei-tzu shou.*" An executioner.

Lee tried another angle of attack. "Who's taking over Tommy One-nut's action, now he's gone?"

"It's up for grabs, the last I heard. You want the players, I could ask around. A week or so."

"You've got two days."

A flash of panic in the junkie's eyes.

"It's not that easy. These are men who keep their business to themselves. Why should I risk my life for you?"

"Your choice. The flip side would be detox, maybe jail time for possession. Either way, you're off the shit, cold-turkey."

"If I help you?"

"Then we're friends again."

"Until the next time."

"Such a worrier. I can't believe your hair's not gray."

"I need my medicine."

"We have a deal?"

Ming nodded like a puppet, snatching at the envelope when Lee produced it.

"Say it, Danny."

"Deal. We have a deal."

"Two days."

"I'll try."

"Don't make me ask a second time."

The brief encounter left a sour taste in Joseph's mouth, but he did not surrender to revulsion. Danny Ming was only one of several snitches he had cultivated on the streets of Chinatown, and he would use them all, if necessary, to secure a solid lead on Robert Chan.

It was a lethal game of hide-and-seek, and Lee was playing in the only way a lone contestant could survive. By making up the rules to suit himself as he went along.

8

It is an oddity among the Chinese tongs that members may refer to their particular society by different names, depending on their place of residence. No subterfuge is seemingly intended, for the links between such "different" groups are not concealed, and yet the naming ritual survives. Accordingly, the largest of America's five tongs is called Bing Kung along the West Coast, while its members in the East belong to a society called On Leong. Their oaths and constitutions are identical, their leadership in daily contact to coordinate all manner of transactions, but they still maintain their "separate" identities with an imaginary border drawn from north to south, bisecting North America.

The other tongs are smaller, but they all have offices in San Francisco, where so many Chinese immigrants first landed in America. The second largest—and the only other tong with members nationwide—is called Hip Sing. Its closest competition, called Ying Ong, is limited in scope to the Southwest, with outposts in Arizona and Nevada. Finally, the smallest tongs—Hop Sing and Suey Sing—are limited to operations in the state of California, keeping small offices in San Francisco and Los Angeles.

Historically, the designation "tong" described a "city hall," the local meeting place where peasants gathered to express themselves on public issues like taxation, famine, crime, and national defense. As Chinese immigrants dispersed themselves around the globe, the title was applied to those benevolent societies created for their protection. In America, the tongs could be relied upon for food and clothing, prompt assistance in securing shelter and employment. If the new arrivals were harassed by racist vigilantes, members of the local tong would mount a guard—and sometimes pay the insults back in kind. When round-eyed politicians courted Chinese votes, the tongs delivered, in return for services received. Their strength was unity, the Chinese rule of silence, and the white man's ignorance of Asian history.

It is impossible to say, at this remove, when the comingling of the tongs and Triad criminal societies began. Created some two hundred years before the Mafia, by Buddhist monks in Fukien province, the society derived its name and basic symbol from a triangle, the three sides representing heaven, earth, and man. Initially a vehicle of self-defense against the hostile legions from Peking, the Triads soon lost sight of Buddha but maintained their sacred oaths and rituals of blood. The leaders coupled profit motives with hard-line politics, becoming fabulously wealthy through extortion, gambling, prostitution, and the sale of opium. While the Sicilian mafiosi were a ragtag band of country rebels battling the French invaders of their homeland, Triad scouts were building outposts in Siam, the Philippines, and the United States.

Somewhere along the way, between the hills of Fukien province and the streets of San Francisco, Triad soldiers found their place within the tongs. It was a perfect symbiosis, charity and crass self-interest merged to form an entity at once more powerful and more sinister than any that had gone before. As immigrants relied upon the tongs for shelter in a new environment, so the Triads hid themselves behind the cover of benevolent societies, establishing their spheres of influence in every Chinatown from coast to coast. They raked in profits from the immigrants and whites alike, through brothels, gambling dens, and seedy *ta yen* parlors, where the junkies of another era came to smoke their opium in peace. The Chinese wall of silence covered Triad operations, and police were paid to look the other way. Conversely, if the round-eyes threatened Chinatown, a flying squad of Triad hatchet men could turn out on a moment's notice to defend their fellow countrymen.

Today the anti-Chinese riots are an ugly footnote in the history of California, but the Triads and the tongs remain, their separate functions—and their close affiliation—more or less unaltered since Gold Rush days. Computers have replaced the abacus in calculating profits, automatic weapons edging out the trusty cleaver as a mode of execution, but at heart, the Triads have not changed. Their driving force is greed, their punishment of enemies relentless, absolute.

In San Francisco, that September of 1995, Robert Chan was near completion of his second term as *mi shu chang* —chief secretary—of the Bing Kung Tong. His reelection in December was a certainty, since he was running unopposed. The last contestant rash enough to vie for Chan's position had been crippled in a daylight hit-and-run on Jackson Street outside his family's florist shop.

Word got around.

Chan's number-two position in the Bing Kung hierarchy granted him free access to the treasury, while simultaneously insulating him against publicity. His nominal superior within the tong, an aging jeweler from Macao, was interviewed for ethnic "human-interest" stories several times each year, but Robert Chan remained unknown to the majority of California newsmen. You could spot him in a published photograph from time to time, part of his round face visible over someone else's shoulder, but the appended captions seldom bore his name. A man of some celebrity in Chinatown, Chan strove for anonymity beyond its borders in the white man's world.

But he was known in certain round-eye circles, all the same. In Washington his name and likeness were familiar to the FBI and DEA. Chan's tax returns were periodically reviewed—without result—by agents of the IRS, and his extensive foreign contacts were a topic of discussion at Customs and Immigration. The California state attorney general's office also kept a file on Robert Chan, but had yet to trace a solid link between the man and any sort of criminal activity. In San Francisco the police department knew his name, but experience had taught them the futility of trying to construct a major case in Chinatown.

Chan's notoriety with law enforcement was occasioned by his membership in Sap Sie Kie, a Triad faction known more commonly and simply as the 14K. According to the FBI's best estimate, it is the second largest in a field of nine competing Chinese syndicates, with twenty-three affiliated gangs and thirty thousand members overall. The 14K is based in Hong Kong, but its tentacles encompass Southeast Asia, Western Europe, Canada, and the United States. Its covert treaties with the Yakuza have opened thriving markets in Japan.

In Triad parlance, Robert Chan was designated as the "Red Pole," an enforcer charged with keeping order and suppressing competition in a given territory. Standing five-foot-five in stocking feet, a slender man of forty-three, well-dressed, Chan did not look imposing. To understand his reputation in the Chinese underworld, one had to know about his skill and years of training in the martial arts, the sheer ferocity that elevated him from common soldier to a captain of the Sap Sie Kie within a span of seven years.

The tales were grim and graphic. Punishment of stubborn merchants who refused to buy "insurance" from the 14K. Sporadic border wars against competing Triad gangs in Chinatown. A bloody clash with mafiosi in the spring of 1991, securing Sap Sie Kie's monopoly on China white imported via San Francisco and Toronto.

Chan's campaigns had earned him the respect of his superiors, and one of them had christened him *hu-li,* the fox.

Chan's soldiers—and his enemies in Chinatown—had given him another name, behind his back. *Tu she.* The cobra.

Brains and lethal fangs aside, no solitary man could oversee the numerous investments and affiliations of the 14K. Chan was assisted in his duties by a pair of skilled subordinates named David Lao and Michael Ng, respectively identified within the Triad as "Straw Sandal" and "White Paper Fan." Lao's function was communication and liaison with the other tentacles of Sap Sie Kie and various affiliated groups, including labor unions, charities, political machines, and street gangs. Michael Ng, a thirty-eight-year-old attorney, served the 14K as Chan's adviser on administrative and financial matters, roughly duplicating the performance of a Mafia *consigliere.* Both men were efficient, affluent, and fiercely loyal to Robert Chan, who held their lives and fortunes in his hand.

The news of trouble came, at first, from David Lao. It started as a whisper on the streets, repeated over mah-jongg tiles and billiard tables, in the seedy cribs where teenage prostitutes eke out a living on their backs and on their knees. Lao heard the whispers in his office, on Pacific Avenue, because it was his job to notice any unexpected change of atmosphere in Chinatown and pass the word along to Robert Chan.

A stranger, asking questions. Prying into Sap Sie Kie affairs without permission or authority. The man was not a round-eye, but he still might represent the white man's law.

It took the best part of an afternoon to learn his name, and David Lao experienced a moment of uneasiness when he relayed the news to Chan.

Joe Lee.

He must have been *sha-tzu,* an idiot. Some people never learned from their mistakes.

Chan bore the news with equanimity. Misfortune came to every man at periods throughout his life, and this appeared to be a relatively minor irritation. A mosquito nipping at the tiger's flank, too small and short of sight to apprehend his danger. Swatted once, but merely stunned, the pest returned to try his luck again.

It made no difference to the tiger, crushing insects, and a narc's life mattered even less to Robert Chan. Still, even insect bites could fester, spread disease, and bring a healthy predator to ruin if he left them unattended.

This time Chan would supervise the pest control himself.

It took the best part of the afternoon for Danny Ming to find a decent car with keys in the ignition. There had been some junkers, fading paint and rusted out below—

the kind their owners *hope* will get ripped off, for the insurance—but he couldn't drop a piece of shit like that on his connections.

Not if he expected to get well.

The junkers could be stripped for engine parts, if there was anything worth taking, but he wouldn't pocket fifty dollars for his trouble. If he didn't make a decent score, he would be forced to work again tomorrow, and his superstitious nature told him not to push his luck.

It would be easier, of course, if he had special tools for opening locked doors and keying the ignition, but he didn't have the extra cash to throw away on toys. Truth was, he wouldn't have a clue how to use the tools if they were in his hand, no more than he could hot-wire any of the newer cars, with their security devices, locking columns, shit like that. He did all right with older models, if he needed temporary wheels, but junkers didn't pay, so he was forced to hang around the malls and supermarkets, waiting for a fool to leave the keys behind.

Like now.

His target was a brand-new Mustang, one of Ford's expensive thirty-year commemorative models, and a stroll-by on the driver's side showed Danny Ming a set of keys in the ignition. Fucking morons. He could see a house key on the ring, before he tried the door, and gave a thought to trying something different for a change.

Forget it.

Burglary was not his line. He didn't have the nerve required for going in a house. The first strange noise, and he would shit himself, tear out of there, and run until he dropped or made it safely back to Chinatown. He had a knack for stealing cars, and knew his limitations. A couple decent cars a week—four, tops—and Danny did all right.

He checked the parking lot again. Nobody staring at him, no one close enough to stop him. He could pick up fifteen hundred dollars for the Mustang, easy.

It would get him well.

He tried the door—some assholes *locked* their keys inside, despite the warning bells and buzzers meant to rule out such an accident—and found it open, slipped behind the wheel. No sweat about his fingerprints. The Mustang would be squeaky clean, new paint, new numbers all around, before it ever hit the streets again.

Ming checked the rearview as he backed out of the parking space. No fender-benders now, for Christ's sake, with a hot car on his hands. He waited for a blue-haired matron who was having trouble with her shopping cart, the front wheels twisted out of line, and finally made it to the exit. He was sweating through his T-shirt by the time he nosed the Mustang into traffic on Dolores, headed south.

Three hours. He was running out of time, and Joey Lee would be around to see him if he didn't call. The fucking narcs were like a bunch of leeches, putting him at risk and giving fuck-all in return.

He had to fix before he spoke to Lee, or he would never pull it off. And for that he needed cash.

The chop shop was disguised as a garage on Havelock, near Balboa Park. The place was always busy, and potential customers—the straight ones—were discouraged with a bullshit line about delivery schedules, waiting lists, the whole nine yards. Four years that Danny Ming had known the owners, they had never done a tune-up or an oil change, never changed a set of plugs or balanced anybody's tires. They had their hands full switching license plates and changing ID numbers, stripping paint and forging registration papers, sometimes looting older cars for parts.

The best part was, they paid top dollar, dealing interstate, and that kept Danny in the shit he needed to survive.

The service bays were closed when Danny got there. Odd, considering the weather, but it didn't pay to advertise around the neighborhood, and Danny wrote it off as simple caution. He left the car and went inside.

Familiar smells of oil and paint and gasoline, but Jesus, it was *quiet.* No one in the office as he entered, circling around the counter, past an army-surplus desk, to enter the garage.

Across the threshold, Danny froze, quick eyes and lazy

brain attempting to coordinate their efforts and interpret what he saw. Four Mexicans in greasy coveralls and Mr. Pfeifer, the manager, in his suit, all lying facedown on the concrete floor, their arms stretched out in front of them like they were flying. On his left, a slim Chinese in mirrored shades and pin stripes had their action covered with a shotgun, sawed off well below the legal length.

The stubby weapon swung up to cover Danny as he entered, bad enough without the gunner's mocking smile. A robbery in progress.

"What the hell . . . ?"

Ming didn't hear the second man come up behind him, but he felt the muzzle of an automatic pistol, cold against the skin behind his ear.

"Somebody wants to see you, Danny." Soy sauce on the gunman's breath. "Let's take a ride."

The stun gun was a marvel of applied technology. Five inches long, its shell high-impact plastic, with a simple thumb switch on the side. Up front, two metal studs comprised the business end, a two-inch gap between them. Seven ounces, with the battery in place, and it would fit inside a handbag or the outer pocket of a coat without a telltale bulge.

Chan smiled and pressed the stun gun's switch, a blue arc bridging the electrodes, crackling while he held the trigger down. His nostrils flared, the scent of ozone registered and filed away.

"I'm glad that we could have this little chat."

His voice was muffled in the soundproof room, absorbed by the acoustic tiles that covered walls and ceiling. In the center of the room a metal serving table had been bolted to the floor. The junkie, stripped and stretched, was anchored to its surface, wrists and ankles bound by heavy leather straps.

"I don't know what you want," the junkie whimpered, sounding on the verge of tears.

"Of course, I haven't told you yet. We're chatting now, that's all."

"I don't know *anything.*"

"You're much too modest. *Everyone* knows *something.*"

"God, if it's about the Mustang, you can have it. How was I to know? The keys were in my pocket when they brought me in."

"That's very generous, but I don't need another car today."

"What, then?"

Chan let him see the stun gun, triggering another arc and smiling as the junkie flinched away.

"Amazing, isn't it? We tend to think that fifty thousand volts should look much bigger, like a bolt of lightning. I suppose it might be more impressive if we separated the electrodes. Still . . ."

"Please, don't."

The first tears spilled across Ming's temples, disappearing in the forest of his sideburns.

"You imagine that I'm angry over something you have done. A stolen car, perhaps, or items pilfered from a shop. If that were true, I simply would have had you killed, as an example to your kind."

Ming's eyes were darting helplessly around the sterile room, his mind in overdrive. "Just tell me what you want."

"Of course, but first . . ."

He pressed the twin electrodes into Danny's armpit, feeling wispy hairs against his knuckles as he hit the switch. No crackling sound or smell of ozone this time, as the current surged through human flesh. The young man lurched against his bonds, the muscles in his upper body twisting spastically, breathless croaking noises issuing from his throat.

Chan held it for a second before releasing the trigger. Ming slumped back against the table, eyes half-closed, his breathing labored, body twitching with a string of tiny aftershocks.

"We understand each other now. I mean to ask you certain questions. You will answer truthfully and promptly, to avoid a repetition of discomfort. Ready?"

"Unh."

"You have a friend. His name is Joseph Lee."

Chan saw a sudden spark of panic in the junkie's eyes.

"He's not my friend."

"A careless choice of words. He uses you."

"Sometimes he asks me things."

"And you provide the information he requires."

"I'm not a stoolie."

Chan was smiling as he placed the metal studs on either side of Danny's nipple, counting to three before he broke the current's flow.

"Let's try again."

A sheen of perspiration made Ming glisten under the fluorescent lights. The red marks on his chest resembled insect stings.

"Lee asks you questions."

"Mmpf."

"You feed him information to protect yourself. This much, I know already."

"Once or twice," the junkie whined. "I swear to God I never gave him anything important."

"I'm concerned about the future, Daniel."

"Future?"

"When you spoke to him on Tuesday, what was on his mind?"

The junkie hesitated, fishing for an answer that would satisfy without endangering himself. Chan planted the electrodes on his testicles and pressed the trigger, hearing Danny scream, and jerked away as Danny pissed himself.

"Should I repeat the question?"

"Ma."

"Again?"

It took a moment for the young man to coordinate his tongue and vocal cords. Chan held the stun gun out of sight and gave him time.

"He ask me Tommy Ma, the names."

"*Which* names?"

"New dealers, over Tommy's action."

"And you told him?"

"Names I didn't have."

Chan wondered if the voltage had disrupted Danny's brain. It would be interesting to study the effects, when he had time to spare.

"I don't imagine he was satisfied with that."

"Said get me names. Three days."

"You have a date to meet him, then?"

"Supposed to call, or he'll come by."

Chan smiled, relaxing. "You can use my telephone," he said. "It wouldn't be polite to keep him waiting."

9

Lee parked his car on Jackson Street, the seven-hundred block, around the corner from his snitch's cheap hotel on Grant. He checked his watch—four-thirty, hours of light remaining, yet—and told himself that it was no big deal to hold the meet in Danny's room.

And yet . . .

His junkie contact had sounded different on the phone:

"I got those names you wanted."

"So? Let's have them."

"Not so fast. I'm out of pocket on this deal. You owe me."

Ming would try to screw him if he saw a chance.

"How much?"

"A hundred."

"Bullshit, Danny. When'd you ever lay a hundred out for anything but smack?"

"I've got expenses, man. Let's call it fifty bucks, okay?"

"If I find out you're shitting me—"

"It's straight, I promise."

"When and where?"

It would be smack, perhaps a shortage of it, making Danny sound like he was winded after running laps. A hard day boosting cars to feed the monkey on his back.

Still, you could never be too careful where a junkie was concerned.

Lee reached inside his jacket and released the double-action Browning automatic from its horizontal shoulder rig. He knew damned well the gun was loaded, but he still went through the motions, checking out the magazine with fourteen cartridges in place, plus one more in the chamber. Two spare clips in pouches, worn beneath his arm, and if he couldn't do the job with forty-three nine-millimeter rounds, he might as well go home.

He left the Browning's safety off and tucked the piece away.

"Let's do it."

Talking to himself, repeating Gary Gilmore's final comment to a firing squad in Utah. Words to live by.

On a whim, he left the car unlocked—no valuables inside for anyone to steal—and crossed the street. He left his lightweight jacket open, easy access to the automatic, pausing at the corner to survey the street.

No one obviously loitering among the various pedestrians on either side, nobody waiting in the cars lined up along the curb. One vehicle—a two-door Cadillac, parked south of Ming's hotel, outside the barber shop—struck Lee as out of place, too classy for the neighborhood, but he dismissed it as coincidence. Somebody visiting a relative or bookie, maybe killing time upstairs with one of several hookers who did business out of Ming's hotel.

Inside, Lee took the stairs and left the ancient elevator to those tenants who could tolerate its smell. Ming's room was on the third floor, rear, and he could use the exercise.

On two he passed a Chinese working girl in all her finery, headed for the street. She looked him over briefly, putting on a listless smile that disappeared as Joseph passed her by.

He could remember days when you would never see a prostitute in Chinatown. They were available, of course, patronized primarily by round-eyes, but they had been kept discreetly out of sight, in brothels called *yao-tzu.* The women did not ply their trade at curbside, and arrests were rare. The pimps, unlike their counterparts in other ethnic ghettos, made a point of living quietly, without conspicuous displays of cash and garish clothes.

Lee reached the third-floor landing, in semidarkness where a couple of the hallway's naked bulbs had been removed. By tenants shaving pennies off the cost of living, or by someone else?

Danny's room, 307, was halfway down and on his left. A solitary light was working there, its meager output amplified by shadows in the background, leaving Joe half-blinded. There were more stairs at the far end of the hallway, leading to an alley in the rear, but Lee could no more make them out than he could see the dark side of the moon.

He felt exposed beneath the single bulb, a sitting duck, but wrote it off to paranoia as he knocked on Danny's door. He recoiled, the automatic in his hand, as it swung inward, neither latched nor fully closed.

"Hello?"

No answer from beyond, a wedge of wall and threadbare carpet visible, daylight leaking in through tattered blinds.

"You in there, Danny?"

Silence.

There were two ways he could go, and tentativeness might get him killed if there was someone waiting for him on the other side. Lee made his choice and slammed the door back, lunging through and ending on his stomach, like a third-base runner coming home to score. He had the tiny bedroom covered, staring over gun sights at the soles of worn-out sneakers, toes up, pointed at the door.

His snitch was laid out on the unmade bed, heels close together, both arms tight against his sides. It was a coffin pose, precise in every detail, from the buttoned collar to the pillow under Danny's head. Lee knelt beside the bed and pressed a hand against Ming's chest to verify the obvious.

No pulse.

No rise and fall of respiration.

"Jesus, Danny."

Short hairs prickling on his neck, Lee bent closer to the body, trying to determine cause of death without disturbing any evidence or leaving fingerprints. He might decide to call it in, but on the other hand—

A scuffling rush of footsteps from the bathroom saved Joe's life. He heard the gunner coming, and flattened himself behind the bed and rolled to his left before an automatic weapon started chewing up the room. A silencer reduced the gunfire to a sound like ripping canvas, bullets smacking into Danny Ming, the mattress, K-Mart furniture, the flimsy walls.

Lee counted to three and came up firing, three rounds off the mark before he had a chance to aim. Two missed his target cleanly, but the third went home and spun the shadowman around, his submachine gun cutting divots in the carpet as he sagged against the wall. Two more, for life insurance, and the guy left crimson skid marks on the plaster as he melted to the floor.

A setup.

He would have no choice about that call to Homicide, but first he had to find a telephone. Ming's junkie budget didn't cover nonessentials, but the manager would surely have a phone, if Lee could track him down. If not, he would be forced to try the barber shop or laundry next door.

He did not hear the backup gunners coming, ears still echoing with gunfire, but the solitary bulb outside betrayed them, casting jerky shadows on the wall. They might have been Ming's neighbors, coming to investigate the sound of shots, but Joseph took no chances, flattening himself against the wall beyond their line of sight.

They caught a glimpse of two men down and came in blasting with a shotgun and another automatic, shattering the window and a bedside lamp, projectiles etching abstract patterns on the wall and ceiling. Blind, Lee poked his gun around the corner, squeezing off four rounds in rapid fire. No thought of scoring on the enemy, but with a ton of luck he just might scare them off.

It worked.

A parting shotgun blast took out a fist-sized chunk of wall beside his head, and Lee went down on hands and knees for two more aimless shots around the corner. He could hear them running now, and instinct made him follow, scuttling in a crouch, bent on saving something from the fiasco.

Lunging through the open door again, reversing his

dramatic entry. A spray of shotgun pellets whipped the air above his head. He sighted on the muzzle flash and started firing, prone, until the Browning's slide locked open on an empty chamber.

Scrambling to his feet, Lee dumped the empty magazine and dug a fresh one out, reloading on the move. He had a live round in the chamber, pistol steady in a firm two-handed grip, before he reached the landing and the body lying crumpled there.

The gunner was Chinese, his leather jacket open halfway down, with crimson blotches soaking through the T-shirt underneath. He might be dead or on his way, but Joseph couldn't spare the time to check it out. He kicked the sawed-off shotgun out of reach and went in search of number three.

The stairs would kill him, if he let them. Every turn and landing was a death trap, a potential ambush with the final gunner waiting down below. Lee wasted precious time on two, and then again before he reached the lobby, covering the empty shadows as he worked his way downstairs.

Too late.

He saw the glass doors swinging shut and bolted for them, instinct forcing him to veer off-course as his assailant fired a long burst from the sidewalk, covering his own retreat. Lee duck-walked over shattered glass and cleared the entryway in time to see his target slide behind the Caddy's wheel and make a stab with the ignition key. The driver's window glided down to clear the submachine gun as another spray of bullets raked the face of the hotel.

The Caddy's engine caught, tires screeching as the driver butted into traffic, but a yellow taxi caught him on the right and pinned him fast against the fender of a station wagon parked against the curb. He tried to power out, but it was hopeless, rubber smoking as the rear tires spun in place. The desperate driver fired another burst at Lee, to pin him down, and took advantage of his slender form to wriggle through the window on the right-hand side. Across the taxi's hood on hands and knees, the driver gaping, horns and tortured brakes responding as he hit his stride and dodged through traffic toward the eastern side of Grant.

His choice made for him, Joseph cursed and followed in the runner's wake.

The shopping slowed her down, but Lisa Reilly knew she still had time as she pulled up outside the small apartment house on Seventh Avenue. The past three days, it had been six o'clock or later when her man came home, and she could still have something special on the stove before he wandered in tonight.

Her man.

The label echoed in her mind, surprising her. They had not come around to talking shared addresses or commitments yet—and she had spent only one night with Lee—but it felt right, somehow.

Her man.

Their home.

At Joe's insistence she had made a copy of his key, and she used it now to let herself inside. An odd sensation, strange but not unpleasant, as she crossed the threshold, feeling Joseph in the room and knowing she was all alone.

Lisa was still hard pressed to understand the way in which their intimate relationship had blossomed, literally overnight. At first, when she was planning her surprise the day of Joe's release from San Francisco General, she had argued ethics with herself, debating whether it was "proper" for a nurse and patient to establish outside contact. She had nearly called it off before deciding that she owed the effort to herself; if Joe had someone waiting for him, or her presence seemed to make him ill-at-ease, she could retreat with no more damage than a wounded ego. If he wanted her to stay . . .

The ethics question did not bother Lisa anymore. It wasn't like a student-teacher thing, for heaven's sake, and both of them were old enough to cope with their desires. If she had any cause for worry now, it lay with Joe himself, and with his job.

Some patients, Lisa knew, developed an attachment

for their nurses and blurred the boundary lines between emotions, losing sight of simple gratitude, mistaking it for love.

Love.

Another label neither one of them had yet applied to their relationship, but it was coming. She could feel it in the air between them.

The job was something else entirely.

Lisa understood his need to find the men who had shot his partner, but the understanding did not cancel fear. Those men had nearly killed him once, when he was carrying a badge, and they were bound to try again if he pushed too hard.

Looking at a stranger in Intensive Care, she had had no personal investment in his life or death; today, if something happened to him . . .

Lisa pushed the morbid thoughts away and started sorting out the groceries. Rib-eye steaks. Asparagus. Fresh mushrooms. Wine. The steaks would be like leather if she started now, but she had brought the makings of a salad, and it wouldn't hurt to start mixing the dressing.

Dressing now, *un*dressing later.

Lisa felt a tingle of anticipation, looking forward to dessert. One appetite relieved, another anxious to be satisfied.

And what if she decided not to wait? She had an apron in her shopping bag, and she imagined Joe's reaction if she met him on the doorstep, wearing that and nothing else.

Smiling to herself, she put the steaks on a broiling rack and opened the wine to breathe, already reaching for her zipper when she spied the mounted pegboard with its row of hooks for extra keys. One smaller than the rest.

The mailbox.

She had meant to check it on arrival, but her hands were full and it had slipped her mind. Five-thirty by her watch, and that left half an hour, at least, before she heard Joe on the stairs. Plenty of time to collect the mail before readying her surprise.

Lisa left the door unlocked and made her way downstairs. The boxes were together, three short rows of five that faced the street. She had to try a second time before the key fitted in its slot. A millisecond of resistance as she turned it, opening the metal hatch.

And then the world exploded in her face.

A sports car nearly tagged Lee as he dodged around the Cadillac to reach the second lane, the driver leaning on his horn and cursing in fluent Cantonese. Too angry to be frightened, Lee avoided the car and reached the curb, pedestrians still reeling from the gunman's passage through their midst.

His quarry had a block's head start, due east on Jackson, but Lee kept the gunner's bobbing head in sight and concentrated on his breathing as he ran. He would not risk a shot along the crowded sidewalk, but his adversary had no such compunction. Glancing back across one shoulder, face contorted in a snarl, the gunman broke his stride and turned to fire a burst along his track.

Lee sidestepped, ducking in between parked cars, as someone started screaming on the street. Returning to the chase, he saw a woman down and bleeding, with a wounded man beside her, other figures huddled on the sidewalk in fear. The triggerman was leaving him behind, and Joseph hurdled prostrate bodies in his rush to close the gap.

More traffic at the Wentworth intersection, and Joe lost contact with the gunman for a moment as a van cut in between them. He followed the runner by the sound of blaring horns and angry voices as he made the sidewalk, veering south toward Washington and Portsmouth Square, beyond.

Lee had reduced the gap to fifty paces as they neared the park, the gunner pivoting to fire another burst. His weapon seemed to jam—or was it simply out of ammunition?—as he squeezed the trigger, jerking backward on the bolt. Retreating, he produced a handgun from beneath his jacket, snapping two quick rounds at Lee before he turned and ran.

Inside the park, it was a different game, pedestrians evacuating at the sound of gunfire, leaving them alone. Lee went to ground behind a hedge, emerging once to spot his target, and a stream of automatic fire ripped through the shrubbery, snipping leaves and twigs.

So much for luck. The gunner had at least one extra magazine, and he was back in business, leaving Joe outgunned.

Lee had a sudden flash of *déjà vu,* the darkness and machine guns hammering away at point-blank range. Warm moisture on his face as Eddie Hovis died.

No fucking way. Not this *time.*

Crawling on his shins and elbows, Joseph worked his way along the hedge until he found an opening. A water fountain blocked his way, but it was made of stone and he was thankful for the cover as he wormed his way around it, prickly branches rasping at his face and neck. Downrange, the gunner played another burst around his old position, firing from the shelter of a children's slide.

Lee swallowed the desire to risk a shot from where he lay, aware that he would have no second chance. The Browning gave him fourteen rounds without reloading, and the move he had in mind might use them all, if he lived long enough to try it.

It seemed to take forever, wriggling across the grass, and he was painfully exposed once he had cleared the hedgerow. Any second now, he expected the triggerman to cut and run while there was time, before the squad cars started to arrive, but nothing happened.

The gunman was waiting for another shot at Lee. A final chance to do his job.

Lee made it to the sandbox, creeping past, briefly out of contact with his adversary, turning right beyond the pit and making for the swings. No real protection there, but he would have an unobstructed angle on the gunner's flank, at something under thirty feet.

Another moment, now.

He couldn't think of any prayers, and so he concentrated on the enemy, the earth in front of him, imagining himself a reptile creeping silently upon its unsuspecting prey.

Except a lizard never tried to take the bugs alive.

If he could bag the gunner—wound him, if it came to that—the police would have a chance to break him down and trace the contract back to Robert Chan. A solid count of murder in the first degree for Danny Ming, at least. Perhaps a bonus, if ballistics matched the weapons back to Tommy Ma and Eddie, or the shooter felt like singing for a deal.

Lee reached the swings and scrambled to his knees, his gun arm braced across a horizontal bar of steel. Surprise was everything, and he would have a heartbeat, give or take, to call the play.

"It's over!"

Startled by the tenor of his own voice, expecting something like a wheeze and coming out with solid authority.

The gunner hesitated for a beat, and Lee could almost read his mind.

"Don't try it, man."

He tried it anyway, the automatic stuttering before he made his turn, a burst that came in high and rattled on the uprights of the swing set, over Joseph's head. Erupting from his crouch behind the slide and nearly losing it before he found his balance, breaking for a line of trees impossibly beyond his reach.

Lee didn't bother counting rounds, the Browning an extension of his fear and anger, giving everything it had in something like three seconds flat. He would remember it in bits and pieces afterward—the sound and recoil, glinting cartridges in flight, the runner staggering and twisting as they found their mark.

Lee's man was down before the Browning's slide locked open and he had a chance to think again. Reloading as he rose, with voices at a distance, traffic sounds around him, coming back. He kept the prostrate figure covered as he closed the intervening distance, knowing it was over, but instinct making him make sure.

"Goddammit."

Staring at the man who had tried to kill him, twisted in

an attitude no living body can adopt. Dark glasses lost on impact with the ground, his eyes wide open, staring at the sky.

"Goddammit!"

Holstering his pistol, Joseph turned away and started back toward the hotel.

10

Two black-and-whites were on the scene when he arrived. The uniforms disarmed him, cuffed Lee's wrists behind his back, and put him in the car. He made no protest, understanding their reaction and responsibilities.

He waited for the suits.

It took them nearly half an hour, but they got there, Mutt and Jeff in outfits purchased off a bargain rack. The short one was Detective Alvarez, an overweight Chicano with a thick mustache and piercing eyes, his black hair lightly oiled and combed straight back. His partner was Detective Fleischer, tall and slender, pale, with thinning sandy hair. His gold-rimmed spectacles were perched on a prodigious nose.

They went through Joseph's wallet first, examining the temporary gun permit that Charlie Maddox had obtained from friends downtown, his ID card for Ace Investigations. Alvarez appeared suspicious of the paperwork, as if it might be forged. His partner didn't seem to care much, either way. The lab men from Forensics were on hand before they got around to the Miranda speech.

"You have the right to remain silent," Alvarez told him, reciting from memory. "Anything you say may be used against you in a court of law."

"I know my rights."

"Shut up and listen." White teeth glinting under the mustache. "You have the right to speak with an attorney prior to any questioning. If you cannot afford a lawyer, one will be appointed for you by the court. You understand these rights that I've explained?"

"I told you."

"Yes or no, goddammit."

"Yes."

"You want a lawyer?"

"No." He glanced at the hotel, its shattered door, the uniforms and suits. "Not yet."

"You've had a busy day," Fleischer said. "Three stiffs here, another one at Portsmouth Square."

"I'm good for three, in self-defense," Joe said. "Room 307's tenant was already dead when I arrived."

"*You* say."

"That's right."

"You work for Charlie Maddox?"

"Off and on."

"He used to be a cop," Alvarez said.

"You see a lot of that, these days."

"What's that supposed to mean?"

"I'm DEA," Joe said. "*Ex*-DEA, that is."

"How long ago was that?"

"Since Monday."

Fleischman cocked an eyebrow. "You're retired?"

"Suspended."

"Ah."

"Four days, you couldn't take the peace and quiet, huh?" Alvarez said. "You had to come down here and shoot some guys to keep your hand in?"

"I was meeting an informant. Danny Ming, upstairs. His door was open when I got here, and I found him on the bed. Before I had a chance to call it in, his playmates came in shooting."

"You were *gonna* call, of course." The short Chicano made no effort to conceal his skepticism.

Joseph shrugged. "Why not? I didn't kill him."

"But you killed the other three."

"In self-defense, just like I said."

"The one at Portsmouth Square, you must've chased him four, five blocks. You call that self-defense?"

"He murdered one man that I know of, tried to murder me, and shot some other people up the street. You'd rather that I let him go?"

"You said this Danny Ming was an informant," Fleischer interrupted. "What's the story there?"

"It's privileged."

"Bullshit. We've got four men dead, three people in emergency receiving, and I'm not accepting any pseudolegal crap from part-time bedroom peepers. Are we clear on that? You try to fuck around with me, your buddy Maddox can start looking for another line of work."

"Okay. I'm looking for the men who killed my partner."

"Joey Lee," Alvarez said. "I *knew* I recognized that name. Last month on Market Street, with One-nut Ma."

"That's right."

Detective Fleischer frowned. "You got some kind of vigilante action going, Lee? Is that what this is all about?"

"What kind of vigilante lets the bad guys hit him with the kitchen sink?"

"A clumsy one, could be."

"It was a setup. Danny told me he had information. Someone *made* him call me. Then they rubbed him out and set their trap. They got a little careless, or you'd have two bodies now, instead of four."

"Our luck," Alvarez said. "You wouldn't know *who* set you up, by any chance?"

Lee shook his head. "Ming wouldn't tell me anything until we met. He said he wanted money. As it is, I figure he was reading cue cards."

"Maybe." Fleischer's tone was wary. "Why'd they cut you loose at DEA?"

"You'll have to ask my supervisor. Call the Federal Building, ask for Raymond Christy. He'll be gone by now, but they can patch you through."

"He isn't in the book?"

"Are you?"

The two detectives stepped aside and whispered back and forth for several moments. When they finished, Alvarez came back to Lee, while Fleischer disappeared amidst the crowd of suits and uniforms.

"We'll make a couple calls," the short Chicano said. "You need to understand that you're in trouble, as it is. I find out you've been shitting me about this federal thing, you ain't seen nothing yet."

Joe waited in the black-and-white while photographs were taken on the street and three bodies were trundled out to hearses branded with the emblem of the county medical examiner. By then the news hawks had begun to gather, Minicams and Nikons aimed at the hotel, a number of them drifting over for a shot of Lee in custody, before patrolmen moved them back.

At one point, ten or fifteen minutes later, Alvarez came back and crouched beside the open door, Lee's wallet in his hand, his square face furrowed by a brooding frown.

"Your driver's license says you live on Seventh Avenue," he said.

"That's right."

"Okay."

He closed the door again and moved away to huddle with his partner on the sidewalk. Running down the angles, making sure their subject was not feeding them a line. If Christy came, in answer to their call . . .

Lee couldn't check his watch, but he was good at estimating time. He calculated forty minutes from the time they put him in the car until he saw Ray's craggy face among the others, near the shattered door of the hotel. Gray dusk had settled on the scene, and it would soon be dark.

Ray made his way past uniforms and newsmen to the black-and-white, with Alvarez and Fleischer on his heels. With rumpled hair and shadows underneath his eyes, no tie, he looked like hell.

"What's shaking, Joe?"

"Somebody tried to make it two for two." Lee said. "They blew it."

"So I hear." He hesitated, cleared his throat. "We need to have a talk."

Lee couldn't read the message in his eyes. "What is it, Ray?"

"These boys weren't on their own, you follow me? They had a backup plan, in case they missed you here."

He felt the short hairs bristling on his nape again, saw Alvarez as he confirmed Lee's address.

"Ray?"

"They rigged a booby in your mailbox, Joe. It takes a while to get the reading back from ATF, but it was probably C-4. They figure half a pound."

"The mailbox?"

"Wired to blow when it was opened. Jesus, man, I'm sorry."

"Lisa?"

"Had your key, I guess. They found her purse in the apartment."

Feeling numb inside, and deathly cold.

"You lying bastard."

Christy turned to Alvarez and Fleischer. "Can we get him out of there? And how about the cuffs?"

"He's still in custody."

"You think he's going somewhere? Jesus H., come on."

They pulled him from the black-and-white, his legs like rubber. Flashing back to San Francisco General, but there wasn't any pain this time. He would have folded, but for Christy's grip beneath one arm. Another moment, and the cuffs were gone. He used both hands to brace himself against the car.

"We have to take a ride downtown," Christy said. "Can you make it, Joe?"

"I want to see her."

"No, you don't."

"Goddammit, Ray—"

"I told you it was C-4, didn't I? Close range. They'd still be guessing if it wasn't for her wallet and the nurse's uniform."

Ray caught him as his knees gave way, held Joseph as the remnants of his lunch came back and splattered on the curb around his feet. A TV newsman spotted them and made a beeline for the action with his Minicam.

"You point that fucking thing at me," Christy snapped, "and I'll shove it up your ass."

Another spasm rocked Joe, tying his stomach in a knot,

but he had nothing more to give. An endless moment later, Christy guided him away.

"My car's right over here."

"I've got my own."

"We'll send somebody back. You're not in any shape to drive."

"Hold on a second!"

Alvarez was in his face, a human roadblock, but his partner muttered something Lee didn't catch, and the Chicano stood aside.

"I'll give you twenty minutes, with the traffic. Any longer, and I'm putting out an APB, you got that?"

Christy shouldered past him, saying, "You're a prince," and led Joe to the waiting car.

It took them a half-hour to reach the San Francisco Hall of Justice, and they still got there ahead of Alvarez and Fleischer. The Chicano glared at Ray, coming in, and Christy said, "I'm glad you made it. I was just about to put your pictures on the wire."

"You're pretty clever, for a fed."

"I study nights."

"It shows. We gave your boy Miranda at the scene, and he don't want a lawyer. Do you?"

"No."

"That's what I thought. We've got a few more questions for him, if you wanna get yourself some coffee, find a magazine to read."

"I'll tag along."

"No fucking way. Four homicides on city turf, right now I don't care whether it was self-defense or not. Your buddy's a civilian, by his own admission. DEA can take a flying fuck."

"I've got the regional director coming down to see your captain," Christy said. "You want a pissing contest, we can waste the time. Fact is, you're looking at a contract job that fell apart. The leading suspect is an asshole we've been looking at for . . . What?" He glanced at Joe. "Two years?"

Lee nodded, kept his mouth shut. Watching Christy work.

"The past five weeks," he said, "you fellas have been getting nowhere with the murder of a federal agent. Now you've got a dead informant on your hands, three shooters on the slab, and you can't wait to bust an agent—"

"Former agent."

"—who's recovering from wounds he suffered in the line of duty. Seems to me that kind of story oughta make the newsboys cream their jeans. You think so?"

Alvarez was fuming. "Wanna know what *I* think?"

Fleischer cut his partner off before he could elaborate. "We're not arresting anybody yet. Your man admits three fatal shootings. Even if they're righteous, we still do our job. You follow that? And now, we've got this bombing thing."

"No problem. All I'm saying is, we should relax until my supervisor gets here. He can help you put things in perspective and explain the federal interest in this case."

"He's on his way, you said?"

"Should be here anytime."

"I don't believe this shit," Alvarez griped.

"It couldn't hurt," Fleischer said. "Either way, we clear this up before you guys take off."

"Hell, yes."

"Okay, let's see if we can find a spare interrogation room. The coffee tastes like shit, but it won't kill you. Crazy fucker trashed the Coke machine last night."

They waited in a room the size of Christy's office, Ray smoking, neither man inclined to speak before the hidden microphones and two-way mirror on the wall. Lee sat with shoulders slumped and stared unseeing at his own reflection in the glass.

It was approaching eight o'clock when Leland Kephart entered, Alvarez and Fleischer close behind. The regional director of the DEA was wearing formal evening dress, a topcoat over all, and he was clearly not amused. He took a seat across from Joseph, the detectives hovering at one end of the table, neutral ground.

"We got preliminary word on Ming," said Fleischer

while his partner stood and glared. "The M.E. says his neck was broken, maybe a karate chop, no way to tell for sure. The bullet holes are all postmortem, anyway. Before he died, somebody worked him over with a cattle prod or something similar. That fits with your suggestion of a setup, I suppose."

"The shooters?"

"Two of them had priors for B-and-E, assault—the usual. Convictions, zip. It's gonna take some time to trace connections, if we ever get that far."

"Outside, you talked about a suspect," Alvarez put in.

"Potential," Christy told him. "Robert Chan."

"The tong guy?" Fleischer looked surprised. "I thought he did chop suey."

"Among other things," Ray said. "Will you be filing any charges?"

"That's the D.A.'s call," said Fleischer. "Off the record, though, I can't see anybody taking this one to a jury. Like you said, a former lawman ambushed on the street, outnumbered three to one. You don't need F. Lee Bailey for a case like that."

"Then Joseph's free to go?"

"We'll need a formal statement, maybe take an hour or so."

Across the table, Kephart cleared his throat. "Would it be possible for us to have a word in private first?"

The tall detective glanced at Alvarez and shrugged. "Suits me."

Ray Christy kept his seat as the detectives left, but Kephart didn't seem to mind. He waited for the soundproof door to close before he leaned across the table on his elbows, pinning Lee with stormy eyes.

"Would you explain to me what you were doing down in Chinatown?"

"I like the food," Joe said.

"Goddammit, Lee, you fuck around with federal cases while you're on suspension, and that phony P.I.'s license won't mean shit. You're out there carrying, endangering civilians—Jesus, *killing* people—and you wind up here. Am I supposed to be impressed?"

"Truth is, I hadn't given that much thought."

"I don't believe you've given *anything* much thought. You're so wrapped up in Bobby Chan, you don't know what the hell you're doing. Christ, six people dead, and there you sit—"

"It's seven."

"What?"

Ray filled him in, the regional director watching Lee, a grim expression on his face. When Christy finished, Leland sat back in his chair and said, "I didn't know. I'm sorry, Joseph."

"One more point for Chan."

"Assuming that you're right, it should be clear by now that you can't touch him on your own. A case like this takes years sometimes. You've been around the block enough to know the way things work."

"I don't have years."

"You won't have any time at all, if you keep pushing Chan. He's missed you twice. Three strikes, you're out."

"I might get lucky, score a run."

"Get real. Your cover's blown in Chinatown. You couldn't make a contact now if you were giving smack away. With Ming and Tommy Ma behind you, you're a goddamned kiss of death."

Lee had no answer for the truth. He settled for, "I'm not about to let Chan walk away from this. Not now."

"All right, hear this. If I find out you're operating Chan —or anybody else in San Francisco—you'll be cited for impersonation of a federal officer. Beat that one, and I'll charge you with obstructing justice, interference with continuing investigations, anything I need to keep you off the streets. I'd rather spend my time on bad guys, but I swear to God I'll break your back, you give me any grief."

Lee stared across the table, silent, wondering what Kephart knew of grief.

"I hope I'm not just talking to myself," the regional director said.

"I hear you, Leland."

Kephart glanced at Christy as he rose, but there was nothing more to say. He moved around the table, looking like a misplaced maître d' in his tuxedo, and the door snicked shut behind him as he left.

"That guy." Ray shook his head. "The trouble is, he's right this time. No way you've got a prayer of taking Chan yourself."

Lee smiled at Christy. "I appreciate you coming down."

"No sweat. Nadine was making tuna casserole."

"Okay."

"You need a place to stay tonight?"

"I've got one."

"Well, I thought . . ."

"It's fine."

"I'll stick around and run you home, then, when you're finished."

"No, I'm fine."

"You sure?"

"Go eat your tuna casserole."

"I thought you were my friend," Ray groused, but in another moment he was gone.

It took an hour and twenty minutes for Lee's statement to be witnessed, typed, and signed, with his initials at the top of every page. When Alvarez and Fleischer walked him out of the interrogation room, they almost stumbled over Charlie Maddox waiting in the hall.

"You guys through rousting my employee?" Maddox asked.

"Another dick," Alvarez said. "That's all I need."

"Make do with what you've got," the fat man counseled, focusing on Joe. "You look like you could use a drink or three. My treat."

Lee reached inside himself and found another smile he didn't feel. "I thought you'd never ask."

11

Lee sleepwalked through the next four days, until the funeral on Tuesday afternoon. They hadn't talked about religion much, and it surprised him to discover Lisa was —had been—a Catholic.

Reilly.

It made perfect sense, and Joseph was embarrassed that he'd never taken time to find out more about the woman he had . . . What? Desired? Made love to? *Loved?*

It hurt too much to put a name on feelings, so he gave it up. If you began to classify emotions, then the pain of loss was amplified accordingly. The last thing Joseph needed was a fresh scar on his soul.

But sometimes, when he wasn't thinking or the alcohol was wearing off, Lee knew that he had loved her. Which did nothing to bring her back.

The services were scheduled for a small church on Vallejo, three blocks north of Alta Plaza Park. The forward pews were full when Lee arrived, a sound of weeping audible beneath the organ music as he waved the ushers off and found himself a seat in back.

Up front, against the chancel railing, Lisa's casket was a bronze torpedo trimmed in gleaming brass and banked with flowers. Thinking of her pitiful remains inside, Lee wished that he had stopped off somewhere on the way, to have another drink.

To keep himself from thinking, he counted mourners, studying their profiles, clothing, hair. He picked out Dr. Beck, Nurse Fairchild, several other faces that he recognized from San Francisco General. Were there other patients present too? Lee pushed the thought aside and concentrated on the members of her family, seated in the second pew. He recognized her parents and a younger sister from the snapshots Lisa had produced one night, in bed, when they had finished making love. She had seemed inordinately proud—her father was a dentist, Joe recalled; the sister did prelaw at Berkeley—but there was a hint of sadness also, undefined, as if she viewed the photos with a sense of loss.

He could have asked, but at the time he needed something else from Lisa, reaching for her with a hunger gnawing at his loins, and they had never gotten back to talking family. His loss, an opportunity to know her tossed away in favor of the heated moment, never to return.

Lee caught himself, before the sadness could degenerate into a public show of maudlin sentiment. Her family didn't know him, and they would be less than thrilled to have the services disrupted by a weeping Chinese. Aside from the embarrassment, a personal display would lead to questions, and he had no answers that would satisfy the family in their grief.

The organ music swelled, and Lee glanced up to find a priest emerging from the wings. The congregation rose as he approached the pulpit, waiting for his signal to begin a hymn Lee did not recognize.

It was the third time in his life that Lee had set foot in a Catholic church. The first two had been weddings, in Los Angeles, and he remembered the impressive stained-glass windows, gilded sculptures of the Virgin Mary and assorted saints, all dominated by a looming crucifix behind the altar. Christ in agony, but managing a smile somehow, as blood rolled down his face and wounded side. Lee marveled at the nerve of a religion that would publicly display the mortal weakness of its god.

When the priest was done, he stood back and one of Lisa's mourners took the pulpit. Joseph didn't recognize the woman's name or face, but she professed to be a friend from college, smiling through her tears as she related anecdotes of Lisa as a student nurse, consumed with zest for life and a desire to serve her fellowman. It was the standard fare of eulogies, but something in the words struck home with Joseph, made him look inside himself.

And it occurred to him that he had barely walked around the edge of Lisa's life. What might he have discovered if their time had been extended? If his own obsession with a dream of vengeance had not cut it short?

Lee forced himself to sit through two more eulogies, a test of will, but slipped away when they began to sing another hymn. Propelled across the narthex on a swell of music, he felt dizzy as he reached the steps outside. His tie was strangling him, and he tugged it down, undid the collar button, sucking in a ragged breath.

Across the street, young girls were playing hopscotch on the sidewalk, laughing as they wobbled on one leg and nearly fell. A pizza van drove past, en route to a delivery.

And life went on.

It had to be the glare of sunlight, Joseph told himself, that brought the sudden moisture to his eyes.

Lee trailed the funeral procession to the cemetery, watching from a distance as the priest went through the motions one more time. The modest crowd from church had dwindled to a handful now, including Lisa's parents, sister, and the several friends who had been moved to speak on her behalf.

Lee stood apart, pretending interest in the Schuster family plot, a stranger to the rest of them as he had been while Lisa lived. He saw the casket lowered out of sight, the mourners on their feet and dropping flowers in the grave before they scattered to their waiting cars. Lee gave them time to pull away before he left the Schuster plot and passed among the rows of headstones toward the open grave. As he approached, two members of the cemetery staff were stripping artificial turf away from tidy mounds of soil, preparing to complete the task of burial.

It was a strange sensation, watching them and listening to shovelfuls of dirt rain down upon the coffin lid. His own religious training left him unprepared to think in terms of afterlife and worlds beyond the flesh, but he was desperate to believe that part of Lisa had survived.

How else, for God's sake, could he ever hope to find forgiveness for his crime?

The diggers hardly seemed to notice Lee as they proceeded with their work, unrolling strips of sod across bare earth when they had finished filling in the hole. A stone would be erected later, but the major work was done, fresh turf staked out to camouflage the wound. Until the marker was erected, Lisa would remain anonymous, invisible. From all the evidence, she might have never lived at all.

He waited for the diggers to collect their tools, the folding chairs and sheets of artificial grass, and stow them all inside a van that bore the cemetery's tasteful logo on the sides. It never hurt to advertise. When they were gone, he stood beside the grave, eyes picking out the lines between old turf and new, imagining it must have been the same when Eddie Hovis was returned to the earth.

Old friends, new lovers, bound together by the common thread of death. One man responsible for both. It had been Joseph's aim to make him pay for Eddie, but the tab was getting higher all the time.

He nearly missed the sound of footsteps on the grass behind him, pivoting to catch Ray Christy in his one black suit and shades that looked like something borrowed from Ray Charles.

"I couldn't hack the church," Ray said. "Too soon, I guess. The service always makes me think I may be next."

"It doesn't matter."

"Anyway, I figured you might be here." Moving closer to the grave. "You see her folks?"

Lee shook his head. "They wouldn't know me."

"Kephart asked me if he ought to come or send somebody out. I told him not to bother."

"Thanks."

Ray shrugged it off. "No big. You almost finished here, or what?"

Joe tore his eyes away from Lisa's grave and scanned

the field of headstones, crosses, Stars of David, spreading out in all directions to the limits of his sight.

So many dead. Strangers except the one in front of him.

"I'm done."

Ray lit a cigarette and said, "So, how about a beer?"

The bar was dark and nearly empty, one of Christy's favorites on Divisadero, south of Golden Gate. They sat in back, a corner where they had the door and rest rooms covered, buying rounds in turn and drinking slowly, speaking only when they felt the need.

"What's going on downtown?" Lee asked while they were waiting for their second round.

"Still checking out the guys you dusted, what it's worth. One of them was a slug named Stevie Han. You bagged him in the park. Turns out, he did some odd jobs for the Bing Kung Tong, a general gofer, shit like that. So far, there's nothing we can use to make a link with Chan."

"The other two?"

"They both had sheets—nine priors between them—but they never took a fall for drugs, and nothing we can turn up makes them Triads."

"Let it go."

"Say what?"

Their drinks arrived, and Joseph paid the waitress, tipping her a dollar and allowing her to leave before he spoke again.

"We both know Chan put out the contract. Kephart knows it, and you gave his name at Homicide. The trouble is, he's too damned smart to leave loose ends for us to play with."

"So?"

Lee sipped his beer and watched a solitary patron feeding quarters to the jukebox, punching his selections. Turning back to Ray, he raised his voice in competition with the sounds of David Bowie, running down the joys and risks of modern love.

"The man was right about my cover being blown in

Chinatown. I couldn't buy a paper there without somebody running back to Chan."

Ray nodded glumly. "Little fucker's got his eyes and ears all over, that's the truth."

"I try to reach him anywhere down there—hell, anywhere in San Francisco—and I'm wasted, right?"

"Okay, so what?"

"I think I need a change of scene."

"It couldn't hurt. Go home and see your folks, kick back awhile. Recharge those batteries. It could be, getting out of DEA's the best thing ever happened to you."

Joseph forced a smile and said, "You may be right."

"Damn right, I'm right."

"One thing. I wasn't thinking of L.A."

"Well, hey, I follow that. A time like this, the family wants to feed you milk and cookies, tuck you into bed, and treat you like you skinned your knee in kindergarten. When my mom was still alive, God rest her soul—the time my youngest broke his leg—she brought *me* chicken soup. It's bad enough I hate the shit, I wasn't even sick."

"Someplace with more excitement."

"Now you're talking. Take a week in Vegas, say. You wouldn't even have to play the tables if you're short. Hang out around the pool all day and catch a couple of the dinner shows. I'm not suggesting anything, you understand, but did you know that prostitution's legal in Nevada? Christ, last week I'm standing in the checkout line at Albertson's, and there's this paperback—*A Guide to the Nevada Brothels.* Fucker wrote it's got them rated like hotels, with pictures, price, the whole nine yards."

"I've been to Vegas, Ray."

"Well, if you've got someplace in mind . . ."

"Hong Kong."

"Aw, shit."

Lee finished off his beer and flagged the waitress down. "Two more."

"I had it right the day you walked. You're fucking crazy."

"I don't see it that way."

"Well, you'd better look again. You think Chan's got a

lock on Chinatown? Right now, the fucking Triads *own* Hong Kong."

"That makes them easier to find."

"I wouldn't be surprised. And once you make connections, then what? Maybe have a cup of tea and chat awhile, before they slit your throat and dump you in the bay?"

Their beers arrived, and Christy paid the waitress, sorting through a wad of crumpled bills to find a five.

"I'm playing this by ear," Lee said when she was gone. "I can't reach Bobby Chan, agreed?"

"For once."

"That leaves me two alternatives. I can forget the whole damned thing—scrub Eddie, Lisa, all of it—or I can go *around* him, tag his contacts."

"Overseas? For what? The last I heard, our badges didn't carry any weight in Hong Kong."

"Ray, we work with locals all the time."

"What *we*? You're on suspension, Joe. The man won't rest until he makes it permanent. Wake up, okay? You're not an agent anymore."

"*You* know that, Ray. *I* know it."

"Jesus Christ."

"But *they* don't know it yet."

"You think it's some big secret? They've got phones in Hong Kong, Joe. They punch the buttons, someone answers in the States, you're history. With any luck, the Brits will throw your ass in jail before the Triads take you out."

"My problem. What I need from you—"

"Forget it, Joe."

"—is someone I can talk to on the force out there."

"You heard me, dammit. There's no way I'm getting into this."

"A name, that's all."

"Oh, well, if *that's* all. What the hell, let's take my twenty-seven years and flush 'em down the john, by all means."

"No one's asking you to make the call."

"My ass, you're not."

"A confirmation, maybe, if they try to check me out."

"And Kephart goes to work on me when he gets done with you. No, thanks."

"No stone unturned, he said."

"It's fucking politics. He tells the papers what they want to hear."

"He promised *me.*"

"Same thing."

"You're writing Eddie off, like he was nothing."

"Hey, fuck you. I knew him five, six years before you came along and partnered up. Don't tell me what I'm doing, how I feel."

"A name."

Christy rolled the Miller bottle back and forth between his nervous hands. "You're crazy, Joe."

"Not yet. I will be if I try to make believe that nothing's happened in the past six weeks."

"They're gonna eat you up alive."

"They have to catch me first."

"That oughta take about an hour. It isn't just the gangs," Ray said. "You think we've got corruption over here? A few years back, the Hong Kong papers got ahold of rumors there was gonna be a crackdown on the force. It was a pipe dream, but they printed it, okay? By midnight they were looking at a couple hundred resignations from detectives, sergeants, right on down the line. One guy with thirty years in uniform, they logged his assets in around six million bucks, American. He didn't make that kind of money fighting crime."

"I'll take my chances."

Christy stared at Joseph while he tipped his bottle, drained it, setting it aside. "Before I cut my own damn throat," he said, "I need another drink."

12

The daily flight from San Francisco into Hong Kong averaged fourteen hours, but the Boeing aircraft gained a day in transit over the Pacific, and the change in time zones made it seem that Lee had spent only six hours in the air. His aching muscles knew the truth, however, and he welcomed the announcement of their imminent approach to Hong Kong International at half-past four on Thursday afternoon.

The airport is unique, located on the Kowloon side, with runways thrusting into Kowloon Bay. Lee had a panoramic view of Hong Kong Island and its teeming harbor as the pilot took them inland, circling to approach his runway from the north. Lee clutched the armrests of his seat as they began their steep descent between two mountains, skimming Kowloon rooftops on their final pass.

A leisurely approach to the arrival gate gave Lee a chance to breathe again. He waited while they docked, then claimed his carry-on from overhead and joined the line preparing to deplane.

With gates for thirty major carriers, elaborate offices, and tourist shops, the Hong Kong terminal is subject to continuous repair and renovation. The arrival area for Joseph's flight seemed curiously incomplete, as if the workmen couldn't get their act together, brand-new carpet on the floor and wiring visible through gaps between the ceiling panels, flat gray primer on the walls. A multilingual sign directed him to Immigration, where his passport and return-trip ticket were examined, Lee assuring the inspector that he did not plan to linger past the one-month limit that was standard for Americans without a visa.

Moving on, he claimed his suitcase from the baggage carousel and checked through Customs, watching as another man in uniform went through the contents of his bags, in search of alcoholic beverages, tobacco, drugs. Aware of the restrictions that prevailed in Hong Kong, Lee was traveling unarmed. If necessary, he was confident that he could find a weapon later, on the streets.

A two-man welcoming committee waited for him on the other side of Customs, standing off to one side in their stylish khaki uniforms. One Anglo, one Chinese, all spit and polish with their caps and badges, brass and service ribbons, pistols on their belts in military leather. Joseph didn't have to guess which one of them had spoken to him on the telephone.

"Inspector Wilson."

"Mr. Lee."

The tall man's grip was firm and dry, his flinty gaze direct, uncompromising. Salt-and-pepper hair, trimmed short above his ears and longer in the back, was visible beneath his cap.

"Detective Sergeant Thomas Choi."

Another solid handshake, not quite testing Lee. The sergeant had a classic poker face, betraying nothing of his inner thoughts. He made no effort at a smile and did not speak, although a scarlet shoulder tab identified him as an English-speaking officer.

"It's bloody rude," Wilson said, "but I am required to ask for your credentials."

"Certainly."

Joe handed him the spare ID he kept around the house in case of loss or damage to the set now held by Leland Kephart.

Wilson barely gave the card a glance before he passed it back. "Formalities, you understand. We have a car outside."

Inspector Ian Wilson was the second in command of the Narcotics Bureau for the Royal Hong Kong Police Force. "If you want to know about the Hong Kong Triads," Ray had advised Lee, "they don't come any better, but you have to watch him. Fuck around with Wilson on his own home turf, he'll chew you up and spit you out before you know what's happening."

They moved along the concourse three abreast, with Joseph in the middle, tourists and employees of the airport cutting sidelong glances as they passed, imagining some real-life drama under way, a prisoner in custody. Lee kept his head down, wishing that his escorts had dispensed with uniforms for the occasion, hoping there would be no Triad spotters in the crowd.

Outside, blue skies and sunshine, with a view of black-eared kites and sea gulls circling over Kowloon Bay. Their car was blue and white, a compact with police insignia emblazoned on the doors, a light bar mounted on the roof. Choi opened the trunk for Lee to stow his luggage, and he rode in back, behind a metal screen that separated prisoners from keepers during transport.

Choi slid in behind the wheel—the car had right-hand drive—and Wilson took the shotgun seat. "We shan't be long," he offered, giving Lee a glimpse of chiseled profile as he settled in and snapped his shoulder harness into place.

Before they covered half a block on Austin Road, Lee knew the Hong Kong streets would take some getting used to. Quite apart from driving on the "wrong" side of the road, you had to cope with an apparent traffic jam of buses, taxis, and innumerable private cars, all interspersed with swarms of bicycles, pedestrians, and rickshaws. It seemed hopeless at a glance, but still they made good time, the traffic flowing at an unforgiving pace. Lee half-expected intersections to be strewn with mangled bikes, the corpses of pedestrians, but everyone appeared to take the crush in stride.

Choi took a left on Salisbury Road, past Kowloon's luxury hotels, the Space Museum, to reach the Star Ferry Concourse. He nosed the squad car into line behind a cargo van and left the engine idling, waiting for a uniformed attendant to arrive and validate their pass. On board, they parked belowdecks, finally shutting off the engine in compliance with instructions painted on the bulkhead.

"It's a panic scene, up top," Wilson said, turning in his seat to face Lee through the mesh. "Not worth the trouble, really, if you don't mind sitting tight."

"No problem."

"You'll have ample time to see the harbor, I should think. Damned near impossible to miss, in fact."

The crossing took another twenty minutes, and the ferry put them out within two blocks of City Hall. Incredibly, the traffic here was worse, with overloaded trams competing for a place in line. Lee kept his fingers crossed and concentrated on the harbor view, ships fat with cargo from around the world, a thousand smaller junks and sampans jostling for space like piglets at a feeding trough.

The city parking lot was spacious and surrounded by an eight-foot chain-link fence with coils of razor wire on top. Choi parked the cruiser in a numbered slot and opened Joseph's door, which had no inside latch.

"Your luggage should be safe here," Wilson said. "We'll leave it, shall we? Right."

The elevator ride to Wilson's fourth-floor office gave another glimpse of Hong Kong's fast-lane life-style. Lee was startled when the doors hissed open and a dozen passengers burst out, their haste reminding him of actors in a 1920's silent film played at double speed. He would have missed the lift entirely but for Sergeant Choi, who blocked the door and waved him in.

"Three seconds, in and out," Wilson said. "We had the doors adjusted slower, but the businessmen complained that they were losing precious time."

Upstairs, they shoved past waiting suits and uniforms, the chief inspector leading Joseph to an office three doors down. Inside, it could have passed for any bureaucratic office in the world, except for signs and posters bearing double messages in English and Chinese.

"A cup of tea?"

"No, thank you."

"Sergeant?"

"No, sir."

"Right, then." Wilson hung his dress cap on a wall hook, next to Choi's, and settled in behind his desk. "You're interested in learning more about our Triads, I believe?"

"That's right."

"We've been in contact with your agency for some time now. Between the published literature and our communiqués, I would have thought you had substantial information at your fingertips."

"It's not that simple," Lee replied. "I'm working on a stateside drug connection that involves the Bing Kung Tong and 14K."

"You've said as much. Go on, please."

"The distributor is Robert Chan, Chinese-American, connected where it counts. His income is ostensibly derived from restaurants and laundries, with the Bing Kung serving as a cover for his outside interests."

"Heroin."

It didn't come out sounding like a question, but Lee nodded, all the same. "We know he's moving major weight, but so far we've got nothing that will stand in court. The past six weeks, he's murdered two informants and a federal agent, covering his tracks."

And one civilian.

"You're looking for a different angle of attack?"

"That's it. If I can't touch the man, I'd like to damage his connection, interrupt the flow enough to make him nervous. Nervous people make mistakes."

"And his connection is in Hong Kong?"

"I believe so, yes."

"You know a bit about the Triads, then?"

"Bare bones. Right now, I'm interested in anything and everything."

"The first thing you must come to grips with is their sense of history." The chief inspector leaned back in his chair and made a steeple of his fingers, watching Lee. "If we accept tradition, the first Triad society was organized by Buddhist monks residing in a Foochow monastery,

Fukien province, about 1674. They saw themselves as freedom fighters, harassed by the oppressive Ch'ing Dynasty in Peking."

"I've wondered how religion got involved," said Lee.

"The monks were Ming Dynasty loyalists," Wilson replied. "To them, the Manchu invaders who captured Peking in 1644 were infidels, barbarians. From self-defense around Foochow, it was an easy step to armed resistance on a wider scale. Peking sent troops to massacre the rebels, but a handful managed to escape and formed a league they called Hung Mon—the Heaven on Earth Society. The modern Triads are descendants of Hung Mon."

"And they've been active ever since?"

"In essence. The Triads were already present when Hong Kong was organized as a crown colony in 1842, and three years later they were banned by law. The legislation's still in force, for what it's worth. In 1851 the Taiping rebellion against 'foreign devils' was launched by Triad gangs in Kwangtung province. It took colonial troops thirteen years to suppress the rebels, but they were never wiped out. Instead, by the mid-1860's they shifted their focus toward criminal enterprise—smuggling, extortion, and piracy."

"They gave up politics?"

"Far from it." Wilson smiled. "The overthrow of Manchu rule remained a top priority for every Triad faction. They got their wish in 1911, when the last Manchu emperor was forcibly deposed by Sun Yat-sen's Young China party. Sun, incidentally, got his start in politics as a Triad enforcer—a 'Red Pole'—and the Kuomintang, his ruling party, was essentially a pack of Triad thugs in uniform. Sun's heir was General Chiang Kai-shek, another hardcore Triad, who unleashed the KMT against Mao's communists. Of course, it didn't quite work out. Whatever one may think about the reds, they have a way of coping with their criminals."

"So, after Mao, the Triads moved to Hong Kong?"

"As I mentioned, some of them were here already. One society, the Wo group, is indigenous to the New Territories, organized sometime in the early 1900's. During

World War II, the Japanese invaders found they couldn't wipe out Hong Kong's Triads, so they did the next best thing and put them on the payroll. Rival factions were combined to form Hing Ah Kee Kwa—the Aid Asia Flourishing Association—with its members armed and paid to keep civilians in their proper place. Much like the Nazi Iron Guard in Croatia, I should say."

"And V-J Day made it business as usual."

"Until Mao. His victory in 1949 was a disaster for the syndicates. Secret societies were banned across the board, and hundreds of gangsters were shot out of hand. Of course, the reds were shooting priests and democrats and honest businessmen as well, which worked out nicely for the Triads. Every freedom-loving country in the world was glad to take them in, regarding them as patriots and freedom fighters. Smoke?"

"No, thank you."

Wilson chose a cigar from the desktop humidor, pausing to light it before he continued.

"Of course, Chiang took his bosom friends and allies to Taiwan, but others made their way to Singapore, Malaysia, Thailand, northern Laos, and Burma. And thousands more wound up in Hong Kong after 1949. The influx brought at least five separate gangs from Shanghai, with the Green Pang Triad dominating smaller groups. They clashed immediately with their ethnic rivals from Swatow, who call themselves Chiu Chou. A state of war existed in the colony through early 1963, when leaders of the Shanghai faction had enough and packed their bags."

"Survival of the fittest."

"Not unlike your gang wars of the 1920's, I suppose. And then, you have the Sap Sie Kie, or 14K. As Triads go, the 14K is still an infant, organized in 1947 by Lieutenant General Kot Siu Wong, of Chiang's nationalist army. Initially, the group was formed to fight a rearguard action against Mao's communists. Wong didn't have the luxury of schooling his recruits in proud tradition, so they simply called themselves the Fourteen Association, after the address of Wong's headquarters at 14 Po Wah Road, Canton. With Chiang's defeat and Kot Wong's death in 1953, the group followed its predecessors into full-time criminal pursuits. The name was changed to 14K in honor of the profit motive, as a reference to fourteen-karat gold."

"I understand that Sap Sie Kie is listed as the second-largest Triad, overall."

"We estimate a worldwide membership of thirty thousand, while the Wo group weighs in closer to the forty thousand mark. However, 14K is better organized, more militant. The different factions of the Wo group are always quarreling among themselves, like jealous children."

"Which leaves the field wide open for the 14K."

"Not quite. The Chiu Chou have been dealing opium around the world since 1844. They still control most of the Bangkok trade, so Sap Sie Kie is forced to deal with Chiu Chou brokers for their poison. Still, it works out well for all concerned. The rich get richer, and the addicts multiply."

"How many Triad members are there in the colony?"

"One estimate suggests it may work out to nine hundred thousand individuals, all told." The chief inspector noted Lee's reaction, smiling as he said, "Of course, the vast majority are old men now, retired, and many doubtless joined the postwar Triads to express themselves politically, with no involvement on the seamy side. Still, every member takes a vow of silence under pain of death. You can understand our difficulty when it comes to witnesses or jurors to support a case in court."

"You're telling me it's hopeless?"

"Not at all. But difficult . . . oh, yes. There are about two hundred active gangs within the colony, each one affiliated with one Triad or another. They corrupt our labor unions, politicians, judges—and, of course, police."

Across the room, Detective Sergeant Choi leaned forward, elbows on his knees, and cleared his throat. "You have been warned about police in Hong Kong, I suppose?"

Lee shrugged, uncertain whether Choi was friend or foe. "Dealers pick up friends, no matter where they go.

For every crooked cop in Hong Kong, I can show you one in New York City or Miami."

"Scum!" The sergeant's voice was taut with anger, color rising in his cheeks. "They must be weeded out and crushed like insects."

Ian Wilson smiled indulgently. "Go easy, Sergeant. Chances are, the weeding will be done by someone else. In fourteen months the colony reverts to mainland jurisdiction, and I daresay the Beijing authorities may have a more direct approach to fighting crime."

"I can't afford to wait that long," Lee said. "In fourteen months Chan's syndicate will find another outlet. Hell, for all I know, they're working on it now. I need to hit them before they get another route nailed down."

"Good luck."

"I hoped you might have something more concrete to offer. Names, let's say?"

"Oh, yes indeed." The chief inspector waved a hand in the direction of his filing cabinets, seven in a row along the facing wall. "We have no end of names, but they won't take you far. Detective Sergeant?"

Choi regarded Joseph Lee with an expression that was both curious and distant. He said, "The Triads are a combination of the old and the new. They feed upon society but dwell outside it, guarded by their ceremonies and traditions. Members are christened with special names and numbers, bound by oaths of loyalty which they hold sacred unto death."

"I need to learn about the 14K."

"Its leader is a man named Yau Lap Wong. In Triad jargon, he is called Shan Chu—the 'Hill Chief'—and his sacred number is 489. Its significance derives from the sum of three digits, totaling twenty-one. That, in turn, is the number obtained by multiplying three—the holy number of creation—times seven, the number of death. The Hill Chief rules by virtue of his power to create new wealth for his disciples and his willingness to punish insolence with death."

Lee frowned and said, "He sounds like your basic Mafia godfather."

"Except that members of the Mafia do not, I think, invest their leader with the aspects of a deity. The Hill Chief's second in command is called Heung Chu—the 'Incense Master.' His responsibility extends to ceremonial initiations and perpetuation of the Triad through its diverse rituals. His sacred number is 438, with addition of the digits yielding fifteen—a product of creation multiplied by five, the sacred number for longevity. The Incense Master of the Sap Sie Kie is Sun Mok Lin."

"They take this number business seriously?"

"As a Catholic takes his rosary." Choi smiled at last, but the expression never reached his eyes. "Beneath the Hill Chief and his Incense Master stands the Red Pole—the enforcer, as you say. The Hill Chief and the Incense Master are unique within a given Triad, but there may be several Red Poles, depending on the Triad's size and range of operations. All are skilled in martial arts—kung fu, specifically—and serve as field commanders when the syndicate does battle with its enemies. Away from home, the Red Pole serves his Triad as the ruler of a local territory."

"Chan?"

"Perhaps. The Red Pole's sacred number is 426, whose digits may be added to produce the number twelve. In turn, that figure is obtained if one should multiply creation by the number four, a designation of the four seas that surround the earth in ancient Chinese legend—thus, an indication of the Triad's universal scope."

"They don't think small."

"In foreign lands the Red Pole is assisted in his duties by officers known as the White Paper Fan and the Straw Sandal. The White Paper Fan is a counselor. A messenger by tradition, the Straw Sandal communicates with different Triad branches and coordinates the syndicate's relationships with outside groups."

"Are there titles for the rank and file?" Lee asked.

"They are anonymous, but each of them is designated by the number forty-nine. The digits, multiplied, yield thirty-six—the number of successive oaths a new initiate must swear before he is accepted into Triad membership."

"With all these calculations going on, it's hard to see how anyone has time for running dope."

"They manage," Wilson told him.

"You seem to know a lot, considering the tight security involved."

"Some time ago, we built a cover for a native officer, fresh out of the academy. He was initiated into Sap Sie Kie and spent eleven months inside, before they found him out. Grim business. He was tortured and emasculated, shot nine times—the Triads love their multiples of three—and dumped in Kowloon Bay on Easter Sunday. Someone's little joke, I would imagine."

"So, you owe them one."

"We owe them several, Mr. Lee."

"I'd like to help you, if I can."

"But you came here to *ask* for help, if I recall correctly."

"We can help each other," Joe replied. "I pin a case on Robert Chan, it leads right back to his connections in the colony."

"And how do you intend to pin this case on Mr. Chan?"

Lee rose and moved to stand before the window, staring down at crowds around Queen's Pier, the bay beyond.

"I'll let you know," he said. "First thing, I need to get down there and have a look around."

"You know Hong Kong?"

"Not yet."

"You'll want a guide."

"Too risky. If I blow it on my own, at least I've got nobody else to blame."

"I hope you know your business, Mr. Lee."

Joe turned to face the chief inspector, frowning. "So do I."

13

Lee had selected his accommodations from the Fodor guidebook, opting for the Harbor Hotel on Gloucester Road. His room faced inland, but he didn't miss the harbor view. His choice of the hotel was founded on its close proximity to Central Hong Kong and the seamy Wanchai district, to the east.

Alone at last, he made a beeline for the shower, stripping off the clothes that he had worn for nearly twenty hours. He turned the shower on as hot as he could stand and lathered twice before he felt a bit more human. Finishing, he spun the knob to bring an icy spray down on his head and shoulders, needles prickling at his chest and back. One minute, counting off the seconds in his mind, and by the time he turned the shower off, the mental cobwebs had been swept away.

His room felt almost muggy, by comparison, and Lee strode naked to the sliding windows facing on a narrow balcony. He slipped the latch and stepped outside, unworried by the prospect that a Peeping Tom might see him on the fourteenth floor.

Below him, Central Hong Kong was a mixture of the new and the ancient, market stalls and beggars overshadowed by the looming spires of chrome and glass. Where new construction was in progress, bamboo scaffolding surrounded steel-and-concrete skeletons, jackjammers and pile drivers filling the air with a sound like distant machine-gun fire. Above it all, the traffic sounds—from aircraft overhead to trams and taxis down below—provided background music, the eternal rhythm of a city that has never learned to sleep.

The name Hong Kong translates to "Fragrant Harbor," and its origin was clear to Joseph Lee, despite his altitude above the streets. Pollution is a problem in the colony, but constant fresh breezes from the sea help clear away vehicular exhaust and the effluvium of heavy industry across the harbor, on the Kowloon side. For Lee, the stench of traffic was immediately overshadowed by the rich and fascinating fragrance of the market stalls and restaurants below.

Examining the crowded streets, the hanging signs of red and gold, he felt no sense of "coming home." His great-great-grandparents had come to the United States before Chinese exclusion, in the late 1870's, and no one in his family had stepped outside the country since. (Lee's overnight excursion to Tijuana, during high school, did not count, although he still leafed through the memories from time to time.) They spoke Chinese at home because it seemed the thing to do, a link with family, but they were all Americans and no one ever spoke of going back. In China, there were communists and famine, waiting to destroy a lifetime of achievement. Why should anyone subject himself to that, when he could have a tract house in the suburbs of Los Angeles?

Had Lee been missing something, all these years? A sense of history, perhaps, that powered Robert Chan and all his Triad brothers, thousands of them working single-mindedly toward preservation of the whole. A far-flung colony of worker ants who fed on garbage, packing lethal stings for use against their enemies.

He didn't buy it for a moment.

Strip away the Triad ceremonies, their compulsive numerology and fond remembrance of a ninety-year-old victory against the Manchus, and you found that you were dealing with a syndicate of ruthless criminals. A Mafia with epicanthic eyelids, steeped in bloodshed and corruption, financed by the sale of tender flesh and heroin. Three hundred years of ritual might breed fanatics for the cause, but it would never make them any more than scum.

If Lee felt any kinship for the crowds below, it was

expressed in terms of outrage at the fact they had been victimized by human predators for sixty generations, never seeing fit to raise a hand in self-defense. He cherished no illusions of his own ability to smash the Triads, but he owed it to himself—to Eddie's memory, and Lisa's—to inflict whatever damage might be possible.

The fighting urge reminded Lee that he was hungry, having eaten nothing since his dinner on the plane. He left the window open, dressed, and rode the elevator to a restaurant downstairs. No point in going out before night arrived, and so he dawdled over pepper steak with rice and mushrooms, salad, a carafe of wine. When he emerged from the hotel, pale dusk had deepened into twilight and the city's lights were coming on, an endless blaze of neon that reflected in the harbor, crowned by orange and yellow streetlights on the Peak, where wealthy *taipans* dwelt apart from common men.

It took Lee two full blocks to spot the tail.

The teeming streets made isolation of a shadow difficult, but he had been expecting company since Chief Inspector Wilson had agreed—a bit too easily, Joe thought—to let him nose around the city on his own. The tail was not in uniform, but he might as well have been. He paused whenever Joseph stopped, reversed directions when his quarry turned around, and jogged to close the gap between them if Lee turned a corner unexpectedly.

Okay.

The first job was to lose him, since a clumsy shadow would be obvious to others, just as it was obvious to Lee. Whatever chance he had of running down the 14K and tracing links to Robert Chan, the odds would be reduced to zero if the Triads saw him coming with a tail.

Lee took his time, no sudden moves, becoming more familiar with the rhythm of the streets as he devised his strategy. A stranger, he would have to take the city's pulse before he tried to shake a native off his track. Finally he flagged down a rickshaw and huddled with the driver, talking price. Like most of Hong Kong's residents, the youth spoke Cantonese—about as similar to Joseph's

Mandarin as English is to Dutch—but Lee was able to communicate sufficiently. The momentary hesitation gave his shadow time to find a ride, and Lee was pleased to see him still in place as they began their trip downtown.

Precision timing was the key, and Joseph watched his landmarks as they circled Statue Square, returning east on Charter Road with the Supreme Court on their right.

The Wanchai district lay ahead, but Lee would not go there directly. First, he needed room to run and time to lose his tail. A busy side street showed him what he needed, and he barked instructions to the driver as they neared an alley, closing on the left. They had a half-block lead, and it would have to do.

The driver made his turn and pedaled briskly through the littered alley toward a cross street at the other end. Lee chose his moment, pushing off and landing in an awkward crouch behind a reeking garbage dump, wincing at a flare of protest from his hip. Dr. Beck had warned him to expect discomfort in the next few months if he attempted strenuous activity.

No matter.

A second rickshaw rattled past him, in pursuit, his shadow snapping at the driver. In another moment they were gone, and Lee emerged from cover, moving back the way he had come, to put more ground between them in the time he had.

The cop would start to backtrack, once he realized that Lee had given him the slip, but it would be too late. Joe waved down a taxi outside the alley's mouth and made directly for the Wanchai district, disembarking on a hectic corner where the garish lights daubed passersby with orange and crimson, setting them on fire.

In front of him, to either side, strains of jazz and pop and heavy metal clashed on streets where young-old hookers lined the curb. Acutely conscious that he had come unarmed, Lee chose a street at random and began his hunt.

• • •

Wanchai has earned its reputation as an Oriental flesh-pot, catering to servicemen and other tourists with a taste for drugs and liquor, sex and high-risk games of chance. In recent years the central business district has expanded eastward, gleaming office towers changing Wanchai's face in part, but businessmen go home at night, and the streets are then reclaimed by other denizens. Along the side streets, sometimes standing side by side with legal offices and travel agencies, nocturnal visitors still have their choice of topless bars and tattoo parlors, porno theaters and "health clubs" featuring erotic variations on the everyday massage. With guidance, a discerning customer may still find brothels, underground casinos, live sex shows and homosexual nightclubs.

In short, Wanchai is still a district where the Triads feel at home.

Lee made his way on foot from one bar to another, checking out the action and politely fending off the "hostesses" who earned their keep by steering customers toward watered drinks and cribs upstairs. It would blow his act at once to ask for Yau Lap Wong or his associates, but he could watch and wait, learning how the local game was played.

In some clubs, patrons sat in deep upholstered booths while naked dancers straddled them and simulated coitus, stopping fractions of an inch from any contact that would place them on the wrong side of the law. The acts were long on titillation, short on payoff, but a customer in need would have no difficulty scaring up a prostitute to douse his fire.

Between bars, Lee passed a squad car on patrol and took advantage of the crowd to hide himself. The shadow he had ditched would be in touch with Choi or Wilson now, but there was no way they could track him down without a blanket effort, and he didn't rate that kind of service yet. A lookout would be waiting for him at his hotel, but there were still precautions Lee could take to keep them from discovering where he had gone. No taxi to his door, for starters, since the watchers could record its number and interrogate the driver to discover where he got his fare. So Lee would walk the last block or two.

But he wasn't finished yet. He still had much to learn about Wanchai before he packed it in. The neighborhood had secrets, and he meant to search them out. The key to Robert Chan's destruction might be waiting for him just around the corner.

Inspector Wilson called for Lee at nine o'clock Friday morning, and they shared a hearty breakfast in the hotel restaurant before departing on a "Triad tour" of Central Hong Kong. Wilson made no allusion to last night or Lee's evasion of his watchdog, and for just a moment Joseph wondered if the tail had been official, after all.

If not police, who else?

He shrugged the problem off, convinced that pride and practicality would seal the chief inspector's lips. It would be painful to admit that Lee, a stranger to the city, had been able to elude a native officer assigned to follow him. And if the scheme had any chance of working on a second try, it would not do for Wilson to confess.

Lee settled for the simple explanation. The alternative meant he was blown already, and might as well pack up and head for home while he was still alive.

The chief inspector drove a different car this morning, dark and nondescript, without the cage in back or the bubble-gum machine on top. It was the classic "unmarked" car, identifiable from any angle by its two-way radio antenna and official license plates, but it was still a visible improvement on the standard blue-and-white. Inspector Wilson's khaki uniform had been replaced by natty tweeds, in deference to their "undercover" mission, but his ramrod bearing set the man apart, no matter what he wore.

"A simple drive-around," Wilson said as he slid behind the steering wheel. "No worries, nothing heavy. Right?"

"I'm in your hands."

"Stout fellow."

Lee had grudgingly acceded to the tour, on Wilson's personal assurance that he would not be exposed to members of the Triad in the company of a policeman. He had hoped cooperation with the chief inspector would forestall an incident like last night's tail, and now he had no option but to carry on with the charade.

"First item, on our right."

Lee craned his neck to glimpse a modern high-rise, smoky glass and burnished steel.

"Not bad."

"Our Chiu Chou friends have owned the land for years," his escort said. "They put the building up themselves, with their connections in the trade, and now they lease the offices to tenants who presumably have no idea about their landlord's shady past. Attorneys, for the most part. One or two have handled Triad cases in the past, but most of them are clean, as far as we can tell."

"You can't go wrong with real estate."

"Unless the land is scheduled for reversion to the reds in fourteen months," Wilson said. "It's a buyer's market, these days, with a number of the Western firms preparing to evacuate. They hate to leave, of course—cheap labor, relatively speaking, and the income tax is still fifteen percent—but none of it means anything if Beijing throws it all in the communal pot."

They rode in silence for a few more blocks, proceeding west along Connaught, until the chief inspector spied another landmark on their tour.

"Just there," he said. "The second on your left."

"The bank?"

"Its chairman of the board is hard-core 14K. We've never caught him with his fingers in the cookie jar, of course, but what's the need? Deposits are accepted—under pseudonyms, if need be—and the cash goes out again as loans. I think you'll find we have as neat a laundry system here as anything in Switzerland or the Bahamas."

"Currency control?"

"Essentially, it's nonexistent. Hong Kong is a free-money market, with various national currencies purchased and sold at the hour's going rate. There's no restriction whatsoever on the trade in currency or gold."

"It must be tricky for you, keeping tabs."

"Damned near impossible. Our drug laws throw the book at anyone convicted of possession or engaging in sales, but we have no provision for the seizure of related assets, such as you lot have at home."

"Mixed blessings," Lee replied. "A few months back, Management and Budget made a survey of the federal seizure program. Turns out we've been losing money when we auction confiscated cars and houses. It costs us more to build a case and bring the dealers into court than we can ever make by selling Jags and condos at bargain rates."

"At least you hit them where it hurts," Wilson said.

"Do we? Most times, Mr. X is out on bail and shopping for a new Rolls-Royce before I finish typing the arrest report."

"And still, you try."

Lee nodded, frowning. "Yes," he said. "Because the day I quit, they win."

He spent the next three hours touring Central Hong Kong with the chief inspector of narcotics, driving south to Aberdeen and back again by lunchtime. Wilson's list of Triad properties included six more high-rise office buildings, one more bank, three posh department stores, plus better than a dozen bars and restaurants. As they returned to his hotel, Lee had the feeling he had landed in the middle of a Triad settlement, with enemies on every side.

"I trust you'll watch your backside," Wilson said, as if he'd peered inside Lee's skull to read his mind. "It's easier to lose oneself in Hong Kong than you might imagine."

"So I gathered."

"In Wanchai, for instance, people have been known to disappear without a trace. Policemen too."

Lee met the chief inspector's gaze. "They tried to kill me twice at home. It didn't take."

"You're in a different game with this lot," Wilson said. "Home-court advantage, as they say. I don't suppose you're armed?"

"In violation of the law?"

"Quite so. More reason to be cautious, then. Avoid heroics, Mr. Lee."

"Why don't you make it Joe?"

"I would do," Wilson told him, "but I've never cared for burying my friends."

That evening, it required more ingenuity for Lee to shake the watchdogs stationed outside his hotel. For openers, they were assigned to work in pairs, one man on each side of the street as Lee set out on foot. If he flagged down a rickshaw or a cab, his shadows went for separate vehicles, prepared to cover any option if he tried another leap in midtown traffic or a darkened alleyway. He took it as an exercise in strategy from the beginning, and was pleased when he found ways to ditch them both.

At seven-thirty, after dining in a restaurant across the street from his hotel, Lee began to lead his escorts through the streets of Central Hong Kong, circling aimlessly on foot, in cabs and rickshaws, prior to hitting on a plan he thought might work. The answer was a large Queen's Road department store, where he invested thirty minutes browsing through cosmetics, handbags, ladies' lingerie, enjoying the discomfort of his followers. He led them next to a department selling cameras and jewelry, where he found a private guard in uniform attempting to look casual as he posed beside the escalator.

Putting on a show of nerves, Lee moved directly toward the guard and asked for help in Mandarin. It took a moment for the rent-a-cop to understand, but finally he nodded, frowning hard, as if a grim expression on his face would ease translation. As it was, he followed Lee's accusing finger, saw the guilty-looking men pretending interest in a rack of necklaces, and understood when Joseph called them both *kuan tsei*—the label for a thief.

"Wait here."

The rent-a-cop had one hand on his pistol, moving to confront the suspects. It was all Joe had to see before he turned and bolted for the escalator, down and out. The guard would fold at once when they displayed police credentials, but Lee still had time, if he was quick about it. He flagged down a taxi at the curb outside and was lost in traffic well before his shadows reached the street.

That night Lee spent his time and money in a search for contacts, taking care to keep it casual, avoiding any hint of urgency. He was a stranger to the city, looking for a little action, pleased to risk his bankroll on an honest game of chance. Casino gambling is illegal in the colony, but clubs exist, regardless. Their survival rests, in equal parts, on the corruption of police and the discretion of selected scouts who troll for players in the Wanchai bars and strip joints.

After three false starts, Lee found his contact in a nightclub called the Lotus Flower. Fifty Hong Kong dollars did the trick, invested with a barmaid who professed to guarantee results. Ten minutes later he was seated at a corner table sipping beer and watching topless dancers grind through their routine, when he discovered he was being watched.

The watcher was a slender ferret of a man, his greasy hair combed across a shiny bald spot in the middle. Smallpox scars had turned his cheeks into a lunar landscape, and the overall effect was not relieved by an expansive grin exposing crooked yellow teeth.

The ferret made a roundabout approach to Joseph's table, stopping here and there around the room to chat with various acquaintances he recognized in transit. Finally he closed the gap, still smiling as he gestured toward an empty chair.

"Are you expecting someone?"

"Possibly."

"A woman?"

"No."

The new arrival sat without an invitation, leaning on his elbows, wrapping slender hands around his cocktail glass.

"You strike me as a man who might enjoy a challenge."

"Oh?"

"A chance to test your skill, perhaps."

"That would depend upon the game."

"Of course." The smile winked off and on. "I might be able to suggest a place."

"In which case, you would have my gratitude."

"Expressed in more substantial terms?"

Lee smiled and shrugged. It was the weasel's play.

"The price would be one hundred dollars, Mr. . . . ?"

"Lee. American or Hong Kong dollars?"

"I have great respect for the United States."

"With payment on delivery?"

"A cash advance is customary."

Joseph smiled and shook his head. "I have been cheated once already. No offense, but I'm a stranger here, without recourse to the authorities."

"Half now, the rest when you are satisfied."

"One-quarter. If I am to lose my money, I prefer to choose the game."

The weasel thought about it, finally nodded, glancing at his watch.

"The hour is late. There are precautions I must take, you understand?"

"You are afraid of the police."

"If I could have the name of your hotel? A simple matter of eliminating risks. You are available tomorrow evening?"

"Yes."

Lee played along and slipped 190 Hong Kong dollars to his contact, the equivalent of twenty-five American.

"Expect my call tomorrow at noon."

"If you should fail?"

The weasel shrugged. "It simply means that we cannot do business, after all."

"And my deposit?"

"Ah."

"I understand."

"Until tomorrow, then."

"Tomorrow."

Alone once more, Lee bought another drink and nursed it while the dancers finished their routine. It would not do for him to hurry off, not while the weasel or his contacts might be watching. Play it cool and watch the naked women for a while, like any bachelor tourist looking for a little fun.

It was approaching three o'clock when Lee got back to his hotel and found his watchdogs sitting in a car outside. They glowered at him, plainly furious, but he ignored them, moving through the lobby to the elevators, finally relaxing as he reached his room and locked the door behind him.

One more day.

This time tomorrow, he would have had a look inside a Triad operation for himself. With any luck at all, the mug shots he had studied Thursday afternoon in Wilson's office might pay off.

If not . . .

14

The call came through at 12:02, and Joseph let the phone ring twice before he picked it up.

"Hello?"

"You recognize my voice?"

The weasel from the Lotus Flower.

"Yes."

"And are you still inclined to try your luck?"

"I am."

"Tonight, same place, at seven-thirty, then."

"I'll be there."

"Excellent."

The line went dead, and Joseph cradled the receiver. Seven-thirty gave him time to plan his moves and shake the escorts he assumed Wilson would have waiting for him on the street. He would allow himself two hours, just in case.

He spent the afternoon at his hotel, a swim and sauna to relax, with television after, in his room. An early dinner in the restaurant downstairs, and he was ready for the streets by half-past five. Still daylight, but the lemming exodus of downtown office workers from their jobs was under way, and if the crowds were not enough to help him lose his shadows, darkness would not make a difference either way.

Emerging from the lobby, Joseph found the lookouts waiting in an unmarked car against the curb. He waited while the doorman hailed a taxi, knowing they would be behind him all the way. He chose a downtown address that would give them all a mile to travel through the worst rush-hour traffic, watching as the unmarked car nosed into traffic half a block behind.

So far, so good.

The move he had in mind would be a daylight variation of the trick he had used to ditch his solitary tail the first night out. No alley this time, but he wouldn't need one if the traffic held. Another block, and then one more, as they began to crawl between the intersections, catching every red light on the way.

Lee checked the meter as the cab pulled up behind a van and waited for the light, the watchers four cars back and going nowhere fast. He dropped some money on the seat and exited without a word of explanation, weaving through the traffic jam on foot before the light had time to change.

Behind him, Joseph heard a car door slam and knew exactly what was happening. The driver would be forced to stay with his machine, and he would never find a parking place downtown at this time of the day. His passenger was in pursuit on foot, and that reduced the odds to one-on-one.

As Joseph had intended all along.

He reached the sidewalk at the corner of Connaught and Ice House, moving past the Mandarin Hotel. Instead of running, jostling those around him, he maintained a steady pace until he reached the hotel entrance, veering left and pushing through a tall revolving door. He crossed the spacious lobby, all green marble with gilded antique carvings, watching out behind him as he punched a button for the central lift.

Luck held; he had the elevator to himself. Behind him, coming off the street, his shadow cleared the entrance as the doors hissed shut.

Three seconds, in and out. The saving grace of speed.

Lee spent a moment pushing every button on the panel, lighting up the different floors. He waited out the stops on two and three, doors opening and closing like a pair of metal jaws that bit off sound and sight. He left the car on four and moved along the hall until he found the service stairs.

One man below, and even if the call for reinforcements had been placed the moment Joseph left his cab, the crush of traffic would prevent them from arriving anytime within the next few minutes. Timing would be critical from this point on.

He tried the service exit, leaning on the heavy door when it resisted, shrugging off a twinge of protest from his shoulder—nothing that he couldn't handle—as he started down the stairs. Lee didn't know if his remaining watchdog would have followed him upstairs or if he would be waiting in the lobby for his backup, but he could not take the risk of leaving in the same way he had entered the hotel.

Emerging from the stairwell, Joseph found himself directly opposite the laundry, with the kitchen farther on and to his left. He passed the swinging doors with portholes in them, glimpsing men in white at work, and stepped out on a concrete loading dock where food supplies and linens were received. A parking lot of sorts, with several older cars and lots of two-wheeled transportation for employees, facing on an alley in the rear.

It was ideal.

He moved along the line of bicycles and tried each one in turn, six down before he found a combination lock that opened at his touch. The owner would have been a hasty type, the sort who left his combination sitting on the final digit so that all he had to do was give the lock a yank and stow the chain before he wheeled away. He would expect the very presence of a lock to warn thieves off, and nine times out of ten he would be right.

But not today.

Lee spent a crucial moment with the ten-speed, worried that his hip might give him trouble on the ride, but it was fine, and by the time he reached the alley proper, he was making decent speed. The side street was a different story, calling on his brakes and skill to navigate through traffic, but it still beat walking. Two miles from the Mandarin Hotel, on Hollywood, he parked the stolen bike outside a flower shop and left it, strolling half a block before he flagged down a taxi.

"Wanchai," he told the driver, settling in his seat. "And take your time."

Lee did not go directly to the Lotus Flower. It would look suspicious if he turned up early, and he saw no point in staking out the bar. An ambush might be waiting for him—anything was possible—but he would run a greater risk of setting off alarm bells if he started acting like a cop instead of a compulsive gambler anxious for a chance to throw his cash away.

The streets reminded him of San Francisco's Chinatown to some degree, but Wanchai amplified the sounds, exaggerated the sensations, letting Joseph know he was a world away from home. Outside the seedy bars and topless clubs, street vendors hawked their "hundred-year-old eggs" and mythic aphrodisiacs, "ghost money" meant for burning to supply lamented loved ones in the spirit world. Streetwalkers worked the curb with one eye on the taverns, primed to pounce on any unattended male who surfaced for a breath of air.

Lee killed an hour on the street and crossed the threshold of the Lotus Flower fifteen minutes early for his date. A hostess wearing silk with nothing underneath was waiting for him, but he waved her off and found an empty bar stool that would let him watch the door. He paid for bottled beer and nursed it while he scanned the crowd in search of a familiar face.

No weasel yet, but he could wait.

His contact entered from the street at 7:29 and thirty seconds, spotting Lee at once and moving toward the bar, his vacant smile in place. The man on Joseph's left was leaving, but the new arrival did not sit, nor did he order anything to drink.

"The rest of my advance?" he said, still grinning like a skull.

"Upon delivery, as agreed."

"When you are ready, Mr. Lee."

Joe set his bottle on the bar and fell in step behind the pockmarked ferret, past a line of waiting hostesses, to reach the street outside.

"How far?"

"A little way," his escort said. "If you would care to ride—"

"I need the exercise," Lee cut him off, imagining a one-way trip to nowhere.

"As you wish."

They covered three short blocks before his guide picked out a narrow alley, stepping from the glare of neon into semidarkness. Lee hung back, his eyes adjusting to the change before he made his move.

"This way."

"I'm coming."

Halfway down, a flight of concrete steps descended to a basement door. Lee's contact led the way and knocked—three raps, a pause, two more, and three to finish. Yellow light spilled through a peephole, adding jaundice to the weasel's problems as he gave the password to a guard inside.

A heavy bolt was thrown, the door swung open, and his escort led the way. Lee found himself inside a kind of airlock, doors on either side, a meaty bouncer watching both of them with gimlet eyes.

"The money?"

Lee produced a wad of Hong Kong dollars, counted in advance, and stood at ease while his connection verified the total.

"Very good. This way."

Beyond the second door, a basement fifty feet in length and twenty feet across had been remodeled to accommodate the fittings of a miniature casino. On Joseph's left, dice tables and a roulette wheel; on his right, a double bank of slot machines, with tables set aside for fan-tan, baccarat, and poker. Women dressed in next to nothing circulated through the press of gamblers, bearing drinks on plastic trays, accepting tips and the occasional caress as they performed their duties for the house.

"Enjoy."

The weasel pumped his hand and disappeared in search of other clients, leaving Joe to find his way alone. Lee worked his way across the smoky room to reach the cashier's cage, a plywood box enclosed by chicken wire, and changed a thousand Hong Kong dollars into betting chips. Another look around the room, and he was drawn to the roulette wheel by a glimpse of a familiar profile.

Cautious now, on hostile turf, where any slip could be his one and only. Sorting through the images of mug shots viewed in Wilson's office, Lee picked out a winner, circling the room until he found a place across the table from his mark.

A short man, balding, heavyset, with steel-rimmed spectacles that magnified his eyes.

A man named Sun Mok Lin.

The Incense Master of the 14K.

Lee fought the urge to stare, examining the table as he found his place, considering the distribution of the bets. He waited through another round, pretending interest in the wheel, before he dropped five chips on red.

And won.

He let it ride, and won again. A girl who might have been eighteen appeared beside him, and he ordered whiskey, shifting his accumulated chips to black before the croupier began his spin.

Another win, his money tripled in five minutes' time. He claimed his winnings, left five chips on black—and lost them as the ball dropped onto twenty-seven, red.

Lee bet another five on evens, winning as the wheel gave up a thirty-six. He let it ride again, and saw his money doubled with a twenty-two.

His drink arrived, and Joseph tipped the hostess well enough to rate a fetching smile. The whiskey had been watered, but he didn't mind. The last thing he needed was a fuzzy head and slow reaction time.

Across the table, Sun Mok Lin was playing carelessly, more interested in his companion's ample cleavage than the dwindling stack of chips in front of him. The money couldn't matter much, assuming the casino was a Triad operation, since the Incense Master would be raking in his share of profits from the house. In essence, Sun was playing for himself, but from the looks he gave his foxy escort, Lee decided that the aging thug had something else in mind for later.

Fair enough. It proved that Sun was human, vulnerable, just like any other man. His thoughts were not on Triad rituals tonight, and if he let his guard down far enough—

Lee's train of thought was interrupted by a clamoring alarm bell and red lights winking at the door and cashier's cage. Before their import had a chance to register, the croupier was raking chips and cash across the table, dumping everything together in a burlap sack, abandoning his post. Lee saw the hostess who had brought his whiskey, short skirt riding up on golden thighs as she sped past him, making for a smallish exit in the rear.

A raid!

Lee cursed and started shoving through the crush, another gambler anxious to escape before the uniforms crashed in. He did not stop to think in terms of timing or coincidence; escape was paramount, before he was identified and questions asked.

Too late.

The first man at the door was jolted backward as a flying squad in khaki bulled their way inside. Lee had a glimpse of truncheons flailing, someone going down, and he retreated toward a neutral corner, trying to become as inconspicuous as possible. There might still be a chance to slip away if—

Someone gripped his shoulder, spinning him around, and he was face-to-face with Thomas Choi. Before he had a chance to speak, the sergeant hit him low and hard, a blow that bent him double and put rubber in his knees. Another jolt between the shoulders kept him there, and Lee was kneeling on the bare concrete, still fighting for a breath, when he felt handcuffs close around his wrists.

Inspector Wilson lit a thin cigar and said, "I'm waiting for an explanation, Mr. Lee."

"I was about to say the same."

The small interrogation room had much in common with its stateside counterparts. A table bolted to the floor and flanked by wooden chairs. Walls painted beige. A mirror on his left that had no purpose other than concealment of an observation team or video equipment on the other side. Lee faced the chief inspector as if they were playing cards; Detective Sergeant Choi stayed on the sidelines, careful not to block the mirror-window when he moved.

"It happens you're in no position to be asking questions," Wilson said.

"Oh, no?"

"I should advise you that anything you say may well be taken down and used against you."

"Great. Terrific. First, your people do their best to blow my cover, now you're reading me Miranda. This is perfect."

"What we've done, so far, is save your life. Your 'cover,' as you put it, had been well and truly blown before we tracked you down."

Lee read the chief inspector's face and understood that he had no cards left to play.

"You talked to Kephart?"

"Agent Christy, as it happens. He was kind enough to verify the information we received from sources on the street."

Lee felt a worm of apprehension wriggling in his gut.

"Which is?"

"The fact of your suspension and impending separation from the service of your government. An idiotic plan to crack the Triads on your own and make us all look foolish in the bargain."

"When you say you got this information from the street—"

"I mean exactly that," the chief inspector cut him off. "We cultivate informants here as well. They're not a bloody Yank invention, Mr. Lee."

"Informants in the Triads?"

"Near enough. I'd rest assured the other side has heard about your little escapade."

The worm had ceased its wriggling, and an icy chill was creeping over Lee, as if the air-conditioning had suddenly been turned on high. He glanced from Wilson to Choi and back again.

"Mind telling me how much they know?"

"I don't suppose there's any harm. Detective Sergeant?"

Choi stopped pacing, dark eyes boring into Lee. "Ex-DEA, Chinese-American, pursuing a vendetta in defiance of the law. They know your name and your departure date from San Francisco."

"When did this come down?"

"This afternoon, around the time you were embarrassing my men."

"You didn't waste much time."

"We had a bit of luck," the chief inspector said, and let it go at that. "Now, if you wouldn't mind—"

"You talked to Ray, you must know why I'm here."

"A bit of Don Quixote, it would seem. I know about your partner being killed."

"There's more."

"The woman." Wilson frowned. "We're not the Wild West here, I should remind you. High noon in the colony means lunchtime, nothing more."

"You've missed the point," Joseph said.

"Have I?"

"If the heavies know I'm here, who told them?"

"Someone in the States, presumably."

"But *who*?"

"Why not this Robert Chan you're on about? If he's a ranking member of the 14K, as you suspect, delivering your head to his Hill Chief would be Chan's duty . . . and his pleasure."

"Same question. Who tipped Chan?"

"I'm told there have been multiple attempts on your life. Surveillance seems a logical solution, in the circumstances."

"No." Lee shook his head. "I spent two hours checking for a tail the day I left. One person knew where I was going."

Wilson studied the accumulated ash on his cigar, then glanced at Choi. "A bit of privacy, perhaps?"

Choi nodded, left the room, and came back moments later.

"Done."

"We'll do without the cameras for a bit," Wilson said. "You were saying?"

Lee was hesitant to let his train of thought proceed. A part of him could not accept Ray Christy in the role of sellout, but the ugly notion would explain Chan's almost extrasensory ability to stay one jump ahead of the DEA the past few months. When Lee was still in San Francisco General, he had questioned Ray about the possibility of leaks, and he recalled his supervisor's words.

I hate to think so.

Covering his ass? Lee felt as if he might be sick. "I could be wrong," he said.

"And then again, you may be absolutely right." The chief inspector spent a moment weighing what he had to say. "For some time now, we've had occasion to suspect a problem in your agency. Conflict of interest, as it were."

"Explain."

"We work in close cooperation with the DEA, as you're aware. Have done, for years. Of late, however, we've encountered . . . difficulties, shall we say. Joint operations scuttled at a cost we frankly can't afford."

"A leak?"

The chief inspector's frown was etching shadows on his face beneath the harsh fluorescent lights.

"The native officer I mentioned earlier?"

Lee nodded. "I remember."

"We have reason to believe he was deliberately betrayed," Wilson said. "I've examined those within my own department who had knowledge of the operation. I believe they're clean. Of course, I could be wrong."

"But you don't think so."

"No."

"And that leaves the DEA."

"It seems our difficulties may be similar."

"If not identical."

"Your Mr. Christy has suggested that I put you on the next flight back to San Francisco."

"And?"

"The problem lies in finding you, of course. You've shown a penchant for evading my detectives. Theoretically, it might be days before we run you down."

"And in the meantime . . ."

"Joseph Lee would disappear."

"I understand."

"Not quite. I must insist that you accept our help this time. Detective Sergeant Choi has kindly volunteered to be your unofficial escort and interpreter."

"You're banking on a leak at the DEA, instead of the Narcotics Bureau?"

Wilson's eyes reminded Lee of granite chips. "No one outside this room will be informed until the operation is completed, one way or another. If it fails . . ."

"You'll know who blew the whistle."

"More or less. Do you accept the terms?"

Lee glanced at Choi. "I don't appear to have much choice."

"We all have choices, Mr. Lee."

"One question. Why?"

"I'm running out of time in which to do my job. A few more months, and I'll be back in England, probably retired. I'd like to feel that I've accomplished something here before I go."

"I understand."

"And as you said, I owe the bastards one."

15

The gun was a Beretta Model 84, .380 caliber, with plastic grips and a capacity of thirteen rounds. It had been confiscated from a pimp who used it to intimidate his competition and impress his girls. A trace, if it should come to that, would link the weapon to a shipment "lost" in France, from which assorted pieces made their way around the world by means unknown. If it was found on Joseph Lee, the pistol's Hong Kong source would be a mystery.

In fact, he had received it—off the record—from Inspector Wilson of the Royal Hong Kong Police Force. Logged as evidence a full year earlier, the gun had disappeared from custody around the time its owner went to jail for seven years on charges of felonious assault. If asked, the property custodian would testify, in all sincerity, that it had been destroyed with other confiscated weapons during April 1995.

It had been Lee's idea to travel armed, this time, and Wilson had agreed with only fleeting hesitation. They had gone too far to balk at trifles, as it was, and Wilson trusted Lee to play his part if anything went wrong.

Assuming he was still alive.

Lee had his reservations about working undercover with Detective Sergeant Choi. For openers, Choi was a veteran on the force, which meant his face might well be known around Wanchai and other districts where the Triads owned the streets. Aside from that, Lee did not know the sergeant well enough to share Inspector Wilson's confidence that Choi was squeaky clean. His life was riding on the line with two men he had known a brief four days, assuming treachery from one whom he had trusted for the past ten years.

No matter. He was in the game to stay, and he would have to play the cards as they were dealt. If he suspected Choi or Wilson was about to sabotage the operation, he would have a shot at taking out the leak before they fed him to the jackals.

Either way, he was a long step closer to revenge for Eddie, Lisa, and the rest. Another step toward pinning something on Robert Chan.

With Wilson running interference, Lee had been checked out of his hotel and reestablished at the first-class Miramar, on Nathan Road, Kowloon. He registered as Arnold Jin, presumably a broker from Los Angeles, employed by first-time buyers who were anxious to remain anonymous. Choi picked the alias of Wonsoo Kee. The ruse was paper-thin, but in the circumstances it was all they had.

Choi's stratagem involved a canvas of the clubs where dealers did their business over high-priced drinks and meals, with high-priced women at their sides. He put out feelers in Wanchai and on the Kowloon side, the Tsimshatsui district, spending the department's cash like it was going out of style. By Friday, Joseph's eighth day in the colony, he had a bite.

"The club is called Lung Cheung—the Happy Dragon," Choi informed him. "I will pick you up at half-past seven."

"Who's the mark?"

"A dealer, Kyung-Hee Su. He is a member of the 14K, confirmed."

"No chance he'll make your face?"

Choi shook his head. "We have not met. It is a pleasure I've been saving for the proper time."

"Till seven-thirty, then."

"A tie would be appropriate," Choi said. "And bring your pistol, just in case."

The Happy Dragon was a combination supper club and strip joint, trying hard to show a touch of class. The topless dancers, instead of strutting along the bar, had been relegated to a central stage, a lighted runway leading to the wings. When they performed, they were surrounded by their audience on every side, the clank of silverware and undertone of chatter constantly competing with the small live band.

Choi and Lee were expected, and the hostess—either Filipino or Hispanic, Joseph couldn't say—conveyed them to a ringside table where their contact waited, sipping wine. He ordered more as they were seated, shaking hands across the table, putting on a predatory smile that felt more like a grimace.

Kyung-Hee Su was short and wide, a human fireplug, with a bullet head trapped in between his meaty shoulders and a flat toupee. The hairpiece might have cost a fortune, but it looked like something from a novice actor's makeup kit, with netting visible along the part. Joe concentrated on not laughing while he waited for the wine, relieved when it arrived. A waitress took their dinner orders—seafood all around—and disappeared.

"I understand you come from California, Mr. Jin."

Lee sipped his wine and smiled. "That's right."

"I have associates in California."

"So I'm told."

"You could have ordered merchandise from them, I think."

"Too risky, at the moment. Too expensive."

"Ah. You wish to undersell my friends, perhaps?"

Lee shook his head. "By no means. Those I represent intend to cultivate new markets, out of state. They understand your loyalty to established clients and would not presume to interfere."

Su turned his deep-set, piggy eyes on Sergeant Choi. "What is your role in the transaction, Mr. Kee?"

"A simple guide for one who does not know the city," Choi replied, the very soul of modesty. "I'm told there may be something in the nature of a finder's fee."

"Indeed?"

"From my associates, of course," Lee said. "A simple cost of doing business."

He was momentarily distracted by a flashbulb on the far side of the room, and turned in time to see a slim young woman in a sequined dress line up another shot of two delighted couples, glasses lifted in a toast. The moment captured, she moved on, some patrons waving her away, while others huddled close and grinned like children on a jaunt to Disneyland.

Su's voice drew his attention from the sideshow. "The commodity you seek is not available at bargain prices, Mr. Jin."

"Of course not, but there are inherent risks in shipment and delivery, which increase the cost. My clients are prepared to share those risks, perhaps assume them altogether, if the price is right."

"And they intend to buy in quantity?"

"If the projected market studies are correct, you may expect a standing monthly order in the neighborhood of ten to fifteen kilos, pure."

Another flashbulb winked in Joseph's line of sight. He saw that the photographer had halved her distance from their table in a few short moments, moving ever closer as she worked the room.

"I only deal in purity," said Kyung-Hee Su. "The price is fifty thousand for a kilo."

"Hong Kong?" Lee inquired, pretending innocence.

The dealer chuckled. "Hong Kong dollars are like toilet paper, Mr. Jin. I need American, or the equivalent in gold."

"Then surely fifty thousand is your price for a delivery in the States. My clients are prepared to offer twenty-five."

Su frowned and shook his head. "Impossible. My own source charges more. Perhaps, for guarantees of future business, I might be able to accept a bid of forty-six."

Lee glanced at Choi and smiled, a businessman engaged in haggling.

"Thirty thousand, with a six-month guarantee," he said. "One-quarter of the total in advance."

"For one year's guarantee, I could accept the sacrifice of forty-one per kilo."

Near the runway, two male customers were on their feet, a stripper kneeling just behind them, one breast framed between their smiling faces as the camera flashed again.

"My clients could not guarantee a year at any figure over thirty-five."

"You rob my children of their daily bread. Perhaps at thirty-nine . . ."

"I have no power to negotiate beyond the sum of thirty-seven-five."

Their food arrived, and Kyung-Hee Su was silent in the presence of their waitress, waiting till she left and both his guests had voiced approval of their meals.

"At thirty-seven-five," the dealer said, "I must require a quarter of the full year's order in advance."

"Of course."

"In that case, gentlemen, we have a deal."

The camera flashed behind their host, one table over. Half a dozen Japanese on tour, all smiles, recorded for posterity. As the photographer approached their table, Kyung-Hee Su put on a scowl and waved her off.

"More wine," the dealer said, refilling Joseph's glass and moving on to Choi. "A toast to our most excellent association."

Su picked up his glass, the momentary scowl discarded as he beamed. "Prosperity and friendship," he saluted. "And the ruin of our enemies."

Lee drained his glass and set it on the table.

To the ruin of our enemies.

The roving camera flashed once more, behind him, and was gone.

The Red Pole's name was Ho Kwan Pang. A product of the Hong Kong streets, at twenty-five he bore no visible resemblance to the urchin who had once lived hand-to-mouth by stealing food from market stalls or pawing through the garbage bins in back of restaurants. His suit was custom-tailored and his jet-black hair was styled; his graceful movements were the product of an expert martial artist's quiet strength. These days, instead of lurking in the alleyway behind a restaurant or nightclub, he was welcomed by the maître d' and treated with respect.

Pang owed it all—his very life itself—to Sap Sie Kie. Without the 14K, he might be dead by now, or marking time as one more faceless, nameless piece of Hong Kong's vast machine.

Pang knew the meaning of respect and duty. When his Shan Chu issued orders, even on a moment's notice, he dropped everything and hastened to obey, as if his life depended on it.

Which, one day, it might.

This evening, he had left a willing woman in his bed to supervise the taking of a snapshot, waiting while the photo was developed, printed, dried. Pang recognized the dealer Kyung-Hee Su by his ridiculous toupee. The other men were strangers, but a Red Pole of the 14K has ways of picking information off the streets.

In this case, Pang avoided middlemen and took his problem straight to the police. His contact was a Chinese sergeant on the Triad payroll, detailed to Narcotics for eleven years before his shift to Personnel. They met outside the sergeant's home on Bowring Street, Kowloon, a house that he could never have afforded on policeman's pay. One glance, beneath the streetlight, and he recognized Detective Sergeant Thomas Choi.

The third man was a stranger, but it made no difference now. He worked with Choi, had no doubt used a pseudonym to meet with Kyung-Hee Su, and he would have to die.

Pang waited only for the Shan Chu's order to be handed down.

They met in Tsimshatsui, on the Kowloon side, one flight above a nightclub owned by Yau Lap Wong. The Hill Chief kept a combination office and apartment there, although he lived in Hong Kong proper, on the Peak. A man of simple elegance, he wore a thousand-dollar suit and diamond tie tack, offering cigars and whiskey, which the Red Pole was expected to decline.

Pang stood before his master, placed the glossy eight-by-ten on Yau Wong's desk, and fingered Thomas Choi.

"The other?"

"Shan Chu, he represents himself as Arnold Jin. Our contacts do not recognize his face. He checked into the Miramar on Sunday afternoon and paid in cash."

Wong tapped the stranger's likeness with an index finger.

"The American."

Pang smiled, impressed. "Quite possibly."

"They mean to damage us, our family."

"It shall not be allowed, Shan Chu."

Wong pushed the photo back across his desk. "I leave the matter in your worthy hands."

"An honor, Shan Chu." Bowing deeply as he palmed the eight-by-ten and turned away, the doorman standing back to let him pass.

Before he reached the stairs, Pang knew how many soldiers he would need to do the job, the weapons they would use. He had a choice of tactics, the direct approach or something subtle, but his instinct told him that the Hill Chief would prefer these slugs to serve as an example. The police would understand, and they would hesitate before they tried such clumsy moves again.

Ho Pang was smiling as he reached the street, his driver waiting for him in the car. He issued terse directions, settled back, and closed his eyes, a signal that he did not wish to talk before they reached their destination.

In his mind, the scene played out like something from a high-tech action film.

As always, when he fantasized, Ho Pang became the star.

Tonight would be his chance to shine, the fantasy made flesh.

And blood.

Detective Sergeant Thomas Choi had never married, for the simple reason that he was devoted to his job. He could not think of any way to serve a family *and* the Royal Hong Kong Police Force well, so he had made a choice. The job came first, and if it meant his branch of the expansive family tree remained a stunted twig for life, so be it.

Most of his colleagues on the force were married, and despite their claims of satisfaction, he had seen the way policemen changed once they had wives and children to support. Some used the job to work out their frustrations, sifting latent anger toward their prisoners and members of the public they were sworn to serve, while others suddenly became a bit too cautious, always last to cross the threshold when a raid was carried out. More often, there were money problems, and he had observed the way a man with hungry mouths at home developed hungry eyes around the office, looking for an easy way to supplement his salary. Choi did not blame the wives and children for corruption on the force, but he remained a man of simple tastes and had no one to satisfy except himself.

When Choi required a woman, he did business with a pimp he had arrested several times while working Vice around Wanchai. The raids had been a business matter, nothing personal, and there were no hard feelings. While the pimp had offered first-class service free of charge, Choi always paid. It was the sergeant's way of drawing lines between himself and officers who lost their focus, taking handouts from the very people they might someday have to place in jail.

Choi did not find his women on the street. Instead, they visited his home, a small house near the Happy Valley Race Course, where he lived alone. Choi could afford a slightly larger home, but he was pleased with what he had. Before agreeing to the purchase, he had consulted a practitioner of *feng shui*, the ancient Chinese art of geomancy that evaluated dwelling sites to see if they would serve the tenant's karma or retard his progress in the years ahead. *Feng shui* kept some wealthy merchants dwelling in the humble neighborhoods where they were born, but it was not the Chinese way to tamper with success, especially where spirits were involved.

Detective Sergeant Choi was not a superstitious or religious man, but he respected the traditions of his people.

Recently that same respect had prevented him from sharing the exaggerated apprehensions of his colleagues as they looked toward 1997 and the shift to communist control. Choi would survive because the state had need of solid, incorruptible policemen under any flag. And if his new superiors attempted to subvert his sense of honor, Choi could always find another place to live, *feng shui* notwithstanding.

Friday night, an hour after dropping Joseph Lee at his hotel, Choi sat at home before his color television with the sound turned off, a glass of seltzer in his hand. The meal had not agreed with him, though it was well-prepared, and he was working on a sour stomach now, determined not to try to sleep before he put his churning gut at ease.

In fact, Choi knew that it was not the food or wine he had consumed that made him bilious now. It was the company he had to keep, from Kyung-Hee Su to the American whom he had been assigned to chaperon. Inspector Wilson trusted Lee to help him plug a leak at the DEA, but Choi had learned that it was best to deal with strangers at a safe arm's length. Lee might be everything he claimed, a persecuted victim of the Triads and a traitor in his own department. On the other hand . . .

The rapping on his door surprised him. It was nearly midnight, and his neighbors would be fast asleep, unless one of them had a problem to discuss. It was the fate of a policeman to attract complaints that rarely fell within his jurisdiction, problems he could solve only by turning casual acquaintances to enemies. Choi made a point of listening (or seeming to) before he tactfully directed the complaints to clergymen or counselors, another family member—anyone at all, to get the burden off his shoulders, back where it belonged.

He quaffed the seltzer, moving toward the door, surprised to find that he was almost grateful for the interruption this time. A distraction would be welcome at the moment, even if it forced him to observe the blemished underbelly of a neighbor's life.

Three strangers waited on his doorstep, and it took a

moment for the sergeant's mind to clear, recalling office photographs, before he recognized Ho Pang.

A Red Pole of the 14K.

Pang gave him time to understand—a heartbeat, more or less—before he slid the shotgun out from underneath his leather jacket, his companions drawing weapons of their own. Choi's pistol was in the bedroom, where he didn't have a prayer of reaching it in time.

Still, he had to try.

He bolted, shoulders hunched against the coming blow, and made it halfway to the bedroom door before his killers opened fire. At fifteen feet, a blind man with a shotgun could have cut him down, not to mention three executioners who had performed this kind of task before. They squeezed off two rounds each and left him crumpled in the middle of the room, a broken thing, beyond repair.

A sports announcer on the silent television witnessed their retreat and smiled.

While Thomas Choi was dying in his living room, Joe Lee was strolling by himself in Kowloon Park, across the road from his hotel. He could not sleep, and did not feel like drinking to anesthetize his nerves. The park was quiet, close at hand, and relatively safe while Joseph wore the small Beretta automatic on his belt.

He was encouraged by their seeming progress with the Triad dealer, Kyung-Hee Su, but it was difficult to chart the next move in their strategy. On one hand, Lee was hopeful that a major purchase might lead Su to grant an audience with his supplier, something in the nature of a good-faith gesture to a valued customer. By contrast, Sergeant Choi was all for busting Su the moment they had drugs in hand, applying heat until he gave them a substantial evidentiary link to someone higher in the 14K. They had not reached agreement by the time they parted, and they would be forced to hash it out tomorrow, prior to meeting Su on Causeway Bay at ten P.M.

With any luck, Lee thought he might win Ian Wilson over to his plan in time, but if the chief inspector went for

Choi's idea, Joe would be forced to play along. He had come close to wearing out his welcome in the colony, and he was not prepared to jettison the only friend he had.

He reached the western limit of the park, on Canton Road, and started back for his hotel. The night was cool but not unpleasant, and the lightweight jacket he wore to hide his pistol was sufficient for his needs. No one accosted him as he made his way across the park. For all he knew, he had the darkened trees and gently rolling grassland to himself.

The first alarm bells sounded in his mind as he was crossing Nathan Road to reach the Miramar. Sparse traffic gave him time to scrutinize the front of his hotel, the doorman in his uniform, a dark sedan just pulling up outside. Three young Chinese got out, a fourth man staying with the car, and Lee was watching them, already on the east side of the street, before the driver spotted him and did a classic double-take.

The lookout glanced at something on the seat beside him, back at Lee, and pressed his horn. His passengers had reached the lobby, but they doubled back as Joseph reached inside his jacket, hauling out the light Beretta Model 84.

The point man wore dark glasses, glinting in the wash of neon, and he had a sawed-off shotgun in his hands as he emerged from the hotel. Lee braced the automatic in a firm two-handed grip and shot him twice before he had a chance to use the stubby weapon, bolting into Nathan Road before the other gunmen could recover from their initial shock.

They tried to chase him, but the darkness was a friend, and they had seen what he could do if he was cornered. Joseph ran through darkness till his burning lungs demanded rest, then crouched behind a sculptured hedge and listened for the sounds of pursuit.

It took five minutes to convince himself that they were gone, and still he kept the pistol in his hand as he trekked north, the full length of the park, to Austin Road. They might anticipate him, lay an ambush there, but Joseph reckoned they would have their hands full with the hotel doorman, passing witnesses, and a dead or wounded member of their team.

If they were waiting for him, Lee would do his best with what he had. If not, then he was free to find a telephone and spread the word.

Before it was too late.

"A neighbor made the call," Wilson said, offering a pack of cigarettes, which Lee declined. "Too late, of course. It was over in an instant. Nothing anyone could do."

Lee pictured Thomas Choi in death and felt an unexpected pang of loss. "We could have seen it coming," he replied.

They sat in Wilson's private car in a darkened bit of parking lot outside the Kowloon railway station. Wilson used the dashboard lighter on his cigarette and rolled his window down to vent the smoke.

"You had a lucky break, all things considered." There was bitterness in Wilson's tone, but Joe was not the target. "If they'd found you in your room . . ."

"I hit one of them," Joseph said.

"You killed him, as it happens. Frightened his companions bad enough that they went off without him." Wilson's frown seemed etched in stone. "His name was Pang. A Red Pole with the Sap Sie Kie."

"So much for tight security."

"No leak this time." Wilson reached in his pocket for a folded eight-by-ten. "Pang had this with him when he went to his reward."

The photograph was cracked and wrinkled, marked with rusty-looking bloodstains on the back. Lee opened it and recognized the cheap toupee on Kyung-Hee Su, as captured from behind. Across the table, Thomas Choi was smiling at the dealer with a wineglass in his hand, Lee turned in profile toward the sergeant who was dead now, lying in a metal drawer downtown.

"They had us spotted going in."

"Apparently. One look at that"—Wilson stabbed a finger at the photograph—"and all they had to do was name the players. Choi would be no problem, though I doubt we'll ever know for sure who fingered him."

"And me?"

The chief inspector shrugged. "You came with Choi, so you were guilty by association. Even if they didn't know your name, it all comes down to cleaning house."

"Goddamm it!"

"We've an order out for Su's arrest, of course, but that won't take us far. A photograph of three men eating dinner won't support a murder case, and he'll have witnesses to prove his whereabouts throughout the evening."

"Maybe if you sweat him—"

Wilson shook his head. "The Triad vows of secrecy are quite emphatic. Violators may expect to die by thunderbolts or 'myriads of swords,' depending on the nature of their lapse. The operative term, in any case, is death. We can't compete with that these days."

"You know the shooter. Trace it back from there."

"A self-employed kung-fu instructor," Wilson told him. "Nine arrests and no convictions. Knowing Pang's connections and substantiating them in court are very different things."

"I don't need scientific proof," Lee said.

"Quite right. You need a ticket out of town, before I have another body on my hands."

"Now, wait a second—"

"No." The chief inspector's voice was firm, his eyes like chips of slate. "I've had the luxury of playing cowboys once already, and it cost a good man's life. I'll live with that, but I will not compound my error by extending the charade. Be clear on that point, Mr. Lee. We have a flight to San Francisco leaving Hong Kong International at nine A.M. If you insist, I can arrange protective custody until that time."

"I have a choice?"

"A wise man would go home, I think."

"Suppose I'm foolish?"

"You will have to leave the colony, in any case. I can't

protect you, and there's nothing more you can accomplish here, except to throw your life away."

"If I were moving on?"

The chief inspector flicked his cigarette butt out the window, staring at the night. "I know a man in Bangkok. Not a friend, exactly, but he hasn't let me down so far."

Lee sat and watched the running lights of aircraft, lifting off and landing at the airport, several miles away. "Right now," he said, "I'll take what I can get."

16

"You look for smoke?"

The barker was a sallow Thai with dark tattoos entwined around his forearms, oily hair worn in an Elvis cut, with wet curls drooping on his forehead.

"Smoke?" he said again. "Real thing, no substitute."

Lee shook his head and brushed the man aside, continuing his trek along the neon runway that was Patpong Road. Before he made ten feet, he heard the barker coming on to someone else behind him, offering the seamy pleasures of the Orient at bargain rates.

By any standards, Bangkok's Patpong Road rates near the top—or bottom—of the scale in Asian nightlife. Although limited in area, a few short blocks between Silom and Suriwongse roads, the district manages to offer hundreds of "massage" facilities and taverns, countless prostitutes available around the clock, and several dozen sex clubs where the shows are neither simulated nor entirely suitable for squeamish patrons of the art form. In comparison with Patpong Road, the Wanchai district of Hong Kong resembles Omaha, Nebraska, on election day.

Thai citizens describe their capital as Krung Thep—"City of the Angels"—but it would have taxed Diogenes to find a glimpse of heaven on the streets.

The scenes of almost desperate gaiety were telling on his nerves, but Joseph had a job to do, and he was not about to be put off by mere fatigue. Six hours on the ground, and early twilight found him working Patpong Road, intent on searching out the one man who might help him on his way.

His contact was supposed to be a Thai, Damrong

Yodmani, who had worked with Ian Wilson in the past. Besides the name and a concise description, Wilson had supplied a British passport in the name of Wen-Ling Shyu, together with a cashier's check amounting to a quarter-million U.S. dollars. Like the pistol he had left behind in Hong Kong, Lee's supply of working capital had been obtained by means of confiscation, most of it from dealers moving China white, and Wilson was prepared to take the heat if its unauthorized disbursement came to light. Upon arrival, Lee had drawn five thousand dollars' worth of baht—a wad of notes that could have literally choked a buffalo—and banked the rest to keep it safe from local predators. The cash would be available at need, and in the meantime he could show the passbook as a demonstration of his *bona fides.*

The Customs officers at Don Muang airport, north of town, had passed Lee on without a second glance, once they assured themselves that he was not transporting firearms or substantial sums of cash. As Thailand's contribution to the worldwide "war on drugs," the government required disclosure if a tourist carried currency beyond the sum of ten thousand American dollars, but no such limits were applied to bank drafts or traveler's checks. The cosmetic effort to discourage heroin transactions had no serious effect upon the trade, and it would not prevent Joe Lee from making contact with his enemies.

Provided he lived that long.

The issue of survival had been driven home in Hong Kong, if it needed any reinforcement, and he knew the Triads would not hesitate to try again in Bangkok, if they saw through his charade. One possible advantage was the momentary shift in targets, from the Sap Sie Kie to the competing Chiu Chou syndicate that held a virtual monopoly on narcotraffic in the City of the Angels, but he realized that it would take one slip to bring the full wrath of the Triads down upon his head.

That knowledge made it all the more imperative for Lee to arm himself, and as he traveled east on Patpong Road, ignoring the suggestive smiles of male and female prostitutes, he had a destination fixed in mind. There was a purchase to be made before he pressed the search for Wilson's contact and began the last phase of his hunt.

The pawnshop was a rat hole set below street level, three brass balls suspended from a sign above to signify the broker's stock in trade. A flight of rough-hewn steps led Joseph to a door inscribed with words he could not read. It opened at his touch, a small bell jangling overhead to herald his arrival, and the shop's proprietor appeared at once, all smiles as he pushed through a beaded curtain in the back.

"Sawat dee khrap."

"Good evening."

"English, yes. I speak."

The broker listened carefully as Lee explained his need, adopting a confused expression until Joseph palmed the hefty roll of baht and indicated he was serious.

"You not police?"

Lee showed his bogus passport, waiting while the broker studied it and gave it back.

"This way."

He followed past the beaded curtain into something like a combination storage room and office, wooden crates and cardboard boxes stacked almost to the ceiling, metal cabinets on the eastern wall secured with combination locks. The broker opened one of them, his shoulders hunched to hide the combination, and removed a smallish suitcase, which he set upon his cluttered desk, unmindful of the papers it disturbed.

Inside, at least a dozen handguns had been wrapped in terry towels, protected against rust and accidental damage when the case was hauled about. The broker took his time unwrapping them, like Christmas presents, lining up his wares for Lee's inspection.

He examined the revolvers first. A pair of Ruger double-action Magnums, one in stainless steel, were laid out with an antique Russian Nagant Model 1895. The Smith & Wesson offerings consisted of two .38's—a Combat Masterpiece and stubby five-shot Bodyguard—together with a vintage Model 1917, chambered in .45 caliber. Britain was represented with a Webley Mark 4, and the six-gun collection was rounded off with two lightweights: Rossi's .32-caliber Model 89, and a Taurus Model 83, in .38 caliber.

The automatics were an equally mixed bag in terms of quality and stopping power. A .45-caliber Colt Model 1911A1 was the first piece displayed, followed closely by a Japanese Nambu dating from the Second World War. The Star 9mm BKM and Browning's Model BDA-380 were a fairly even match, as were the Soviet 7.63mm Tokarev and its identical Chinese knockoff, the Chicom Type 51.

Lee chose the big Colt .45 for knock-down power and reliability, despite its age. A decade had elapsed since the Beretta Model 92F was selected to replace the Colt as America's standard-issue military sidearm, but the G.I. .45 was still a killer in the proper hands.

"Tao rye?" he asked the dealer, nearly using up his Thai vocabulary.

"Thirty thousand baht."

Twelve hundred dollars, give or take.

"Paeng mark." Lee shook his head and put the pistol back. "Too much."

The broker frowned and chewed his lower lip. "Hokay," he said at last. "Four magazines and one box ammunition, you pay twenty-five."

The price would still raise eyebrows in the States, but it was fair by Bangkok standards, for a gun in decent working order. Lee did not respond immediately, reaching out to lift the .45 again.

He pressed the magazine catch to eject the empty clip, and used his thumb to test its spring. The broker watched him as he drew the slide back and confirmed an empty chamber with a glance through the ejection port. Releasing tension on the recoil spring, he freed the barrel bushing and the slide stop, lifting off the automatic's slide and its components to survey the crucial working parts. Before he finished, Lee had stripped the firing pin and the extractor, checking each in turn before he put the weapon back together, satisfied that it would function on command.

The dealer's smile was back in place as Lee produced his bankroll, peeling off a stack of red and purple notes that signified one hundred and five hundred baht, respectively. When 140 bills were stacked in front of him, he nodded like a chicken pecking grain and backtracked to the metal cabinet, fetching three more magazines, together with a box of cartridges.

The box held fifty shells, and Lee used twenty-eight of them to load the magazines, plus one round in the pistol's chamber. With the .45 tucked through his belt in back, he balanced out his jacket with the extra magazines and partial box of shells on either side.

Emerging from the pawnshop, Lee did not deceive himself by thinking he was ready for a one-man war against the Triads, but at least he could defend himself against a personal attack. If he required more hardware later, he could always shop around.

The automatic's solid weight felt reassuring as he moved along the crowded sidewalk, rubbing elbows with the servicemen and randy tourists, junkies, pimps, and whores. He had already put out feelers in a score of "better" nightclubs, asking for Damrong Yodmani, scribbling his chosen name and that of his hotel on the blue fifty-baht notes he passed out to barkers and bartenders.

Sowing the seed.

Tomorrow, when he was rested from his journey, he would start again.

Lee hailed a passing *samlor,* one of the nimble three-wheelers that featured a seat for the driver and one for his passenger, the whole contraption powered by a motor scooter's engine. It was not that far to his hotel—the Montien, facing onto Patpong Road—but he was tired of walking for the moment, and the *samlor* offered him a chance to verify that there was no one on his trail.

So far, so good.

Lee kept his fingers crossed, and told himself his luck had turned.

• • •

It turned again at the hotel, as he approached room 415.

The phony passport should have covered him, and there was nothing in the room that he could not afford to lose in case of theft, but Lee was interested to know if anyone had come calling in his absence. He had taken the precaution of applying talcum powder to the doorknob, underneath, where it would be rubbed off by any uninvited visitors. A first-class prowler might detect the powder on his fingertips, too late, but a precise replacement to conceal the entry—one dab here, another there—was virtually impossible.

Lee stooped to check the knob before he used his key, and froze when he beheld the brass wiped clean. A glance along the empty corridor, each way, before he straightened, shifting hands, the room key in his left, the right inside his jacket, wrapped around the warm grip of the .45.

A search was one thing, but the prowlers might still be inside, prepared to take him as he wandered in, oblivious of danger. If they tumbled to the powder trick, his enemies would be on guard, but Lee did not intend to ditch his room and luggage on the off chance that an ambush might be waiting there.

His hand was steady as he turned the key, unable to prevent the latch bolt snapping on release. He threw the door back hard enough to stun a prowler hiding with his back against the wall, the automatic cocked and leading him across the threshold as he entered.

To confront a well-dressed stranger, seated on the bed with both hands empty, resting on his knees.

"You won't be needing that."

He kept the stranger covered while he closed the door and checked the bathroom, making certain it was one-on-one. Lee pegged his uninvited guest at forty-something, six-foot-two, around 190 pounds. His hair was dark and short, not quite a crew cut, and his face was deeply tanned from long exposure to the sun. The tanning emphasized a scar beside one eye—the left—that marked him like a pale parenthesis.

"Who are you?"

"Gordon Flack. Assistant chief of station, CIA."

"Take off the coat," Lee said.

"I never carry in the city."

"Then you shouldn't mind a search."

The stranger shrugged, stood up—make that six-three—and stripped his jacket off. No sign of any weapons as he made a pirouette for Lee's inspection, taking care to fold his jacket neatly on the bed before he sat.

"Credentials."

Flack produced a leather wallet and delivered it to Lee. As far as Joe could tell, the simple ID card looked genuine. He gave it back and eased the automatic's hammer down before he occupied a chair across from Flack, well out of reach.

"You make connections in a hurry," Flack remarked, his eyes locked on the .45.

"I didn't know the CIA was interested in local firearm laws."

"We have all kinds of interests, Mr. Lee."

"The name is Wen-Ling Shyu."

"Let's not play games, all right? I've been in touch with San Francisco, and your people aren't amused. Mine either, as it happens. They'd be shitting bricks at State, if anybody knew what you were up to."

Lee considered keeping up his show of ignorance, but saw no point. The pistol in his hand was proof enough of criminal intent, regardless of his name.

"Is this where I'm supposed to plead for mercy, so you won't tip off the cops?"

"I'm not concerned about your dress code, Joseph. May I call you Joseph? Hell, you want to lug that thing around the streets, it's fine with me."

"Then we've got nothing more to talk about."

"Strike one." Flack crossed his legs, a small frown tugging down the corners of his mouth. "I may not mind you packing, but I can't afford to have you fucking up my action with your Rambo games."

"What action might that be?"

"You know our mandate, Joe. Intelligence collection as an adjunct to American security. I understand you've got this hard-on for the Triads, but there's no way I can let some vigilante bullshit jeopardize the national defense."

"You're counting on the Triads for a helping hand in case we go to war?"

"We're sitting on a powder keg in Thailand, Joe. Have been for twenty years, since Saigon fell. You read about the war in junior high, I guess."

"It rings a bell."

"Okay, so you can understand that Washington is anxious to maintain the friends we've got in Southeast Asia, few as they may be. We're tired of watching dominoes fall down, you get my drift."

"A little compromise?"

"A little common sense. We don't win any friends by barging in and telling people how to run their country, Joe. It's not polite."

"As I recall, that's never slowed your people down before."

"The cold war's over, in case you haven't heard. These days, we've got cooperation on the menu. Freedom-loving people, working side by side to build a better world."

"Free enterprise for one and all?"

"I'd like to think so."

"Even when the product winds up killing children in the States."

"We know about the drug war, Joe. You want to talk priorities, it rates right up there."

"Just so long as no one rocks the boat."

"I see you've got your mind made up to look at things one way."

"I've tried the other viewpoint, Flack. It sucks."

"Word is, you couldn't handle teamwork at the DEA. You lost it when your partner bought the farm, and then the woman. What was her name?"

"Be careful."

"Sure. You need to understand the way things work in Bangkok, Joe. You run amok, we've got three options."

"Only three?"

"One way, we let the cops take care of you like any other criminal, but that gets messy if they make your old connections. Maybe someone at the palace thinks we're running games and takes it into their pointy little heads to cut us off below the knees."

"That's one."

"Another school of thought, we keep our fingers crossed and watch the folks you're after do the job themselves. They've got a couple hundred years' experience and all the tools they need, believe me."

"Number three?"

"Or I could make a phone call, take you out myself. We're talking off the record here, so I can tell you that it wouldn't be the first time someone had an accident while he was pulling one on Uncle Sam."

"You seem a little short on muscle, Flack."

"Don't get me wrong." Flack's oily smile clicked on and off. "I'm talking hypothetically, you understand. The way I'd like to see it go, make everybody happy, is for you to pitch that hogleg in the first canal you see and catch the next flight home. Wise up on this, you just might find the home team's had a change of heart about your premature retirement."

"Bullshit."

"You don't want the job, okay. At least you've got a choice. Last time I checked, career advancement was restricted to the living."

"I just got here," Joe reminded him. "It seems a shame to leave before I've seen the sights."

"Depends on what you're looking for, I guess. Three hundred temples in the city, all the pussy you can eat. Hang out a couple days, for all I care. Enjoy yourself. But don't lose sight of what you are."

"Which is?"

"A two-time loser, bucking odds you'll never beat. The way things stand, your life means less than zip. The only friend you've got in Bangkok's right there in your hand."

"How many friends have you got, Flack?"

"I gave up counting, Joe. Don't push your luck, unless you want to meet them."

"Thanks for stopping by."

"My pleasure." Flack stood up and slipped his jacket on, adjusting it to show the proper bit of cuff on either side. "You get the urge to talk or book that one-way home, I've got a number at the embassy. We're in the book."

"I'll let you know."

"Don't take too long. A couple days, my CO might not care. Beyond that, well . . ."

"The door," Joe said.

"How's that?"

"Don't let it hit you in the ass."

Alone once more, he set the automatic on the nightstand, stretched out on the bed, and tried to study the unanswered questions, one by one.

Who had tipped the CIA that he was moving on to Bangkok?

Did Flack represent the Agency?

If so, was his commitment to the cause of "national security" enough to forge a flexible alliance with the Triads?

Would he see Joe killed—or have it done, himself—to stop the precious ship of state from being rocked by stormy seas?

On that score, anyway, Lee had no grounds for disbelieving Flack. Assassination was supposedly beyond the pale for agents of the CIA, as third-degree techniques were barred for the American police, but such rules had a way of getting broken in the crunch. It might not happen every day, but the infrequency of "wet work" posed no consolation for a target, once the job was done.

Lee recognized Flack's threat for what it was: an effort at intimidation, backed by lethal force.

Okay.

He had a better view of all the players now, and Flack was right about the odds. No matter how Lee measured them, he came up short.

And that was fine.

He might not walk away from Bangkok, but he wasn't running either.

Flack had given him a day or two to think it over and decide. A toss-up, choosing life or death.

If he could last that long, Joe thought it just might be enough.

17

Lee passed the daylight hours in Bangkok as an ordinary tourist might, examining the Chapel of the Emerald Buddha and the National Museum, browsing in the Thieves' Market and boating on the Chao Phraya River, watching kraits and cobras milked for venom at the Chulalongkom University's snake farm, across the street from his hotel. If he was being followed by the CIA or someone else, they knew their business better than the Royal Hong Kong Police.

And with the darkness, he returned to Patpong Road.

Another dozen clubs by half-past nine, his working name and that of his hotel inscribed on bills that disappeared the instant Joseph finished writing, vanished in a wink, as if they had been sucked up by the bar itself. He knew that he was wasting money, probably his time as well, but there appeared to be no other way of making contact with the man he hoped to find. Yodmani had no listing in the telephone directory, and Ian Wilson had been forced to get in touch through contacts on the force in Bangkok—an approach that neither of them wished to use in present circumstances.

Lee would have to find Yodmani on his own, somehow. And if he failed, then what?

Then nothing. He would have come as far as he could go alone, and he would have to pack it in, retreat to San Francisco with his tail between his legs. A failure, toting better than two hundred thousand dollars in his wallet, all unknown—so far—to Uncle Sugar and the IRS.

Dream on. If Flack had traced him this far, and so quickly, there was every chance he knew about the

Bangkok bank account. If so, would he attempt to freeze Lee's assets? Starve him out and force him home that way, without a further show of strength?

Unlikely.

Losing cash he never really owned might stop Lee dealing on the streets, but it would hardly silence him. He could approach the press, if all else failed, and rock their boat in headlines for a while unless they shut him up for good.

Flack still might seize the money if he thought it would help his cause, but for the moment Joseph had a feeling it was safe. He had to keep his fingers crossed and pray for contact soon, before he crossed Flack's hazy deadline and the roof fell in on him.

"You look for smoke?"

A different barker, different club, same come-on.

Joseph shrugged. "Why not?"

"Ten baht."

He made it roughly forty cents, one of the brown notes changing hands before he stepped inside. The music was a blend of pop and rock, less frantic than the heavy-metal neighbors, but they cranked it up just loud enough to make the patrons and their "hostesses" shout back and forth at one another over tables that were more the size of stools. The smoky room looked SRO, but Joseph let a slender hostess take his hand and lead him to a table halfway down. She tried to order mixed drinks from the barmaid, but he canceled them in favor of two bottled beers and let her pout, resembling a small child trapped inside a woman's body.

On the stage, two dancers—male and female—had already stripped to jock and G-string, going through a sexy-slow routine that seemed to simulate a lovers' quarrel. He tried to woo her back; she pushed him off. She changed her mind; he shouldered her away and sneered . . . until she knelt before him on the stage and pulled the sequined jockstrap down around his knees.

The hand on Joseph's leg did not surprise him. Hostesses in Bangkok clubs were mostly prostitutes who did their best to push the house's watered booze and kicked back part of anything they made from horny customers who followed them upstairs or down the street to work it off. Joe sipped his beer and watched the dancers getting down to business, somewhat startled by his own reaction to the scene.

He wrote it off to loneliness, fatigue, frustration.

And he left the warm hand where it was.

Another round of beers arrived before the couple finished onstage, and Joe decided he would have to pace himself. At twenty baht per bottle, it was fair enough—the girl's time would be extra, thank you very much—but getting shit-faced in a bar on Patpong Road was not a part of any plan his mind had formulated in the past two days. A little grope, okay; he'd even tip the girl, if she deserved it. But he had to keep his wits about him, just in case.

Onstage, the man was finished, pulling out—an errant dollop landing on a ringside table, where a round-faced Japanese and his companion of the moment stared and grinned—but his companion drew him back, and he kept working, red-faced, to the end of the routine.

The hostess slid her hand up Joseph's thigh and found him, squeezing to acknowledge contact. When he glanced at her, she smiled and licked the beer foam off her lips.

Why not?

He had compiled a mental list of half a dozen reasons, starting with disease, before the music shifted to another beat and Joseph's eyes were drawn back to the stage.

The solitary dancer wasted no time on amenities. She came out in a filmy robe, gapped open in the front, and quickly shed it to confirm that she was naked underneath. The robe was draped across a folding metal chair that formed—or helped support—the central feature of her act.

Half-slouching in the chair, she braced her heels against the front edge of the seat and spread her legs, exposed to an extent that Joseph would have thought impossible without some dislocation of the hips. He felt a twinge of sympathy, then something else, before he pushed the stroking hand away.

Another pout, and his companion left to find the rest room or the barmaid. If she came back with expensive drinks, he would accept one round, but that was all. Meanwhile . . .

The girl onstage—no more than sixteen, surely, though her eyes looked older—had produced a foot-long dildo from a pocket of her robe, applying it to smallish upturned breasts before she brought it lower, to the shaved part of her that hypnotized her boozy audience. A teasing stroke along her naked slit before the fat head disappeared, and she began to roll her hips, eyes closed, the plastic dildo vanishing inside.

When it was gone, she raised her arms and locked both hands behind her head, the posture of a prisoner surrendering. She arched her back and twisted, pushing with her heels against the seat until her buttocks cleared the flabby cushion, levitating. Tendons on the inside of her thighs stood out like cables underneath the velvet skin.

Lee was prepared when she expelled the dildo, one hand swooping down to catch it as it fell. She did the trick again, and then began to masturbate in earnest, one hand working on her nipples while the other slid the dildo in and out. A sheen of perspiration glistened on her body by the time she simulated climax, moist lips swallowing the dildo one more time and holding it, concealed, before she gave it back.

Joe was aware of his companion coming back, her shadow on his face, the warm hand on his leg. The barmaid came around a moment later, bringing two more beers, and that was fine.

The dancer stashed her dildo in one pocket of her robe, retrieved a pack of cigarettes and plastic lighter from another. Smiling at her audience, she tapped the open pack to free a filter-tip and put the cigarette between her lips. She flicked her Bic and took a drag to get it started, adding one more plume of smoke to the polluted atmosphere.

The audience was nearly silent now, expectant, as she dropped the pack and lighter on the stage. One hand slipped in between her legs, investigating, opening the swollen lips as she reached down and stuck the filter-tip in her vagina. A minute adjustment, and she left it there, eyes closed again as she began to work her stomach muscles in and out. Lee watched the cigarette glow bright and fade, glow bright again, a perfect ash accumulating on its tip. A wisp of smoke escaped, and Joseph understood why she was forced to shave: without the buzz, she might have set herself on fire.

Another moment, and she took the cigarette away, hips rising as she smiled and blew a perfect stream of smoke directly toward her audience. Applause was growing as she cut it off and started making tiny clouds—smoke signals from a porno western—for the crowd's amusement. Joe was wondering if she could manage rings, when she ran out of steam and lit another cigarette to try again.

The warm hand captured Joe, its fingers strong and sure. He turned to face his hostess, startled to discover she was gone, a different woman in her place. The light was chancy, but he made her in the mid-late twenties, more mature, but still without the flinty edge so many whores adopt with time.

"You like the show?" she asked.

"It's interesting."

Her fingers teased him, quick and sly.

"I think you rather play than watch."

Again he asked himself: Why not? At least with this one he wouldn't feel like a pedophile.

"I clean," she said, as if in answer to his thoughts, no vestige of embarrassment. "You like, I show you health certificate."

"How much?"

"Five hundred baht."

Another bargain. Joseph shifted to accommodate her hand and spent another moment thinking.

"Where?"

"I have a room," she said, "or maybe you like better your hotel."

"I'm at the Montien."

"Not far." She smiled and squeezed.

Lee felt his last ounce of resistance crumbling and forced a smile. "Okay. Let's go."

The taxi was a gamble—tourists frequently reported strong-arm robberies by drivers when they made arrangements on their own, instead of booking cabs through their hotels—but Lee was carrying the .45, and he was not averse to showing it if they "got lost" along the short drive back to his hotel.

Besides, Joe didn't feel like walking at the moment, cramped inside his slacks that felt at least one size too small. His escort saw the problem, but her efforts to relax him in the cab were only making Joseph's difficulty more pronounced.

Her name was May Tansiri, she informed him, and her hands were magic, quick and leisurely by turns, a tantalizing blend of hard and soft. Lee was about to show her his appreciation, when the cab pulled up in front of his hotel and she released him, leaving him to pay the driver while she waited on the curb.

Inside, they had the elevator to themselves, and she surprised him, opening his fly and taking him in hand. She freed him from the prison of his clinging shorts and bent to run her tongue around the head of his penis, teasing him. The echoes of his pulse were like a drumbeat in his ears, the cadence marking time without a tune that he could recognize.

His eyes came open with the elevator doors, relieved to find an empty corridor beyond. May straightened, smiling, leaving him exposed, and leaned outside to check the corridor. Returning with a glint of wicked mischief in her eyes, she pressed one button, waiting for the doors to close, then keyed another—this one red and labeled "STOP!"

For all Lee knew, it might be sounding an alarm downstairs at the reception desk, but he no longer cared as May hiked up her miniskirt and slid one arm around his neck, thighs clasped around his waist. Her naked buttocks filled his hands, his fingers probed the cleft between them, as her free hand found his shaft and brought it home.

Control was not the issue any longer. Lee had all that he could do, just staying upright, as the undertow of climax carried him away. May's body gripped him like a velvet fist, unyielding, leaving him no choice but to advance and pummel her with his remaining strength. He filled her up, allowed himself the luxury of hoping that the little passion sounds she made were real.

They separated ages later, straightening their clothes as Joe released the elevator doors. A stodgy British couple met them in the corridor, and May could not help giggling as they passed.

"Which room?"

He showed her, reaching for her as they crossed the threshold, wanting her again before the door was closed and double-locked.

"I need a shower," May informed him.

Jumbled images of Nancy, Lisa Reilly, banished as he said, "I'll scrub your back."

Undressing in the bedroom while she fixed the shower's temperature, Joe left his automatic in the nightstand's single drawer, beside a Gideon New Testament with text in Thai and English. Steamy condensation had obscured the bathroom mirror by the time he got there, joining May inside the shower stall.

He let her bathe him, slow and easy, lathering his chest and shoulders, legs and buttocks, working back around until she knelt before him, soap in hand. May took her time with his erection, rinsing twice before she satisfied herself that he was squeaky clean. Despite the shower's heat, the gliding motion of her hand, Lee knew the difference at once when she bent forward, taking him inside her mouth.

A side effect of their explosive coupling in the elevator was endurance, Joseph leaning back and savoring the sweet sensations of her lips and tongue, absolved of any burning need to rush. He guided her, one hand behind her head, and May began to tease his scrotum with her fingernails, a maddening assault that sparked new fires of urgency inside.

Afraid of wasting it, he pulled away and drew May to her feet, his fingers trembling as he turned the shower off. Outside, he hooked a bath towel from the rack and buffed her dry, May squirming as he dried her breasts, between her legs.

Joe led her to the bedroom, there surrendering a measure of control as May positioned him across the mattress, mounting him, her face toward Joseph's feet. The posture gave her leverage, elbows braced against his upraised knees, and heightened sensitivity for both of them as Joseph's shaft made contact with her pubis.

Starting slowly, gliding up and down like she was riding on a carousel, May gradually increased her tempo, working at it, perspiration beading on the smooth plane of her back. Joe used a fingertip to probe between her buttocks, searching, and she shifted to accommodate him, shuddering at the invasion. Doubly filled, she started rocking back and forth with greater energy, the friction bringing Joseph off again before he had a chance to brace himself. He heard and felt May right behind him, maybe faking this time, maybe not, and either way he didn't give a damn.

She took another shower afterward, while Joe lay naked on the coverlet and let the air-conditioning revive him. He was starting to regain a measure of his strength when May Tansiri stepped out of the bathroom, naked to the waist, the towel around her hips resembling a sarong.

"When you are able, I will take you to the man you seek."

Joe pushed up on his elbows, staring in surprise.

"Yodmani?"

"You may bring the pistol from your nightstand, if you wish."

18

Returning to the lobby took much longer than the trip upstairs, or so it seemed to Joseph Lee.

"You knew about the gun?" he asked, not quite surprised, but checking on himself, to see where he had failed.

"I felt it, earlier," May said. "And then, the drawer was open this much"—fingers spread to roughly half an inch—"which it was not, before."

"No trick at all, I guess."

"No trick."

He felt like Dr. Watson, needing everything explained to him by Sherlock Holmes. But it was worse, somehow, because Holmes had never taken Watson to his bed, pretending to be satisfied with his performance, scheming all the while.

Lee recognized the symptoms of a wounded ego, and he tried to shake them off. What else had he expected from a whore? Distractions could be fatal in a place like Bangkok, where the enemy was damned near everyone he met.

One more surprise: May's English was considerably more refined than she had led him to believe. Joe wondered if the cover was a mere defensive mechanism, used with strangers, or if she was playing Mata Hari, living out her role.

It hardly mattered, either way. If she could take him to Yodmani and they made a deal, it would be worth the ego knocks. If she was working on a setup—something for the Triads, say, or Gordon Flack—well, there was still the .45, and Lee would do his best to make her pay for any treachery.

Downstairs, they let the doorman hail a taxi, charging it to Joseph's room. May rattled off directions, and the driver took them west from the hotel on Sipya Road, until they reached the riverfront. A quick left there, and left again on Suriwongse Road. Lee understood that they were circling the block, and when he turned to question May, he found her staring out the back.

"We're being followed," she explained before he had a chance to ask.

Lee swiveled in his seat, the headlights painful in his eyes. Another Bangkok traffic snarl.

"You're sure?"

"The third car back was waiting for us, and it turns when we do. Yes, I'm sure."

She gave the cabbie new instructions, and he made a right-hand turn on Patpong Road, then right again, to catch a narrow side street where the autos were outnumbered by pedestrians. Behind them, slowed by traffic, Joseph saw the chase car copy every move.

May rolled her window down a foot or so, enough to slide her hand out, flourishing a handkerchief. The gesture was elusive, there and gone, like someone waving to a casual acquaintance on the street, but Joseph noted it and kept his eyes peeled as their driver picked up speed.

The hunters tried to match them, closing, but a *samlor* suddenly appeared from nowhere, veering right across the chase car's path. It wasn't much of a collision, really, but the frail three-wheeler capsized and its driver came up cursing, putting on a twisted Quasimodo walk for the excited witnesses who flocked around. The chase car was surrounded in an instant, totally cut off.

"That's done," May said, and changed the cabbie's orders, speaking rapidly in Thai. Joe watched their track for several blocks, until they turned off Patpong Road again.

"Who were they?"

May Tansiri shrugged, apparently uninterested. "Police, perhaps. Or someone else."

It was that *someone else*, the range of lethal possibilities, that worried Joe. Did Flack have spotters on him, after all, assigned to mark his contacts for reprisal? Had the Triads been supplied with information here, as in Hong Kong? And how much would the opposition—*any* opposition—know of Ian Wilson's contacts in the city, prior to Lee's arrival?

Pointless questions. For the moment, he was clear, and all he had to think about was May Tansiri. Whether she was helping him make contact with Yodmani, as she said, or leading him into an ambush laid by *someone else.*

Their taxi pulled up in the middle of a narrow street where sidewalk vendors plied their trade outside massage and tattoo parlors. There was neon here, of course, but less than on Patpong Road, and its reflection seemed to amplify the dark instead of holding it at bay. The driver kept his engine running as they disembarked, but May said something to him, laughing, and he settled back to wait.

"This way."

Joe couldn't read the small shop's sign, but the artistic renderings of nearly naked women in the window left no doubts about the services available within. Massage, in Bangkok, was a well-established form of entertainment, parlors ranging from the opulent to the degenerate. May's choice fell somewhere in between the two extremes, but it was obvious the rubdowns practiced here were not confined to simple therapy for aching muscles.

They were greeted in the foyer by a plump young woman dressed—almost—in navy silk. The outfit buttoned at her throat, but cutouts bared her cleavage, navel, back, and sides, with thigh-high slashes in the skirt to show her legs. Stiletto heels completed the effect and added several inches to her height.

A brief exchange in Thai got May and Joseph past the lobby, numbered doors on either side of them along an empty corridor, until they reached the stairs. On two, a bouncer built like Mr. Universe and carrying a pistol in his waistband studied Lee with passing interest, but he made no move to block their way.

More doors, this lot unnumbered, but they had been painted different colors as a simple code. May chose the blue one, second on her right, and opened it without a knock. Lee had a hand inside his jacket, covering the automatic, as he followed her inside.

The room was small, by office standards, but it would have made a spacious walk-in closet. Joseph was examining the furnishings—a couch and coat hooks on the wall, a battered army-surplus desk and swivel chair with duct tape on the seat—when May excused herself and closed the door behind her.

"Mr. Shyu?"

The man who stood before him was about Joe's height, perhaps a half-inch shorter, slim and wiry-looking in his baggy linen shirt and slacks. The sandals on his feet were leather, with a heavy rubber sole. His hair was long in back, below his collar, shorter on the sides. His eyes missed nothing, scanning Joe from head to foot.

"Damrong Yodmani?"

"In the flesh."

Yodmani's smile had more in common with a grimace, but his English was exceptional, the accent barely noticeable. He was quick, this one, and Joe decided he would have to use a measure of the truth to make it work.

"My name is Joseph Lee."

Yodmani cocked an eyebrow, leaning back against his desk.

"Have I been misinformed? The man who asks for me on Patpong Road is known as Wen-Ling Shyu. Room 413 at the Montien Hotel."

Behind Yodmani, on the desk, Lee picked out several ten-baht notes with writing on their faces.

"The name's a cover. It was given to me recently, in Hong Kong, by a friend of yours."

"A friend who gives out names. And does he keep one for himself?"

Lee thought about it briefly, and decided he had come too far to stonewall. "Ian Wilson."

"Ah." Yodmani frowned. "How is the chief inspector?"

"Well enough, last time we spoke. I couldn't say the same for some of those around him."

"Times are hard. Be seated, please."

Lee took the couch; Yodmani sat down in the swivel chair, the old leather patched with duct tape creaking underneath his weight.

"I have some work to do in Bangkok," Joseph said. "Perhaps a trip outside the city. Wilson thought you might be willing to assist me."

"Why?"

"I understood you've worked with him before, on matters that were . . . similar."

"Such rumors strain a friendship. If I knew their source—"

"The horse's mouth."

Yodmani's frown produced the only major wrinkles on his timeless face. "With all respect, if what you say is true, the chief inspector has been indiscreet."

"He's running out of time—his words. A working colleague—and a friend, I think—was killed two nights ago."

"Because of you?"

Lee shrugged, a worm of guilt uncoiling in his gut. "We had a mutual objective," he replied.

"The killers?"

"They were Sap Sie Kie."

"Perhaps, if you explain from the beginning . . ."

Joseph let him have a thumbnail version, dropping Lisa from the narrative but noting Eddie Hovis, Robert Chan, the death of Thomas Choi, his own suspicions of a leak at the DEA.

"And now," Yodmani said, "you wish to try your luck again, in Bangkok."

"With a twist."

"Your quarrel is with the 14K. Their chief resides in Hong Kong. Wilson should have told you that, instead of sending you to me."

"The twist I mentioned."

"Yes?"

"I want to hit their source," Lee said. "Shut down the pipeline long enough to make them nervous, anyway. With luck, I may find something that will lead me back to Chan."

"One man?" Yodmani was amused. "You will need more than luck."

"I'll go up-country if I have to."

The amusement faded from Yodmani's eyes. "Are you a fool?" he asked. "Or do you simply want a witness to your suicide?"

"Right now, I'd settle for some information."

"Very well." Yodmani made a steeple of his fingers and cocked his feet across the corner of his desk as he began. "You are familiar with the link between Chiu Chou and 14K?"

"Chiu Chou supplies the 14K with China white for export overseas."

"Correct. But they are not the *source*, by any means. 'Up-country,' as you say, it is another world."

"The Triangle?"

"Such concepts have no meaning in the north. Forget what you have learned of states and borders. Guns and money are the only law, above Lampang."

"I understand the situation."

"Do you? Native tribesmen in the north—the Meo and Lahu—have been farming opium for centuries in what you call the Golden Triangle. The crop allows them to survive. Since 1949, their masters have been warlords of the Kuomintang, who sell the drug abroad for money to support their war against the Chinese communists. Our government pretends to rule the northern territory—just as Laos and Burma claim to manage their domains—but no one stands against the warlords. No one."

"And the link?"

"The opium is sold to Chiu Chou brokers for refinement into heroin at mobile plants in Burma and the northern provinces of Thailand. When the Sap Sie Kie or other buyers need a fresh supply, they visit Bangkok and consult with Chiang Min Fai."

"He runs the show?"

"Chiang serves his Triad as a Red Pole. Do you recognize the term?"

"A local underboss."

"In essence. Chiang has masters in Kowloon, but they

would starve without him. Soon, I think, their roles may be reversed."

"And Chiang maintains his Triad's contact with the KMT."

"One contact, in particular. There are two armies in the north, both Kuomintang and staunchly anticommunist, but they compete through sales of opium. The larger of the two is led by General Shih Yeuh Sheng."

"Chiang's source?"

"*A* source," Yodmani said. "His fields produce about two-thirds of Chiang's supply in any given year."

"A deal this size, there must be someone running interference with the state."

Yodmani dropped his feet and crossed his legs.

"Our situation is precarious," he said. "The communists hold Laos and Kampuchea, to the north and east. Our western neighbor, Burma's so-called socialist republic, has been torn by civil war for over thirty years. Since 1985 our sovereign borders have been violated several times by the Vietnamese."

"More dominoes."

"Survival, Mr. Lee. It's not a children's game."

"And where does Chiang fit in?"

"He does what others like him have been doing for the past half-century. When labor unions strike or dissidents attack the state, he helps restore a kind of order, using methods barred to the authorities. The government is duly grateful, in its way."

"And you?"

"A simple businessman. I deal with Chiang's associates from time to time."

"Can you arrange a meeting?"

"Possibly. It would depend on your intentions, the extent to which my own involvement is exposed."

"I want to get beyond Chiang's network, to the source. I've thought about it, and I can't see any other way to crimp the flow that keeps the 14K in business, stateside."

"So, you *are* insane."

"Not necessarily."

"You count on Chiang to give you General Sheng's

address, perhaps? And when you all sit down to tea . . . then what?"

"I haven't taken it that far. I'll think of something."

"You won't have to. Chiang protects his sources like a miser hoards his pocket change. The repercussions of exposing General Sheng would be disastrous."

"Not if he was dealing with another businessman."

"Explain."

"I've got a quarter-million U.S. dollars sitting in a bank downtown. As far as Chiang's concerned, it's earnest money for a deal he can't refuse."

"With one condition?"

"Right. I make the bid contingent on an introduction to his source. My people aren't prepared to play unless I take a look around the operation first. Make sure it's really happening."

"You may insult Chiang if you question his ability. I don't advise it."

"For a quarter-million down and weekly payments of the same amount, year-round, I have a feeling he'll indulge me."

"If you're wrong . . ."

Lee shrugged. "It wouldn't be the first time."

"Possibly the last."

"I understand the risk. I'm asking for an introduction, not a life-insurance policy."

"And for my trouble?"

"I can spare three thousand baht right now. It isn't much, I know—"

"A pittance."

"—but if things work out . . ."

"How much?"

"Let's say whatever's left of my account."

Yodmani's eyes lit up, and this time when he smiled, it seemed a trifle more sincere.

"The quarter-million?"

"Any part of it I haven't spent. Why not?"

"Indeed, why not? But if you have an accident . . ."

"That's life," Joe told him with a narrow smile. "Are you a praying man?"

"Devout."

"Well, there you are. Just drop a hint that maybe nothing ought to happen to me for the next few days."

"In Bangkok, even God consults Chiang Fai. Above Lampang, he lets men take care of themselves."

"I guess you're gambling, then."

Yodmani frowned. "The introduction is a simple thing. Beyond that point, we must rely upon your powers of persuasion."

"We?"

"Of course. It would be hazardous for me to foist a total stranger on Chiang Fai." His smile came back. "In any case, I would not miss it for the world."

Yodmani had a cab waiting outside when they were finished, and Joseph didn't bother checking for a tail as he rode back to his hotel. They passed the point where May's contrived distraction had disposed of one pursuer, and he hoped the clumsy shadow had been CIA. If not . . .

It took only one leak to blow his cover with the Triads, and his risk was multiplied by every human contact on the journey east. Ray Christy was a suspect, and the Royal Hong Kong Police Force was infested with patrolmen and detectives on the Triad payroll. Here in Bangkok, Gordon Flack might burn him for the hell of it, an easy way to wipe the slate, and Lee was far from certain of Damrong Yodmani's loyalty. If someone made the Thai a better offer, chances were that he would snap it up without a second thought.

Departing from his room that night with May, he hadn't taken time to dust the knob with talcum powder. As it was, he heard the television playing in his room before he found his key, and he knew damned well they had not turned it on while they were making love.

Get real. While they were *fucking.* Love and tenderness had played no part in anything he'd done since Lisa's funeral.

Time for fun and games.

He drew the .45 and cocked it, shaking off a sudden flash of *déjà vu* before he turned the key and crossed the threshold in a crouch. The TV program—an American police show, dubbed in Thai—helped cover his approach, but May was ready for him as he entered, sitting up in bed, the sheet tucked underneath her chin.

"You want to shoot me?" Teasing him, but still unsure. "I do not have a weapon."

Proving it, she dropped the sheet and let him see that she was naked to the waist.

"You're off the clock," he told her, stepping back to check the bathroom, just in case. "I've done my business with Yodmani."

A professional, she did not take offense. A touch of the remote control turned off the TV set.

"I was employed to find you, nothing more. The rest was my idea."

"Five hundred baht, as I recall." He stuck the pistol in his belt and palmed the roll of cash, peeled off a purple note. "It almost slipped my mind."

May frowned. "I've hurt your pride."

"Not even close. We had a business deal. You did your part." He left her payment on the nightstand. "Now we're even."

"You believe Yodmani sent me back to spy on you."

"I don't much care. Right now, I need some sleep, and you're just in the way."

She kicked the sheets back, sleek and naked as she turned to face him, sitting on the mattress edge.

"You still have business on your mind. You should relax."

Deft fingers at his fly. A warm, familiar touch.

"No sale."

"I'm off the clock, remember?"

"Sure." Despite himself, he was responding.

"You could always buy me breakfast."

"And?"

"And dinner, if you like."

"I may not be around."

"In that case"—lapping at him like a cat with cream—"we shouldn't waste the time we have."

19

They breakfasted in bed and spent the morning there as well, Lee dozing, roused from sleep at intervals by May's impulsive lips and magic hands. He slept again while she was in the shower, knowing that he had all day to wait for Yodmani's call, but when she crept back into bed, the smell of soap and powder on her skin excited him once more. He lost track of their couplings, the positions they explored together, and he knew his staying power had as much to do with nervous energy as any passion she inspired.

The call had not come through by noon, so they got dressed and went downstairs to let the maid make up Lee's room. The restaurant was nearly empty, and they dined on curried beef with rice, washed down with strong domestic beer. The conversation rambled, Joseph letting May spin fairy tales about her childhood in Pattaya and her later life in Bangkok, fending off her random questions with laconic generalities. When they went back upstairs, the message light was winking on his telephone.

The switchboard operator told him that Yodmani's call was logged at 12:18. There was no message, but a number had been left for Lee to call at his convenience. Taking time to slip the pistol from his belt and place it on the nightstand, Lee sat down and dialed again.

"Sawat dee kha?" A woman's voice.

He spoke Yodmani's name and waited most of forty seconds, listening to empty air, before his man came on the line.

"Sawat dee khrap."

"My sentiments, exactly."
"Ah."
"I hope this line's secure."
"I guarantee it."
"Fair enough. What's happening?"
"We have a dinner invitation," Yodmani said.
"Where and when?"
"There is a nightclub two blocks east of your hotel. The Tiger's Paw. Be on the curb, in front of it, at eight o'clock."
"We're going for a ride?"
"Security, you understand."
"Of course."
"Our host would like to see the cash."
Lee smiled. "I'd like to see the sunrise. If a passbook doesn't satisfy him, we can scrub the meet right now."
"Your choice."
"I've made it. Eight o'clock, the Tiger's Paw."
He cradled the receiver, feeling May beside him as she settled on the bed.
"Good news?" she asked.
"I won't know that until tonight."
"You are uneasy?"
"I'll get by."
She took his hand and brought it to her breast, warm flesh beneath cool silk.
"A little something for your nerves," she said.
The bedside clock confirmed that he had almost seven hours to kill.
"Why not?"

The orphan Chiang Min Fai was twelve years old when student demonstrations led to bloody confrontations with police and soldiers in the streets of Bangkok, leaving ninety persons dead. An interested observer, Chiang took full advantage of the chaos to direct his younger cohorts in a string of window-smashing raids on Phya Thai Road. He moved past bodies lying in the street, saw several finished off at point-blank range by military firing squads, but he felt nothing for the slain. Chiang knew that students were selected from the privileged class, spoiled brats who never lacked for food or spending money while they made a game of preaching revolution to the poor and dispossessed. In Chiang's opinion, sudden death was all that they deserved.

At age fifteen, when new unrest was spawned at Thammasat University, Chiang joined the paramilitary "Village Scouts" to fight for his adopted country, bearing arms against the leftist scum who had insulted Crown Prince Vajiralongkorn. Three hundred students died in the assault, three thousand more crammed into reeking jails, an estimated million books hosed down with gasoline and set afire before the mob formed chanting ranks to march on Government House. Chiang still remembered the crown prince, resplendent in his captain's uniform, as he addressed the crowd and thanked them for their patriotic service to the nation.

Most of all, however, Chiang Min Fai recalled the students he had killed that afternoon. A boy and girl, no longer sneering as they huddled in each other's arms, behind the cafeteria. They had already seen enough to know their cause was lost, and they were pleading for their lives. Chiang felt like God, with humble subjects bowed before him, groveling.

He shot the young man first, one round between the eyes, and listened to the female scream awhile before he slugged her with his pistol, opening a gash below one eye. Chiang made her strip and stand before him, naked in the sun, raw power surging through him in the moment left before he shot her down.

Chiang Fai had always been a patriot, and his reward, through nineteen years of military rule, had been phenomenal advancement in his chosen field. A man who served his friends and earned their loyalty in return, by twenty-one he had cemented friendly contacts with the military junta and expanded his horizons to the north, among the rural provinces. When left-wing dissidents began to rant against the government, Chiang fingered them for the police. If workers struck for higher pay, Chiang's thugs encouraged a more reasonable attitude.

On more than one occasion he directed military strikes at rebel strongholds in the countryside, endeavoring to cleanse the land of communists and other social parasites.

Along the way, Chiang tried his hand at pimping and moving opium, which pursuits put him in competition with the Triads. For the Chiu Chou leadership, it came down to a choice of killing Chiang—and thereby risking conflict with his friends in uniform—or recruiting him to serve the higher cause. Chiang was approached, the offer made, and on the weekend of his twenty-second birthday he had flown to Hong Kong for initiation in the lodge.

By dead of night he was conducted to a warehouse where the Incense Master waited with his retinue of guards, all bearing swords. On hands and knees, a joss stick burning in his fist, Chiang crawled beneath crossed blades and knelt before the sacred altar, waiting while the Incense Master spilled out cups of tea and wine upon the floor, with mystic incantations over each. Upon command, he echoed the thirty-six oaths required of a Triad initiate, pledging his loyalty and life to the brotherhood, finally snuffing his joss stick in water to symbolize death of a traitor. The water and ash were then seasoned with blood from a freshly killed cockerel, and Chiang was required to contribute some blood of his own for a potion he shared with the Heung Chu and guards.

It seemed childish at first, but Chiang felt himself changing midway through the ritual, shedding his sense of embarrassment, gaining a brand-new perspective. Instead of feeling asinine, he thrilled with pride at being part of something greater than himself, a brotherhood of blood that magnified his strength a thousandfold.

Chiu Chou became the family Chiang had never known when he was living on the streets, surviving hand-to-mouth. He took the Triad's power as his own, expanding operations while he kept up close relations with the army and police. Instead of running opium by night, a kilo at a time, he dealt in hundredweights and tons. He had managed several dozen whores alone, but he now collected cash from hundreds, leasing clubs and cheap hotels for them to ply their trade in relative security.

From time to time he organized a private show for "special" customers, with peasant women who would not be missed if things got out of hand. His wealth surpassed the wildest fantasies of urchins in the street, but Chiang was never satisfied. A hungry child at heart, he always wanted more.

And still, he served Chiu Chou, his masters in Kowloon.

Despite persistent rumors to the contrary, Chiang Fai did not believe he should be Hill Chief of the clan. He *knew* the post was his—or would be, soon. Who else had done as much to win the brotherhood a virtual monopoly on heroin produced in Thailand, rubbing out the competition with a ruthless zeal that made his name a legend on the streets? Who else maintained such close relations with the ruling junta and the warlords of the Kuomintang?

Soon, now, the scepter would be passed, and Bangkok would become the Triad capital of Southeast Asia. All Chiang needed was a little time and ready cash enough to back his play, in case the Shan Chu's loyalists in Kowloon decided to resist. A few more major deals . . .

Chiang frowned, remembering his conversation with Damrong Yodmani earlier that day. The little Thai was no more than *chung jen*—a middleman—but even peasants could be useful, in their way. Tonight he brought Chiang Fai a brand-new customer, an independent from America with money in his pockets and a taste for China white. If they could strike a decent bargain, it would put Chiang that much closer to his goal.

If not . . .

Chiang knew from personal experience that there were many paths to ultimate success. He would attempt to deal with the American like any other customer, determining his strengths and weaknesses, examining the men behind him as potential friends or enemies against a day when allies in the States might be essential. If he found them weak and wanting, Chiang would simply take the money for himself, by force.

Outside the family, survival of the fittest was the only law in Chiang Fai's world.

And anyone outside the clan became fair prey.

At 7:55 P.M. Lee stood outside the Tiger's Paw on Patpong Road and watched the hookers work. He did not speak their language, but he recognized their style. Revealing outfits, flashy costume jewelry, heavy makeup with a dash of glitter to accentuate the eyes. In daylight, most of them would come off looking tired and used, but neon served its purpose here, creating a surrealistic scene where fantasies might almost come to life.

Lee had prepared himself by doing absolutely nothing in the past few hours. There was no one he could call for backup if the meet went sour, and he had left his pistol in the hotel room with May. The bankbook in his pocket might not be enough to cinch the deal with Chiang, but cash in hand could get him killed, another careless would-be dealer bumped and dumped when he began to play beyond his league.

Whatever else the evening held in store, he would not be the victim of a simple rip-off.

Not tonight.

At 8:01 a gray Mercedes limo pulled up to the curb, its driver bailing out and circling the car to scatter several waiting prostitutes. He held the door and Lee climbed in, to find Yodmani seated in the back. A pair of stone-faced gunners occupied the jump seats opposite, one of them gesturing for Lee to raise his hands as they began to roll.

The frisk was businesslike and thorough, hitting all the spots where Joseph might have stashed a hideout gun if he was being clever. Crotch and armpits, ankles, even in the hollow of his back, where lazy cops sometimes forgot to check. The stone-face clearly knew his job.

Before they made a block through traffic, blindfolds were produced and carefully secured with snug elastic bands. Lee told himself that it was merely a precaution, Chiang Fai dealing with a customer he didn't know first-hand. He tried to banish images of standing with his back against a wall before a firing squad, but he could not entirely shake the childish sense of being lost, abandoned in the dark.

At first, he counted turns: two left, a right, another left. At twenty miles per hour, give or take, he thought they must have traveled six or seven miles before the limo stopped again and they were ushered out. It was a trifle cooler here, the traffic sounds remote, and Lee could smell a river or canal nearby.

The Chao Phraya waterfront? What difference did it make?

His escort kept a hand on Joseph's elbow all the way, alerting him to concrete steps, an elevated threshold, guiding him along an air-conditioned corridor. Yodmani and his watchdog seemed to be in front, or else acoustics in the hall were playing tricks with Joseph's ears.

They rode an elevator up, perhaps three floors, and were relieved of blindfolds as they reached their destination. Muted lights were easy on the eye, and Joseph found himself inside a spacious suite of rooms that seemed to be an office and apartment all in one. The goons hung back and let them find their way across a deep shag carpet, past the stylish bar and water bed with video accessories, to reach the slightly elevated office space directly opposite.

They might have had a striking view, but drapes had been pulled shut across what seemed to be a window wall behind Chiang's desk. The man himself was on his feet and waiting for them, with the curtains at his back, a pose that Lee imagined he had practiced for effect.

"Good evening, gentlemen."

Chiang Fai was five-foot-nine, late thirties, trim and fit. His tailored suit was sharkskin, with a silk shirt open at the neck and Gucci loafers on his feet. As with Robert Chan, Lee had a hard time picturing this man in combat, going one-on-one with enemies and spilling blood himself. Still, there was something in his attitude that intimated power just below the surface, held in check by a veneer of charm.

Yodmani made the introductions, and Chiang offered Lee his hand. The Red Pole's grip was firm and dry.

"Be seated, please. Would either of you like a drink? Some wine, perhaps?"

Lee played along and settled in a seat across the desk from Chiang, Yodmani on his left. One of their escorts made the rounds with chilled Chablis and faded back in the direction of the bar. Chiang sipped his wine and set the glass aside before he spoke.

"I'm told you have a business proposition for me, Mr. Shyu?"

"That's right."

"You represent a group of California buyers, I believe."

"Old money, looking for a new direction."

"So. I take it they have no experience in handling pharmaceuticals?"

"They deal with Mexican supplies from time to time, but as you know, the quality leaves much to be desired."

"Of course. In the United States they call it 'mud,' if I am not mistaken."

Joseph forced a smile. "You got that right. It's Number Four, the same as China white, but riddled with impurities that make it difficult to cut. On top of that, the government of Mexico is under pressure to eradicate the traffic and preserve its foreign aid from Washington."

"I deal with politicians every day," Chiang said. "At times they seem like children, stubborn and immune to reason."

"As you say. However, trade goes on . . . or will, if I can find a new supplier for my clients."

"Ah, your clients. If I may presume to ask—"

"I'm sorry," Joseph cut him off. "They cherish anonymity and pay top dollar for the privilege of maintaining distance from their source. I understand your hesitancy at dealing with a stranger, particularly one sight unseen, but I am authorized to tell you only that they have no convictions and face no indictments or investigations at the present time."

"You say top dollar?"

"Forty thousand for a kilo, on delivery at the Bangkok waterfront. My clients take responsibility for shipment overseas and guarantee a monthly minimum of fifteen kilos for the next two years."

Chiang blinked, already calculating decimals and dollar signs.

"Three hundred sixty kilos?"

"Minimum. If the demand picks up, there may be more."

"I see."

"You've been informed, I trust, that I've established an account at one of Bangkok's leading banks. The quarter-million dollars on deposit there is yours, a gesture of good faith, if you accept my proposition. Sadly, business matters kept me from retrieving it today, or else—"

"I understand, of course."

If Chiang was pissed, it didn't show. His mind was miles downstream, imagining what he could do with 7,000,000 extra dollars in his pocket.

Joseph cleared his throat. "There is, however, one condition placed upon this offer by my clients."

"Yes?"

"I'm not sure how to say this, Mr. Chiang. I promise you that any insult is the last thing I intend."

"Speak freely, please."

"My clients are insistent that I meet your source and verify his capability of filling orders on this scale. They call it 'touching base.'"

"The meeting you suggest is most irregular. My reputation surely must suggest—"

"Again, I must apologize for any insult. Several years ago my clients dealt with a supplier in the state of Tamaulipas, Mexico. His reputation for delivery was unrivaled on the border, and for thirteen months we had no problems whatsoever. Then, without a hint of warning, officers investigating the abduction of a Texas college student called upon our friend and dug up fifteen bodies on his ranch, outside of Matamoros. It appears that he was totally insane, obsessed with sacrificing human beings in some kind of voodoo ritual."

"And your investment?"

"Lost. Two hundred kilos seized by Mexican police,

along with one-point-five million in cash. An unqualified disaster."

"What became of the supplier?"

Joseph smiled. "He hanged himself in jail . . . or so they say."

"You realize that I would need permission from my source before I could arrange a meeting."

"Certainly."

"I cannot promise his cooperation."

"We can only try," Lee said.

Chiang shot his cuff and checked a bulky Rolex for the time.

"I'll need to make some calls at once," he said. "If you would care to wait . . . ?"

"By all means."

There were two phones on his desk, but Chiang was on his feet and moving toward a door on Joseph's right. "Please, help yourself to more wine, anything you like. I won't be long."

In fact, it took the best part of an hour, during which time Joseph sipped another glass of wine and studied Chiang's expensive furnishings. Yodmani recognized the need for silence—they could not be certain whether microphones were planted in the room or if the gunners by the elevator had some means of overhearing them—and the uncomfortable quiet had begun to drag when Chiang returned.

"Sincere apologies for the delay," he said. "Communications in the north are primitive, at best."

"No problem." Lee was getting antsy, but it would be a grave mistake to push.

"I have surprised myself. The powers of persuasion found in money, yes?"

"Are we in business?"

"My supplier has agreed to your request, on two conditions."

"Namely?"

"First, you must be ready to begin your trip tomorrow."

Joseph shrugged. "No problem. I can leave tonight."

"Tomorrow is soon enough. And, second, your clients must appreciate the privilege they are being granted. Contact with my source will be—how would you say it in America?—a onetime thing."

Lee smiled. "That's all we ask."

"Then let us toast our partnership"—Chiang beamed—"before my driver takes you back to your hotel. You will be needing rest, to face the days ahead."

Lee's mind was clicking as the stone-faced shooter poured more wine.

A onetime thing.

One time should do the trick, if all the pieces fell together. And if not . . . well, it was still the only move left open in a game of life and death. He would proceed because he had no viable alternatives.

20

The call came through to Gordon Flack while Joe Lee and Damrong Yodmani were en route to keep their date with Chiang Min Fai. Flack's home—a small but stylish house off Ploenchit Road, ten minutes from the U.S. embassy—had guards outside and various built-in security devices to ensure the CIA assistant chief of station's safety, but he still got nervous sometimes, after dark. The city was a hostile place, and what could his two lookouts *really* do in the event of a determined terrorist attack?

Flack lived alone (the watchdogs didn't count), and had for seven years, since he was posted overseas and Dorothy, his ex, refused to leave their house in Georgetown. The divorce was bitter, but it worked out for the best, with manufactured evidence about her lesbian affairs allowing Flack to wriggle out from under alimony payments in the end. He took the snapshot album out of mothballs now and then, remembering the good times they had logged in fourteen years of marriage, but the good times had been relatively few and far between. Above all else, Flack cherished solitude, his precious privacy.

Except, sometimes, at night.

It was ironic, Flack decided, that the darkness had never bothered him in Washington. A town like that, you couldn't walk the streets by day *or* night without a risk of being mugged, or worse. Still, it was home, and he had grown up with a native's understanding of the blacks and homeless, welfare dregs who would not even qualify as third-class citizens on any scale Flack recognized. In

Washington, at least the animals spoke English and the cops were on his side.

Bangkok was different. Bad enough that hours—or days—could pass without a white face seen outside the embassy. It was the local attitude toward life itself that made Flack travel armed, installing new security devices in his home each time a fresh report of urban terrorism made the headlines. Thailand's murder rate, with twenty-seven persons killed for each hundred thousand of the population, was quadruple that of the United States, and hired assassins were available in Bangkok at a going rate of twenty dollars for a hit. Flack was aware of "special" clubs, ignored by the police, where patrons laid out heavy bread to see a woman brutalized and killed onstage. Participation by the audience cost extra, and was strictly optional.

In Bangkok, Gordon Flack had come to terms with personal mortality. His predecessor had been wounded in a drive-by shooting, on a visit to Bangsaen, and Flack himself had been the target of repeated threats since his arrival in the City of the Angels. He did not regard himself as paranoid—not yet, at least—but he had elevated caution to an art form, dealing with his native contacts at a safe arm's length whenever possible.

Just now, the phone call took him by surprise.

Flack was expecting a report from the surveillance team assigned to Joseph Lee, but it was early yet. Who else? They had his number at the embassy, of course, and there were half a dozen private parties who could ring him up in an emergency, but none of them would ever call at night to share good news. It was a fact of life that phone calls after-hours meant trouble, nine times out of ten.

Reluctantly he picked up on the seventh ring. "Hello?"

Long distance humming in his ear. "You recognize my voice?"

"Of course." How could he miss?

"I'm scrambling."

"Right."

The scrambler on Flack's private phone was standard

issue for the Company, a carbon copy of the one he used at work. No larger than a pack of cigarettes, it canceled any risk of interception on the line, unless the tappers had a corresponding set tuned in to Flack's selected frequency. The odds against successful interception of a given call were astronomical, but Flack knew they would speak in cryptic generalities, regardless, to be doubly sure.

"Okay?" The caller's voice was firm and clear despite the intervening miles.

"All set."

"What's happening?"

"We had a talk."

"Results?"

"He didn't seem impressed."

"I see. You're covered there?"

"So far. He's made some local friends, but nothing heavy. I've got eyes in place."

"We can't afford to take the chance. You understand? There's too damned much at stake."

Flack felt the short hairs stirring on his nape. "I hear you."

"Options?"

"I was thinking that a word to our associates could do the trick. Their town, their problem. Let them clean it up."

"The problem's ours, if someone starts to think we can't hold up our end."

A chill had settled in Flack's bones. "I'm listening," he said.

"You still use independent jobbers out your way?"

"From time to time."

"Reliable? We don't need any comebacks."

"I can handle it."

"Well, there you go."

"Is there a deadline?"

"Yesterday."

"I'll see what I can do."

"Clean sweep, agreed?"

Flack grimaced. "That's affirmative."

"Good man. No point in troubling our associates with this. We're simply cleaning house."

Flack felt a sudden urge to wash his hands. "I'll keep you posted."

"Soon."

"ASAP."

The hollow sound became a dial tone, silenced as he cradled the receiver, and the scrambler disconnected automatically.

We're simply cleaning house.

Despite his years in harness with the Company, Flack never ceased to marvel at the euphemisms used to cover violent death. They called it wet work, executive action, surgical excision, termination with extreme prejudice—and still, it all came down to killing.

Gordon Flack was cleaning house, and that meant Joseph Lee would have to die. Along with his confederate, Yodmani. Two dead for the price of one.

He lifted the receiver, punching out a local number from memory. It was the kind of number Flack would never dare write down.

Another phone call after-hours, spreading bad news all around.

And death, for some.

With Chiang's apologies, they donned their blindfolds in the elevator and were herded back along familiar-smelling corridors until they reached the building's exit, passing on through muggy darkness to the waiting car. Their escort dropped Lee off outside the Tiger's Paw, avoiding his hotel, and vanished with Yodmani in the traffic thronging Patpong Road.

Joe loitered on the curb for several moments, scanning for a tail, but finally gave it up and trekked back to the Montien, past the barkers and the whores. Upstairs, he used his key without a knock and found May waiting for him in the bedroom, with the big Colt automatic leveled at his chest.

"What's this?"

She ran to him, surrendering the pistol as she threw her arms around his neck.

"A phone call. There was no one on the line. I thought perhaps . . ."

Lee knew what she was thinking. Hotel switchboard operators almost never hit wrong numbers. That left someone checking out the room to learn if he was in. And when they got no answer, then what? Searching Bangkok was a hopeless case. That left a stakeout or a welcoming committee in the room itself, prepared to strike when Lee appeared.

And the appropriate response?

"We're getting out of here," Joe said. "A new hotel. I only need tonight."

"I know a place," May said.

"Okay." Already tossing items into a suitcase as he spoke. "I'll phone Yodmani once we're clear, and let him know—"

His train of thought was interrupted by a rapping at the door.

Lee drew the automatic from his belt and cocked it, pushing May in front of him until an angle of the wall protected them from any shots fired through the door.

"Who is it?" Peeking back around the corner as he spoke.

"Room service, sir."

"I didn't order anything."

"Champagne," the disembodied voice replied. "A gift."

"Who from?"

"I have not read the card."

"Please do."

A moment's hesitation, time enough to set a bottle down and rip into an envelope, perhaps. Unless . . .

"Damrong Yodmani," said the voice.

Which proved exactly nothing, dammit.

"I'm not dressed. Just leave it by the door."

"I'm sorry, sir. There is a signature required."

Lee had a choice to make. He could reject the gift and see what happened next, or he could take a chance.

"Stay here," he whispered, leaving May behind and creeping toward the door on tiptoe, painfully aware of every sound he made. A burst of gunfire through the door right now would drop him in his tracks.

The bathroom on his left, immediately off the foyer. Open. Dark. Joe switched the automatic to his left hand, flattening himself against the wall, and slipped inside. The doorknob was within his reach, if he was quick enough to pull it off.

A lunge, his fingers slick with sweat, and Lee ducked back again before the caller had a chance to tag him with a lucky shot.

"Okay, it's open."

Watching as the door swung inward to admit a husky Thai, mid-twenties, with a silver bucket and a bottle of champagne in one hand, a confused expression on his face. His free hand slid beneath the crimson bellboy's jacket, going for the pistol in his belt, and he was almost there when Joseph stuck the big Colt in his ear.

"What's this? A little something extra?" Easing a Beretta from the shooter's belt, May taking it to cover him. "I'll ask you once: How many?"

"No one else."

It had a hollow ring, but Joseph had no time to waste on an interrogation. He relieved their captive of the champagne bucket, left it on the nightstand, and retrieved his bag.

"We're leaving now," he told the gunman. "Play it smart, I'll drop you off somewhere along the way. Fuck up, and I'll be pleased to kill you where you stand."

The shooter nodded, sullen, turning something over in his mind as Joseph nudged him toward the door.

"You first."

They were waiting, as Lee knew they would be, two men loitering around the nearby elevators with their right hands tucked inside their jackets, coddling hardware. The appearance of their designated hitter, empty hands thrust out in warning or in supplication, took them by surprise and gave Joe Lee the heartbeat that he needed to respond.

And even so, it nearly wasn't good enough.

His first round winged the gunner on his left, a puff of blood and fabric from his sleeve, but nothing that would bring him down. They both had automatics out before Lee fired again, and he was startled by another pistol cracking just behind him, recognizing the Beretta's sound as May joined in.

Downrange, their opposition was returning fire, the "bellboy" taking some of it and dropping to his knees. A bullet drilled Lee's suitcase, jogging him off-balance, and he paid the gunner back with two quick rounds that punched him over backward in a twitching heap.

The third man might have nailed him, had it not been for May. Joe couldn't vouch for her experience with firearms, but she did all right, unloading half a magazine in rapid fire and wounding her assailant twice before he fell. Lee gave him one to make it stick, and led May past their fallen opposition toward the service stairs.

If there were lookouts in the lobby, Joseph couldn't pick them out. They caught a taxi on the street, and May supplied the driver with an address as they pulled away. Behind them, on the sidewalk, no one seemed to give a damn.

"Where are we going?"

"Someplace safe," she said, still flushed from the explosive confrontation in the corridor outside Lee's room.

"Such as?"

"My home."

The cabbie let them off a block away—no point in giving out the right address, if he was grilled—and Joseph gave the lady points for thinking on her feet. No indications of pursuit as they slipped into her apartment building near the boxing stadium, off Wireless Road.

May's flat was on the second floor. She seemed to have no fear of an intruder, but Joe kept his .45 in hand and checked the three small rooms once they were safe inside. His next objective was the telephone, to warn Yodmani of his danger.

If they weren't too late.

The point man at the Montien had known Yodmani's name, expecting it to open Joseph's door. That didn't mean another team would be dispatched to tag his contact, necessarily, but Joseph didn't feel like taking chances. If Yodmani was at risk . . .

The phone rang twice before a woman picked it up.

"Sawat dee kha?"

"Damrong Yodmani, please."

"A moment."

Watching May and waiting on the line, his stomach tied in knots, until he recognized the cautious voice. "Hello?"

"Are you all right?"

The edge came off Yodmani's voice as he relaxed. "There was an incident. I tried to call your room at the hotel."

"It got a little crowded over there. I had to leave."

"Are you secure?"

"For now. I think we need to talk."

"Agreed, but not like this."

"I understand." Yodmani had begun to doubt his own security, beginning with the telephone.

"Where can we meet?"

Lee thought about it for a moment, frowning. "Do you know the boxing stadium?"

"Of course."

"South side?"

"In half an hour. Be on guard."

The line went dead, and Joseph dropped the handset in its cradle. May Tansiri had been watching him, and now she picked up her handbag, the Beretta snug inside.

"I'm going with you."

"May—"

"The others knew Yodmani, and they might know me. I won't stay here alone."

Joe saw her logic, but he hesitated, dreading the necessity of putting her at risk a second time.

"There is another reason," May informed him.

"What?"

"Yodmani."

It was all she had to say. The thought had crossed Lee's

mind as well, while they were covering the mile between his lodgings at the Montien and May's apartment. What if the assassins knew Yodmani's name because *he* sent them?

"Let me see your gun."

It was a Model 86, .380 caliber, with wooden grips. He pulled the magazine and checked the tip-up barrel to confirm the weapon's load.

"Four shots," he told her, handing back the pistol. "If you have to use it, make them count."

Before they left, he fed the Colt another magazine and topped the first one off with bullets from his dwindling supply. He thought about his suitcase, knowing it would draw unwelcome notice on the street, and wrote it off. The clothes he wore would have to be enough until he had a chance to shop. Lee made a final inventory of his pockets—bankbook, cash, spare magazines, loose cartridges—and they were ready to begin.

A half-block from the stadium, they separated, May Tansiri hanging back to cover Joe from thirty feet away while he ranged up and down the curb with hands in pockets, waiting. It was risky, but at least they had a fighting chance this way, in case Yodmani brought a firing squad along. Lee hoped it would not come to that, but he had done his best to guard against a new surprise.

The BMW was a 1990 model, still in decent shape considering the Bangkok traffic. Joseph didn't recognize the driver, but he saw Yodmani in the shotgun seat and flicked a glance at May, confirming recognition as the car pulled up beside him, headed north. Inside the right-hand pocket of his coat, Lee held his automatic cocked and leveled at Yodmani's face.

Yodmani's driver kept the engine running as his passenger got out to speak with Lee.

"How many were there?"

"Two."

Yodmani circled to the BMW's rear and rapped his knuckles on the fender, waiting while his driver used an inside lever to release the lock. He raised the lid and

Joseph had a glimpse of bodies curled together, stiffening in death, before it closed again.

He eased the automatic's hammer down and beckoned May to join them.

"You suspected me?" Yodmani did not seem to take it as an insult.

"I'm on guard, just like you said."

"Of course." His contact cut a sidelong glance at traffic, flowing past. "We should not linger here."

Lee sat in back with May; Yodmani swiveled in his seat to face them while his driver watched the road and checked their track for shadows.

"Who?" Lee asked when they were rolling.

"I suspected Chiang at first, but he would not have let us go. Perhaps an enemy of yours, from Hong Kong?"

"It's a possibility." Lee watched the neon blurring past his window. "Or it could be Gordon Flack."

"The CIA?"

"You know him, then."

"By reputation only."

"We had words the day I landed. I've been wondering why he let it go at that."

"You still intend to travel north?"

"I haven't got much choice."

Yodmani frowned. "Nor I."

"What's that supposed to mean?"

"This is the second time in fifteen years of business that assassins have been sent to take my life. The first time, I expected it; my enemies were known. Tonight I find that strangers wish to have me killed. I will not be secure in Bangkok until they have been identified and neutralized."

"You said yourself, there's no way either one of us can neutralize the Triads. That goes double for the CIA."

"Then I must leave, in any case. I may as well go north, and seek my answers there."

Lee was surprised by a sensation of relief that he would not be traveling alone. "You're sure?"

Yodmani shrugged and forced a smile. "Why not?" he said. "I have a vested interest in your safety, after all. But come, there are arrangements to be made. I think it best if we reorganize our travel plans, as you would say, from scratch."

The telephone again. Flack listened to its shrilling for a moment, scowled, and finally lifted the receiver to his ear. "Hello?"

The voice began and ended with apologies, the bad news sandwiched in between. A total cluster-fuck, across the board.

Flack felt his stomach churning, and he closed his eyes. "I understand."

Two hitters dead, a third man badly wounded, two more lost without a trace. The caller knew that he was in deep shit, determined not to let it stick. He was prepared to make it right, if only Flack would give him one more chance.

"First thing," the CIA assistant chief of station said, "you need to tidy up. We can't afford your walking wounded spilling everything he knows to the police. Take care of it."

Assurances, with more limp-dick apologies.

"Next item," Flack cut through it with a snarl, "we need a tracker. Someone who can run them down outside the city and resolve this mess. Can do?"

He listened to the moron telling him: no problem, everything he wanted would be taken care of perfectly the second time around.

"I hope so, guy." He let an edge of menace creep into his voice. "One more like this, I'll have to scrub your franchise, if you get my drift."

He broke the link before his contact had a chance to grovel anymore, deciding he would wait a day or two before he placed the call to San Francisco. Better if he had a positive report, instead of stirring up a hornet's nest to no effect.

Flack's tolerance for failure was not high, but some of his associates were positively rabid on the subject, and he did not care to make them think he was letting down the side.

A day or two—no more than three, by any means—and he could put their minds at ease. Flack did not even want to think about the flip side, where the options simply went from bad to worse.

A man who didn't watch his step could get cut off below the knees, and that made things hard when it was time to run away.

21

Yodmani's preparations for the trip included rugged hiking clothes and weapons for defense along the way, between their starting point and General Sheng's home base at Mae Salong. The Thai picked out a Ruger Mini-14 semiautomatic rifle for himself, and Joseph settled for a Savage twelve-gauge pump, with buckshot rounds to minimize the need for pinpoint aim. He knew enough about the territory they were facing to be confident that any violent action would be fought at something close to point-blank range.

With final checks complete, the weapons were dismantled, packed along with ammunition and their sidearms, hiking clothes and gear, in matching leather bags. En route to Don Muang airport, they dropped May Tansiri at a safe house and received her grudging promise that she would not show her face outside until she had some word of their success or failure in the north. In the event that neither one of them returned—a possibility they could not ignore—Yodmani had a friend on tap who would supply the necessary cash and travel documents to get May out of Thailand for a while, until the heat died down.

Domestic flights at Don Muang use a separate terminal, and passengers are not subjected to the strict security precautions visited on international arrivals and departures. They could not have gotten by with packing pistols on the plane—and Lee felt naked in the waiting room, aware that gunmen would be searching for him, even now—but no one gave their loaded bags a second glance.

Joe felt a little better once their early-morning Airbus flight was off the ground and headed north. He knew what lay behind them, and their destination—though obscure—at least held out a prospect of survival. Lee had no clear plans for dealing with the general, once they met, but he would play that part by ear. For now, it was enough to have escaped from Bangkok with his life.

How many dead, so far, because he dared to challenge Robert Chan? Lee gave up counting when he got to Lisa, concentrating on the days ahead, the enemy he was about to meet.

If Chiang Min Fai was playing straight—and Joe agreed the mobster would have had them killed at once, instead of wasting time and having gunners wait for them at home—they were about to take a privileged look inside the single largest source of opium and heroin in Southeast Asia. Granted, it would be a worm's-eye view, but Lee was carrying a note of introduction to the ranking warlord of the Kuomintang, a man whose word was life and death in Meung Nam province and across the line, in Burma.

As the Airbus took them north, Joe Lee reviewed his knowledge of the Golden Triangle and smuggling operations on the ground. The "Triangle"—so called not for its shape, but for the geographical convergence of Thailand, Laos, and Burma—covers some 150,000 square miles of mountainous jungle populated by nomadic tribes who cultivate their lethal crop in forest patches cleared by ax and fire. Despite a legal ban that dates from 1958, Thailand produces some three hundred tons of opium per year, with like amounts turned out in Burma, Laos, and China's southern Yunnan district, where the communists have failed to put a damper on free enterprise.

Raw opium—from *opion,* Greek for "poppy juice"—is harvested from late December through early March, purchased for fifty to fifty-five dollars per kilo by Chinese traders who double their money on resale to Triad brokers in Tak, Lampang, or Chiang Mai. From March to June the opium is moved by pack trains, using elephants or mules, to reach the covert drug labs tucked away in Burma. By July the fruit of peasant labor has been transformed into heroin, which dealers designate as either

Number 3, "Chinese brown sugar," or the potent Number 4, dubbed "China white." Traditionally smoked in pipes, the rocky Number 3 is favored by Chinese around the world, while Number 4 is mainlined by the addicts of America and Europe. Western dealers likewise favor China white, with its initial purity of ninety-odd percent, which lets them "cut" their poison prior to sale and multiply their profits several thousand times.

In any given year, the Golden Triangle—or quadrangle, if you include Yunnan—supplies an estimated seventy percent of heroin on sale worldwide. General Shih Yeuh Sheng produces perhaps one-fifth of that, and ranks among the major dealers in the world, but is legally untouchable from the United States. His presence in Meung Nam is tolerated by the Bangkok government because his seven thousand mercenary troops are pledged to fight the communists wherever they're found, and General Sheng has thrown his weight against Thai rebels in the north on more than one occasion. On the other side, in Burma, he has made war against the Shan and Kachin "liberation armies," thereby earning gratitude from nervous politicians in Rangoon. Whenever Washington suggests extradition or concerted moves against the poppy fields, the overtures are met with helpless shrugs from presidents, prime ministers, and kings.

Joe Lee was going in without illusions, eyes wide open to the grim realities of greed and terror which had let the Kuomintang survive without a homeland for the better part of half a century. He recognized the odds against him, knew his hopes of coming out alive were marginal at best, but he had come too far to give up now. Behind him, there was only death and failure, while ahead lay . . . What?

The end, he thought, whichever way it goes.

The Airbus dropped them at Chiang Rai, four hundred miles due north of Bangkok, and their guide was waiting in the small terminal. He looked Chinese, except for darker skin, and Lee had been forewarned that they were dealing with the Meo, dominant among the several tribes that cultivated opium above Lampang. He wore a simple linen shirt and slacks, with leather sandals on his naked feet. Yodmani introduced the man as Tranh, but they did not shake hands.

Tranh had an open jeep outside. He stowed their bags and slid behind the wheel, Yodmani staking out the shotgun seat and leaving Joe to sit in back, hunched down between the luggage and an extra can of gasoline. The ride was smooth enough in town, despite some potholes on the outskirts, but his spine and pelvis took a beating as they left the settlement behind and started climbing on a narrow unpaved road.

The engine noise and gnashing gears discouraged conversation, giving Lee a chance to study his surroundings as they drove. The track was steep and winding, deeply scarred by runoff and erosion, with jungle growing thick and dark on either side. Three seasons are acknowledged by the Thais—hot, cold, and wet—the latter corresponding to monsoons that bring torrential rains from June through mid-November, but in truth the temperature is seldom less than warm. Humidity makes eighty-five degrees feel like a hundred in the shade, with periodic cloudbursts offering the only measure of relief for those compelled to live without the benefit of air-conditioning.

The rain caught up with them a few miles north of town, and they were drenched in seconds, Tranh continuing to drive by instinct as the visibility was cut to six or seven yards. He shifted into four-wheel drive and kept on going, fording ruts that flowed like rivers in the downpour, Joseph hanging on in back and wondering if he would have a chance to jump when Tranh misjudged and took them off the road.

It didn't happen, though, and in another moment the deluge evaporated, leaving only heat and steam behind. Clouds parted, and the sun beat down relentlessly upon a forest sparkling clean, so vibrant it was almost painful to the eye.

Then, two hours from Chiang Rai, they lost the road. Tranh drove for several yards along a rocky streambed, veering off through ferns and thorny undergrowth before he parked the jeep.

"From here," he said, "we walk."

They spent a quarter-hour changing clothes, assembling weapons, loading up, while Tranh cut limbs and fronds to camouflage the jeep. Tranh's load consisted of a water bag and a machete, with their street clothes and the luggage left behind. Yodmani said it would be no loss if someone stole their dirty laundry, and the thought of hauling leather bags beneath a broiling sun made Joe agree.

Their trail was hidden from the road, but Tranh knew where to look, a narrow goat path through the trees that kept Joe leaning forward at the best of times, occasionally clutching roots and branches as he climbed. The second time he dropped the twelve-gauge Savage, Lee decided it was hopeless and he slung the piece across his back, devoutly hoping he would not be called upon to fight a battle on the trail. His hip and shoulder had begun to throb before they made a hundred yards, and a nagging cadence echoed in his skull, but Joseph clenched his teeth and forged ahead.

In time, the track grew wider and a trifle less severe. Tranh set a pace his troops could live with, and they marched on through another cloudburst, Joseph grateful for the drenching that refreshed him on his feet. He threw his head back, let the rain beat down on his face, eyes closed and mouth wide open, drinking greedily. The rain was warm and not especially sweet, but at the moment it rejuvenated Lee like ice-cold beer.

No sooner had the rain subsided than the muggy heat redoubled. Tranh didn't seem to feel the heat, but Lee was gratified to see Yodmani sweating through his stiff safari shirt and mopping at his forehead, with his rifle hanging muzzle-down and thumping listlessly against his hip.

Tranh called a break at noon and passed the water bag around, then followed it with strips of tough dried meat that Joseph made no effort to identify. More water for dessert, and they were on their way, Joe's hip renewing its objections as the gradient increased.

They met the cobra fifteen minutes later. It was five or six feet long, stretched out across the trail, and showed no inclination to retreat at their approach. Instead, the reptile coiled and reared its head, the forked tongue darting in and out, its hood flared to reveal the lighter ventral scales. The warning hiss was loud and clear.

Yodmani faded to the left and leveled his rifle, Joseph reaching for his .45.

"No shooting," Tranh commanded, edging toward the serpent in a semicrouch with his machete thrust in front of him.

The cobra waited, swaying gently back and forth as Tranh began to weave, refusing to present a stationary target. When the gap between them had been cut in half, to six or seven strides, the reptile hissed again, defiant in the face of overwhelming odds.

Tranh feinted with his blade, the cobra following as if unable to resist. And back again, as Tranh reversed the move. Almost in striking distance now. Another step . . .

The cobra chose its time and struck, the upper body whipping forward just as Tranh stepped back and brought the heavy blade of his machete down. It caught the snake an inch or so behind its lunging head, flesh parting with a whisper as a jet of blood erupted from the open neck and sprayed Tranh's muddy feet.

Lee stood and watched the reptile's body thrashing on the trail, a frantic chain of figure-eights that lost momentum seconds later, winding down into a final twitching roll. Tranh scooped the lethal head up on his blade and skimmed it toward the trees, then seized the flaccid body by its tail and cracked it like a whip, to clear the last remaining blood, before he hung the snake around his neck.

"Good food," he said, and turned away, continuing along the trail.

Lee thought about the salty strips of meat they had consumed at lunch and waited for his stomach to complete a lazy barrel roll. He found Yodmani watching him and smiling as he slipped the automatic back inside its holster.

"Dinner, do you think?"

Yodmani shrugged and slung his rifle, lowering his voice as he replied, "With Meo, who can say?"

"If we get the choice," Lee said, "I think I'll try the salad bar."

They broke twice more for rest and water on the trail, at two o'clock and half-past four. The ache in Joseph's hip had faded slightly, as his calves and thighs began to throb in unison, reminding Lee that he was out of shape for mountaineering. Overhead, the brutal sun progressed from east to west without a noticeable drop in temperature, until it cleared the trees and shadows loomed across the trail.

Lee checked his watch again and found that it was nearly six o'clock. In front of him, Tranh showed no signs of slowing down. Yodmani had begun to sag, but Joe thought he would struggle on behind their guide until he dropped, to prove himself.

Eight hours on the trail, including drive time in the jeep, and Joseph had begun to doubt that he could last another hundred yards. He was about to question Tranh about their ETA when it occurred to him that they were hiking over level ground. Another bend, and he could see a village in the middle distance, shadows long around the bamboo huts and cooking fires.

No place like home, Lee thought, and gave the final quarter-mile everything he had.

The huts were large, with overhanging eaves, and Joseph counted seventeen before they reached the village proper, trailing dusk behind them all the way. Two fires were burning, one at either end of what he chose to call a street, for want of a better term. In fact, it was a strip of muddy earth that wound between the huts, worn bare by constant traffic over several months.

They were expected, and the villagers showed no alarm at their approach. It was a good thing, too, since several of the men were armed—Lee saw a vintage M-1 carbine, a Garand, a pair of modern M-16's—and he suspected they would be crack shots if called upon to prove themselves. The women tended cooking fires or crouched outside their huts, industriously sewing beads and brightly colored feathers onto strips of cloth for the adornment of their tribal garb. A dozen children, give or take, were running in and out among the huts, the young ones naked, older boys bare-chested, wearing baggy trousers, while the girls wore simple shifts cut just below the knee. As they discovered strangers in their midst, the games were broken off and they disappeared inside the huts.

It was the odor of the village that impressed Joe at first. These were simple people, living off the land, and precious water hauled for hours up the mountainside in hollow bamboo tubes would not be wasted washing clothes or bodies. Still, there was a feral smell about the tiny settlement which no one else appeared to notice, and he did not understand until he saw the animals—emaciated dogs and small black pigs—that roamed the village unrestrained. The mongrels came as a particular surprise, more mouths to feed, but from the look of them, they had not taxed the village larder much in recent days.

The village chief was waiting, and greeted them with the solemnity reserved for honored guests. Tranh made it clear the chief would be their host that evening, granting them the privilege of sleeping under his roof. Considering the smell, Joe would have settled for a blanket on the ground outside, but as it was, he bowed and forced a smile, Yodmani offering effusive thanks.

Upon the chief's command, a young man hurried forward to receive their weapons. Joseph understood it was a sign of friendship, mandatory in the circumstances to preserve their welcome, but he hated parting with the shotgun and his .45. Tranh seemed to have no qualms about surrendering his arms, but Lee made sure to note the dwelling where their weapons were deposited. If anything went wrong, the simple clasp knife in his pocket would be useless against the village guns.

They were invited to sit down around the larger fire,

and Joseph waited for the chief to choose his patch of dirt, then peeked inside the cooking pot. As far as he could tell, the evening meal was soup or stew, composed of native vegetables and spices. There was no meat visible, so far, and Joseph stole a glance at Tranh in time to see him greeted by a woman four huts down, the headless cobra changing hands. She disappeared inside, and Joseph breathed a small sigh of relief.

Too soon.

A frightened yelp behind him, and a rangy mongrel scurried past, a young boy on his heels. Before Lee had a chance to blink, the hunter caught his prey with one hand on the mongrel's tail, a hatchet glinting in the firelight flashing down against the canine skull.

The Meo wasted no time on preliminaries in the preparation of their meal. As Joseph watched, Yodmani making small talk with the chief, the hunter and another boy picked up the twitching dog and dropped it on the second cooking fire, then settled back to wait.

At once a stench of burning leather overpowered the other village smells, as hair and hide were seared away. The youthful chefs had clearly done this kind of thing before; they knew exactly when to prod the smoking carcass free and turn it over to a pair of women waiting in the wings. With knives and nimble hands, the women gutted their pathetic roast and stripped its flesh, which was immediately added to the evening's stew.

The stew was served in wooden bowls, with bamboo hearts and tea. By that time Joseph's stomach had begun to growl from hunger, but he still had trouble with the stringy dog meat, nearly gagging on the first few bites. Yodmani helped him through it by distracting him with stories of the Meo and their lives, explaining how the tribes remained in one place, clearing poppy fields at greater distances, until the farthest crop might lie a full day's march from home. The Meo kept about one-fifth of the opium they raised for personal consumption, rearing addicts from the cradle, but they did not show the various debilitating symptoms of a junkie hooked on heroin. If they gave any passing thought to how their crop was used, the misery it caused worldwide, the knowledge never made it to their eyes.

Somehow, Lee's bowl was empty, and he managed to avoid a second helping, concentrating on the rich, dark tea. It nearly killed the taste of dog-meat stew, and he was not concerned about the strong brew keeping him awake. Despite the strange surroundings, the stiffness in his back and legs, the sunburn pulsing on his neck, he knew he would have no trouble sleeping like the dead.

As promised, they were rooming with the chief, his hut the largest in the village and the one in which their firearms had been stored. Inside, they lay on woven bamboo mats with cushions underneath their heads, Lee fighting to remain awake, Yodmani graciously accepting as the chief invited them to join him in an after-dinner smoke. Three slender pipes—elaborate silver stems and tiny bowls—were lifted from a cedar chest and laid before the chief as he began the preparation of the opium.

A long, thin needle speared each crusty ball of sap and held it near a gas lamp's flame for softening. When it was soft enough, he made the transfer to a waiting pipe and held its bowl above the flame, inhaling acrid smoke to demonstrate for his guests. Yodmani didn't seem to need the lesson, smoking like a pro and grinning at the chief, while Joseph did his best to fake it, certain that tomorrow would be challenge enough without a groggy mind and bleary eyes, but there was no way short of suffocation to avoid the smoky atmosphere inside the hut, and somewhere in the middle of Yodmani's second pipe he lost it, drifting in a warm, surrealistic dream world where the children carried hatchets and the dogs ran for their lives at suppertime.

Dogs woke him in the morning, fighting over scraps outside the hut, their snarls providing sound effects for Joseph's dream until a shaft of sunlight speared his eyes. Yodmani hailed him from the doorway, calling him to breakfast, and his stomach twisted at the thought of choking down more mongrel stew.

Joe made his way outside, remembering to leave his

guns behind, and was relieved to find the women slicing fruit on wooden trays. The protein was apparently reserved for evening meals, and Lee felt better as he dined on mangoes and bananas. It would never last, once they were on the trail, but after last night's meal, Tranh's no-name jerky would be something to anticipate.

It was half-past eight before a boy was sent to fetch their guns and Tranh rejoined them, carrying a rifle now, besides his water bag and the machete in his belt. Whatever might be waiting for them on the trail, their guide was covering his ass.

Lee watched Yodmani going through the ritual of thank-yous with their host, inserting bows and gestures where appropriate. No cash changed hands, but Joseph had no doubt the Thai was promising some favor in return for hospitality received, a show of friendship and acknowledgment of obligation stopping short of insult.

No one but the chief, Tranh's woman, and a pair of scrawny canines watched them go. The trail was fairly level for another fifty yards or so, and then they started climbing, Joseph's muscles picking up their symphony of aches and pains where they had let it go the night before. When he turned back to check their distance from the Meo village, it was lost to sight among the trees, a solitary mongrel standing guard.

They marched for ninety minutes straight before another trail crossed theirs, and Tranh veered off to lead them west. The track was steep, with gnarled roots underfoot that offered toeholds when they weren't engaged in snagging Joseph's feet and tripping him. At one point, where the grade was nearly forty-five degrees and Lee was down to crawling on all fours, they passed a mountain waterfall that bathed them in a cool, refreshing spray.

They rested for the first time on a rocky crest that proved to be their halfway point, with blue skies overhead, the jungle sweltering beneath a layer of mist as far as they could see. Tranh passed the pemmican and water bag around, Lee finding that he didn't care if it was dog or snake this time, as long as it was in his hand.

"From here, all down," Tranh said, one bony index finger aimed at the descending trail.

"How far?" Yodmani asked.

"Not far. Five hours, maybe six, unless we stop."

It looked like easy work, the downhill run, but Joseph soon discovered brand-new problems as the mud and gravel slipped beneath his boots, stiff muscles in his back and legs protesting loudly as he fought to keep his balance on the trail. A tumble here would bowl the others off their feet and carry all of them a hundred feet downhill unless a tree or boulder broke the fall. In places, Lee was forced to turn around and travel backward, like a fireman climbing down a ladder, clutching roots and vines until his nails were chipped and caked with mud, fresh blisters burning in his palms.

A grueling hour into their descent, the trail played out and dumped them on a stony ledge that overlooked a river valley several hundred feet below. Tranh led them north along the goat path, Joseph hugging rock and fighting vertigo until they reached the west end of a long rope bridge across the chasm.

"This is it?" Lee's mind played vivid images of frayed ropes snapping, broken bodies plunging through the void.

"We cross," Tranh said, already moving out before Lee could object.

Yodmani glanced from Joseph to the swaying bridge and back again before he shrugged. "We cross."

"That's what I thought he said."

Yodmani let Tranh make his way across the bridge, proceeding only when their guide was safely on the other side. Lee watched and waited in his turn, aware that it was probably all right for several men to cross the bridge at once, but unwilling to experiment when the result of failure would be not-so-sudden death.

And then he was alone, the two of them regarding him from safety, on the distant ledge.

The classic line from old adventure movies—*Don't look down*—made sense, but how in hell was he supposed to watch his step on narrow, weathered boards if he kept staring at the clouds? He clutched the guide ropes in a death grip, measuring his strides and praying that a gust of wind would not arrive to set his frail perch swinging like a pendulum. Attempting to distract himself, he wondered who had built the bridge, and *how.* Would they construct the whole damned thing on one side of the chasm and contrive a way to launch it off through space? Was someone waiting on the other side to catch it, and if so, how did he get there? If another method was employed, who volunteered to creep along the guide rope, laying wooden planks and binding them in place?

The game of twenty questions saw him through, but he was trembling by the time he reached the eastern face. Tranh offered him another break, but Joseph shrugged it off and they continued on their way, a gentler slope that wound through rocky crags, with trees and ferns encroaching until it became a jungle again.

They stopped again at half-past three, beneath a wooded ridge that screened their view of the surrounding countryside. Behind them, rugged slopes they had negotiated hours earlier seemed leagues away, impossibly remote. A measure of fatigue, Lee thought, exaggerating progress in a bid to put the trek behind him while he still had strength enough to move.

Tranh did not offer meat this time, but water was enough. Their resting place was relatively open, ringed with boulders like a giant's camp, with grass and drooping ferns inside the ring. It would have made a pleasant camp if they had not been pushing on, but Joe looked forward to a roof and decent food tonight. With any luck at all, the menu would not feature dog.

Yodmani passed the water bag to Tranh, their guide recapping it and setting it beside him on the ground. Tranh seemed to need no rest, and it was all the more remarkable when he sprawled backward, twitching on the grass, as if his feet had been jerked out from under him.

Lee blinked and stared, a precious moment lost before

he focused on the hole between Tranh's eyes, the crimson trail across his forehead, lost above the hairline.

Jesus Christ!

A second bullet stung him with chips of stone before his ears picked up the rolling sound of rifle fire.

22

Lee dropped behind the nearest boulder, swiping at the bloody pinpricks on his cheek. In front of him, Yodmani had found cover in the shadow of another giant stone, while random rounds cracked off the boulders or came whispering through the grass.

Pinned down.

Lee's mind was racing, trying to identify their enemy by guesswork, knowing it was a hopeless task. There were three of them at least, from the converging angles of their fire, but there might be a dozen or a hundred others in the trees, already circling to flank them while the snipers did their job of holding down the front.

He flicked the safety off his shotgun, knowing it lacked the range to kill efficiently beyond a hundred feet. The snipers were secure at twice that distance, covered by the trees, but there was still a chance, if he could pull it off.

He whistled softly to Yodmani, catching his attention on the second try. Afraid of risking words, he sketched his plan in pantomime, repeating it until the Thai responded with a jerky nod. It was a relatively simple scheme, by no means certain of success, but it was all he had.

And it could get him killed if he made one false step along the way.

The nearest boulder on his left was fifteen feet away, and Joseph timed his break to fall between the scattered shots that peppered their position. It was risky, second-guessing strangers that he couldn't even see, but a diversion was essential for Yodmani to pop out and spot their muzzle flashes—if he could—and bring them under fire.

Lee checked Yodmani, found him ready, waiting. Images of Eddie Hovis jerked and screamed inside his brain, and Joseph shook them off. He knew exactly how the slugs would feel if any of the snipers scored a hit, but he would not be paralyzed by fear.

He lunged across the bit of open ground, remembering to dog it just enough that all of them would want to try a shot. He fired a shotgun blast in the direction of the trees, a flagrant waste of ammunition, and the snipers were responding when Yodmani's Ruger joined the argument. The Thai squeezed off five rounds before they drove him under cover, but at least he had them spotted now.

Until they moved.

It was the obvious approach, with shadows lengthening among the trees, full darkness due in two hours' time. Lee reckoned the snipers were alone; their backup surely would have sprung the trap by now if they were coming. Nightfall would allow their quarry to escape, unless the gunmen had a Very pistol and a bottomless supply of flares.

In short, they had to strike while light remained, and Lee was waiting, peering cautiously around his rock from time to time, when they began their serpentine descent.

The way to do it, he decided, was to leave one man in place for cover fire while two crept down the slope and took up new positions at the base. Once they were both in place, their spotter would be free to make his move with cover from below, in preparation for a pincers movement to surround their prey.

Another peek, and Joseph caught a glimpse of movement in the woods, descending. Twenty feet away, Yodmani saw it too, and fired three rounds before the sniper drove him back. Lee didn't waste his ammunition on a target that was out of range and screened by trees.

Who were they, dammit?

Bandits came to mind, but Lee had lost his faith in mere coincidence. They might as easily have been dispatched by Gordon Flack, Chiang Fai, or General Sheng. Whichever way it played, survival was the first aim, and Lee knew they would have to take their adversaries out before they had the luxury of speculating on identities and motives.

One way or another, it was coming down to do-or-die.

The next time Joseph risked a glance, two rifles fired in unison, their muzzle flashes winking from the tree line, thirty yards away. Above them, working down the slope, their backup made no effort to conceal his progress from the enemy. They knew what they were doing, and it was apparent that they had no fear of letting Joseph or Yodmani slip away.

At least the bastards were in range now, even though their cover made them relatively safe from buckshot. Lee squeezed off a round, regardless, throwing it away in his desire to feel that he was doing something to slow the hunters down and make their work more dangerous.

How long before they had the clearing covered with triangulated fire? No more than thirty minutes, if they dawdled; half that time if they were brisk and bold. The best Lee and Yodmani could achieve was nuisance fire, unless one of the snipers lost his mind and showed himself ahead of time.

Fat chance.

Once they were all in place, retreat cut off, the gunmen could decide if it was worth their while to rush the clearing. Theoretically, if they selected their positions properly, a charge across the open ground would be unnecessary. They could do their killing from the trees and never break a sweat before the job was done.

Lee shot a glance at Tranh, deciding he should try to reach the dead man's rifle, give himself some range while there was time. He was about to make his move when automatic fire erupted from the forest, short staccato bursts from several weapons overlapping into one protracted blast. Lee hunched his shoulders, waiting for the angry swarm of bullets, but it never came. Another heartbeat passing as he realized that someone else was under fire.

The snipers?

What the hell?

He glanced around his rock in time to see a figure clad

in camouflage fatigues emerging from the tree line, running for his life. Lee held his fire, uncertain as to who or what the runner was, but someone in the trees behind him entertained no doubts. As Joseph watched, two automatic weapons opened up in unison, the runner spinning through a jerky little dance of death before he fell.

Someone was mopping up back there among the trees. Lee heard the crack of a familiar rifle, aimed at other targets now, before its voice was swallowed up and silenced by the automatics.

He was waiting when the new arrivals showed themselves, a dozen figures clad in olive drab and tiger-stripe fatigues, all armed with M-16's or Russian AK-47's. Joseph knew there would be others watching from the trees, and he was wondering how many he could kill before they cut him down, when one of them cupped his hands around his mouth and called across the open ground in English, "We have come for Wen-Ling Shyu!"

Joseph saw Yodmani braced to rise and fire, but he signaled him to wait. "Who sent you?"

"General Shih Yeuh Sheng," the uniform replied. "He waits for you in camp. Your enemies are dead."

"I'm not alone."

"How many are you?"

He could see no point in lying, when the troops in front of him could easily surround and kill them both.

"Just two. Our guide is dead."

"You have no further need of him."

Lee caught Yodmani watching him and raised an eyebrow, questioning. Yodmani shrugged, and Joseph nodded affirmation, knowing that their range of choices finally came down to none at all.

He rose and held the shotgun ready at his side, for all the good that it would do. "We're coming out."

September made it forty-seven years since General Shih Yeuh Sheng had seen his home in Xiangtan, China, but his memories were crisp and clear, as if mere days had passed, instead of decades. When his birthday came next month, he would be seventy years old, but he was strong and healthy for a man his age—for *any* age—and he could still command the loyalty of his troops.

No matter if the leftist press insisted that his cause was lost and branded Sheng a criminal. He knew the secret of endurance, and he would keep the faith with fallen comrades while he lived.

Sheng had been twenty-three years old, a green lieutenant in the Kuomintang, when Mao's red army drove them out of Kweichow province, south and west across Yunnan, with the artillery like thunder at their backs. There had been blind panic in those early days, when the reality of grim defeat had risen up to mock the soldiers who were promised they would never lose, not while America and God were on their side. By mid-October 1949, Sheng realized that most Americans were cowards; God, for His part, simply chose to look the other way.

That fall, five thousand soldiers of the Kuomintang escaped to Indochina, where they were imprisoned by the French, repatriated to Formosa in the spring of 1953. Sheng's band, some fifteen hundred strong, pushed into Burma from Yunnan, establishing their stronghold in the rugged Mong Hsat district, where the Burmese army was unable to dislodge them. In the first two years of exile, they increased their strength tenfold, absorbing refugees from communist oppression in Yunnan. The district's thirty-four hereditary chieftains were absorbed or killed, depending on their state of mind, as General Li Mi's troops spread out to make the eastern Shan states their preserve.

In 1951 the CIA began to show an interest in the Kuomintang's forgotten army, massed along the southern Chinese border. It was hoped that General Mi's command might help contain the communists and block them from invading Southeast Asia. Arms and other military gear were readily available for friends in need, the shipments funneled through Formosa or direct from Bangkok, dropped around Mong Hsat by parachute, from unmarked planes. In time, a jungle airfield was constructed by the KMT, to cut down wear and tear on their supplies.

On paper, General Mi's command—with Shih Yeuh Sheng promoted to the rank of captain at the age of twenty-four—was meant to screen intelligence from mainland China, standing by in case of armed aggression from the north. In fact, the general and his troops were never satisfied with sitting on their hands and waiting to defend themselves on foreign soil, while home lay close enough for them to smell rice cooking in the Mekong villages below Changning. Between the spring of 1950 and the autumn months of 1952, Mi's forces crossed the Yunnan border seven times, and were repulsed each time, with heavy losses, by the People's Liberation Army. In the process, Captain Shih Yeuh Sheng became a colonel, rising through the ranks as battlefield attrition cleared his path.

By winter 1952 the KMT had given up on going home. If General Mi was trapped in Burma, he would make the best of it, but his decision to remain indefinitely raised the hackles of uneasy politicians in Rangoon. The latter took their case to the United Nations, but their timing was unfortunate; a plea for help in ousting refugees from communism raised a storm of worldwide indignation, leaving Burmese troops to do the dirty work themselves.

They failed.

Rechristening his force the "Anti-Communist Army of National Safety," General Mi easily annihilated the Burmese strike force, using the attack as an excuse to cross the Salween River and secure Mong Shu by Christmas Eve. Mi forged a battlefield alliance with the rebel Mon and Karen tribes, already waging war against the Burmese government, and traded modern weapons for supplies of tungsten, which the Karens mined at Mawchi, eighty miles above Rangoon. In league with Karen rebels, KMT advance troops seized Pagun and Panga, thirty miles from Burma's capital—and there, at last, they were contained.

Confronted with the prospect of extinction in the next few days or weeks, the Burmese government threw everything it had behind a massive counterstroke, repulsing General Mi and forcing him across the Salween in the early days of March. Objections were renewed at the United Nations, branding Chiang Kai-shek as the aggressor, and in April 1953 the Burmese Kuomintang was censured, ordered to disarm and leave. Negotiations in Bangkok provided for evacuation of two thousand KMT guerrillas to Formosa, courtesy of the CIA's Civil Air Transport, but General Mi still had a few tricks up his sleeve. The "troops" who boarded planes that fall were really local tribesmen dressed in surplus uniforms and bearing rusty, antique arms. The backbone of the Kuomintang, with all its modern military gear, remained in place.

The Burmese government, beside itself with rage, launched new assaults against the KMT in early 1954. Mong Hsat was bombed and overrun, two thousand Chinese Nationalist troops disarmed and forcibly escorted to the Thai frontier. Reluctantly, Taiwan agreed to take five thousand more, along with some eleven hundred family members, but the sweep still left six thousand soldiers on the ground, recruiting from the local native tribes until their strength was doubled in the next six years. By 1961 the Burmese government was desperate enough to form a brief alliance with the Red Chinese, eleven thousand soldiers of the People's Army pushing south from Yunnan province to corral the KMT and drive them east, toward Laos and Thailand. When the push ran out of steam, eight thousand KMT survivors put down roots and cast about for ways to earn their daily bread, while keeping up their endless war against the traitors in Peking.

The answer lay in opium.

The homeless army might have picked a different course, with General Mi in charge, but he had fallen on the grim retreat from Burma, his demise attributed in various accounts to snakebite, fever, or a broken heart. Mi's death produced a vacuum at the top, and Colonel Shih Yeuh Sheng was quick to recognize his opportunity. Promoted to the rank of general by his own authority, he made a fortress out of Mae Salong, a mountain village ringed by jungle on all sides. Before the year was out, Sheng had extended his benevolent protection to a score of native villages, establishing connections with the Chinese dealers who procured their opium for resale in the south.

Sheng's self-promotion in the Kuomintang did not amuse his closest rivals for command. Before Sheng had a chance to wear his brand-new general's stars, he was confronted with dissension in the ranks, a rift that threatened to destroy the KMT. Around Tam Ngop, a stronghold in the wilderness beyond Chiang Mai, Lieutenant Colonel Li Wen Huan proclaimed himself a general in his own right, drawing off three thousand troops to form an army of his own. Encouraged by the trend toward independence, self-appointed General Ma Ching Ko led fifteen hundred men away to set up camp near Fang, along the Burmese border, going into business for himself. Ostensibly cut off from CIA support, despite persistent rumors to the contrary, the fractured KMT recruited heavily from Meo, Lahu, Shan, and other tribes. The leadership remained Chinese and staunchly anticommunist, but as the different factions peddled drugs and fought among themselves for territory, slowly reestablishing their Burmese outposts to the west, the rank and file was drawn increasingly from native tribes, among whom cultivating opium was an established way of life.

Sheng's lucky star shone bright in 1969, when several thousand troops of General Huan's gave up the fight and were repatriated to Taiwan. From there, it took only a minor shove to topple Huan, allowing him to salvage face by entering a "partnership" with Sheng, to form a new "Chinese Irregular Force" under Sheng's general command. In nearby Vietnam, meanwhile, the year-old Tet offensive had destroyed the CIA's inherent confidence in its ability to stem the tide of communism single-handed. Allies were required in Laos and Thailand, even if their price was calculated by the kilogram, with potent China white flown back to the United States in military body bags. Sheng fattened on the profits from his lethal cottage industry, cooperating with the Chiu Chou dealers to ensure delivery abroad, and if the CIA made money on the side, what of it?

General Sheng had spent a lifetime fighting communism, to defend free enterprise. The totals in his several foreign bank accounts assured him there was ample cash to go around.

But there would never be *enough.*

In thirty years of dealing drugs and almost fifty years of warfare, Sheng had learned one thing about himself and all the other members of his race: no man was ever truly satisfied.

Religious trappings and political affiliations came to nothing in the end, where human greed and hunger were concerned. The Chinese communists spent billions on defense and massacred their dissidents like sheep because they feared the loss of power. The United States supported brutal puppet states because a third-world revolution jeopardized established interests, flushing precious dollars down the drain. The revolutionaries hijacked planes and murdered innocent civilians in a bid to seize the wealth and power they had so long been denied.

All greed. All vanity.

Sheng smiled when Western journalists described him as criminal, corrupting children he would never meet, a world away from Mae Salong. He knew the politicians and policemen who secured their own positions by declaring "war on drugs" around election time, relapsing into apathy and opening the gates again when they had finished counting votes. It was a game with basic rules and million-dollar stakes, which General Sheng had mastered at an early age.

Tonight he would be sitting down to play the game with strangers, but he had no fear of being beaten by a wild card in the deck. Sheng made the rules himself, around Meung Nam, and he had never learned to lose.

Once Joseph and Yodmani were disarmed—"for reasons of security," the KMT guerrilla leader said—they were escorted through the trees for several hundred yards to reach a string of mules the troops had waiting. Wen-Ling Shyu had been expected, so a sturdy animal was waiting for Joe, but Yodmani was the odd man out. Instead of forcing him to walk, the leader of their escort had Yodmani double up with one of the guerrillas, straddling the donkey's rump and grinning ruefully at Joe as they began their final march.

It took three-quarters of an hour, and the sun was fading fast before they cleared the tree line and began their climb toward Mae Salong. The mountain village called up mental images of something from medieval times, a feudal baron's stronghold overlooking his domain, but the illusion vanished as they passed by sentries packing M-16's, a guard post that included stacks of sandbags and a big M-60 light machine gun covering the road.

Dismounting on the outskirts of the village, Lee and his companion were surrounded by a team of six guerrillas while the others led their mules away to food and water. Feeling rather like a prisoner in custody, Joe trailed the leader of their team along an unpaved street, past busy market stalls, still climbing toward the center of the town.

At first glance, Mae Salong appeared to be a village under siege. The uniforms were everywhere, some of the occupying soldiers bearing arms, as if they feared an enemy was on the way to challenge them. A closer look, and Joseph caught a different feeling—more like San Diego when the fleet was in and several thousand sailors hit the streets in search of ways to spend their time and money. The civilians represented several mountain tribes, existing side by side in what appeared to be perfect harmony.

Sheng's military compound was the centerpiece of Mae Salong. It occupied the high ground, with machine guns and a pair of vintage howitzers commanding homes and shops along three sides; the north flank, Joseph knew from briefings on the trail, was guarded by a sheer rock face that rose three hundred feet above a plunging river valley, with the forest floor another thousand feet below. The compound was enclosed by concertina wire, with lookout towers spaced one hundred yards apart, and sentries armed with automatic weapons flanked an open gate that faced the village marketplace. On Joseph's left, a line of jeeps and half-ton trucks were lined up with their tailgates to the wire.

The inner compound was a patchwork quilt of metal Quonset huts, bamboo and plywood structures, and a line of canvas tents along the east perimeter. A fair-sized generator sputtered near the center of the camp, with insulated cables strung from poles like spokes in an exaggerated spiderweb. Across the compound, near the barracks buildings, Joseph saw a military chopper crouching on its helipad.

The general's CP was an elevated structure, riding on stilts above the barren earth, a four-foot crawl space underneath. They lost three guards as they began to climb the wooden steps, two more on Sheng's front porch as they were shown inside. Above their heads, an antique ceiling fan worked doggedly to stir the muggy air.

Lee had expected General Sheng to fall somewhere between the mythic characters of Fu Manchu and Genghis Khan, inscrutable and cruel. Instead, the man who stood before him was a thickset senior citizen in faded khaki, five-foot-five, with thinning iron-gray hair combed straight back from his face. He wore no military decorations, but the gold stars on his collar glinted in the light from naked fixtures overhead.

Their escort snapped a clean salute and made the introductions, Joseph and Yodmani bowing to their host in lieu of shaking hands. Lee handed Sheng the letter from Chiang Fai, in Bangkok, watching as the general read it through and placed it on his desk.

"Your journey from the south was satisfactory?"

"We had some trouble near the end," Lee said. "Our guide was killed. We would have joined him if your soldiers hadn't come along."

Sheng listened as their escort rattled off a brief description of the firefight, noting that the dead had been relieved of weapons, ammunition, and a walkie-talkie one of them had carried on his belt.

"Do you have enemies in Thailand, Mr. Shyu?"

Lee shrugged. "They didn't introduce themselves," he

said, "but they were on the trail ahead of us, not following. Hill bandits, I suppose."

"Perhaps." The general did not sound convinced. "In any case, you have arrived and you are under my protection now."

"I wish to thank you, on behalf of those I represent, for granting me the privilege of a visit to your home."

"A small thing," General Sheng replied. "But Mae Salong is not my home. I am without a country, doomed to finish out my days in exile."

"You have triumphed in adversity," Joseph said. "Even in the West, your name is spoken with respect by men of influence."

"A wise man cultivates his friends and leaves no enemies behind." The general smiled and shifted gears without a hitch. "We had expected you to come alone."

"I thought it best to bring a friend with knowledge of the local tribes and customs. I apologize for any inconvenience my presumption may have caused."

Sheng fanned the air with chubby fingers, frowning. "Not at all. A stranger would be foolish to proceed without a guide, on unfamiliar ground. You are fatigued? In need of rest?"

"Perhaps a shower."

"Certainly. A banquet has been laid, to celebrate your visit, but we still have ample time. Refresh yourselves. An hour, shall we say?"

More bowing as they took their leave of General Sheng and were escorted to their quarters near the motor pool. Along the way, Lee managed to identify the armory and the communications hut, located near the generator. He had no idea how either one could serve him yet, but they were points of passing interest, all the same.

Their private quarters measured twelve by fifteen feet, with plywood walls and floor, a corrugated tin roof overhead. The furnishings consisted of two cots, a pair of camp chairs stacked together in one corner, and an oil lamp hanging from the central beam. Fresh khakis, size approximate, lay folded on the cots.

They took the clean clothes with them as their escort

led the way to the communal showers. Once inside, they stripped and gratefully gave up their filthy hiking outfits to be cleaned and pressed. The chunky soap was rough on Joseph's skin, but after two days on the trail, the steaming shower felt like heaven, helping him relax.

Almost.

Two sets of khakis waiting.

Why had General Sheng feigned surprise at finding two guests in his camp? Of course, his gofers could have rushed to lay out the clothing while Joseph and Yodmani visited the general in his office. Still . . .

Watch out.

It would not do to take the obvious for granted here, on hostile ground. Lee had to think ahead, anticipate the unexpected where he could, and be prepared to roll with any punch General Sheng might throw.

He turned the shower off and grabbed a towel.

For openers, he didn't plan to keep the old man waiting. They had been invited to a feast, and if it turned out that sudden death was on the menu, Joseph was prepared to eat his fill.

23

The general's banquet hall was a pavilion near the helipad, a canvas roof and bamboo poles, constructed in the fashion of an army mess tent. The tables were plywood supported by sawhorses and flanked by wooden benches, with seating for at least a hundred diners. At the north end of the tent, Sheng's private table occupied an elevated platform, facing the pavilion where his officers would soon assemble.

Lee had given up on trying to surmise the general's troop strength. The official estimates ranged anywhere from seven thousand to eleven thousand men, but Joseph guessed that barely half the smaller number would reside at Mae Salong. The central compound would accommodate five hundred, maximum—including most of Sheng's command staff—while the others spent their nights with wives or lovers in the village proper. Boil it down, Lee made the odds at roughly fifteen hundred to one, assuming he could count upon Yodmani for assistance in the crunch.

Their escort from the trail was sporting captain's bars when he returned to fetch them for the banquet, going through the snap-salute routine again when they met General Sheng. The Kuomintang commander wore a full dress uniform, complete with braid and combat decorations, polished brass, an automatic pistol on his hip. He waved the captain off and led them to the dais, seating Joseph on his right, Yodmani on his left.

"I seldom entertain," Sheng told them, seeming perfectly at ease. "The last time was, I think, two years ago. A

Burmese delegation, seeking my assistance with the Shans."

They traded anecdotes about the business as a group of native women made the rounds with fruits and salad, steaming broth, great serving bowls of rice and curried shrimp, roast pork, and stir-fried vegetables. The food was excellent, and Lee tried some of everything, his appetite enormous after two full days of pemmican and dog-meat stew. He let their host direct the conversation back and forth from politics to the narcotics trade, discovering that they were two sides of a single coin for General Sheng. The KMT commander hated communists, specifically the ruling party in Beijing, and he would fund his war against the infidels by any means available. If leaders of the free world would support him as they had in bygone days, before the left-wing liberals seized control of Washington, Sheng would be perfectly content to halt the trade in opium.

Or so he said.

Lee recognized the speech for what it was, a mincing sidestep to avoid responsibility for personal involvement in the narco trade. Some forty years had passed since leaders of the Kuomintang abandoned dreams of "liberating" China, but the general still used slogans from the 1950's to conceal his greed.

With variations, Joe had heard the argument a hundred times before. Colombians were not to blame for turning out cocaine, since Mother Nature predetermined crops and climate in their native land; the peons had a choice of growing coca leaves or sitting back to watch their children starve. In Turkey, opium supported peasant families and allowed their government to stockpile arms against the cruel Bulgarians and Yugoslavs. When agents of the CIA shipped heroin from Vietnam to the United States in military transport planes, they served a higher cause by propping up the pro-American regime.

All bullshit, covering a lust for money, power, and prestige.

Their plates were cleared away, and coffee had been served, when General Sheng stood up to make a speech.

His officers fell silent, breaking off their private conversations, waiting for the great man to hold forth.

"Tonight," Sheng said, "we have been honored by the presence of a guest from the United States. Not all Americans, it seems, have sold their birthright and their souls to communist aggressors in the name of peace."

A murmur from the audience, with several captains and lieutenants rapping on their tables in appreciation of the general's words.

"Unfortunately," Sheng continued, "I must also sound a solemn note this evening, for I have been warned against the presence of a traitor in our midst."

A different kind of rumble from the crowd this time, and Joseph felt the short hairs bristling on his nape. Instead of seeming shocked, he tried to show the proper interest for a stranger in the midst of lifelong comrades, listening while secrets are revealed.

"One here tonight has been accused of acting as a spy for the authorities," Sheng said, "attempting to destroy us from within. His name is known to me, and I have promised trusted friends that I will supervise his punishment myself."

The general glanced at Lee—another chill—then swiveled toward Yodmani with a brooding frown. The Thai was staring back at Sheng with nervous eyes, the color draining from his face. His hands were trembling, and he tucked them out of sight.

"The traitor is—"

Yodmani bolted, toppling his chair and nearly going down before he caught himself and saved it, lunging off the dais with a strangled cry of panic. Uniforms were waiting for him there, two corporals pinning him between them as a sergeant stepped in close and drove his fist into Yodmani's gut. The fight went out of him with that, and he was dragged away, boots scraping in the dust.

Lee kept his seat, already wondering if he could reach Sheng's throat before they beat him down. It seemed improbable, but if he had no other choice . . .

He swallowed hard and played his final ace. "How did you know?"

The general cocked an eyebrow, as silent as the others in the mess tent.

"I did not. A friend in Bangkok warned me to beware of new acquaintances. I played a hunch, as you would say in the United States. Your friend betrayed himself, through cowardice."

"My friend? I barely know the man."

"Of course." The general's frown betrayed a healthy dose of skepticism. "Some would say that only a policeman travels with a known informer. As for me, I always give a new associate the chance to prove himself."

"I'm listening."

"You are my guest tonight. The traitor will be questioned, to identify his contacts and discover how much damage he has done. Tomorrow morning, you will earn my gratitude by serving in the role of *kuei-tzu shou*—his executioner. When it is done, we shall have business to discuss."

"My pleasure." Lee put everything he had behind the smile.

"Until tomorrow, then. I know you must be weary after traveling so far."

A sergeant with an AK-47 accompanied Joseph to his quarters, and he lingered at the door, on guard, once Lee was safe inside.

So much for trust.

The guard confirmed Sheng's suspicion and prevented Lee from slipping out while they were working on Yodmani, milking him for everything he knew.

How long could he expect Yodmani to hold out?

Not long.

It would depend upon technique, of course, the tools employed by Sheng's inquisitors and their zeal to finish off the job. If they enjoyed their work enough, he might have hours, but if they were anxious to be done with it and find themselves some women, he imagined that

Yodmani could be broken rapidly, the crucial information sifted from his early screams.

Lee had noted the hut where Sheng had penned his prisoner, the same two corporals standing guard outside. It stood between the general's own CP and the communications hut, set back some distance, toward the armory.

A plan was taking shape in Joseph's mind, but he would have to think it through before he made a move. The general and his sentries would be counting on impulsive action, ready for a reckless break to brand their second guest as an accomplice in Yodmani's crime. To save himself, Lee knew that he would have to gamble, bide his time, and trust Yodmani to delay the end as long as possible. If he could spare an hour or two . . .

Lee turned the oil lamp down until it barely cast a glow, afraid of dousing it entirely, since he had no matches of his own. He stretched out on his cot, still fully clothed, and focused on the rafters overhead. Inside his mind he carried out a dress rehearsal of his plan, anticipating its problems and enumerating its hazards.

Five hundred men in camp, perhaps three thousand more outside, plus the civilians who depended on their trade. Lee's only ally was a captive, like himself, who might be seriously injured by the time they met again—if Joseph ever got that far.

The odds were too damned long to even qualify as odds. It seemed a clear-cut case of suicide, but sitting on his hands would buy only a few more hours, at best. When he had finished with Yodmani, General Sheng would start on Lee, dissecting him by inches while his answers to innumerable questions were recorded for posterity.

No fucking way.

If he was bound to die, the least he could do was try to take a couple of the bastards with him. Raise a little hell and shake them up a bit before they cut him down.

Lee waited for an hour, counting off the seconds in his mind and sweating through his khakis as he lay there in the semidarkness. Running down the details of his half-assed game plan one more time. Convinced, for what it might be worth, that he had done his best with what he had.

It was approaching ten-thirty when he got up, turned up the lamp, and clomped across the plywood floor to poke his head outside. The guard was on alert, Lee's footsteps having given him away, and he made no objection when his charge expressed a need to visit the latrine.

Lee knew the way—his destination was near the showers—and his watchdog followed silently, uninterested in conversation with a guest-prisoner. At the latrine, he took up a position in the doorway, leaving Joe to choose a toilet stall and shut himself inside.

Lee spent a moment fumbling with his trousers, making bathroom sounds as he withdrew the clasp knife from his pocket, opening the three-inch blade. He ran a thumb along the cutting edge to satisfy himself, and went down on his knees before the polished wooden seat, delivering his most sincere rendition of a seasick baritone.

Again.

Behind him, boots approaching. Joseph gave it everything he had, a finger down his throat to take the place of method acting, tasting bile and remnants of his supper on the second time around.

Outside his stall, the sergeant asked him what was wrong. Joe let the answer gag him, thrashing with an arm against the thin partition on his left. The doors were not equipped with locks, and Lee was ready when the sergeant crowded in behind him, huddled with his face above the hole where countless buttocks had rested in their time.

The hand on Joseph's shoulder was a trifle tentative, his watchdog still uncertain how—or whether—he should help. Lee gauged the distance, waiting for the sergeant to repeat his question, leaning closer with his rifle pointed at the floor, his throat exposed.

Lee struck, both hands around the clasp knife as he twisted, slashing left to right across the sergeant's throat, snagging on the windpipe for an instant, blinded as a pumping jet of blood exploded in his face. The sergeant staggered backward, trying desperately to raise his weapon, but his hands would not cooperate, and Joseph slapped the muzzle down.

He struck again, the short blade disappearing on the left side of the sergeant's neck, fresh blood exploding from the ragged wound. His enemy was dying, robbed of any chance to speak, but he had strength enough to kick Lee in the chest and drive him back against the toilet seat with bruising force.

Rebounding, Joseph dropped his knife and used both hands to grapple for the AK-47, twisting it away and hammering the butt against his adversary's forehead. Twice. A third time. Stopping only when he knew the sergeant was unconscious, seconds short of death.

Lee stood above his kill and waited with the automatic rifle in his hands. A passing soldier might have heard the struggle, but his options would be limited: investigate or raise a general alarm. When nothing happened after sixty seconds, Joe decided it was safe enough to hit Phase Two.

The sergeant was a slightly smaller man, his khakis snug and badly bloodstained, but the uniform would have to do. Lee shoved his own clothes down the open toilet, propped his late assailant on the bench seat, knees drawn up against his chest, and took a final look around the stall before he left. The bloody floor was hopeless. He would have to keep his fingers crossed and pray that no one wandered in to notice it before he reached Yodmani and the inquisition team.

Outside, Lee kept his head down, sticking to the shadows when he could, the AK-47 slung across his shoulder. Casual. There was a chance some roving sentry might have seen him bound for the latrine, and the emergence of a guard without his prisoner would sound alarms. If he was intercepted now . . .

He slipped the rifle off its sling and tucked it underneath his arm, for quicker access in case of an emergency. He passed the generator shack—no opposition yet—and moved behind the structure housing the camp's radios. Ahead of him, the armory and the interrogation hut, a solitary corporal standing guard.

How many others were inside? Lee reckoned two, at

least, for an efficient job, but he would never know for sure until he stepped across that threshold and confronted them. He loitered in the shadow of the general's CP for a moment, making sure he had the corporal to himself, before he ducked his head and set off on a rough collision course.

The lookout saw him coming, but he missed the crimson stains on Joseph's shirt and pants until the new arrival stood within arm's reach. Too late, he seemed to have a question on his lips when Joseph raised his head and swung the AK-47 like a club, the wooden stock connecting with a solid *thunk* that dropped the corporal in his tracks.

Lee didn't bother with a follow-up. Already running out of time, he tried the door and found it open, pushing through and closing it behind him, standing with the rifle braced against his hip.

Damrong Yodmani, pale and naked, occupied a wooden chair positioned in the center of the room. He was surrounded by three KMT guerrillas, one of them with captain's bars, another with the chevrons of a sergeant on his sleeve. The captain wore a pistol on his belt, the holster flap secured, while his companions were apparently unarmed.

No matter. They were dead the moment they set eyes on Joseph Lee.

He shot the captain first, the AK-47 set on semiautomatic, two rounds blowing him away before he had a chance to reach his sidearm. Pivoting, Lee nailed the private with a chest wound, left of center, and was ready for it when the sergeant used his only option, diving for the gun.

It was a decent effort, but he never had a prayer. The AK-47's spout was eighteen inches from his face when Joseph squeezed the trigger, and the slug drilled through his septum, tumbling by the time it blew a fist-size exit wound behind one ear. Momentum kept the sergeant moving, even so, and Lee was forced to back-step, butting up against the doorjamb as the body thumped against his knees.

Time blurring as he flicked the clasp knife open, working on Yodmani's bonds. Lee registered the more outstanding burns and bruises, glittering utensils laid out on a tray beside the straight-backed chair. They had been working up to major surgery when he arrived, but the preliminaries had been bad enough. Yodmani's face was swollen and discolored, eyes half-closed, and he was sluggish in response to Joe's demand for speed.

Lee found Yodmani's clothing wadded in a corner, helped him dress while keeping one eye on the door. How long before the gunshots brought a troop of reinforcements down upon them? Was the rifle team already there, lined up and waiting for a target to reveal itself?

Yodmani's shirt had lost its buttons, hanging open to reveal his mottled chest, but he was standing on his own as Joseph reached the door. Emerging from the hut, Lee braced himself, his weapon set for automatic fire, but there was no one waiting for them.

Yet.

"Nah lee?"

The question posed in Mandarin, its answer instantaneous.

"This way!"

Lee saw them coming, half a dozen uniforms, and hosed them with a burst of cover fire that emptied half his magazine.

"The armory!" he snapped, propelling his companion with a shove between the shoulder blades. "Let's move!"

It was the only chance they had, and Lee would have bet that it wasn't good enough.

The long, low building's sliding doors would admit a vehicle, and they were guarded by a sentry with an M-16. Lee stitched a burst across his chest from twenty yards and grabbed his fallen rifle on the run. The sliding doors weren't heavy, and they were not locked. He left one of them open wide enough to serve Yodmani as a gun port, handing him the M-16 and moving on to look for something they might use to save themselves.

The armory was like a lethal supermarket, automatic

rifles lined in standing wooden racks along one wall, the corresponding crates of magazines and ammunition labeled in Chinese and English. Shopping in a hurry, Joseph found grenades (American and Russian), crated submachine guns, an M-60 with its belts of ammo neatly folded into boxes marked USMC. The heavy shit included mortars, flamethrowers, and RPG's—the Russian one-man rocket launchers favored by guerrilla fighters from the Middle East to Nicaragua and Namibia.

Yodmani was providing cover fire as Joseph made his choice. The RPG's weighed roughly fifteen pounds apiece, unloaded, and they measured something over three feet long. Lee tucked one underneath each arm and left them near the open door, returning for a crate of high-explosive rounds. The RPG "grenades" weighed five pounds each and loaded by insertion in the launcher's muzzle, with the bulbous tip exposed. Lee knew from law-enforcement briefings that the rockets sprouted stabilizing fins in flight, and were designed to penetrate at least a foot of armored steel.

The job he had in mind should be a snap, if he could only keep from getting killed before he pulled it off.

Outside, a group of riflemen returned Yodmani's fire for several seconds, but a shouting officer restrained them. Joseph guessed that he was sweating out the risk of stray rounds sparking an explosion that would tear the armory apart, along with much of the surrounding camp. The momentary lull gave Joseph hope; they might be trapped inside the armory, but they could get a few licks in before they died.

He braced one of the rocket launchers on his shoulder, edging toward the partly open door. "Watch out for backflash," he advised Yodmani, nodding toward the open crate of rockets on the floor, "and keep me loaded if you can."

Lee didn't need to think about a target for the first projectile. Sheng's command post would have been deserted at this hour on a normal evening, but a clutch of riflemen were huddled in its shadow now, awaiting orders to advance or hold their ground. Joe framed the stilted building in his sights, squeezed off, and listened to the *whooooosh* of the departing high-explosive round.

It wasn't quite a bull's-eye—he had jerked the trigger, throwing his aim off a bit—but the results were still impressive. General Sheng's CP appeared to swell before his eyes, like an inflatable cartoon house, the illusion shattered by a combination thunderclap and fireball, literally bringing down the house.

Lee passed the empty launcher to Yodmani, shouldering the second RPG and shifting to his right. The generator hut was smoldering, where fiery bits of wood had landed on the roof, and men in uniform were scrambling around to fetch a ladder and douse the flames before they had a chance to spread.

Good luck.

His second rocket turned the generator into scrap and blacked out the compound except for oil lamps here and there. Exchanging launchers with Yodmani, Joseph marveled at the absence of return fire from his enemies. How much of their facility were they prepared to lose, to save the armory?

He reasoned that the radios were dead without the generator, but there might be backup batteries, so Joseph used his next explosive round on the communications hut. Another hit, his stomach rolling as a human torch came out of nowhere, trailing flames as he ran. Somebody grabbed the runner, and they went down in a thrashing, screaming heap.

"Again."

He took the loaded RPG and knelt to give himself a better angle on the only lookout tower he could see. Its spotlight had been neutralized, but the machine gun perched up there would have a perfect field of fire as they emerged. Joe lined it up, squeezed off, and watched the comet race to meet his enemies.

Not perfect, but it did the job—a flash of red and orange, immediately followed by the *crump* of the explosion. Bodies and equipment airborne as the tower came apart, one leg sheared off, the structure flattening a section of the barbed-wire fence when it collapsed.

He dropped the RPG and found Yodmani with the second launcher primed and ready. "Can you fire it?"

"I don't know."

"Find out. Waste anything you want, except the vehicles, and then reload. I've got a shopping list to check."

He moved along the standing rack of rifles, picking up an M-16 and making sure its clip was full. Two bandoliers of extra magazines and one of hand grenades. A single-action Browning automatic tucked inside his belt. Lee passed the flamethrower, then doubled back, deciding it was too good to resist.

Yodmani's practice round had missed the general's helicopter and destroyed a nearby Quonset hut, but he was grinning ear-to-ear, another rocket set to fly.

"Suit up." Lee handed him two bandoliers and fed Yodmani's M-16 a new magazine. "You'll have another shot outside, then ditch it. And for God's sake, don't shoot me."

"No problem." Grinning. Tickled pink to pay the bastards back.

Joe slung the M-16 across his chest, the strap around his neck. It was an awkward fit, especially with the bandolier, but it allowed him to accommodate the flamethrower's harness, adjusting the shoulder straps that secured twenty-pound tanks of fuel and compressed air on his back. A hose connected fuel tanks to the wand, equipped with double pistol grips. The rear grip twisted like a motorcycle's throttle, to control the flow of fuel; its forward mate was fitted with a trigger, for ignition on command.

"Hang on a second."

A blunder would be fatal, once they made their move. Reluctantly Joe faced the nearest empty wall and gave the weapon's throttle half a crank, remembering to press the trigger just in time. A hissing tongue of flame erupted from the nozzle, lighting up the whole damned wall before Lee shut it down.

"Sweet Jesus!"

Now they *had* to leave, before the licking flames spread far enough to feed on ammunition and explosives. Moving toward the door, Joe braced himself for what he knew might be the last few moments of his life. Yodmani followed with the RPG, his shirt still open, burns and bruises seemingly anesthetized by violence.

It was payback time.

"On three."

When Joe cleared the doorway, Sheng's rifle squad was nearly in position, creeping nearer in an effort to surprise their enemies and save the arsenal. Their leader tried to get a shot off at the moving targets, but he never had a chance as Joseph set the night on fire. Stick figures rolling on the ground and screaming as they fried.

He swung the nozzle left to right and cut a fiery swath in front of him, igniting canvas, plywood, human flesh. The screaming seemed to come from miles away, and then Yodmani joined the chorus with his final rocket, taking out another barracks on the run.

"The trucks!"

Yodmani ran ahead of him, already firing with his M-16 at shadow men along the wire. Lee torched a line of tents and caught a pair of sentries in the open as he followed, crisping them with liquid fire. He felt the searing heat reflected on his hands and face, but he gave no thought to easing off the throttle as he trailed Yodmani toward the motor pool. A few more seconds, now . . .

The tanks began to fail him as he reached the trucks. He launched a final plume of fire along his backtrack, dumped the harness where he stood, and flicked the safety off his rifle as he moved along the line of vehicles.

"No keys!" Yodmani shouted from the cover of a half-ton, firing off a burst at the remaining sentry tower.

Joseph checked the nearest jeep, heart pounding as he recognized a vintage model dating from the days of the Korean War. It was a virtual antique, but well-maintained —and best of all, it needed no ignition key. He slid behind the steering wheel and punched the starter, hanging on and offering silent thanks as the engine caught and held.

"Get in!"

Yodmani threw himself across the shotgun seat as Joseph popped the clutch, and they were rolling, past the other vehicles, beneath the tower, with a swarm of bullets snapping close behind. The windshield frosted over, shattered, and was gone. Yodmani fired a burst at sentries on the gate, then lobbed a frag grenade behind them as the jeep cleared the wire. Its flash and thunder flattened several khaki soldiers following on foot.

The village was awake, by now, but its defenders were disorganized, responding cautiously to sounds of battle from the general's compound. They were slow to act, confused as Joseph and Yodmani passed them in the speeding jeep, and no one tried to bar their way until they reached the marketplace.

Somehow, perhaps by walkie-talkie, word of their escape had spread into the streets of Mae Salong. A group of riflemen ran out to block the narrow road, but Joseph flicked his headlights on to blind them, bearing down on the accelerator while Yodmani used the last rounds in his magazine to clear the way. One soldier fell, and several others scattered for their lives, a solitary private standing rooted in his tracks by fear until the jeep rolled over him and left him crumpled in the dust.

Another block at breakneck speed, and they were taking hits from every side. Joe doused the lights and hunched down in his seat, Yodmani alternately spraying short bursts from his M-16 and tossing hand grenades in answer to the hostile fire. If they could last another ten or fifteen yards . . .

The sentries outside Mae Salong were waiting, laying down a wall of automatic fire at their approach. Joe braced his rifle on the dashboard, holding down the trigger as they blasted through the checkpoint, with the steep track dropping off in front of them.

The road was worse than he remembered from the mule ride hours earlier, with ruts that jarred the vehicle and threatened to unseat him as they sped along. Beside him, Joseph had a brief glimpse of Yodmani clinging to his seat with one hand and the dashboard with the other, looking green around the gills. Instead of slowing down, he pushed the jeep to even greater speeds, aware that Sheng's guerrillas would be organizing their pursuit by now.

The jeep was blowing steam and clanking ominously three miles out of Mae Salong. It died before they hit the four-mile mark, and Joseph steered it over to the shoulder of the winding mountain track. The river gorge was on their left, perhaps three hundred yards below. It seemed a rugged climb, but once they reached the river, Joseph knew that they could follow it until it joined the larger Te Kok, flowing just above Chiang Rai. Their options were to linger on the road and wait for Sheng to overtake them, and to strike off blindly through the trackless jungle, praying that they struck a friendly settlement before they starved to death or Sheng's guerrillas and civilian allies ran them down.

"I hope you're up to climbing," Joseph said.

Yodmani grimaced. "Do I have a choice?"

"We all have choices."

Glancing back along the road to Mae Salong, the Thai appeared resigned. "Let us begin."

24

The slope was gentler than it looked at first, with roots and branches offering support on their descent. With rifles slung across their backs, they scrambled down the bank at something like an average walking pace, allowing for the darkness and the wildlife scattering around them in the undergrowth. Joseph would have liked to rush, but knew they must not risk a slip that would send one or both of them careening down the hill.

A hundred feet below the road, the grade began to steepen. Joseph lost his footing twice on mud and sliding stones before he gave it up and turned around, descending ladder-style. With every sliding step, he paused to listen for vehicles above, a signal they were out of luck and out of time. When it remained quiet, he started wondering if General Sheng was wounded, even dead, but would not allow himself the luxury of hope.

Halfway between the road and river gorge, they struck a game trail that provided them with better footing, even though its angle of descent meant they would take more time to reach the water's edge. Lee's muscles cried for rest as they began to double-time along the trail, pain jolting through his hip, his knees and ankles, but he could not take the time to rest. Their lead was minimal, and Sheng had trackers who could stalk them through the forest like a hunter trailing game. Lee would think in terms of personal security only when they reached Chiang Rai.

And then?

How far did General Sheng's authority extend? He would have agents in Chiang Rai, of course, and with the

Triads on his side he could reach out to tag his enemies in Bangkok just as well. It struck Lee that he might not find a decent hiding place in Thailand—or in Southeast Asia—but the grim acknowledgment did nothing to relieve his sense of urgency.

They had escaped Sheng's clutches, seriously damaged his facility, and they were still alive. So far. The general had to run them down before he could avenge himself, and in the meantime they could score a few more points against their enemy.

They jogged along the trail for some two hundred yards before it disappeared without the slightest warning, swallowed up by jungle thick enough that it reduced their visibility to six or seven feet. Disgusted, Lee was on the verge of doubling back to seek another way when his companion pointed out a break in the surrounding undergrowth.

"Down there."

In fact, the trail had not run out, so much as it had changed direction, plunging down the hillside at an angle close to sixty-five degrees. It was a descent that would tax a mountain goat, but they were running out of time.

Would Sheng wait for daylight to begin the hunt? Could he afford to give his prey that much of a head start? It would take a good half-hour to double back along the trail in darkness, and Lee didn't know who might be waiting for them there.

"Let's do it, then."

Joe took the lead, devoutly wishing they could wait for dawn to light the way. He tested every step and handhold before committing to a move. Above all else, he concentrated on the descent and tried to make his mind a blank, forgetting they were absolutely helpless if a squad of snipers showed up on the game trail overhead. Lee didn't want to think about the rugged drop beneath his feet, or reaching out to grab a root and finding it was a pissed-off snake.

The slope was bad enough, if he could just—

Yodmani's cry of terror drove an icy spike between Lee's shoulder blades. He heard the scuttle-scrape of sliding earth and braced himself, pressed flat against the hillside, tasting moss and dirt. Yodmani tumbled past him in a blur of twisted arms and legs, rebounding from a shelf of jagged rock, a bootheel cracking Joseph on the skull.

He nearly lost it then, his left hand slipping on a trailing vine as he was spun around to face the void. Lee hung suspended by his right arm, one heel braced against a jutting stone, and watched Yodmani fall.

It seemed to take forever, though he knew it must have been mere seconds, hearing one more scream before the crumpled body disappeared from sight. The jungle swallowed him, but Joseph marked Yodmani's progress by the sound of crashing undergrowth, a heavy impact somewhere far below.

How far?

He couldn't guess, and there was only one way to be sure. When he was able, Joseph twisted back around, retrieved his grip on Mother Earth, and started down the slope. The snail's pace had him cursing under his breath, impatient to be finished, but his rage was tempered by anxiety. He wondered if Yodmani's desperate cry had carried in the darkness, whether someone else was homing on the sound and using it to track his prey.

At any moment he expected gunfire from the trail, a bullet drilling through his skull to finish it and send his lifeless body tumbling down the slope. Another small-time loser, screwed for playing with the big boys when he didn't even understand the rules.

It might have taken twenty minutes or an hour to complete the descent; when he set foot on level ground again, the feeling of relief was almost sickening in its intensity. He staggered like a drunken sailor searching for his land legs, leaning on a handy tree until his equilibrium had nearly stabilized.

He called Yodmani's name three times before he got an answer from the shadows, following the voice and nearly stumbling over his companion in the dark. Yodmani lay where he had fallen, his shoulders braced against a log, his legs splayed in front of him at crazy angles.

Broken.

Joseph didn't need a medical degree to know the left leg had been snapped above the knee, and once again below. The right was something else, not fractured quite so much as it was twisted out of shape. It took a second glance for Lee to realize Yodmani's heel was facing toward the front, a man prepared to walk both ways at once.

Except, in this case, Joseph knew Yodmani could not stand, much less continue on their march.

"How is it?"

Wasting time because he could not think of anything to say.

"No pain," Yodmani said. "My back, I think. There is no feeling in my legs."

Small favors. Instead of saying it, he told Yodmani, "I can carry you."

"For thirty miles?" Yodmani shook his head. "Impossible."

It could be more than thirty, Joseph knew, and jungle all the way unless they found themselves a stray canoe. He would be lucky if they made a hundred yards, Yodmani riding piggyback.

"You're right." He brought the rifle off its sling and checked the safety. "We can face them here."

"Do not be foolish." As he spoke, Yodmani shed his bandoliers, extracting two spare magazines and two grenades, depositing the rest at Joseph's feet. "I can delay them long enough to be of some assistance, I believe."

Lee choked on his reply. "Goddammit!"

"You must go now. Even with the darkness, you have little time."

Joe glanced around at ferns and rocks, another fallen tree. "You haven't got much cover here."

"It makes no difference. Go."

Joe stood and slipped the extra bandoliers around his neck, still hesitating. "Listen—"

"There is nothing more to say."

"Okay. I'll see you."

"Yes, perhaps."

Reluctantly he turned and struck off to the south, along the riverbed. Five minutes later, when he turned to check his trail, Yodmani had already disappeared.

"God*dammit*!"

Moving with a purpose now, he took himself away from there, the darkness opening before him, closing tight again once he was past.

Despite the earphones, it was noisy in the helicopter's cockpit. The general sometimes wished he could obtain a newer model, with the rotor blades constructed out of fiberglass to minimize their racket, but he would make do with what he had.

The gunship circled over Mae Salong, a quarter of the camp in flames, before the pilot leveled out and headed south. Below them, on the winding mountain road, his troops were following in jeeps and trucks, prepared to bag the enemy alive if possible, but pledged to bring them down at any cost. Sheng hoped he would have a chance to question them himself, prolong their agony until they prayed for death, but he would settle for a quick, clean kill if necessary.

Just so long as it was not *too* clean.

He still had trouble understanding what had happened back in camp. The soldiers who had bungled their assignments were beyond his reach forever, now, and Sheng was forced to speculate on their mistakes. It made no difference in the long run—only time and money would repair the damage—but the general thought it might have helped, somehow, to know exactly where his troops went wrong.

If nothing else, it would have eased his mind to know the fault was not his own.

Of course, it would have been a simple thing to kill both men immediately, after he received his warning from the south. Still, there was money on the table, and the prospect of a major sale to new clients in America. Sheng's greed had caused him to delay, take chances, and the game had blown up in his face.

It was a good thing, Sheng reflected, that he answered

only to himself. As for his "friends" in Bangkok who had sent the traitors north, they would have much to answer for when he had finished cleaning up the problems in his own backyard.

Beneath them, once they cleared the mountain peak and Mae Salong, the jungle was a vast expanse of midnight shadows, more like sea than solid earth. A herd of elephants could hide beneath the trees down there, and pass unnoticed as the helicopter skimmed above them, searching aimlessly. Two men would be impossible to find, unless . . .

He knew they were following the road, or had been, when they left the village. If they kept on driving, it should be a simple thing to track them down and cut off their escape. If they were forced to leave the jeep, at least his infantry would have a starting point from which to launch their search.

The general took a breath and held it, trying to relax. He told himself that there was nowhere for his prey to hide. The native villagers throughout Meung Nam depended on his army for protection and liaison with their buyers in the south. They would do nothing to protect his enemies.

It all came down to time and patience, in the end. Experience and ancestry had taught Sheng how to wait for perfect opportunities and seize them when they finally arrived. He had survived this long because he never made impulsive moves or let his guard down, even in the presence of a friend. It had been said, and more than once, that General Sheng was cautious to a fault.

Except tonight.

His anger called for action, and he had joined the helicopter's crew against the stern advice of his subordinates, because he could not—would not—let another huntsman claim his prize. If Sheng could not dispatch his enemies in person, he would be there soon enough to revel in their death while they were warm, their blood still fresh upon the earth.

And if he found them first . . .

Behind him, in the chopper's cabin, sat four soldiers.

Three of them were armed with automatic rifles; number four was wrapped in belts of ammunition for the big M-60 braced across his lap. As members of the general's private guard, they had been chosen on the basis of their martial skills and sheer ferocity.

A perfect killing team.

Now, all they needed was a target.

Sudden static in the earphones as the pilot spoke to him and pointed through the windscreen toward the narrow road below. Sheng saw the jeep at once, their spotlight stabbing through the night to show him it had been abandoned.

Closer now, but where?

He keyed his microphone and started barking orders to his people on the ground, informing them of the discovery, demanding speed. They would begin to sweep the darkened jungle while his infantry moved in to launch a more efficient, systematic search.

They had all night, and then all day tomorrow, if it came to that. How far could two men travel in the darkness, one of them a stranger to the jungle, the other weakened by interrogation?

Not far.

Damrong Yodmani heard the hunters coming from a half-mile out, their progress marked by snapping branches, tumbling stones, a muttered curse when one of them came close to falling on the hillside. Pushing with his arms, still numb below the waist and thankful for the fact, he made himself more comfortable with his back against the fallen log.

Lee had been right about the cover; it was pitiful, but it would have to do. Yodmani had been frightened by the prospect of a move, afraid that it would rouse his sleeping legs and set them screaming in their pain, deprive him of the chance to pay Sheng's soldiers back in kind.

He checked his M-16 again. A full magazine in place, and two more in his lap, where he could reach them in a hurry if he got the chance. The frag grenades were wedged beneath his buttocks, one on either side, their safety pins already loosened. When he judged the soldiers were within two hundred yards, Yodmani pulled the pins and tossed them both away.

No turning back, from that point on.

The two grenades were trapped beneath his useless legs, deadweight preventing the ejection of their safety levers and the detonation that would follow seconds afterward. If someone moved him, the lethal canisters would spray their shrapnel in a killing radius of thirty feet.

No problem.

While he lived, Yodmani was not going anywhere.

He estimated thirty yards between the hunters and their quarry, shouldering the M-16 and sighting down its barrel into darkness, following their sounds. If only they had dragged their feet until sunrise helped him see . . .

A moving shadow near the tree line. Yodmani fired a measured burst, the rifle's muzzle brake emitting star-shaped flashes in the dark. An awkward thrashing in the undergrowth encouraged him to think that he had scored a hit.

The others opened fire at once, some of them aimlessly, a couple sighting on his muzzle flash. The bullets hummed around him, clipping ferns and drilling through the log behind him. One round struck his leg, and then another. Still no pain, but he was conscious of a tacky wetness soaking through his khaki pants between crotch and knee.

If they could sight on muzzle flashes, so could he. Yodmani raked the hillside, working through one magazine and slapping in another, firing nearly half of that as well before a round scored above his waist.

Pain now.

His stomach was on fire, the acid spilling out to gnaw at other organs in his body cavity. Yodmani threw his left arm out to keep himself from falling, firing with his right hand at the moving shadows. Then another bullet struck him, and another.

It was curious, he thought, that multiplying lethal wounds only reduced the suffering. He recognized the signs of shock and took advantage of the creeping numbness, firing off the last rounds in his magazine and reaching for the one that still remained.

He nearly had it mated to the M-16's receiver when a member of the hunting party stepped in close and shot him in the face. Yodmani never felt the rough hands grip his wrists and ankles as the troops surrounded him and lifted him between them, laughing.

The concussive shock waves overtook Joe Lee a mile downstream. He hesitated, glancing back, and knew there was nothing he could do to help Yodmani. On the other hand, if he survived and made it back to Bangkok, there was still a chance that he could see the Thai avenged.

He had a fair idea of where to start, but getting there was something else again.

The notion of a boat had been a bitter jest between Yodmani and himself, a touch of gallows humor in the face of overwhelming odds, and Joe couldn't believe it when he stumbled over four canoes lined up along the riverbank. He scanned the forest, half-expecting someone to emerge and challenge him, before he realized the craft were doubtless left onshore to spare the owners toting them repeatedly between the river and their settlement.

All four had wooden paddles tucked inside, and Lee selected one at random, loading up his arms and bandoliers before he dragged his chosen vessel to the water's edge. He floated it by wading out until the water rose above his waist, then nearly tipped it as he hauled himself across the gunwale on the starboard side. The current spun him once, then pointed him downstream before he found his place—remembering to kneel—and started to apply the paddle, quickly alternating strokes on either side to speed the boat along. Sheng's commandos would be coming, now that they had finished with Yodmani, and he had no doubts about their wish to see him dead.

The helicopter found him fifteen minutes later, following the river like a giant prehistoric dragonfly in search of prey. Lee heard the rotors from a distance and was making for the eastern bank when he was blinded by a floodlight from above.

He dropped the paddle, reaching for his M-16 as a machine gun opened fire, the bullets marching past him in a line of tiny waterspouts. Lee fought the urge to duck, knowing he would capsize the canoe, and concentrated on returning fire.

The floodlight, first. Without it, they would be on more or less even terms with him, the darkness hindering his enemy and helping cancel out the twin advantages of elevation and mobility. He missed it on the first pass, forced to wait until the gunship turned and made another strafing run. At thirty yards he saw the muzzle of an automatic weapon winking at him from the open starboard door and heard the angry bullets whipping toward him, churning up the surface of the river.

The chopper's undercarriage would be armored, so Lee concentrated on the floodlight first, expending half a magazine before he blacked it out. The other half was wasted on trade-off with the faceless gunner, dueling with him as the helicopter passed almost directly overhead. At that, his adversary had the better of it, several bullets gouging splinters from the prow and gunwale of his boat before they struck the water and were lost.

Lee fumbled for the nearest bandolier, reloading, turning awkwardly to face the chopper as it made another pass from north to south, the airborne gunner measuring his bursts and firing for effect. Joe left him to it, sighting on the windscreen and the unseen pilot just behind it, holding down the trigger for a burst that emptied out his magazine within three seconds flat.

No time for judging the results, as half a dozen bullets hammered through the hull of his canoe, emerging well below the waterline. One of them grazed his thigh and burned across his calf in transit, but the sudden pain meant nothing. Lee was groping for another magazine, reloading on the move, as water spouted through the bullet holes and started pooling up around his knees.

In front of him, a hundred yards downstream, the helicopter had begun to pitch and yaw erratically, the rotors nearly stalling as it hovered for an instant, losing altitude and veering left, its nose aimed toward the trees. Lee felt the crash as much as heard it, gliding into range before the rising water reached mid-thigh. His M-16 was leveled at the gunship, covering the open door, in case the crash had been some kind of an elaborate ruse.

In retrospect, Lee thought it was the blast that finished him, the shock wave reaching out to slam him backward out of the canoe that was about to qualify as a submarine. He lost his rifle in the river, nearly lost himself as he forgot to breathe and then remembered underwater, gagging on the taste of silt and algae as he broke the surface, thrashing helplessly.

And he might still have lost it, but for pure dumb luck. Another twenty yards downstream, when he had more or less resigned himself to death by drowning, Lee was startled by the jolting impact of a buoyant object brushing past his face. He panicked for an instant, thinking crocodiles, but reached for it instinctively and then clung fast when it did not attempt to tear him limb from limb.

By slow degrees he realized it was a bench seat from the helicopter, vinyl over foam, designed for double duty as a life preserver if the pilot had to ditch his craft at sea.

Or in a river.

Lee hauled himself aboard as best he could, legs trailing in the water. He was leaving blood behind—did they have anything like South American piranha in the East? —but there was nothing he could do about it, short of giving up and letting go.

Not yet.

He was alive, and he still had work to do.

Lee held on tight and let the river carry him away.

25

"Let's move it, shall we?"

Gordon Flack was sick and tired of waiting, and he took it out on those around him, starting with his guards at home, progressing to his secretary and the gofers on his staff. At five o'clock it was the driver's turn to grin and bear it, hoping that the normal crush of Bangkok traffic would not force him to remain with Flack a moment longer than was absolutely necessary.

"Shouldn't be much longer, sir." Flack glaring at him from the rearview mirror. *Fuck you, very much.*

"I hope not."

Two blocks from the embassy on Wireless Road, and they were creeping like a goddamn snail, with cars and bicycles and *samlors* all around them, pressing close. Flack kept a sharp eye out for trouble, knowing it would be the perfect time and place for terrorists to strike. His car nearly immobilized, a sitting duck they couldn't miss.

Of course, the limousine was bulletproof from tires to windows, theoretically immune to hand grenades and dynamite, unless the little fuckers found a way to wire their charges up inside. Flack had the guarantees in writing, from the manufacturer, but whom would he complain to from the grave?

Ten days of silence, going on eleven, were responsible for Flack's hellacious case of nerves. He had been waiting with his fingers crossed, expecting news, since Joe Lee and his sidekick left the city, headed north. A native mercenary team had been recruited to eliminate them on the trail between Chiang Rai and Mae Salong, but there had been no word of a successful strike—which meant the mercs had failed. Reluctantly Flack had been forced to fall back on Plan B.

The other news, as sketchy as it was, had all been bad. Flack doubted they would ever know precisely what had happened at Mae Salong, but General Shih Yeuh Sheng was dead, along with an uncertain number of his men. Flack's personal relations with the Kuomintang were strained, to say the least, and he could not decide if they were truly ignorant about Joe Lee or if they were maintaining stubborn silence as a ploy to piss him off.

Where *was* the bastard?

Was he even still alive?

"Goddammit!"

"Sir?"

"Just drive."

"Yes, sir."

Flack checked his watch again, disgusted with their lack of progress and the thought of sweating out another wasted evening, waiting for the goddamn phone to ring. In front of them, a *samlor* and a taxi had collided, damaging the three-wheeled vehicle and bringing traffic in the right lane to a halt.

"Turn here."

Flack pointed to a side street just ahead, his driver making it with two wheels on the curb. It was a longer way around to reach his home, but Flack was hoping they might gain some time by ditching several thousand cars and buses back on Wireless Road. Most of the traffic for the next few blocks would be pedestrian, and they could damn well stand aside or take their lumps.

He didn't see the woman coming, and she obviously did not see the limousine, the way she blundered off the curb directly in its path. Too late, the driver cursed and hit the brakes, and Flack could feel the impact as they clipped her, watching her go down.

"For Christ's sake, man!"

The driver was outside and kneeling in the street before a crowd had time to gather, pressing close around the limousine. Flack knew what they were thinking; he could read it in their faces, and his diplomatic plates would stand for shit if someone started whipping up a storm against the Yankee pigs.

Two ways to play it, and he swallowed hard before he left the safety of the car to check the damage himself.

Flack's driver had the woman on her feet before he got there, speaking to her gently as she slumped against the fender of the limousine. The crowd was muttering, and that was fine; Flack wouldn't need his gun unless they started shouting, crowding in. Perhaps, if he could muster up a show of sympathy, he just might turn the incident around.

"Are you all right?" he asked in Thai.

The woman took another moment, working on a shaky smile and almost getting it. "I think so."

English. Well, now.

Taking inventory in a rush, Flack couldn't pick out any glaring injuries. The hair was mussed, her face a little flushed, but she was still a looker. There had been some damage to her clothes—the stockings torn, skirt soiled, a button off her blouse that gave him just a glimpse of tit and lace—but it was nothing a C-note wouldn't fix.

Still, there might be internal injuries or shock, perhaps a mild concussion. It would make him look like slime to simply pay her off and leave. If something happened to her afterward . . .

"We'll take you to the hospital," Flack told her, putting on his best concerned expression for the crowd. "The embassy will pay for everything, of course."

"Oh, really, no."

"You've had a nasty shock. A checkup—"

"I'm all right," she told him. "Honestly."

Flack frowned. If he allowed her to escape, no matter what she said, the crowd might place its own interpretation on the scene. Another rich American evading his responsibility.

"I really must insist. A thing like this, my insurance . . ."

"Oh, very well."

Flack slid an arm around her waist, warm flesh beneath the silk, and helped her to the car. She climbed inside, allowing him a flash of thigh before she tugged her skirt down, and he settled in the seat beside her. Sitting close that way, without the other street smells to distract him, Flack was suddenly aware of her perfume.

His driver slid behind the wheel and put the car in motion, tapping on the horn to clear their path.

"The nursing home on Convent Road," Flack said when they were under way.

"I'm not hurt, really," she insisted, turning in her seat so that her blouse gaped wider. "You just took me by surprise."

Flack raised his eyes to meet her level gaze. If she was feeling any pain, it didn't show.

"I can't just put you out this way," he said, relenting. "At the very least, an outfit to replace the one we ruined."

"Well . . ."

"It's settled, then. You name the shops, and I'll get on the phone first thing tomorrow. Anything you like, just charge it to the embassy."

"You work there?"

"Gordon Flack. Assistant to the U.S. cultural attaché."

"You are very kind."

"The least I can do. I hope you'll let me see you home."

"I planned to take a taxi."

"Nonsense. Save your money for a rainy day."

"If you insist."

"I do."

"I really don't know how to thank you."

Flack was dazzled by her smile. She placed her left hand on his thigh and left it there just long enough to start his engine racing.

"One more thing," he said. "Or two, I guess."

She looked confused.

"Your name and address."

"Ah." Her smile came back full-force. "Maneeya Pan Saray. I live at 62 Soi 20, Gaysorn Road."

"Forget about the nursing home," Flack told his driver. "Make it 62 Soi 20, Gaysorn."

"Yes, sir."

They negotiated side streets for a time, Maneeya eyeing Flack, and when she touched his leg a second time, she did not pull her hand away.

"I'm lucky you ran into me."

"The pleasure's mine."

Or will be. This may be exactly what I need.

May had been waiting half an hour for the limousine before it finally arrived. The phony accident on Wireless Road had done its job, with the American's impatience helping out. The rest was easy, acting absentminded as she stepped out in the street, the fall a stunt that she had learned in childhood for extorting food and money from the tourist trade. She hadn't used the trick in years, but it came back to her without a hitch.

At first she had thought the driver might be left to deal with her alone, but when the crowd began to gather, Gordon Flack was moved to lend a hand. He had an image to maintain, and once May had him in her sights, she trusted in her style—strategic buttons missing, a bewildered look—to do the rest.

Agreeing to the hospital had put her in the limousine, and it was relatively easy to dissuade him afterward, once they were on their way. He wanted her; May saw it in his eyes, and never mind about the man's alleged preoccupation with security. When he began to let his penis do his thinking for him, he was lost.

The Gaysorn Road address was new, secured with money from the bank account Joe Lee had opened on the day he came to Bangkok. There was plenty left, and he had promised some of it to May Tansiri, but her mind was not on money now.

Lee had been gone eight days before he turned up at the safe house, wearing mismatched clothes and looking like a man who's had a glimpse of hell on earth. May didn't weep when he informed her of Yodmani's death, nor did she hesitate when he requested help in punishing the man responsible. He briefed her on the risks, unwilling to deceive her, and she let him think the money was enough to make her go along. That night, in bed, their coupling had been more an affirmation of survival than an act of lust.

May knew the man beside her, recognized his type from Lee's description and the way he spoke. Flack was accustomed to dispensing lies as if they might be favors to the persons he misled. If forced to tell the truth on pain of death, she thought he might prefer to die.

Before they got to Gaysorn Road, Flack's hand was on her knee. May left it there, allowing him his fantasy—a man so irresistible that even women knocked down by his car on public streets were smitten with his charm. She felt the heat that radiated from his loins and knew that she could bring him off with just a touch, a stroke or two, but he would have to wait.

A rather different climax was on tap for Gordon Flack today.

"Right there."

She pointed to the tall apartment house and smiled at Flack again, his driver taking pains to find a parking space nearby. The limo was conspicuous, but Flack was unconcerned about appearances or personal security just now. He was imagining the pleasures of her flesh, anticipating ecstasy.

"Well, thank you for your help."

"I'll walk you home," he told her, managing a boyish grin.

"This *is* my home." Naive enough to keep him guessing.

"To your door, I mean."

"That really isn't necessary, Mr. Flack."

"It's Gordon. Please?"

"Your driver?"

"Oh, he'll wait. You don't mind waiting, do you?"

"Not at all, sir."

"There, you see?"

"All right, then."

He stood close beside her in the elevator, not quite touching, saving it until they got inside her flat and she felt free to shed her inhibitions with her clothes. Whatever else this man might be, he was not short on confidence.

The brand-new key turned easily, and May Tansiri led the way inside. No furniture in any of the rooms, except a single straight-backed chair positioned in the middle of the living room. Flack blinked, the Spartan layout a surprise.

He took a guess. "New place?"

"I moved in yesterday."

"You haven't finished, by the look of it."

May smiled, retreating, watching Joseph as he stepped out of the closet. Coming up behind Flack with a pistol in his hand.

"I think," Lee said, "you'll find that we have everything we need."

Flack's stunned expression had been worth the risk, if he accomplished nothing else. Lee gave him several heartbeats to inspect the .45, its muzzle lengthened by a bulky silencer, before he pointed to the chair.

"Sit down."

Flack didn't move. "If somebody had told me you were this dumb, I would've laughed in his face. Talk about mistakes—this takes the prize."

"Sit down," Lee said again.

"I've got a man downstairs. You don't believe me, ask the bitch. If I'm not back in five—"

Joe clipped him with the silencer, a backhand chop that staggered Flack and left him drooling blood across his chin.

"You bastard!"

Joseph cocked the .45 and pointed it. "Which knee? Your choice."

"You wouldn't fucking dare."

"Okay, the left."

Flack scuttled to the chair and sat, knees pressed together, covered by his hands as if he thought the knuckles might be tough enough to stop a bullet. "There, you satisfied?"

"Not quite. I need some answers first."

"You may as well start shooting, then. I took an oath."

"The one about protecting God and country?" Joseph asked. "Or did you have another one in mind?"

Flack's eyes were cold. "I don't have anything to say. You want to pull that trigger, go ahead. And while you're at it, kiss your ass good-bye."

Lee frowned. "I might be doing you a favor, Flack. I'm not sure I could live with that. Why don't I drop a dime, instead, and tell the boys at Langley all about the business you've been running on the side."

"You got a dime to spare, call up your next of kin and tell 'em you're committing suicide. The easy way would be to shoot yourself right now."

"I'm having too much fun. I want to see the network coverage on a CIA assistant chief of station dealing heroin."

"Dream on." Flack's voice was firm, but he was looking pinched around the eyes and mouth. "If you had anything—and I say *if*—the Company would never let it air."

"You're indispensable, is that the party line?" Joe laughed and shook his head. "I'm betting when they catch a whiff of you, they'll toss you out like last month's dirty laundry."

"Say you're right. Why aren't you on the phone right now? You want to see me sweat, you should've brought your lunch."

"I've seen a maggot sweat before. It's no big deal. A little information, you could walk away."

"I'll bet." But Flack was calculating, now. "What kind of information did you have in mind?"

"For openers, I'm interested in how you got word to General Sheng."

"What word is that?"

"You set us up. It got Yodmani killed."

"Tough break. What makes you think I blew the whistle on your little dog-and-pony show?"

"You tried to tag us both the night before we left. When that fell through, you had a fallback option waiting."

"Did you ever stop to think it might've been your buddy Chiang?"

"No sale. He had a stake in keeping us alive, at least until he got the earnest money in his hands. If Chiang had wanted us, we never would have left our first and only meeting."

"So, that still leaves someone from the 14K. You didn't make a lot of friends in old Hong Kong, from what I hear."

"The Sap Sie Kie cut all their deals with Sheng through Bangkok, meaning Chiang. The general wouldn't take on a contract from strangers."

"Well."

"I'm asking why."

Flack shrugged. "Why not? I tried to warn you off, in case it has slipped your mind. You haven't got a fucking clue what's on the table here. When you sit down to play with men who can't afford to lose, your ass is on the line."

"How long have you been dealing, Flack?"

"I deal in information, Joe. Sometimes, along the way, you have to give a little if you want to get results."

"Ends justify the means?"

"Grow up, for Christ's sake. We've been doing business in an open sewer here for close to forty years. Try wading in the shit awhile, you may not smell the same, but you can hold your nose and keep on doing what you're paid to do."

"And if you get paid twice, so much the better, right?"

Flack smiled. "My mama always told me charity begins at home."

"Terrific. You're not wading in the sewer, Flack, you're snorkeling."

"I do my fucking job, goddammit! And I've never touched a kilo in my life. A phone call here and there, okay. I'm playing travel agent. If you're looking for the guy with dirty hands, old son, you should've stayed at home and checked your own backyard."

"I'm listening."

"I'll bet you are." Flack sneered. "The fucking DEA, so busy popping Chinks and Mexicans, you never figured out you've got a heavy hitter on your own damn payroll, undercutting every move you make."

"I want a name."

"So, what's it worth?"

"Your life."

"In fucking Leavenworth? No, thanks."

"And if the tip proves out, nobody hears the source from me. You walk."

"Your word? Don't laugh. I recognize an honest man."

"My word."

Flack smiled and let him have the name, delighted with Joe's visible response. "Is that a bitch, or what?"

"I'll check it out," Lee told him, tight-lipped. "If you're lying, I'll be back to see you. Not the crew from Langley. Me."

"I think you would."

"We understand each other, then."

"Indeed, we do."

The older man was on his feet before he made his move, the right hand gliding back, inside his jacket, digging for a compact automatic worn behind his back. It was a move he had practiced countless times before a mirror, and he almost got it right.

Almost.

Joe's first round drilled Flack just above his waistband, right of center, knocking him off-balance and defeating his attempt to aim. The silencer chugged twice in rapid-fire before he toppled backward, tangled in the chair and sprawling like a giant rag doll on the floor.

Lee stepped around him and retrieved the automatic Flack had drawn but never fired. He used his foot to turn Flack over, dead eyes staring at the ceiling in a fixed expression of dismay.

"What now?"

He glanced at May. "We leave him. Take the back way out. His driver gets fed up with waiting, he can call the cops himself."

"And give them my description?"

"You won't be here," Lee reminded her. "Pick any city in the world. You can afford it now."

"And you?"

Lee's face was grim. "I'm going home."

26

Ray Christy parked his federal four-door on Pacific, near the cemetery, walking back from there. Another goddamned foggy night, like that was news, but he was thankful for the cover as he reached the cemetery gates and tried them, found them locked.

The obstacle didn't surprise him, what with all the vandalism in the news these days. You thought the subways caught it, with their gang graffiti and the rest, but that was nothing. Small time. Cemeteries drew the *real* bizarros after dark. Grave robbers. Satanists and heavy-metal freakoids. Fucking Nazis looking for a Jewish headstone they could tip or cart away. From time to time, a vampire hunter, working out his private kinks with crucifix and wooden stakes.

No way around the lock, and Christy knew he would have to climb.

I'm getting too old for this.

The gate resisted him at first. Its wrought-iron bars were moist and slippery, but Christy took advantage of the ornate scrollwork, cursing all the way as he climbed up and over, dropping on the other side.

"Too goddamned old," he said aloud.

A month since he had seen the grave, but Ray remembered where it was. The gate that he had climbed was one of three, selected for convenience, and he wouldn't have too far to walk. A hundred yards or less, along the blacktop drive that circled left from where he stood, and he would be there.

After that, what happened next was anybody's guess.

Too late, he stopped to wonder if the cemetery might

use guard dogs after dark, but he immediately shrugged the notion off. They would have had his ass by now, with all the time he took—and all the noise he made—just getting in. He wouldn't be surprised to find a watchman on the grounds, but with the fog and darkness, so much area to cover, it was doubtful they would meet unless he started making some god-awful noise.

As a precaution, Christy drew his snub-nosed .38 and checked the weapon's load. Six live ones, hot to trot. He prayed he wouldn't need it, but the pistol's weight against his hip was comforting, an edge against the great unknown.

You're acting like a first-year rookie on a stakeout.

It almost worked.

But almost didn't make the grade.

Five weeks without a word from Joey Lee except for bullshit secondhand reports, and Christy had begun to think he might be lying dead somewhere. In Hong Kong, maybe, or a morgue in Bangkok. Maybe farther north, where half-assed rumor had it he had raised some hell around the Triangle. Hard facts were tough to come by, half a world away, but Burmese sources cheerfully confirmed the death of General Shih Yeuh Sheng, a longtime irritant and enemy of the Rangoon establishment. The cause of death had variously been ascribed to training accidents, a brooding power struggle in the KMT, assassination by the Chinese communists, and wounds inflicted by a raiding party of Vietnamese. There wasn't anything on paper to connect Joe Lee with General Sheng, and yet . . .

It could have been coincidence, the CIA man killed in Bangkok ten days after Sheng went down. As far as Christy knew, no suspect had been named, though Sekigun, a faction of the Japanese Red Army, had released a bulletin accepting credit for the kill. It was an easy out, but no one in official Washington was buying it, especially since the seventeen known members of the JRA were all accounted for—and miles away from Bangkok—when the hit went down.

Ray had no solid reason to connect Joe Lee with Bangkok. Ian Wilson had been cagey on the telephone the last few times they spoke, insisting he had warned Lee off and then lost track of him, assuming Joe was homeward-bound. No reason to believe the chief inspector would be holding out, but there was something in his tone—a distance? caution?—that was new in their professional relationship.

Tough shit.

The call he had to think about right now had been logged at 6:15 P.M. It had caught him halfway to the door, and he had turned around reluctantly, his aspect changing when he recognized the caller's voice.

"How are you, Ray?"

Like that, without a hint of anything unusual, as if they were resuming a routine discussion started over lunch that afternoon. Ray managed to resist the obvious, like saying Joseph's name out loud or grilling him to find out what the hell was going on. Surprise could make you careless, just like anger, fear, or sexual excitement. Nice and easy did the trick, pretending it was no big deal to get a call from someone you supposed was dead.

Lee wasn't giving anything away, of course. It was a standing joke at the DEA that no one knew for sure which office phones were bugged, or when the bugs were operational. As far as Christy knew, the joke was merely that, but you could never tell. Police departments regularly taped incoming calls, and presidents were known to bug their own damned conversations in the Oval Office. Nothing could be accepted on faith.

"We need to have a talk."

The cool, familiar voice as smooth as glass. Ray Christy cautious, but agreeing instantly.

"Remember where I saw you last, outside?"

Ray had to puzzle over that one for a moment, but he got it. After Lisa Reilly's funeral, the graveside.

"Yeah, okay."

"You want to meet me there? Say, midnight?"

Sure, why not? Joe didn't have to tell him he should come alone. The cryptic conversation was enough to set the stage. He didn't know what Lee was up to, but Ray would have bet his pension that it all came back to Bobby Chan.

Who else?

The night was cool, but Christy left his jacket open, ready with the .38 in case Joe came out shooting, or some other crazy thing. No telling what had happened to him overseas, or how the trip had jerked his mind around. Ray knew about the fireworks in Kowloon, some punk and a detective sergeant dead, but all the rest of it was guesswork. He was flying blind, and after Hong Kong—maybe Bangkok—Joe might be a stranger, someone he had never met before.

Christy's Timex showed 11:53 as he found the plot. No flowers, this time, but people tried to put that kind of thing behind them. Hanging out at graves and chatting with the dead was definitely out of style.

There had been no headstone, last time, and he couldn't read it now without a light. The usual "beloved-daughter, faithful-friend" routine, no doubt. Perhaps some doves or angels carved in stone, if anyone had felt like laying out the bread. It wasn't like the occupant would care much, either way.

The fog seemed thicker here, reminding him of something from the movies, where you never saw a graveyard free of mist. It felt like souls were leaking through the ground, somehow, and hovering around the places where their earthly shells had come to rest. A night like this, you half-expected ghosts to be on hand. The headless horseman riding past, or a Lugosi look-alike in fancy evening clothes, with marbles in his mouth.

Goddammit, quit!

Ray wondered if a person ever really shed those childhood fears and superstitions. Was there a way to disconnect the buttons that you pressed to terrify a child? Was *any* single quirk of personality discarded absolutely, or were others simply added on to cover up the rest, with fear of death and taxes standing in for bogeymen like Dracula and Frankenstein?

If there had been a choice, Ray would have preferred the childhood terrors, any day. Like standing in a graveyard as the clock struck midnight, your imagination coughing up the sound of footsteps closing from behind. The muzzle of a handgun pressed against your neck as someone whispered in your ear, "Don't even think about it, Ray."

"I'm here to talk," Christy said. "Nothing else."

Lee slipped his free hand underneath Ray's jacket, feeling for the snubby .38 and palming it. "You won't need this." He backed away and kept Ray covered with the double-action Browning. "Turn around."

"What's this?" Christy asked, staring at the gun. "You gonna shoot me, Joe?"

"I thought about it."

"What did you decide?"

"I changed my mind."

"That's good to know."

"You came alone?"

"Was I supposed to bring a date?"

Lee didn't have to ask. He had been trailing Christy through the fog since he scaled the gate. If there had been a tail, he would have spotted it by now. And still, there seemed to be no point in taking chances by allowing Ray to keep his gun.

"I tried to find you, after Hong Kong," Christy said, "but Wilson wouldn't tell me shit."

"I'm not surprised."

"What's that supposed to mean?"

"He thought he might be talking to a mole."

"Oh, yeah?" Despite the darkness and the mist, Lee thought he saw a flush of angry color rising in Ray's cheeks. "Whatever gave him that idea?"

"Coincidence," Lee said. "I might've helped a little."

"Great."

"Fact is, I had you figured dirty when I split for Bangkok. Looking one way, all the indicators read the same."

"Do tell. Is this where you play jury, judge, and executioner?"

"It might have been, except I had a little chat with Gordon Flack."

"The dead guy? CIA?"
"Was he a friend of yours?"
"Hell, no. He made the papers. Terrorists, they think."
"They're wrong."
"I had a feeling."
"It was unavoidable."
"I hope so."
"He had connections with the KMT, some of the heavyweights in Bangkok, supervising shipments to the States. I guess he figured if it worked in Nam, why not?"
"You heard about the general and his accident, up north?"
"It rings a bell."
"I don't suppose you'd care to fill me in?"
"Another time. I'm running short right now."
"How's that?"
"Before Flack pulled his Gary Cooper act, he let me have a name."
"He gave you Bobby Chan?" Ray frowned. "It's gonna be a bitch to make a dead man testify."
"Chan wasn't mentioned. I'm not sure they even knew each other."
"So?"
"Flack gave me Chan's connection, Ray. The bastard who's been making sure his shit comes through without a hitch."
"I'm listening."
"It's funny. Back in Hong Kong, Wilson had been wondering about the DEA for months. Joint operations blown, informants dead or missing. Nothing he could put his finger on, but still, it makes you think. I can't help wondering why we were so damned slow to pick it up."
"Goddammit, *I* was working Wilson."
"Right."
Ray's shoulders slumped. "We're back to that? You string me out with bullshit, and you *still* think I've been leaking to the other side?"
"It looked that way. Your link, your operations—all the big ones, anyway. It seemed like everything you put your hands on turned to shit."

"And Eddie? I suppose you're blaming me for that?" Ray stiffened, glaring back at Lee. "The girl. That's why you called me here."

Joe shook his head. "I told you Flack gave up a name."

"So, fuck it. I don't give a shit. You've got your mind made up, let's get it over with."

Lee eased the Browning's hammer down and tucked the pistol in his belt. "The name was Kephart."

"What?"

"Who else? He knew each move before you made it. Names and places, everything. You pop an independent, someone 14K can live without, he lets it slide. Colombians or bikers take a fall, no problem. Clean up all the blacks and *marielitos* you want. The bastard knows which side his bread is buttered on. When there's a major shipment due—"

"Hold on a second. Flack and Kephart? Are you telling me the man *imports* this shit?"

"Why not? You know a better cover?"

"Not offhand." Ray Christy sounded like a man who's just been told his wife is bending over for his closest friend.

"We've got a problem, going in," Lee said.

"No evidence, you mean? I thought of that. Flack wouldn't get us anywhere, unless you had the guy on tape."

"Who says I don't?"

Ray looked confused. "Well, *do* you?"

"No."

"So, what the hell?"

"Kephart doesn't know that."

"And?"

"I've got a plan, but there's a risk involved."

"What else is new?"

"It all boils down to who you trust."

"Right now, myself . . . and maybe you," Ray added grudgingly.

"We'll need a couple more."

"You wanna tell me why?"

"That all depends. You in?"

"Hell yes, I'm in. You think I'm gonna let this motherfucker walk?"

Lee handed back the snubby .38 and watched Ray tuck it out of sight. "Okay," he said. "Here's what you do. . . ."

27

At eight o'clock on Friday morning, Leland Kephart waited in his sixth-floor office for Ray Christy to arrive. In front of him, he had arranged a steaming coffee mug, manila files on half a dozen pending cases, and a pad of notes on correspondence for the day. A stranger looking at the desk with every item perfectly arranged would not have realized that Kephart had been on the job for half an hour. By appearances, he might have just arrived.

It pleased the regional director of the DEA to set a good example for his troops, and punctuality had always been a high point of the lectures he dispensed to new recruits. In fact, if Kephart's record was examined, he arrived ahead of time most days and stayed an average of thirty minutes overtime, his secretary often clocking out before the boss was ready to depart.

Somewhere, perhaps in college, he had read about the feud between the Kennedys and Jimmy Hoffa, which, according to reports, had placed at least three famous men in early graves. One incident, specifically, had fixed in Kephart's mind: Bobby Kennedy was riding home from work one night, already late, when he passed by the Teamsters building and observed a light in Hoffa's window. "Turn around," he told his driver, scowling. "If that bastard's working, so am I."

Determination was the key, without becoming a compulsive workaholic. In the end, Bobby Kennedy's obsession got him killed, and there were lessons to be learned from *that* as well.

Determination, with a taste of compromise.

It didn't hurt to let the troops see Kephart's car downstairs when they began to straggle in. He also liked for them to know that he was still upstairs, still working, when they scattered to their homes or favorite bars. Of course, he didn't work the all-night stakeouts anymore, but that was not his function. An administrator was expected to assign responsibility for shitty jobs and make sure everybody washed his hands when it was over. No one seriously thought the regional director of the DEA should be out busting dealers on the street.

From time to time, he almost missed the bad old days of packing heat and sitting up all night in cars that smelled like someone's dirty socks. There had been moments of excitement, salted in among the hours of tedium and paperwork, that made him feel like he was *doing* something with his life. It took a little time to grasp the full extent of his mistake, but Kephart was a willing pupil in the school of hard realities. Whenever possible, he learned from the mistakes of those around him and was spared from sharing their humiliation.

Eight-fifteen.

The intercom announced Ray Christy, and the regional director took a sip of coffee, savoring its taste before he deigned to answer.

"Send him in."

As usual, Christy looked like something the cat had dragged in. His suit was rumpled, with a tie that clashed and shoes that never seemed to hold a shine. His hair was windblown, and you could have packed a lady's fall ensemble in the bags beneath his eyes.

He looked like hell, and Kephart told him so.

"Late night," Christy said, reaching for a cigarette before he caught himself and wound up tugging at his shirt instead.

"Appearance figures into your evaluation, Ray. Remember that. You represent the government of the United States, not Ethiopia. For God's sake, comb your hair."

"Yes, sir. The reason that I asked for this appointment—"

"Something urgent, so you said."

"It's Joey Lee."

The regional director's hand was steady as he reached out for the coffee cup, but there was something in his throat that was choking him.

"You've had some word?"

"He called me up last night, at home."

"From Hong Kong?"

"San Francisco. Wouldn't tell me where, but it was local, sure enough. I checked it out."

"What's on his mind?"

"What else? He claims to have the goods on Chan, dead-bang."

"That's interesting. I don't suppose he gave you any details?"

"One or two, yes, sir."

"Well, Ray?"

"Do you remember Gordon Flack?"

"The name's familiar, but . . ."

"Assistant chief of station, Bangkok, for the CIA. Somebody burned him down last week."

"Ah, yes. The networks covered it, I think."

"Joe claims he had a talk with Flack beforehand. Says the guy was dirty, moving smack between his duty posting and the States."

"For Chan?"

"That's where it gets a little tricky, sir. Lee wouldn't give me all the names, but he was talking heavy hitters. Maybe someone in our own backyard."

"In law enforcement?"

"In the DEA."

"I see."

"Yes, sir. First thing, I tell him there's no way to run with hearsay. Flack could tell him he was moving kilos through the White House, and it wouldn't mean a thing."

"That's true, of course." Relaxing slightly, sipping at his mug.

"So then he tells me that he's got it all on tape."

"And you believe him?"

Christy shrugged. "Who knows? I worked with Joe ten years, before this other thing. He always did his job and nailed the loose ends down. Since Eddie and the woman, though . . ."

"I understand. You didn't hear the tape?"

"He wouldn't play it on the phone. To tell the truth, he sounded kinda paranoid to me."

"I wouldn't be surprised."

"Thing is, he says he'll let me *have* the tape, I meet him on my own, tonight."

"Sounds dangerous."

Ray thought about it for a moment, finally shook his head. "He's got my address, my unlisted number. If he wanted to, he could have taken me last night, or anytime since he's been home. It doesn't smell like ambush time to me."

"You want to keep the date?"

"I'd like to, yes, sir. Joey might be holding shit, but if there *is* a tape—"

"We'll want to follow up, of course. You pick the backup team."

"I wouldn't want to risk it, sir. He'd see them coming from a mile away and think I set him up. The only way he'll play is if I let him make the rules."

"My inclination is to let it go. A hostage situation is the last thing we need."

"He's not about to bag me, sir. It comes to that, I'll take him out myself."

"If you're determined . . ."

"Absolutely."

"Where and when?"

"He's calling back this afternoon, to fix the meet. At home, that is. He doesn't trust the office phones. I thought, if I could punch out after lunch . . ."

"Of course. I'll want the details in advance, you understand. Insurance, just in case you're wrong."

Ray Christy frowned. "You wouldn't try to sneak a backup on me, would you, sir?"

"I promise you," the regional director said, "it never crossed my mind."

• • •

The selection of a home in Daly City had been a conscious move by Robert Chan, away from Chinatown, but he maintained an office at his largest restaurant, on Jackson Street. From nine o'clock till noon, most weekdays, Chan was on the job, receiving visitors and coping with the details of a business that included three more restaurants, six laundries, and a theater. By one o'clock, except in cases of emergency, he was at home preparing for a swim, a round of golf, or simply resting up before the varied banquets, cocktail parties, and liaisons with attractive women that comprised his social life.

On rare occasions, when the need was great, his schedule went to hell.

That Friday afternoon, despite a scheduled dinner celebrating the retirement of a friendly jurist, Chan was working overtime. He was prepared to wait all night, if necessary, for the crucial phone call. Anything to mend a situation that had graduated from a nuisance to a possible catastrophe.

He was surrounded by incompetents, Chan thought, their failures jeopardizing everything that he had worked for through the years. From San Francisco, all the way to Hong Kong and beyond, the curse of negligence and inefficiency had dogged him, wasting golden opportunities and damaging his critical connections, while his enemy appeared to have no problem, striking here and there at will. It might be weeks before the Bangkok pipeline was repaired, and in the meantime, he was losing money by the hour. All because his soldiers had failed to carry out the contract on a nosy fed.

If they were not already dead, Chan thought, it would have made his day to strangle them himself.

And what about the fed's own people, full of promises that he would be contained and neutralized? So far, "containment" had entailed a trip halfway around the world, resulting in the deaths of Gordon Flack and General Shih Yeuh Sheng, with subsequent disruption of the pipeline bringing China white from Bangkok to the States.

It was impossible to say what price the general's ultimate replacement would demand for reestablishing

Sheng's trade agreement with the Sap Sie Kie, but it would not be inexpensive. Robert Chan, meanwhile, had suffered damage to his reputation in the Triad, losing face when he could not prevent a single man from wreaking havoc on his own preserve. It made no difference that the Shan Chu and his troops in Hong Kong had been every bit as ineffective; Chiang Min Fai, in Bangkok, dealing with the traitor as a friend and passing him along; the general failing even to preserve his life, despite an army at his beck and call. It all came back to Chan, allowing Joseph Lee to slip away instead of crushing him at once.

But not this time.

The call alerting him to Lee's return had been a godsend, giving Chan an opportunity to put his house in order and preserve his standing in the 14K. Concessions would be necessary—cash and other favors to the Hill Chief, even to the distant Kuomintang—but with a bit of luck, Chan might survive without a loss of rank. A few more years, to let old wounds and insults be forgotten, and he had an outside shot at winning back the reputation he had lost.

It would have pleased Chan greatly to abduct Joe Lee and torture him to death, protracting his exquisite punishment for days, but practicality demanded swift solutions. He would have to make the tag without a hitch this time, and put the whole damned incident behind him. His superiors were interested in profits, and a Red Pole who could not produce would soon be out of work—or dead.

And so he waited, sipping ginseng tea, impressing those around him as a man without a problem in the world. Chan concentrated on his trifling paperwork and did not raise his voice to the subordinates who served him. He ignored the telephone until it rang at three o'clock, and even then he let his secretary take the call.

"It's Mr. Dean again, sir."

"Thank you, Lin."

He lifted the receiver like a man who half-expects the instrument to blow up in his hand. "Hello?"

"It's set." The anxious voice of Leland Kephart, calling from a public phone booth to prevent a trace.

"Go on."

"Pier Forty-six, at midnight."

"Ah." He would require a boat, but it was easily arranged. "The tape?"

"He's bringing it. Supposed to be a one-on-one. His friend refused a backup."

"Excellent."

"That's it, then?" Kephart sounding hopeful, thinking he had wriggled off the hook so easily.

"Not quite."

"Is there a problem here? You asked for time and place, I got it for you." Kephart sounded peevish, like a frightened child.

"No problem, Leland." Knowing Kephart grimaced at the mention of his name. "I plan to supervise the job myself this time, to guard against mistakes. With one of yours involved, I knew you'd feel the same."

"He *isn't* one of mine," the regional director said defensively. "I canned his ass two months ago, if you recall."

"It didn't help."

"Your problem, Robert." Getting in a small dig of his own. "Besides, the wet work's not my thing."

"It is tonight. I'll pick you up outside the Paper Lion, ten o'clock. Don't keep me waiting."

Chan hung up on Kephart's angry protest, knowing he would fuss and fume awhile before he kept their date. But Kephart would be waiting on Pacific Avenue at the appointed time, because he feared the consequences of refusal. He had given up his right to independent thought and action when he took the first fat envelope of cash from Robert Chan, and he would follow orders to the bitter end.

Tonight.

Nine hours left before Chan washed his hands of Joseph Lee and all the problems he had caused.

Tomorrow, bright and early, everyone connected with the 14K would know that he was still in charge, a man who crushed his enemies and smiled upon his friends.

But first, before Chan started celebrating, he would have to deal with Joseph Lee.

And this time he would do it right.

The meeting place—Pier 46, at China Basin—had been chosen with an eye toward relative seclusion, as a means of minimizing risk to late-night passersby. The pier was too remote for joggers with a grain of common sense, and Lee was trusting that the hour would assure that everyone except a few night watchmen would be clear, in case it went to hell.

For backup, Christy had selected Milliken and Rudd, two hot dogs who were not averse to using muscle on a raid or shooting first and asking questions later. Armed with M-16's and night scopes, they were posted on the roof of a convenient warehouse by the time the fog rolled in at half-past eight, prepared to wait it out and cover any action that went down.

Joe Lee was early, parking his Toyota on the pier a little past eleven, getting out to stretch his legs and smell the ocean close at hand. He wore a navy pea coat over denim shirt and jeans, a stubby Ingram MAC-10 submachine gun riding underneath his right arm in a swivel harness and the double-action Browning in his belt. Spare magazines for both were weighting down his pockets, and he had a bootleg copy of *The Bee Gees Greatest Hits*, in case somebody got around to asking for a tape.

Fat chance.

The hit team would be under orders to eliminate Joe Lee and check his pockets afterward, when they were certain he was dead. No slipups this time. No loose ends. An extra fed on hand would simply mean another body when the workmen came around tomorrow and phoned it in. One murder, more or less, was no big deal to Bobby Chan.

If they were lucky—meaning that they walked away instead of winding up downtown in a refrigerated drawer—it would be Christy's job to pin the tail on Kephart. No one else had been informed about the meet, and it would take a Ph.D. in bullshit to convince the men in Washington that Chan had tumbled to their setup on his own.

Connecting Chan with any action on the pier could take a bit more work, except that Joseph had a hunch the bastard might be dropping by to supervise the hit himself. A Red Pole's reputation rested on the fear that he inspired among his fellow Triad members and civilian residents of Chinatown, a grim mystique dependent on his own ability to cope with problems on his own, when necessary. So far, Chan had delegated all the dirty work to others, with disastrous results.

If he exposed himself to make the tag, they had him cold.

If not . . .

The headlights of another car lit up the foggy pier, and Joseph stepped behind his own Toyota for a little extra cover, just in case. It was 11:55, according to his watch, and he was hoping that the mist would not defeat the night scopes Milliken and Rudd had mounted on the flat roof overhead.

The new arrival doused his lights and killed his engine. Joseph had his coat unbuttoned, one hand on the Ingram as a door slammed, footsteps drawing closer in the dark and fog.

"You there, Joe?"

"Jesus, Ray."

"I couldn't very well come rolling up with lights and siren, could I?"

"Never mind. You have a tail?"

"I couldn't spot one," Christy answered, standing with his big hands in the pockets of his overcoat. "It shouldn't matter, if you're right about the man."

He was correct, of course. The shooters would not have to follow anyone, if Kephart had relayed the rendezvous coordinates to Chan. They might be on the pier already, or . . .

"Hey, listen—"

"Wait."

"What is it?"

"Sshhh!"

A sound, familiar to his ears, but unexpected. Coming from behind him, toward the bay. "A boat."

"Okay, I hear it."

Christy speaking, even as another car rolled toward them, running dark along the pier. Joe cocked his head and listened. *Two* cars, by the sound of it. One hanging back and waiting, while the other one advanced.

"I didn't figure on a fucking boat." As Christy spoke, he drew a compact riot shotgun from underneath his coat. The shoulder stock had been removed in favor of a pistol grip, the barrel shortened to a foot or so for maximum concealment.

"I'll take the boat," Lee told him, swiveling to face the water with the submachine gun in his hands.

"You guys awake up there?" Ray asked the microphone affixed to his lapel.

If there was any answer, Joseph missed it, staring at the misty darkness where the bay should be and sweating through his clothes despite a creeping chill.

He heard the unseen boat make contact with the pier, feet scuffling on the concrete as a landing party came ashore. How many men? Three or four, according to the engine's sound. Chan wouldn't send a cabin cruiser out when he could use a motor launch to do the job.

"You ready, Joe?"

"Let's do it."

"Stop right there!" Ray shouted, facing the cars.

And there was barely time to hit the deck as automatic weapons opened up from left and right, their muzzle flashes winking in the fog.

Joe scraped his knees and elbows on the pavement, hearing bullets ripple through the air a yard above his head. He sighted on the muzzle flashes, squeezing off a measured burst before the gunners showed themselves, uncertain whether he had scored or not. Above him, on the warehouse roof, two rifles set for semiautomatic fire joined in, the hot dogs scoping targets with their infrareds.

Lee heard his small Toyota taking hits—the windows,

bodywork, a flat tire bleeding air—and it meant nothing as he concentrated on the weapon in his hands, the shadows racing toward him in the dark. He counted three, but thought he might have been mistaken as he took one down, a short burst from the Ingram rolling up the gunner on his right.

Behind him, concentrated fire and angry shouts, Ray Christy's twelve-gauge sounding like the voice of Judgment Day.

Two gunmen came at Lee together, firing as they ran, their bullets striking near enough to spray his face with slivers of concrete. He caught one of them with a rising burst that made him dance, a jerky little pirouette, and then the Ingram's bolt locked open on an empty chamber, leaving him with one to go.

The shooter must have tasted triumph, breaking stride and taking time to aim from twenty feet away. Lee fumbled for another magazine and knew he didn't have a hope in hell of making it, unwilling to surrender even in the face of certain death.

The rifle shot came out of nowhere, and his adversary staggered, dropping to his knees, a dazed expression on his face. He might have made the tag, regardless, but a second round from Rudd or Milliken ripped through his chest a second later, dropping him before his brain and trembling hand could get their signals straight.

Joe managed to reload the Ingram, waiting for another rush until he heard the power launch retreating, racing back the way it had come. Behind him, Ray was looking at a standoff with a pair of diehard gunners crouched behind their riddled car, a prostrate body slumped between them on the open ground. The vehicle was going nowhere, but they still hung on and traded shots with Christy, firing off a burst at Rudd and Milliken from time to time, intent on breaking for the second car that waited in the fog, just out of sight.

Joe wriggled past the leaking hulk of his Toyota, smelling gasoline and antifreeze, the pungent vapors giving him a notion on the move.

"I have to get inside the car," he called to Ray.

"What for?"

"Just watch it, when the light comes on."

He got the door latch on his second try and squinted in the dome light's sudden glare. The crouching gunners opened up in unison and raked the car from end to end, but Joseph kept his head down, probing underneath the shotgun seat until he found the box of safety flares he carried there. Retreating, he was poised to push the door closed when a bullet took the dome light out and brought the darkness back.

Lee scuttled to the rear end of his car and stretched out prone on the concrete, examining his target from a worm's-eye view. He did not recognize the make of vehicle, but it was a domestic four-door, which would put the gas tank in the rear. With any luck at all . . .

He braced the Ingram in a firm two-handed grip and held the trigger down, its awesome cyclic rate of fire dispatching thirty-two rounds in a second and a half. They don't make cars the way they used to in Detroit, and he could almost see his bullets ripping into flimsy paneling behind the wheel well, followed by a steady drip of gasoline against concrete.

He took a moment to reload the Ingram, then picked up a safety flare, unscrewed its cap, and struck it on the pavement like a giant match. It sputtered into life, sparks peppering his face, and Joseph pitched it backhand toward the car, where two of his assailants were returning fire with everything they had.

The flare bounced once, then rolled beneath the dark sedan, a spreading pool of gasoline erupting into flame. One of the shooters bolted instantly, still firing, and a shotgun blast from Christy dropped him in his tracks before the gas tank blew. A fireball swallowed up the second gunner and his vehicle, the stutter of his automatic weapon trailing off into a dying scream.

Downrange, a pair of headlights blazed, the backup car retreating as the driver whipped it through a smooth one-eighty, rubber smoking on concrete. Lee chased it with a burst of hot nine-millimeters, knowing it was well beyond effective range.

"Goddammit!"

"Quick!" Ray snapped. "My car."

They made it more or less together, Joe reloading on the run, and Christy slid behind the wheel.

"You set?"

"Just punch it, Ray."

He didn't bother with a turn, but took the hundred feet of pier at fifty miles an hour in reverse, the four-door scraping bottom as they jumped the curb and veered across two lanes of Berry Street.

"Down there!"

A pair of taillights winking as the driver made a wide left onto Second, nearly losing it.

"Hang on," said Christy as he dropped it into gear and roared off in pursuit.

The chase led north on Second Street, across the railroad tracks at King, past Townsend, blasting through the light at Brannan with a blare of horns from Christy and the driver of an eastbound station wagon. Rolling north on the five-hundred block, a gunner in the lead car stuck his head out on the driver's side and started taking potshots at them with a heavy Desert Eagle .44. The first two Magnum rounds missed Ray's car entirely, but a third glanced off the hood and drilled the windshield, clipping off the rearview mirror on its way to gouge the ceiling panel.

"Jesus Christ!"

Joe cranked his window down and leaned out far enough to brace the Ingram's muzzle on the radio antenna, squeezing off a burst that blistered paint across the lead car's trunk. The driver started weaving back and forth across the center stripe, but if he spoiled Joe's aim, he also kept the dead-eye with the .44 from scoring any further hits as they approached the Bryant intersection, holding speed despite the lights. Across the intersection, Second Street ran underneath the freeway, running arrow-straight for half a mile until it vanished into Market, three blocks east of Union Square.

"He needs that turn to make the freeway," Christy

said, and flinched involuntarily as two more Magnum rounds came at them, missing by a yard on Joseph's side.

Lee emptied out his magazine, rewarded by a burst of sparks as one or two rounds clipped the window molding on the driver's side. It was enough to make the gunner pull his head back, giving Joe a chance to ditch the empty magazine and fit a fresh one in its place.

As if on cue, the driver hit his brakes and cranked his steering wheel to make the right-hand turn on Bryant, two wheels lifting off the pavement as he screeched around the corner, rocking like an exhibition driver at a county fair. Lee didn't have the time or opportunity to aim, but he was with them all the way, his Ingram ripping through another magazine before he had the chance to mouth a prayer.

He never knew how many rounds struck home, or what they hit—maybe the driver, something underneath the hood, a tire—but it was good enough. Beside him, Ray was standing on the brake and blurting out "Sweet Jesus!" as the lead car toppled on its side and slid for close to half a block before it came to rest across the freeway entry ramp. Joe's pulse was pounding as he came up with another magazine—his last—and snapped it into place before he left the car.

"Watch out," Ray cautioned, edging toward the junker with his shotgun braced against his hip.

"No sweat."

When they were thirty feet away, the right-rear door popped open, and a battered scarecrow hauled himself outside.

"That's far enough!"

Lee recognized the gunner as he made them, groping for the Desert Eagle he had tucked inside his belt. Ray shot him first, a blast that punched him back against the greasy undercarriage of the car, but Joe was close behind, the Ingram spitting half a dozen rounds before it jammed.

Lee worked the bolt without result, and ditched the useless weapon in the middle of the street. He had the Browning automatic in his fist before a pair of empty hands thrust into view and someone called, "Don't shoot! I'm coming out."

"Your move," Ray told him, leveling his shotgun at the open doorway from a range of twenty feet.

Despite the manicured nails and thousand-dollar suit, it took a second glance for Joe to recognize his enemy. The crash had mussed Chan's hair, and he was bleeding from the nose, fresh crimson spattered on his shirt and jacket.

"Well, now."

Lee could hear the smile in Christy's voice, but he was trembling, both hands wrapped around his pistol, with the sights on Chan. It would be so damned easy just to drop him where he stood.

Ray seemed to know what he was thinking. "Take it easy, Joe. This fuckhead isn't worth hard time."

"I think he is."

"Don't do it, man."

A furtive movement, nearly out of sight behind the car, distracted Lee from Bobby Chan, the pale face staring back at him with the expression of a man who recognizes death. There was *another* man, behind the vehicle, and Joseph wondered if he could have crawled out through the broken windshield while the gunner and his boss were drawing their attention to the rear.

"We've got a holdout, Ray."

"Say what?"

The crouching figure broke from cover, running east on Bryant toward the shelter of the concrete pylons that supported Highway 80 and its feeders overhead. He stopped midway to fire a pistol shot in their direction, framed beneath the glare of vapor lamps before he turned away.

"Is that . . . ?"

"It's Kephart, dammit!"

Squeezing off a shot, too late, Lee saw his target disappear, and followed in a rush, ignoring Christy's warning shout and racing toward the darkness underneath the interstate.

• • •

Joe nearly lost his footing on the slope, loose dirt and gravel costing him a precious moment as he scanned the shadows for his enemy. He might have spent an hour searching back and forth if Kephart hadn't fired a shot just then, his bullet whining off a pylon several feet to Joseph's left. The muzzle flash gave Lee a target he could aim for, but his two quick shots were wasted in the dark, and he heard Kephart scrambling out of range above him, making for the freeway overhead.

Dumb bastard.

If he made the interstate, then what? The traffic would be moving too damned fast for him to commandeer a car, and if he thought that half a dozen concrete lanes would stop Joe Lee, then Kephart didn't know his man.

Another wild round from the darkness, missing by a yard, and this time Joseph did not bother firing back. The Browning still had thirteen rounds in place, with two spare magazines, but he was saving all of it until he had a target fixed in view.

Three shots from Kephart, so far, and he thought the regional director's weapon was a standard .38, but Lee was past the point of taking any chances. Even with a six-gun, Kephart might be packing extra rounds, and there was no percentage in a banzai rush against an unseen enemy equipped with unknown weapons. Joseph was content to follow, for the moment, knowing that his adversary couldn't make the interstate without emerging from the darkness that had sheltered him so far.

To reach the highway, Kephart had to show himself *and* scale an eight-foot chain-link fence. When he was on the wire . . .

Lee froze, a sound of scuffling footsteps changing his direction slightly, audible despite the late-night traffic droning overhead. His man was moving, roughly north to south, noise amplified within the manmade echo chamber underneath the highway.

Joseph followed, caught a glimpse of Kephart as he broke from cover and began to run along the fence designed for keeping stray pedestrians and animals from wandering across the interstate. Lee's former boss glanced back in time to see him following, and fired another shot that kicked up dust behind him, somewhere down the slope.

It was a .38 for sure, and Joseph broke his promise, squeezing off a single round to keep the bastard moving, certain he would miss before he fired. A tactical investment in the game of cat-and-mouse, with Kephart ducking, digging in for traction as he raced along the fence. Nowhere to go, and when he tried to climb . . .

The break was there before Lee knew it, chain mesh sagging where some tramp or gang of kids had cut the links and wriggled through. He tried a shot as Kephart reached the makeshift gate, but tripped and slithered ten feet down the bank. It cost him time, but saved his life as Kephart hesitated halfway through and fired another round that sizzled overhead where Joseph had been standing seconds earlier.

Lee fired one back, to ruin Kephart's aim, and he was startled when he scored a hit, his target sprawling on the far side of the fence, one leg still hung up on the wire.

Too easy for a kill, he thought, and saw his first impression verified as Kephart came up cursing, kicking as he tried to extricate his leg. He lost the shoe and ripped his trouser cuff, but he was rolling out of range before Lee had the chance to fire again. A flesh wound, maybe, but at least the hit had slowed him down.

Lee scrambled to his feet and followed, falling twice before he made the crest and staggered toward the long rip in the fence. His former boss was halfway out and dodging traffic, one hand pressed against his side, the other clinging to his pistol.

"Kephart!"

Turning to confront his nemesis again, the .38 exploding in his fist as Joseph gave him three nine-millimeter rounds in rapid-fire. The impact staggered Kephart, pitching him off-balance, and he never saw the blue Chevette that clipped him, spinning him across another lane.

The pickup truck was braking when it hit, but fifty-five was still enough to flatten Kephart, pulling him beneath the wheels. The next three cars in line ran over him before the drivers had a clear idea of what was happening, and by the time the half-ton U-Haul got there, Joseph couldn't watch it anymore.

Ray found him throwing up against the fence, a three-car pileup blocking eastbound traffic on the interstate in front of him. Lee heard the scraping footsteps coming closer, out of darkness, and he had the Browning aimed at Christy's face before he recognized a friend.

"We're back to that?" Ray asked him, sounding weary.

"No."

Ray stood against the fence and saw the headlights glistening on trails of crimson.

"Jesus Christ."

"Where's Chan?"

"I cuffed him to the car. He isn't going anywhere."

"Nobody else?"

"The driver lost it when they rolled." Ray looked at Joseph kneeling in the dust. "You hit?"

Lee shook his head. Converging sirens pierced the haze inside his skull as Christy helped him to his feet.

"Sounds like the cavalry," Ray said. He pressed a leather wallet into Joseph's hand. "You'd better take this, just in case."

"What is it?"

"Your ID. I think we ought to keep this in the family."

"You're a little late," Lee said.

"Forget about it. Way it reads in my report, the man was squeezing you to keep his own ass covered. By the time they sort this out in Washington, you'll be a fucking star."

"Don't hold your breath."

Ray stopped and faced him underneath the vapor lamps. "Your call," he said. "But I can tell you, it's a goddamned shame to come this far and then just throw it all away."

"That's your opinion."

"Right. So, fuck it, huh? Thing is, I've got this piece of

shit I have to book on something like a hundred major felonies before I hang it up tonight. You wanna tag along, or what?"

Lee was surprised to find that he could smile. "Why not?"

If you enjoyed *China White*, Book 2 in THE ASIA TRILOGY, by Michael Newton, you won't want to miss Book 3 in this explosive series:

Ronin

by
Michael Newton

Turn the page for an exciting preview of *Ronin*, Book 3 in THE ASIA TRILOGY. On sale January 1992 wherever Bantam books are sold.

1

Tokyo, November 199-

After five days in the woman's shadow, following her every move, Tanaka didn't need the photographs to recognize his prey. He would have known her laughter in a darkened theater, the easy rhythm of her stride on any bustling street. The outline of her figure, framed against an open door in silhouette. The way she tossed her head, sometimes, to sweep the long dark hair back from her perfect face.

The snapshots did not do her justice, after all. They could not let Tanaka look inside.

On paper, she was two-dimensional, the shrunken likeness of a pretty girl who might be bright or stupid, tedious or fascinating, frigid or a raving nymphomaniac. Tanaka guessed that the photographer had done his best, all things considered, but the girl was living proof that cameras could not touch the soul.

The photographs were merely tools, in any case, to help him recognize the girl at first, and they had done their job. Tanaka made his mind up to destroy them—tear them up and flush them down the toilet—when he got back to his room that night.

But first . . .

Five days, and he had yet to speak her name aloud. The silence stood between them like an antiseptic shield, prevented him from reaching out to touch her, groping for the answer to a riddle that had carried him four thousand miles from home.

That evening, on the train, their eyes had met, but she

immediately turned away. Not frightened or embarrassed, he was sure of that. She simply had not registered his presence, any more than she would note a hundred thousand other strangers who surrounded her on any given day. In Tokyo, as in the other teeming cities of the East, the quest for privacy began within.

Her name was Sachiko Sugamo, and Tanaka knew that she was twenty-one years old, although she might have passed for seventeen or twenty-five, depending on her mood and choice of clothes. She was unmarried, seemed to have no steady lover, and she was employed part-time at a boutique in the Shibuya district, though she did not need the money. Her apartment, in the Shitamachi residential quarter, was a three-room walk-up renting for five thousand yen per month.

The day before, instead of following his quarry to her job, Tanaka had remained behind to prowl the flat. He had no difficulty with the locks, and once inside, he spent a moment on the threshold simply breathing in her scent and studying the furniture before he started checking out the drawers and cupboards. One small closet in the bedroom, tight with clothes that she could not have easily afforded on her salary; perfumes and lotions on the dresser, most of them expensive, subtle, like the lady's taste.

Tanaka was especially careful with the bedroom chest of drawers, replacing every item that he touched exactly so. He felt a twinge of something—not precisely guilt—as he began to sort through bits of underwear. Bikini briefs in neon shades and simple cotton panties thrown together carelessly; a sports bra and a lacy bit of nothing you could read through, in a pinch.

What was she wearing now?

Inside the tiny shower stall, a washcloth draped across the nozzle and a single twist of pubic hair adhering to the bar of scented soap.

Not guilt, but close enough.

Tanaka worried that the girl—this stranger—had begun to come alive inside his mind. The purpose of his quest was crystal-clear, unwavering, but he could not deny that under different circumstances, Sachiko

Sugamo would have posed a different challenge all her own.

Imagining the undergarments filled, the gliding bar of soap on supple flesh, Tanaka felt ashamed. Perverse.

Until he brought his mind back to the job at hand.

No diary in the drawers or nightstand; nothing in the way of picture albums, save for half a dozen family photos in the living room. He studied each in turn, comparing them with others he had memorized and filed away. A family portrait with her parents and a young man he assumed to be her brother. Yet another of the men alone, with old man Kenji flanked by son and grandson, smiling for the camera. The other shots were casual, depicting Sachiko and girlfriends at the beach, amidst the cherry blossoms of the Heian Shrine, at a *matsuri* festival. If there were secrets locked behind her smiling eyes, Tanaka could not search them out.

This evening, he had followed her from classes at the university to Ueno Park, and on from there by train to reach the Kanda district, disembarking for an easy stroll down Jimbo cho. The Street of Booksellers was picturesque by lanternlight, its many shops and stalls attracting several thousand browsers to the neighborhood. Tanaka kept the girl's red scarf in view and gave her room to run, deciding he would have to wait for the approach until he found a place where he could speak to her without a crowd for company.

But, either way, it had to be tonight.

Five days in Tokyo, and part of him acknowledged he was wasting time. Another part suggested that it might have been too late before he came, and yet, a nagging sense of urgency remained.

Tonight, for good or ill, he had to make his move.

The first day had been spent establishing himself, attempting to become familiar with the hopeless urban sprawl. Days two and three were used to track the woman down, discover her routine, and fall in step. The fourth day, he had prowled her flat in vain and later joined her at the cinema with friends, wedged in between a fat man and a wriggling child three rows behind. A pastry afterward, and home to bed. Alone.

Sachiko had no bodyguards, but there were still police to be considered, and Tanaka did not need a public scene. The first approach required a measure of finesse, deception that would let him slip inside her first line of defense before she shut him out. A chance to win her confidence, if that was possible.

He slowly closed the gap between them as she toured the shops and stalls, Tanaka feigning interest in an illustrated history of sumo wrestling here, a volume on kabuki further on. He scanned the Noh masks mounted in the window of a corner shop, hand-carved and painted to depict a random sampling of the classic gods and demons, interspersed with mortal men. Their faces glowered at him through the glass.

Tanaka felt his stomach tighten when Sachiko met a girlfriend on the street, afraid their meeting might be prearranged. His mind's eye followed them to restaurants and coffeehouses, possibly a party or the theater; another evening lost, unless he loitered on the street outside, to finally accost her like a mugger in the dark. And what if she did not intend to sleep at home tonight?

Ten minutes later, he relaxed and watched them separate with smiling promises to keep in touch. The stranger passed within a yard of where Tanaka stood, oblivious as he fell into step behind her friend. The thrill of a reprieve redoubled his determination to proceed.

Tanaka saw it in his mind, a variation on the patented technique for meeting girls that he had learned in high school. If Sachiko made a purchase, it would take only a nudge, immediately followed by profuse apologies as he retrieved her parcel from the ground. If she was merely window-shopping, as it seemed, Tanaka would remain alert and strike next time she cracked a book, pretending interest in the subject or the author to initiate a friendly dialogue. A winning smile would help, and he was banking on Sachiko's curiosity when she discovered he was an American.

The twist of nationality aside, Tanaka had enjoyed a fifty-fifty record with the tried-and-true approach. The ladies did not always wind up in his bed, by any means, but he had no intention of seducing Sachiko Sugamo. He would settle for a smile at first, her trust to follow, access to a priceless pearl of information somewhere down the line.

The crowd was thinning as they neared the north end of the street, Tanaka hoping she would cross and scout the bookstalls on the other side, to give him time. He failed to register the dark sedan at first—a Honda four-door, several men inside, the driver pacing Sachiko—and when the watchers made their move, Tanaka saw his plans go up in smoke.

Three goons in business suits unloaded in a rush, their driver staying with the car. Sachiko never saw them coming, and they had her in an instant, one on either side to grip her arms, the odd man out assigned to hold the crowd at bay.

He could have saved the angry scowl, for all the good it did him. Startled shoppers made no move to help Sachiko as her captors lifted her and bore her toward the car, feet kicking at their shins and empty air. A few more steps, and she would disappear inside, the Honda lost before Tanaka had the chance to flag down a taxi.

No time to waste.

He took the rear guard from his blind side, like a football lineman, all his weight behind a shoulder to the ribs. Momentum drove his tackling dummy back against the car, the impact letting Sachiko's abductors know that they were not alone.

Tanaka caught the thin man on her right as he began to turn, a sucker punch that snapped his head back, jarring loose the shades that hid his eyes despite the hour. Boring in, he hit his adversary with a forearm to the throat and left him gagging as he finished with a left below the belt.

Two down, and he was turning to confront the third when something like a freight train struck him in the chest. Tanaka staggered, tears of pain obscuring his vision as he caught a glimpse of Sachiko escaping, plunging headlong through the crowd. A second roundhouse kick came at him from the left, and there was barely time to save his face, a shoulder turned and arm upraised to take the jarring blow.

Get out of here! his ringing brain commanded, knowing that the girl was safe and he had nothing more to offer her by standing fast. *Haul ass!*

Too late.

The rear guard met him as he turned to run, the curved blade of his *tanto* slicing through Tanaka's coat and shirt like they were made of tissue paper. Sharp enough that there was no initial pain as it sank home between his ribs.

The crimson blade withdrew—*That's me . . . oh, God*—before a snap kick caught Tanaka in the lower back and dropped him to his knees. Then pain, in blinding sheets and waves that took his breath away and left a roaring like the ocean in his ears. He felt the pavement rough against his cheek, warm liquid plastering the J. C. Penney shirt against his skin. One of Tanaka's adversaries slammed another kick into his wounded abdomen before they fled, a woman screaming in the crowd, as though the sight of blood had finally freed her vocal cords.

Tanaka did not struggle when they turned him over on his back, strange faces looming over him, examining the specimen discarded in their midst. A curiosity, both strange and dreadful.

"Tasukete kure!"

Wondering if anyone would hear the whispered plea for help, much less respond. In New York City or Los Angeles, they would have turned his pockets out by now, in search of cash and credit cards.

Tanaka thought: So this is how it feels to die. The flash of insight failed to stir him. At the moment, he was satisfied to feel the pain retreating slightly, leaden numbness radiating from the epicenter of his wound.

From nowhere, Sachiko Sugamo's face swam into focus, snapping at the crowd for someone, anyone, to call an ambulance. *"Denwa de yasen-boyin wo yonde!"*

She clutched one of Tanaka's bloody hands in both of hers and pleaded with him to hang on. *"Tsudzuku kudasai!"*

"I'm with you," he replied, too weak to translate in his mind.

Tanaka heard her shouting for the ambulance again before the roaring in his ears eclipsed her distant voice and sucked him downward into darkness, seeking warmth and respite from the pain.

2

Tanaka dreamed a city, dark and desolate. He prowled the empty streets without a clue to where he was or why the tall, surrealistic buildings were devoid of life. The only thing that mattered was his job, the lure that drew him on, and he could feel it growing stronger now. He hesitated, waiting for the silent beacon to provide him with direction, startled to discover that the pulse was emanating from beneath his feet.

Tanaka found a manhole in the middle of the street and skinned his fingers raw before he managed to dislodge the cover. Darkness waiting for him, down below; aromas wafting up at him that made his stomach turn. The exhalations of a sleeping carnivore.

"No fucking way."

But even as he spoke the words, Tanaka knew he had no choice. The quest had brought him this far, and he could not turn away when victory was finally within his grasp. The pit held answers that he could not live without.

He started down the ladder, metal rungs that soiled his hands with rust and other things he did not care to name. The darkness was alive below him. Fetid water lapping at the concrete banks that held it prisoner. The skittering of rodents on an endless search for food.

An urgent whisper that prevented him from turning back.

At last Tanaka stood beside a flowing stream of sewage twenty feet below the level of the street. It had been dark out, and the tunnel was a separate world, completely isolated even from the meager starlight, but Tanaka found that he could see. The logic of his dream prevented him from questioning the fact as he began to study his surroundings.

There was fungus growing on the walls and on the ceiling overhead, but rats had kept the runway clear with their incessant pacing. The tunnel seemed to slope downhill, a gentle grade that kept the dark river moving, and Tanaka visualized its terminus. A reservoir of waste that spread for miles beneath the city, its miasma permeating the abandoned shops and offices, invading homes to make them uninhabitable.

Same old shit, he thought, and might have chuckled if he had not seen the river come alive.

At first he blamed the surface turmoil on escaping gas—a great fart, once removed—but then a slimy sort of fish-thing broke the surface, thrashing spastically before it disappeared. Tanaka estimated it was six feet long, at least, its skin a sickly green beneath the darker stains and clinging solid waste. The gaping jaws were lined with teeth like broken razor blades, its eyes vestigial and blind.

He waited for the monster fish to reappear, and slowly realized that there were dozens, hundreds of them gliding through the muck, occasionally breaching to reveal themselves. As far as he could tell, they swam downstream exclusively, compelled to travel with the tide.

Distracted by the fish, Tanaka nearly missed the watcher on the far side of the shit stream. Silently the woman had approached to stand directly opposite—or had she been there all along? He squinted in the murk to recognize her, the ID retarded by her ratty hair and filthy clothes, but there was no mistake about the face.

Tanaka spoke her name, tears coursing down his cheeks. In place of a reply, she raised one hand and beckoned him across.

He froze, unable to advance or turn away. "I can't." The words were acid on his tongue.

Still silent, she began unbuttoning her blouse. Tanaka knew it had been expensive—she always dressed in style—but now it was a shapeless rag that barely qualified as clothing. Still, despite the situation and surroundings, he was captivated as her fingers slipped one button free, another, and the next. Familiar flesh revealed by inches, teasing him, demanding a response.

She slipped the garment off and tossed it out in front of her, the brindle current drawing it away. No bra—Tanaka didn't think she owned one—and her nipples stiffened with the slow manipulation of her fingers, bringing him erect as if the hands were stroking his flesh, rather than her own.

The skirt was short, some kind of faded denim, with a zipper on the side. Instead of dropping it, she took the hem and hoisted it around her hips to show him she was naked underneath. Her pubic hair was shaved in a bikini cut, trimmed close enough to show her sex before a hand got in the way. Slim fingers delving, picking out a rhythm as her hips began to move in time.

Her eyes were closed now, but Tanaka felt her watching him. His hunger took him to the precipice, about to leap, before a thrashing in the shit stream drove him back.

"I can't." His tone somewhere between a whimper and a snarl.

You must.

A silent voice inside his brain, as strong hands gripped his shoulders from behind and forced him toward the brink. Tanaka felt a surge of panic, digging in his heels, for all the good it did him. Lashing out at the invisible, compelling hands.

"Goddammit, no!"

"Mr. Tanaka?"

This voice different from the last, accompanied by a gentle touch that saved him seconds shy of splashdown in the reeking stream, among its blind, voracious denizens.

His eyes snapped open, focused on a woman standing close beside him on the left. Unlike the round-eye in his dream, this one was Japanese. She wore a starched white nurse's uniform and kept a firm hand on his shoulder till the fantasy released its hold.

"Good morning."

As she took his pulse, Tanaka registered that she was speaking English. She had called him by his name. He felt a rush of apprehension—*the hotel, the photographs*—until he realized they must have checked his pockets for ID. His passport and the Honolulu driver's license would have pegged him as American.

"A dream," she told him, making a notation on his chart. "You should not be concerned."

"What time?" he managed, croaking in a parchment voice.

"Eleven-twenty-five." She helped him sip cool water through a plastic straw. "The doctor will be with you soon."

With consciousness and clarity of thought, the pain returned in waves. His shoulder, chest, and back felt bruised and swollen, throbbing in conjunction with his pulse. The bastards knew their stuff, but haste had stopped them short of breaking bones. A shifting movement lit the fire between Tanaka's ribs—*the blade*—and he had sweated through his flimsy gown before the surgeon wandered in, all smiles.

He introduced himself as Dr. Kiyonaga, and he took Tanaka's pulse again, as if he did not trust the chart. "How are you feeling?"

"Like I've just been beaten up and stabbed."

"You have a lucky wound," the doctor said.

"How's that?"

"No vital organs were involved. The knife blade grazed your lung, but missed the spleen and stomach. Very fortunate."

"It hurts like hell."

"Of course." The doctor's smile remained in place. "To suffer, one must be alive."

"How long until I'm on my feet?"

"To walk? Tomorrow, or perhaps the next day. For release, a few days more, I think."

"About this private room—"

The doctor raised a hand to cut him off. "Expenses are provided for. Your job is to relax and heal."

"Who's picking up the tab?"

"Perhaps a friend."

"I don't have any friends in Tokyo."

"A grateful stranger, then." The question obviously did

not trouble Dr. Kiyonaga. "Are you strong enough to speak with the police?"

Tanaka was expecting it. Attempted murder on the street would rate an interview, at least.

"I may as well. Are they around?"

"Eat first," the doctor said. "You need your strength. I will suggest they come this afternoon."

The midday meal was rice and vegetables, with strips of beef he had to search for in a milky sauce. Hospital food, nutritious to a fault, with all but a suggestion of the flavor steamed away. He picked around the edges, eating just enough to satisfy the nurse, and left the rest. When it was cleared away, the nurse brought tablets in a paper cup, with juice to wash them down.

"Rest now," she ordered. "The police will not be here for several hours."

Time enough for him to think about the questions they were bound to ask and worry over what they might have learned already. If they dug too deep—especially if they started making calls to Honolulu—he would have to sweat his cover out and pray for it to hold. One leak, a single slipup, and the "grateful stranger" who was picking up his medical expenses might become a mortal enemy.

The sedative kicked in a moment later, blurring boundary lines between reality and wishful thinking. Concentrating on his pain until it slipped away, Tanaka wondered if he still had any cover to preserve. The thought of dying in Japan was something he had come to terms with in advance, but he would not give up without a fight—assuming he could find the strength to stand. But first, incontrovertibly, he needed sleep.

Tanaka dreamed a city, dark and desolate.

The two police inspectors looked like Mutt and Jeff, one short and square, his partner tall and lean, eyes magnified by horn-rimmed spectacles. Seicho Amato—"Mutt"—appeared to be the senior member of the team, in charge of asking questions, while his partner, Chobei Takamori, frowned and stared.

"You are American," Amato said.

"That's right."

"Nisei?"

"Sansei," Tanaka said. "Third generation. It's my first time here."

"What brings you to Japan?"

"Vacation time. You might say I was looking for my roots."

Amato let the ethnic comment pass. "Vacation? How are you employed?"

"Computer sales," Tanaka lied. It would be someone else's job to make the cover stick, if the police were curious enough to call and check.

The answer seemed to satisfy Amato. "You have friends in Tokyo?"

Tanaka shook his head. "I'm on my own, just checking out the sights."

"And last night, Jimbo cho."

"Is that a problem?"

The detectives looked like finalists in an Olympic frowning competition.

"Not at all," Amato said. "If anything, your presence at the scene was most fortunate."

"Coincidence. Five minutes either way, I would have missed the show."

"You may have saved a woman's life."

Tanaka shrugged, the effort costing him a jolt of pain beneath his arm. "I don't know what the heavies had in mind, but no one else was doing anything, so I jumped in. Dumb move, I guess. Too many Rambo flicks."

Amato missed the joke, or chose to overlook it. "We have gathered various descriptions of the men involved, but you were nearest."

"Too damned near, I'd say."

"If you feel able to describe them . . ."

"Right."

Tanaka rattled off the bare essentials, concentrating on the rear guard, who had stabbed him. Young and wiry, with a dagger hidden underneath the jacket of his tailored suit. The other two gorillas had been somewhat older, in their early thirties, wearing shades at night.

"That's it, I guess."

"You did not recognize these men?"
"How could I? I already told you, it's my first time in Japan."
"Of course. But if you met again . . ."
"A lineup? Sure, why not? You round them up, I'll take a look."
"We have no suspects yet."
"A thing like that, with all those witnesses?" Tanaka feigned amazement. "No one even got the number of their car?"
"A stolen vehicle, unfortunately."
"I'll be damned. So, that's the end of it?"
"We shall continue our investigation," Amato said, "but in Tokyo—as in Los Angeles—such incidents are sadly commonplace. Without a suspect, there is little more that we can do."
Tanaka took a shot, deciding he should push it. "What about the girl? She must have seen their faces when they dragged her to the car."
A curtain fell in place behind Amato's eyes. "Apparently the men were strange to her as well."
" 'Strange' doesn't cover it," Tanaka answered, backing off. "You've got a gang of psychos on your hands."
"Perhaps they only meant to rob."
Another time and place, Tanaka would have laughed out loud, but as it was, he held the urge in check. "You may be right, at that," he said. Not choking on the words, somehow.
"By all accounts, you showed great courage," the inspector told him, finished now and looking for a graceful way to disengage.
"Next time, I look before I leap."
"I trust there will not be a next time."
"Not if I can help it."
"So. Good health," Amato said. "Enjoy the rest of your stay in Tokyo."
"I'll do my best."
The nurse came in to check him moments later and prescribed more rest, but he dissuaded her from trotting out the sedatives. He sampled television for a while—frenetic game shows and a rerun of *Bonanza*, dubbed in

Japanese—then paged through several magazines until the evening meal arrived. More rice and vegetables, with pork this time, although it tasted much like lunch.

"Bon appétit," he told the empty room, and forced himself to eat it all.

Another round of medication for dessert, but they omitted knockout drops this time. Alone once more, Tanaka flicked the television on and searched until he found a Dirty Harry film, the violent action serving as a kind of therapeutic antidote for the frustration he experienced at being stuck in bed.

And still, the residue of physical exhaustion haunted him. Tanaka dozed before the villain of the piece had time to make Clint Eastwood's day.

He woke to find a new face at his bedside, Sachiko Sugamo studying his face and blushing slightly when he caught her at it.

"I did not mean to disturb you." Perfect English, no doubt learned and practiced in the best of schools.

"Disturb away. It seems like all I do is sleep."

"You need your rest."

"So everyone keeps telling me."

She wore a dress he recognized from prowling through her closet, navy blue, with buttons made of ivory. He gave a passing thought to what was underneath, remembering the options, and she blushed again, as if she had the power to read his mind.

"I came to thank you."

"That's not necessary."

"Yes it is, Tanaka-san. You saved my life."

"My pleasure."

"I don't think so." Studying the bruises on his face, the narrow bandage on his arm, where intravenous tubes had been attached the night before.

"Let's say my privilege, then."

A smile lit up her face. "The room is satisfactory?"

"It's fine."

"If there is anything you need—"

"I'd like to know who's picking up the tab," Tanaka said.

"Excuse me?"
"Paying for the room and all."
"My father. He is greatly in your debt, Tanaka-san . . . as I am."
"Make it Harry, will you?"
"Harry?"
"It was an experiment."
"Americans." Sachiko shook her head and smiled. "My name is Sachiko Sugamo. You must call me Sachi."
"That's a pretty name. It fits."
She blushed again, but this time there was pleasure in it.
"I suppose you talked to the police," he said, and watched her smile begin to fade.
"They questioned me. Unfortunately, there was nothing I could tell them."
"Same with me. They seemed to think I ought to know the guys by name."
"You were very brave," Sachiko said, disturbing him with the directness of her gaze.
"That seems to be the consensus. Can you keep a secret, Sachi?"
"Secret?"
"I was scared to death. If I'd been thinking . . . well, I might have turned around and run the other way."
"I don't believe that. Only fools risk danger lightly. Brave men recognize and overcome their fears."
She touched his hand, a gentle pressure there and gone almost before it registered. He was relieved to see the serious expression on her face give way to the accustomed smile.
"The doctors found a key to your hotel room," she informed him, and Tanaka felt the short hairs rising on his neck.
His bags.
The photographs.
"My room?"
"It's been reserved until you're on your feet again, and for as long as you should care to stay in Tokyo."
"Your father's laying out a lot of yen on my behalf."
"He can afford it, Harry."

"Well . . ."

"What brings you to Japan?"

It was the second time that question had been raised within the past few hours, and Tanaka edged a little closer to the truth this time as he replied, "I'm looking for a woman."

Sachiko Sugamo met his gaze and said, "You've found one."